If it had been
found him, Se
who she was

It was clear she'd gone to decent lengths to transform herself. Different hair color, different style, shortened name.

"So..." Ellie looked up at him. "What now?"

The window behind her shattered.

"Get down!" Seth was breathing like he'd just been running, the stress overwhelming him.

The walls of the public-use cabin were rough-hewn wood, solid logs. Likely Sitka spruce. They would slow a bullet in some calibers. Maybe stop one in others.

And in some of the bigger calibers, they'd offer no protection at all.

God, please make this go away, Seth prayed.

Minutes passed. No more shots.

Had the last shot, through the window, been a warning?

Or was someone out there waiting?

SECRETS AT THE SUMMIT

SARAH VARLAND

&

USA TODAY Bestselling Author

ELIZABETH GODDARD

2 Thrilling Stories

Alaska Secrets and *Covert Cover-Up*

LOVE INSPIRED
INSPIRATIONAL ROMANCE

LOVE INSPIRED®
INSPIRATIONAL ROMANCE

ISBN-13: 978-1-335-46369-2

Secrets at the Summit

Love Inspired
22 Adelaide St. West, 41st Floor
Toronto, Ontario M5H 4E3, Canada
www.LoveInspired.com

Recycling programs for this product may not exist in your area.

Printed in U.S.A.

CONTENTS

Sarah Varland lives in Alaska with her husband, John, their two boys and their dogs. Her passion for books comes from her mom; her love for suspense comes from her dad, who has spent a career in law enforcement. When she's not writing, she's often found dog mushing, hiking, reading, kayaking, drinking coffee or enjoying other Alaskan adventures with her family.

Books by Sarah Varland

Love Inspired Suspense

Treasure Point Secrets
Tundra Threat
Cold Case Witness
Silent Night Shadows
Perilous Homecoming
Mountain Refuge
Alaskan Hideout
Alaskan Ambush
Alaskan Christmas Cold Case
Alaska Secrets
Alaskan Mountain Attack

Visit the Author Profile page
at LoveInspired.com for more titles.

ALASKA SECRETS

Sarah Varland

Not as though I had already attained, either were already perfect: but I follow after, if that I may apprehend that for which also I am apprehended of Christ Jesus. Brethren, I count not myself to have apprehended: but this one thing I do, forgetting those things which are behind, and reaching forth unto those things which are before, I press toward the mark for the prize of the high calling of God in Christ Jesus.
—*Philippians* 3:12–14

To the people who have taught me about mushing sled dogs. Thanks for sharing your advice, enthusiasm, dogs and equipment. We are forever grateful to be part of such a great community.

And as always, to my family.

ONE

Ellie Hardison's cheeks were freezing in the minus-twenty-degree weather, and she was terrified her hands had frozen to the grips of the snow machine miles ago. But while turning back might look appealing, she wasn't going to let down someone who was counting on her search and rescue team.

She kept her eyes on the horizon, scanning for any shapes that could be a missing musher and his dog team. Apparently the man, Seth, was overdue from a training run, and his neighbor had called in the Raven Pass Police Department. The PD had requested the help of Raven Pass Search and Rescue, as most people who went missing in Alaska's backcountry were simply victims of the elements, unpreparedness or plain old bad luck.

Whatever the reason this man was missing, Ellie refused to let the weather stop her from doing her duty.

She strained her eyes, still able to see very little in the moonlit Alaskan night. This was one of the coldest nights of the year so far, substantially lower in temperature than the night before, and if the man had already been out for hours longer than planned, he might already need medical attention. They needed to find him fast.

A tap on her back from the second searcher and Ellie's friend, Piper Adams, drew her attention back, and Ellie glanced back. "What is it?" She yelled the words over the roar of the engine, slowing down slightly to try to quiet the wind. She didn't want to stop, because if she stopped, she might fully realize how cold she was. Sure, she was uncomfortable, but someone's life might be hanging in the balance right now.

And Ellie was far too familiar with how fragile life was. If there was a chance the missing man could be saved, she was going to save him.

She was going to save every single person she could— no matter what.

Even though it would never be enough to bring Liz back.

"I see something!" Piper yelled back.

Ellie did slow now, afraid that if she missed whatever Piper had seen, they might not be able to spot it again. "Where?"

Piper reached her right arm forward and motioned to the right, in front of them. Yes, Ellie could see what her friend had pointed at.

The spruce trees were dark in the moonlight and the snow surrounding them was thick powder. In a small clearing ahead was something that didn't look like a tree. A black cluster of something in the snow. Could be their missing man and his dogsled. Could be the shadows playing tricks on them, making a fallen tree seem like the person they were so desperately seeking.

It was worth checking. Just in case.

Ellie steered the machine through the snow, off the trail they'd been on. They'd been following the trail system near the missing musher's house, but whatever

Piper had seen was off the trail, so now they were in who knew how many feet of ungroomed snow. The engine was more than able to perform in these conditions, but the handling was different. Ellie had only been driving snow machines for a few years. Her former life, in a small town in western Washington and then in Anchorage, hadn't lent itself to much of that activity.

As they approached the blurred lumps ahead, the shapes became more recognizable, and yes, it was a turned-over sled and several curled-up, sleeping dogs.

No sign of Seth yet.

Ellie parked her machine. Shivered. It felt like someone was watching her...the missing musher? Someone who'd attacked him?

No, that was unreasonable. They were the only ones out here. And as of right now there was no reason to suspect an attack or any kind of foul play. She was letting her own past crowd in and cloud her judgment. The moonlit shadows on the scrubby spruce trees were playing tricks on her. Her unease was simply a product of her overactive imagination and the vast sense of loneliness the Alaskan wilderness could convey.

Still, she felt *watched*, no matter how much she tried to talk herself out of it. Every sense was heightened. Her shoulders tensed as she readied herself to react.

Was this PTSD from a time when she'd reacted too slowly, when she'd been too late?

Or could there be a human threat involved in this situation?

Ellie had wanted a fresh start when she came to Alaska. But no, she'd never expected her fresh start to take her to Raven Pass, to Liz's hometown, a place that reminded Ellie of her best friend every day and tugged her right back into those nightmares.

"There he is." Piper's words were slurring slightly in the cold. Ellie hated that feeling, when frigid temperatures started to affect your speech. Ellie needed to get all of them—the musher included—back, as quickly as possible. With that in mind, she climbed from the snow machine and made her way in the direction of what looked like the sled. Reaching up, she clicked her headlamp on and immediately caught the glow of at least half a dozen pairs of eyes in the dark.

She could see the dogs now. They were in harnesses, connected to a main rope—called a gangline, she'd learned on a dog mushing tour once—connected to the sled, by smaller ropes on their harnesses and collars. Some of them were lying down, and Ellie wondered how long they'd been here. The sled should be hooked up behind them. She turned her head that direction and confirmed. Yes, it was there, but on its side; no musher that she could see.

Steeling herself against the discovery no SAR worker wanted to make, she walked closer.

"Seth?" She swallowed hard. "Seth?" The caller who had reported him missing hadn't given a last name…but the missing musher shared a first name with her former fiancé. They didn't always even know a first name for the people they were rescuing. All that mattered was that someone was lost and needed SAR to find them.

Ellie saw the sled bag—the fabric compartment that rode on top of the dogsled and gave the musher a place to store gear—which looked torn apart. There was no other evidence of a struggle that she could see to imply it was human-caused, but she didn't see any terrain here where a crash could have caused that kind of damage, but maybe Seth had hit something farther back on the trail system somewhere.

Or what if her thought earlier hadn't been way off base? What if he had been attacked?

What if someone was watching, still?

Chills crept up her shoulders, too deep inside to be the cold, as she reached for the sled bag.

Clean slices. Consistent with a knife. Intentional destruction? Possibly, a suspect could have wanted to access the contents of the bag quickly and had foregone the likely frozen zipper in favor of a knife.

Either way, this was starting not to look like an accident to her.

"Seth!"

Ellie heard Piper's yell and the way her voice changed tenor and hurried toward her as fast as she could.

There, crumpled in the snow behind the sled, was a human form. Ellie swallowed hard, but there was no panic. No, that would have been a welcome reminder of the hopelessness she'd looked in the face before; it would have provided her with some way to feel, to connect to her past.

Instead, since the day her best friend had been taken from her, Ellie had felt nothing.

Well, except regret. And a desperate determination to save every single person she could.

"Is that him? Is he breathing?"

The first question was pointless—neither of them had seen a picture, but the man was dressed for dog mushing and looked like the kind of Alaskan Ellie could picture on the back of a sled. Large parka with a warm ruff around the hood, which was pulled over his head. Strong face with a jawline edged with a five-o'clock shadow. Broad shoulders and arms that should have been strong enough to get himself out of…whatever situation he'd found himself in.

Except…

"He's bleeding." Piper was the one who said it first, but Ellie had already noticed the dark stains in the snow.

Ellie was debating whether it was worth the risk of exposing him to the cold to look under his parka and see what kind of damage the wound in his side was. There was a moderate amount of blood. Enough that it was more than a scratch, but not so much that he was in danger of bleeding out.

Shock, maybe. Especially if she risked exposing him to more cold. Better to see about the wound later.

She'd just decided when the man moaned and reached a hand down by his side.

Then his eyes blinked. Opened, and locked with hers.

"Who are you?" he asked, and Ellie couldn't answer.

Because the bright blue gaze staring back at her had the exact color of her best friend's eyes.

And the man in front of her was the only man she'd ever loved. Liz's brother, Seth Connors.

Even though she shouldn't be so surprised—she'd known that Liz and Seth were from Raven Pass—a shiver still ran down her spine. She'd known he had moved out of Anchorage, as she'd kept an ear out for what was going on with him even after she'd left him. So yes, it wouldn't have taken too much thought to realize he might have gone back to his hometown.

When the job had opened up in Raven Pass, Liz's hometown…

Well, Ellie had taken it. She hadn't thought about

Seth, or at least she'd tried not to. Instead, she had kept on living the life her friend should have had.

Because Liz shouldn't be dead. Wouldn't be if it weren't for Ellie. Ellie should have been able to stop it, or she should have at least been able to save her friend's life.

"Who are you?" the man asked again.

He might not know the answer to that right now. She'd shortened her name, so he wouldn't recognize that. She'd changed her hairstyle. And she was layered in enough winter gear her mom might not recognize her at the moment.

But she knew exactly who he was. Even in the gear.

And every bit of the safe world she'd carefully built for the last three years was threatening to come apart.

Agony shooting through his head and side fought for attention. And Seth was cold… He opened his eyes and saw a woman kneeling over him.

"My dogs!" He remembered he had his dogs with him. Years of training, care; he couldn't lose those dogs. Rule number one of mushing was to never let go of your sled, and he'd apparently passed out at some point and lost them.

"Lie down. You've lost a lot of blood, and you can't just get up like nothing—"

He pushed himself up on the snow, just enough to sit and see the dark shapes ahead of him. His sled, on its side.

His dogs?

Yes, *there* they were. Like she knew he was looking, his lead dog, Spots, lifted her nose and howled in the high-pitched way only she could.

"Your dogs are right here," a second woman said.

"Are they okay?"

"We haven't checked on them yet." The first person, the one with eyes darker than the Alaskan midnight itself and the bossy voice, was talking again. "We were a little busy trying to decide if the man we'd been sent to find was alive."

Seth blinked and tried to make sense of her words with the timeline in his head as he knew it. He'd left for a training run just as it got dark. It was still dark, so it couldn't have been too many hours…

Who had reported him missing?

Surely not the men who'd…

More snippets of memory came back. "I was attacked." He swallowed hard, embarrassed to admit it, since he'd clearly been on the losing end of that, but his rescuers needed to know. "Someone was standing by the trail, next to a snow machine. I assumed they needed help and slowed down." He shook his head. "And when I did, they hit me over the head with something, I guess…" He trailed off.

Someone was apparently after him. Because the three of them were miles from any other kind of help, and if those men came back, he'd be no match for them wounded. Unless either of these women was packing a bear gun, they probably would not be a lot of help fighting off criminals, either.

"We need to get out of here. We aren't safe." What had happened to his sister was never far from his mind. People were capable of all kinds of evil and violence and he had to get these women to safety.

Sure, they were here to rescue him, but he'd been

raised to respect others and anyone getting hurt because of him didn't sit well.

The second woman looked surprised, Seth noted, but the other's face never changed. Almost like she'd expected that?

The first woman nodded, gestured with her head toward his sled bag. "Your bag is slashed apart. It didn't look accidental."

Much as he wanted to sort through that, try to figure out what he thought, he had a different focus right now. He had to take care of his dogs.

"I've got to see about my team." He pushed against the snow, his side screaming at him. He placed a hand against it, brought it away. No fresh blood. But he saw what looked like blood in the snow, the moonlight and the women's headlamps just enough to give them some light.

He felt his head, came up empty. "I lost my headlamp." The throbbing in his head intensified. He needed to get them out of here, but right now he was painfully aware he was the weak link in this group. Every extra bit of hurrying only seemed to make him slower in the long run.

The first person reached into her pocket and handed him one. "I'm Ellie Hardison. This is Piper Adams."

"Seth Connors." He blew out a breath, frustrated that the woman's voice was still so calm.

Ellie stepped away, and he saw something pass over her face. They hadn't met before, had they?

"Your team is this way," she said and turned around.

"I'll look for your headlamp," Piper offered.

"Please be careful." He didn't want to be responsible for anyone getting hurt. Life was fragile. Memories of his sister, an EMT in Anchorage who'd been killed here years ago, flashed through his mind. Her loss had left a hole in his life. Of course, when she'd died his life had blown apart in more ways than one. His sister's best friend, who was also his fiancée, had left soon after. No explanation. Just a hollow *I'm sorry* and then nothing.

Another thing he couldn't afford to focus on right now.

The dogs were curled up in the snow, some of them lifted their heads as he walked by. He started by checking the wheel dogs, those closest to the sled. "Vinson, Jarvis." Next the team dogs, closer to the front. "Riley, Maya." Part of a litter named after some TV show that his sister used to like. They both seemed okay. "Chaos, Mouse. Havoc, Waffle. Scooby, Shaggy. Emmett, Spots." He exhaled. All twelve were okay.

At seeing him, standing and seemingly ready to go, they all stood up, and Seth's eyes widened. "The sled was not hooked in? Unless the hook fell out and caught in the snow and that's what stopped them…" He hurried as fast as he could in the deep, powdery snow back to the sled. He grabbed the handlebar and righted it in one motion, like he'd done many times before, and pressed down on the brake. It caught against the dogs' jerking. They were all ready to run, pressing forward in their harnesses.

He remembered now: yes, the snow hook—the specially designed piece of metal that functioned like an anchor, which dug into the snow to keep a team stopped if necessary—had fallen and caught enough to slow the dogs down and convince them to stop. That would explain why his team was still with him.

"We need to get out of here," he muttered to himself, remembering the heavy weight of the punches his attackers had landed. Mostly unconscious by that point, he hadn't been able to fight back. He'd heard them rip the fabric of the sled bag, prayed that his dogs would be okay. Thankfully they'd left the animals alone. He didn't know who was after him or what they wanted, but one thing he was sure of…he wasn't going to be responsible for anyone getting hurt.

Seth looked ahead at his team, jumping forward in excitement. They'd had a long rest, and they were ready to go.

"I have to go back to town on the sled." He raised his voice over the excited voices of the dogs. The pain in his side was intense but not bad enough that he couldn't take care of his own animals. "You guys can follow on the snow machine or go ahead, whichever you prefer."

Ellie raised her eyes. "You're injured. You need to be with someone who knows what to do if you go into shock."

He'd been taking care of himself for quite a few years now. While he didn't say anything in response to her, his raised eyebrows and set facial expression must have been enough to convey his point, because she shook her head, then followed up with the only thing she could have said to make him consider it.

"What about your dogs? If you do go into shock, you're right back where you started." She nodded toward the sled. "And your snow hook might not hold this time."

She knew enough to call it a snow hook, which was more than most people knew.

"Fine, you can ride with me." He let go of the sled with one hand, motioned for her to step in front of him on the runners.

She raised her eyebrows and just stared. Something about the way she did it caught his attention, like something so familiar, yet she wasn't. He hadn't met her before today.

Had he?

She looked away from him. Too quickly. Yes, the woman was hiding something.

Her friend spoke up. "You'd better go with him, Ellie. Someone needs to make sure he gets all the way home and to the hospital, but another missing person just got called in."

Seth saw the indecision on Ellie's face. She was still resisting for some reason. Dislike of dogs? Or was she uncomfortable riding with him in such proximity? They each had on about a foot worth of snow gear, so that shouldn't be an issue. Though Seth would be lying if he didn't admit to having his heart skip a beat or two thinking about riding double on the sled. She intrigued him in a way that no woman had since…well, since Ellerie had skipped town. She carried herself in a certain way. Soft, but confident. Strong. Beautiful eyes, full of expressions he couldn't quite read.

"Fine." She stepped onto the sled and wrapped her mitten-covered hands around the sled handlebar.

"All right," he said to the dogs, giving them the command that they knew was permission to run. Some people had the idea that dogs had to be given a sharp signal to go, but with his team, giving them permission to do what they loved best was enough. They didn't need any extra encouragement. It came naturally to them.

Having someone on the runners in front of him wasn't a familiar feeling for Seth. The warmth and closeness of Ellie was distracting, but not unpleasant. He was so aware of her, but knew she was just doing a job. This proximity wasn't intentional. Seth tried his best to ignore it, pretend he was alone. For all the good that would do. He wasn't sure he was that good at faking. He never took people along with him. For Seth, his time alone with the dogs was when he recharged. Having someone else with him got in the way of that.

"Are you sure you're okay?" Ellie asked, turning her head slightly so her words wouldn't get lost in the swish of the runners on the snow.

"I'm fine." If *fine* included stab wounds. It hurt to breathe, because of the wounds in his side, under his ribs. He was fairly sure they were shallow because he was still breathing. But they hurt, a deep pain, some of the worst he'd felt in his life, but not the very worst. He was fairly sure he was okay, but he wasn't going to fight her when Ellie suggested he go to the hospital when they got back to Raven Pass.

She didn't ask anything else, which was fine with him. He was watching the trail ahead of them, mindful of typical hazards on any run, like moose, but also watching for a sign of the men who had attacked him and left him for dead. There had been more than one of them, Seth knew that. Because one had been hitting while another stabbed. Maybe a third to go through the sled? His memories were fragmented, broken glass that made an incomplete picture. He'd been struggling to keep control of his team, keep them safe, and trying to fight against more than one opponent. The loss of consciousness hadn't helped sharpen his memory, either.

They mushed along in silence, and he found himself glancing at her. After a little while of reading her body language, he realized he was wrong. She was nervous, she just tried not to show it. Her shoulders were tense, though, her eyes scanning the terrain.

She read more as a cop to him than a search and rescue worker, but his imagination was running overtime right now. Maybe it was wishful thinking, because he could use an officer here.

The run had been going well. What had the men wanted? It still wasn't clear to him. If they'd wanted to kill him, they could have. But they'd left him alive. Why? His sled bag was slashed. Because they'd been looking for something?

"Do you see this a lot in your SAR work?" he asked Ellie, suddenly wondering what she thought. He didn't know why. Seth wasn't usually one to need to bounce his ideas off someone.

"Not often. Most of the rescues we make are pure accidents."

Her voice was soft. Almost like she was trying to disguise her voice? And her identity?

Seth *knew* her. He was sure of it. He just didn't know how.

But before they parted ways tonight, he was going to find that out.

And find out who had been after him. The attack must relate to his sister, because this couldn't be random. There was no other explanation he could come up with that would account for someone attacking him and acting like they were looking for something. Crime wasn't high in Raven Pass. They had incidents now and then, like any other town, but assault wasn't commonplace. Therefore the connection to Liz was his best guess at why someone would be after him now.

If he was right, then it made him even more determined to figure out who was behind it. It had never sat well that Liz's killer had gone free. If there was a link, Seth would figure out who the attackers were and how to stop them—and get justice for Liz.

TWO

A sudden, earsplitting explosion made Seth jump, shift his weight on the sled and almost cause them to tip. He had to throw his weight to the other side to correct, steeling himself against the sharp stabs of pain in his side where he'd been wounded. He gritted his teeth and did his best to ignore the pain. Several of his dogs reacted, too, ears perking up, looking around even as they kept running.

"Gunshot." Ellie's voice was still quiet, but also steady, bored almost. He would have expected most women, most *people*, to dive off the sled for cover, but she was looking around now more than ever. "Did you see where it came from?" she asked. "I didn't notice muzzle flash."

He'd loop back to that curiosity about her being a cop later, because the idea was seeming less crazy the more he thought about it. For now, he was glad she was the one he was left with.

Wait.

Cop. Familiar voice.

His heart skipped, squeezed, and he looked at her again. Of course. Yes, he knew who this woman was. Once upon a time, she'd been the one who knew him better than anyone in the world, and he'd have said the same for her. And then tragedy had struck, she'd left with little explanation and he'd been left with a broken heart and more questions than answers.

And here she was. Close enough to touch. To hold.

And not his anymore.

How had he not realized who she was earlier? She looked different and was bundled in so much gear he could only see about half of her face, but this was a woman he once would have said he knew better than he knew anyone else. He blinked, shock still rippling through him, desperate for a chance to slow down. Process. Think about the fact that she was here. With him.

But he couldn't figure out how he felt about any of that right now, not when the situation demanded his focus. Their safety, as well as the safety of the dogs, depended on it. He looked at his dogs again. *God keep them, and us, safe.*

"We've got to get out of the open." They were mushing through a swampy area, one dotted with some trees, but not many, where there were not many obvious places to take cover.

While Seth wouldn't judge Ellie—he'd known her as Ellerie back then, but she apparently now used a nickname and had dyed her hair—for diving behind a spruce tree right about now, he wasn't going to leave his dogs as potential targets.

Even with the hair dye and the name change, she was still the same, though. He'd have recognized her sooner were it not for the aftereffects of the attack. He likely had a mild concussion.

Still, he knew who she was now. And was even more determined to keep her safe.

"Haw." He tried to keep his voice as calm and self-assured as he could. The dogs could sense a lack of confidence, and it made them slower to respond. In this situation, which had the potential to cost all of them their lives, it was even more important than usual.

The dogs responded to his instruction to veer left, and he leaned his weight into the turn.

"What's your plan?" Ellie asked, her voice carrying more tension than it had earlier.

"Still working on that."

She said nothing. Likely she'd been hoping for a more encouraging response from him, but it was the best he had.

The dogs raced down the trail, and he kept his eyes open and ready to notice any potential threats.

Another gunshot rang out, this one even louder. Either the shooter had changed position and had gotten closer to them, or their aim was better this time.

They hadn't had guns, or hadn't used them, when they attacked him before.

"If you could work on the plan a little faster, I'd appreciate it."

They were midway through the swamp by now, and his house was still ten miles away. He needed to get to a hospital, but taking care of his dogs had to be his first priority. Home was close, but not close enough when his dogs were only traveling ten miles an hour and someone was shooting at them.

Sixty more minutes of this was unacceptable.

If he turned left again up ahead, the trail would double back a little, but half a mile ahead or so was an old public-use cabin that the state had stopped keeping up. It should be empty this time of year, as winter camping wasn't very popular in this area.

It would fit both of them and all the dogs. The biggest struggle would be having to let Ellie help him unharness the dogs and get them inside. He knew she could be counted on in a crisis. Or at least he knew that used to be true of her. Then again, when their worlds had crashed down and she'd disappeared, she hadn't been the person he'd thought he'd known at all.

Dogs could sense emotion. If Ellie was too stressed, they were liable to be harder to handle.

He had no choice but to trust her.

"Haw!" he called again when they reached the crossroad and he stepped a little closer to Ellie on the runners, leaving little space between them, trying to ignore the now-obvious remnants of familiarity. How tall she was compared to him, the smell of her shampoo that was some mix of fruity and flowery—all of it.

"What are you doing?"

Another shot, and he stepped even closer. He wasn't going to let her get shot on a mission she had been on to rescue him.

"Trying not to let you get hurt."

She didn't argue.

"There's a cabin up here. I think that's our best chance." Seth looked around but still saw nothing that could be a sniper. Of course, he also saw half a dozen places a sniper could easily be hidden. Especially with the way the trees clumped together in parts, casting shadows a man could easily hide in. None of them provided enough cover for him, Ellie and the dogs to shelter behind, but one man with a gun could be easily hidden.

They weren't safe here. Not against a threat he couldn't see.

"And the dogs?"

"We will need to unhook them from the gangline and bring them into the cabin with us. I need you to help me do that. Can you do that?"

"Yes."

No hesitation. He appreciated that.

The cabin came into view, and he urged his dogs on. They picked up speed, sensing their run was almost over.

Whoever was shooting at them should be out of view right now, unless they'd followed them. That was the other benefit of this trail. It had taken them out of the direct area where the shots had been fired, whereas continuing on to his house would have kept them in open swamp for another mile or two.

As they pulled in front of the cabin, he pressed his foot on the brake, called *whoa*, and his dogs responded and slowed to a stop.

"Start with the ones in the back," he told her as he set his hook in the snow and stomped it down.

"Got it."

She worked to unhook Vinson as he did Jarvis.

"Just put them in the cabin and shut the door?" she asked, looking up at him.

Her eyes were dark. Deep.

If it had been daylight when she'd found him, he'd have known who she was immediately, even with his possible head injury. It was clear she'd gone to decent lengths to transform herself. Different hair color, different style, shortened name.

But it was *her*.

He nodded and finally answered her question. "Yes."

They unhooked the rest of the dogs, then took shelter in the cabin.

Ellie slid down against the wall and sat, immediately surrounded by dogs wanting attention. She petted Waffle behind the ears. "So…" She looked up at Seth. "What now?"

The window behind her suddenly shattered, glass raining down on the wooden floor.

"Get down!" he yelled, but she'd already pressed her body against the floor and on top of Waffle.

"We shouldn't have come in here. Now we're at a disadvantage. Whoever is shooting at us knows we are pinned here, and we can't see anything."

"Just wait," Seth said between breaths. He was breathing like he'd just been running, the stress overwhelming him. She had a point, they were vulnerable here. But not any more than they'd been out in the open.

The walls of the public-use cabin were rough-hewn, solid logs. Likely Sitka spruce. They would slow a bullet, in some calibers. Maybe stop one in others.

And in some of the bigger calibers, they'd offer no protection at all.

God, please make this go away, Seth prayed.

Minutes passed. No more shots.

Had the last shot, through the window, been a warning? Or was someone out there waiting? It was impossible to say. But all they could do was wait. Seth crossed his arms. It was colder inside the cabin than it was outside. Even the rough plywood floor felt cold beneath him.

"What now?" Ellie asked.

Seth shook his head. "Now, we just wait."

"Defend our position?" She seemed to consider it, then nodded. "All right." He studied her face, and she looked away.

So she still thought he hadn't recognized her. She had to know who he was, right?

A few minutes went by. No more gunshots. Seth wanted to ask her to radio in to SAR or the police department and update them on their situation, but he also didn't want to risk giving their position away if the shooter was in the swamp somewhere, trying to find their trail.

It hadn't snowed in a few days, which meant there was no powder, and the dogs' paw prints would be less noticeable, blending in with many other tracks. Even someone who knew what they were doing would have a difficult time tracking under these conditions, and that was exactly how they needed it to be. This was their safest option at the moment.

Almost enough to make a guy believe God hadn't forgotten him.

But not quite. Seth had way more standing between him and faith than one good turn of events could make up for.

His sister's death.

His subsequent struggle to continue on with his life, the way the people who he'd have thought would have helped him through the depression had abandoned him.

Like Ellerie—*Ellie*. He had to remember that was the name she was going by now, had to change how he thought of her. No longer the woman he had loved, now a woman he didn't even know.

Where had God been then?

And why had Ellie left him?

He studied her. Waited.

She sighed. "You know, don't you?" Her eyes flickered with sadness and a hint of something that might have been regret.

How could she have thought she could hide from him?

"Yes."

"I can explain…" she started.

He shook his head. No, she couldn't. She couldn't explain disappearing the way she did, not in a way that would erase the past. And even if she could, he wouldn't ask her to. They both needed to be able to put the past behind them.

He'd thought he'd stopped being sad years ago, that only anger remained, but he'd been lying to himself. He felt almost hollow, seeing her here in front of him, knowing all they'd lost.

The only positive thing he could say about her right now as he studied her was that she was still beautiful, and that she didn't look away. Her dark green eyes didn't flinch from his gaze. She didn't make excuses. Instead, she just sat there on the floor with more than one of his dogs curled up into her side and waited. She'd taken her hat off and her hair was dark and shiny, falling around her shoulders. It had been medium brown when he'd known her before, but this suited her well.

The air, once cold and empty, was now thick with emotions that he couldn't even name. Here was someone else who understood some of what he'd been through these last few years, but instead of informing him when she'd moved to town—she'd hidden.

Three years. Liz had been gone for *three years*.

The whole time, Ellie had been here, in his hometown, where he'd sought refuge. Of course, he tended to stay out of the town itself, preferring the solitude of his cabin.

Had she known he was here, too?

Why did it matter? he reasoned with himself. The outcome was the same. She hadn't made an effort to reach out to him. He'd never seen her in town, though admittedly his house was a bit outside town and he avoided going into the community whenever possible. He grocery shopped, of course. But he didn't go to town events, or really anywhere else that he would have seen her.

Seth admitted to himself that it did matter... *She* mattered to him. Always had. Always would, probably, even though he knew that was a foolish thought. He took a deep breath, let it out and waited to hear what she had to say. Tried not to lose himself in her jade-colored eyes.

Knowing that, whatever it was, wouldn't help the empty pain inside him heal. But it might give him enough anger to make sure that the walls in his heart never came down, that he could never get hurt again.

Judging by the anger on his face, she'd been right to keep who she was from him.

Or was it sadness? His jaw was hard, clenched. His eyes unreadable.

Ellie rubbed her arms; the cold in the room had gotten worse in the last few minutes, and she felt more alone than she could remember feeling in years.

Strange that she should feel that way with the one person who might understand the hole someone's death could leave in your life.

"Yes. It's me." The words felt funny leaving her lips, speaking to him this way, like they were still close.

Like they used to be.

Like they could have been if it weren't for her. She'd left him while they were both grieving, and she knew her actions were indefensible. But Liz's death was something she should have been able to prevent. Liz had been his sister, his family. There weren't enough apologies in the world to cover that, and Ellie had drowned herself in her guilt.

Left because she couldn't handle feeling it every time she looked at Seth, knowing he'd lost Liz because of her.

"You're in my town." He stared. Waited. "Why?"

She shook her head. "Long story."

"And we have nothing but time."

Ellie stood and walked to a window, cracked it open an inch and looked out. She saw nothing but the dark landscape. The moon had gone partially behind a cloud, making it more difficult to see. That was good; it might mean they were safer sheltering in place here than they would have been otherwise.

Without talking about it, she and Seth had both shut their headlamps off after entering the cabin. There was just enough light streaming inside to read enough of his facial expressions to know he wasn't pleased.

"Please shut that."

He was upset. Because she'd opened the window? Or because of the way she'd left things?

She looked back at him and shook her head. What did he want her to say? That she'd left him because his sister's death had been her fault? That if she'd taken Liz's fears and suspicions more seriously, maybe Liz would still be alive? That Ellie was rewriting her life and her dreams to somehow make it up to her friend?

No, that was a truth he could never know. It was one she didn't even like to admit.

Worst of all of it, she'd lost Seth. The man she'd loved, wanted to spend the rest of her life with. Her gaze flitted to his jaw, the rough stubble that always grew along the edge of it. She'd cupped that jaw in her hands while she'd kissed him, run her fingers along it, admired it.

Now it was the face of someone she didn't even know. Once upon a time, she and this man had been achingly close to living happily-ever-after.

Now they were strangers.

Death was final, irrevocable. Ellie had been a good police officer. She'd always had excellent observational skills, and she wasn't afraid of much. She should have been able to figure out who'd wanted to hurt Liz when her friend told her she was getting threats, but she hadn't been able to. Liz wouldn't give her much to work with; her friend had been hiding something.

Years later, Ellie still didn't know why. Why hadn't Liz told her everything? She didn't believe her friend had been mixed up in anything wrong, but maybe she'd been protecting someone who was? Or maybe she'd been protecting Ellie. What had happened? What had she missed? Why hadn't she been enough? She *should* have been able to protect her nearest and dearest…and that included the man she'd intended to spend her life with.

She looked over at Seth again. Frowned. Something she should have realized before finally tickled at the back of her mind.

"You were attacked…" She trailed off because the pieces still didn't fit in her mind. Nothing made sense. Liz had been gone for three years. Were the same people who had murdered Liz the ones responsible for Seth's attack? Why come after Seth now?

"Do you know who might have attacked you? Any enemies?"

He just stared at her.

"I'm trying to help here."

"You're not a police officer anymore, Ellie."

She frowned.

"And no. No idea why someone would be after me." He swallowed hard.

He was wondering if there was a tie to Liz's case, also. It couldn't be a coincidence that someone had left him for dead. There was a connection. And Ellie was going to find it.

"What about it? Please don't change the subject. Ellie, I want to know why you're here. And why you didn't tell me."

She sat back down against the wall and shifted. Nothing she did made her more comfortable. She let out a breath and tried to calm her breathing and slow down her heart rate. The last thing she needed was to have some kind of breakdown in front of Seth, but right now she felt like she'd downed an entire pot of coffee and a cup of sugar.

Nervous. Anxious. Edgy.

"What do you know about how your sister died?"

The question was fully out there now, not tactful, not gentle, and Ellie knew it, but she needed to know.

How she handled the next hour or so would be dictated by his answers.

"I was told it was a freak thing. Just a random, drive-by shooting in Anchorage. Wrong place, wrong time." His face was unsettled.

Ellie shook her head.

"I didn't think so, either. But no one knew any different, and I couldn't find you to ask what you thought…" He trailed off.

"You looked for me?"

Seth slammed his fist down on the floor. "Of course I looked for you, Ellie. What kind of question is that? We were going to get married. You think my sister died and I just forgot I had a fiancée? That I somehow didn't notice that you disappeared into thin air without saying goodbye? Without talking about Liz? Without coming to the funeral? One minute I'm hearing about my sister, you're with me, hugging me, crying with me, and I think that it's awful and it hurts, but you and I were going to get through it together. And then twenty-four hours later you were gone."

He exhaled, leaned back against the wall and refused to meet her eyes.

Ellie blinked. She hadn't expected that after all this time she'd elicit that much of a reaction from Seth. She'd thought…what? That he wouldn't come after her? That he would let their relationship go without trying to find out why she'd walked away?

She had known him better than that. Those were lies she'd made herself believe intentionally, though maybe not consciously, to ease her conscience about her choices. Lies that were all too easy to believe because she'd never had anyone in her life before Seth and Liz who cared that much if she stayed or left. It didn't excuse her behavior, but it did help her understand herself.

And she had come to the funeral. She'd just stayed away from Seth.

"She was murdered. I'm almost sure of it. She'd been acting strange and had started receiving threats, but she wouldn't tell me any more than that at the time."

"Why didn't you tell me?"

"She made me promise not to and, Seth, there was no reason to."

"You should have told me."

Ellie opened her mouth to argue and finally met Seth's eyes. The weight of their past, the realization that he was right, that this was yet another mistake she'd made, hit her so hard she almost felt out of breath.

"You're right. I should have told you."

Several seconds passed in silence. Then Seth spoke again.

"She wouldn't tell you what they were about or why?"

"No." Ellie had to shake her head. "She didn't say. I couldn't figure it out. She was supposed to tell me that night. We were meeting for coffee and pie at a little diner she liked."

Ellie had been late, and not for any good reason. She'd just lost track of time, been careless. Late for pie and coffee. Then late for everything.

Her fault. Her fault. Her fault.

It echoed every day when her heart beat in her still-living chest. When her friend was still dead.

Ellie knew it should have been her. Or really, it should have been neither of them. Life was cruel. Unfair.

Seth met her eyes. He felt her pain, she could tell. Even after all the intervening years and all she'd put his family through, she felt indescribably connected to this man, and it unseated her in every possible way. Vulnerability meant pain. And she was so very tired. So tired of hurting.

Maybe this connection could be a good thing. If they could almost read each other's thoughts, then surely they could work together to figure out who had been after him and what they'd wanted.

Seth seemed to ask a question with his eyes but then followed it with words. "You think the people who attacked me killed her?"

She nodded. "If you're right that you don't have any enemies, then it makes more sense than anything else. The odds of both of you being targeted for different reasons, by different people, are slim. Since Liz's murder was never solved, it makes more sense that it has to do with that. But I don't know why. Why now?"

He shook his head, unable to answer, either.

"If it is, will you help me find them?"

Ellie nodded an answer. Looked at him with her decision in her expression.

And he nodded his agreement. "Good."

They were going to bring whoever did this to justice. Maybe finally find some closure.

And move on with their individual lives…apart.

THREE

"Why are you here? Why Raven Pass?" he finally asked, in the quiet of the night. Ellie shifted, moving one of her legs out from under a dog who had fallen asleep on her.

Should she tell him the real answer? It revealed too much. But she was tired of all the hiding. For years she'd avoided getting close to anyone. Her search and rescue teammates had noticed but not pushed. Jake, the leader, knew more about her past than anyone did, but he'd had his own secrets and had understood how much it mattered to her to keep them quiet.

And yes, *quiet* described the last few years. She told people the minimum about herself. Had no personal life.

She'd left to avoid hurting Seth more… If she'd only been on time, only taken the threat against Liz more seriously, the woman they'd both loved might still be alive.

And she'd left to start over. To try to have a life again.

But she hadn't been living. Not really. She'd been existing.

Seeing Seth again made her feel alive. Hurting, yes. Uncertain. Awkward. Because he knew her, really saw her.

She'd met him when he'd come by Liz's place when

Ellie was there. They'd hit it off immediately and had so much in common. That first night they'd talked til after three in the morning, laughing at the fact that Liz had fallen asleep on the couch between the two of them, laughing at everything really, because that's what you did when you were just falling into the first stages of love and everything was shiny and new and perfect.

Ellie had loved his confidence, the fact that he wasn't threatened by her own strong personality. She'd loved his laugh. His jawline. His eyes. His faith. She'd loved who she was with him and had been counting down until their forever started.

He didn't just know her past, he *was* her past.

With that in mind, surely she could just answer his question and tell him the truth. "I came here because this town meant something to Liz. And you. And as much as I try, I can't forget either one of you. Especially you. I guess I'm not very good at moving on."

His dark eyebrows rose. She swallowed hard and waited.

He said nothing.

Ellie's heart pounded in her chest, foolishly. She hadn't been trying to get him back. But it hurt to know that she'd handed him that kind of conversational trail to follow and he hadn't taken it.

Ellie cleared her throat, changed the subject. "About the case. Some of the things Liz said... I don't know. Even though I don't know what she'd gotten involved in, or found out about, she was certain she was in trouble. And she was worried you could be, too. Especially in the future. More than once she told me that if she didn't figure out soon who was threatening her, they might come after you in the future."

She hadn't remembered that detail until just now. It had been a long time since she'd let herself think about Liz or Seth or anything in her past.

He face eased into a frown. But not like he was just angry. Like he was thinking.

"What is it?" she asked, almost afraid to hear the answer.

"I got an unexpected package earlier today," he began, leaning toward her. "It was from a lawyer's office in Anchorage."

Her heart caught in her throat. "And?"

"What do you mean?"

"What was it?"

He shook his head. "I don't know. The mail came when I was in the middle of harnessing my team for this run, so I put it away and then left."

That was one of the areas where they'd always been different. Seth never pushed. Sometimes Ellie had been sure it was because he was trying to be kind, not intrude into someone's private business against their will. And sometimes it drove her crazy.

Right now it was the latter.

"From a lawyer's office." She stood, the dogs who'd been lying on her looking at her with an offended spark in their eyes as she woke them up. "Sorry," she mumbled at them. "But we have to go. We have to get back to your house and that package."

Finally he caught up. "Because whoever was after me and tore up my sled bag probably wants that package. Or at the very least, came after me today because I got it."

"Yes, we have to go. We have to—"

"Ellie."

Her head whipped around, her eyes locking with his.

Hearing her name from his lips again, even the shortened version, was the strangest thrill and tugged at her heart. She swallowed hard. It was probably easier to walk away and forget someone if you hadn't been in love with them... That wasn't the case for her.

It had all been *her*. Her fears. Her guilt. But even now, she didn't think she was strong enough to see him every day, knowing that if only she'd been better at her job, his sister would still be alive.

"If they followed me, chances are good they already searched my house. There's no reason to rush over there when we may still be in danger. We need to stay here longer. I'm not risking my dogs."

Over her years in Alaska, she'd known enough dog mushers to not be surprised at his dedication. But that didn't mean it didn't mess up her plans. Risk was nothing new to her, and this one seemed worth it.

Or it would if it was only her life.

Now that she stopped to think, she wasn't willing to risk Seth's.

Her heart almost ached at how difficult it was to be this close to him and not having things the way they used to be. She'd ruined her chance with him. But she needed to know he was alive, safe. Happy.

Somewhat happy, anyway. Try as she might to be gracious and reasonable, the idea of him settling down with another women who wasn't her, having babies with someone who wasn't her...

Ellie still wished it could have been her. But she knew nothing would change the past.

They needed to be careful, focus on this case, and she had to not let her anxiety get the best of her and force her into rash decisions. Seth was right to suggest that they wait.

She paced back and forth, helpless frustration coursing through her veins. Her mind was willing to admit that he was right about the package being gone already. But he might not be, and it was still easy to let her emotions get the best of her. Instead she drew a few breaths, tried to let them out slowly and force herself to calm down.

"When do *you* think it's safe to leave?" she made herself ask. Never mind that she was the one with law-enforcement experience…

Immediately Ellie felt bad for the thought, for acting like she knew so much more than Seth. Yes, she had law-enforcement training and that counted for something. But Seth was smart, and she especially trusted his instincts.

If he said they needed to stay, she needed to listen to him.

He was watching her now. The look on his face said that he'd caught her emphasis, the slight snark in her tone, but rather than be angered by it, he was ignoring her outburst and just preparing to answer the question.

That was something she'd loved about him, once. She tended to be passionate to a fault and sometimes spoke before she thought. Seth was easygoing, forgiving.

"I think we should wait until closer to daylight."

She considered his words. It was a solid plan. People tended to trust darkness when they were trying to avoid detection, so leaving now meant they could possibly be walking into a trap.

Why had someone shot at Seth? They wouldn't have known that Seth hadn't seen what was in the package.

Was whatever it was worth killing over if someone saw it? And what was in it? A package from an Anchorage lawyer...

New evidence in the case? Liz.

There were a lot of options for what could be in the package. All of them urgent. Intriguing.

Worth killing for, if you were the person the information could incriminate.

"So..." Seth began. "I'm going to get that package when we get home."

"Obviously.".

"And then we're going to the hospital because I'd like to make sure the knife wounds don't get infected. And then I'm going to figure out who killed my sister and would come after me, too."

A shiver crawled down her spine. She wished he was bluffing. She'd already lost her best friend to whoever this invisible enemy was. She didn't want to lose him, too.

But hadn't she already lost him? Of her own free will?

She glanced in his direction and knew with certainty that walking away from him was one thing, but knowing she could have prevented his death would be another.

She wouldn't let it happen, not if it was within her power. Which meant sticking close to him. Keeping him safe to the best of her ability, though he was a capable Alaskan, adept in the backcountry, who really didn't need her protection. Yes, that was part of what she'd do, but ultimately if she wanted to keep him safe, do what she hadn't done for his sister...

She had to walk back into this case. Face the past. Her own guilt.

This aching loss she couldn't get rid of.

Because Seth's life, and maybe hers, depended on it.

Daylight came slowly this time of year, and Seth watched it arrive from just outside the cabin door, where he'd quietly positioned himself about an hour ago to watch and see if anything caught his attention. So far no signs of danger remained. The threat may have passed for now. He'd tried to convince Ellie to get some sleep, but she'd stayed awake, just quietly sitting there, petting his dogs.

He had so many questions for her. How much time was a guy supposed to give a girl who'd come back into his life unexpectedly like this before he asked her about it?

She'd walked away once, and Seth wasn't the kind of man who couldn't respect a woman's decision. She didn't want him. She'd made that perfectly clear by leaving. He thought back on her surprise at his reaction earlier, when he'd talked about searching for her after she'd left. Could she really have thought he'd just let her go? The nights he'd stayed up, missing her, feeling the emptiness in his heart like a never-ending ache, the nights he lay awake in bed, wondering what had gone wrong…

They'd promised to marry each other and instead she'd abandoned him. He'd ridden a roller-coaster spiral of grief, betrayal and numbness.

She'd broken her promise to him and his life had never been the same. He still ached. Especially now that he'd seen her, talked to her again and remembered all that he'd lost.

But friends?

He'd settle for that if it meant having Ellie back in his life again.

Seth sighed and leaned back against the door. He was pathetic. If he was one of his friends, he'd smack himself on the back of the head for being this turned around in his head over a woman. But it wasn't just any woman, it was *Ellie*, the woman he'd believed was *the one*.

The door eased open behind him, and Ellie stepped out. Her eyes were sleepy, and she was blinking. Good. Maybe she'd finally rested at least a little when he'd come outside.

"See anything?" she whispered.

He shook his head. "I think we're clear." The sky was lightening on the edges, to the gorgeous, deep cerulean of an Alaska sky. "You ready to go?"

"Well, if I could have grabbed a quick shower, I would have, but strangely I can't find one here," she teased.

Seth laughed, tension in his shoulders relaxing some, though the pain from his wound made it impossible to fully relax. Much as he hated to, he needed to see a doctor when he got back to town. But right now he was in the woods, alone with Ellie, thinking for the first time they had a shot at being friends again. Before now, he would have said they wouldn't be able to reclaim any of that casual familiarity that made it okay to joke with someone. But they had, like they'd stepped back in time, but glossed over everything deeply personal. Friends. Maybe they really could do this. "Okay, sure, so there's nothing to do to get ready except hook the dogs back up. I get it."

She smiled up at him.

They prepared the dogs and started off. Seth was too busy looking around to talk to Ellie. Besides, she was holding herself as close to the sled as she could, away from him where he stood behind her. He guessed the proximity was more awkward for her today, now that she knew that he knew who she was.

As they made the ride, he kept his attention trained on his dogs, noting that everyone appeared to have rested well despite their unconventional stop at the cabin. Last night hadn't been their routine at all, but they'd behaved well in the cabin, no behavior conflicts, and they all had slept well. They looked fantastic this morning. He was proud of this team he'd put together.

When he wasn't watching the dogs, he watched the trail, the woods around them, for any sign of suspicious activity. Seth wasn't naive. He knew the danger hadn't passed, but they had to make progress. Had to get back to town.

Still, he found himself flinching at shadows, standing even closer to Ellie out of a desire to protect her. She was fiercely independent and would say that she could take care of herself. And she could.

But that didn't stop Seth from wanting to take care of her, anyway.

As they approached the trail to his house, he called out *gee*, the command to go right. His leaders reacted immediately, and he leaned into the turn.

"You ever mush before?" he asked. She hadn't years ago, but a lot had changed since then.

She shook her head. "No. I've always wanted to,

though. I usually try to volunteer at Iditarod as a handler when I can."

"Maybe one day you can learn," he said without thinking and immediately wished he could pull the words back, reel them in like a fish in summer. He hadn't meant to imply that they'd keep in touch. Sure, they lived in the same town, but they hadn't run into each other yet. He had to assume she'd done that on purpose. She was going to help him find whoever was after him, he knew that much. But after that?

"I'd like that," she said, surprising him into silence.

They pulled into the yard, and he set the snow hook, kicking it deep to hold the team in place. Ellie stepped off the sled and started to walk away.

"Wait," he told her, uneasiness churning in his gut. The yard looked quiet. Empty. But looks could be deceiving.

"You think someone's here?" she asked in a whisper, stopping beside him.

Seth listened. Watched his dogs for any kind of fear reaction, but they showed no signs of danger and Seth didn't see any, either.

They were safe.

For now.

"I think we're all right," Seth tried to reassure her, but kept his gaze fixed on the dark woods at the edge of his property. Circumstances could change at any moment and he wanted to be ready. He'd been unprepared last time. He couldn't, wouldn't, let that happen again.

Their safety secured for now, Seth went about his routine. He petted every dog, told them how well they'd done, and then unharnessed them and hooked them back to the tethers near their houses. The pain in his side where the knife wounds were had faded to a dull throb, but he knew he needed medical attention.

"They don't mind the chains?" Ellie asked from where she stood watching.

"It's good for them to have the option to run around and exercise, actually. And to socialize with other dogs." He smiled at his leader, Spots, and rubbed her behind the ears as he glanced around again, still checking for any sign of intruders.

When the last dog was secured, he started toward the house, Ellie on his heels. The door of the house was closed, but not locked as he'd left it. His chest tightened and he felt his heartbeat quicken. Seth paused, took a slow breath and looked in Ellie's direction, shook his head. "I left this locked."

"And it's not locked now?" she confirmed.

He shook his head and slowly eased the door open, staying on the front porch while it swung full open.

He waited, let his eyes adjust to the darkness of inside.

The scene was worse than he'd expected. Overturned tables, emptied drawers and mess everywhere. He was a fairly neat guy and liked to think he didn't keep a lot of junk, but the place was destroyed. Definitely not how he'd have preferred Ellie to see his house for the first time.

But no sign of anyone still inside. He kept himself on the alert just in case.

"We need to clear the house and make sure no one is in here. I'm not going to wander around and be caught off guard." Ellie was using her cop voice and Seth would have smiled at how quickly she went back to her old self when the situation called for it, but nothing about right now was a smiling kind of situation.

"You're right. One problem. Neither of us has weapons."

"Do you have any inside?"

"My bedroom."

"Let's go there first."

He did as she told him, moving silently through the darkened rooms, listening for any signs of movement and hearing none. When they were in the room, he opened his gun safe, handed her a 10mm and chose his favorite .45 for himself. Both handguns stayed loaded.

"This room is obviously clear. Next room."

They worked their way through the house. All clear.

In the living room, they lowered their weapons out of ready stance.

"They had to have found it," she said, and he could feel how close she was to giving up.

"Hey." He pulled her toward him, then startled and pulled his hands away from where they'd rested on her upper arms. "I—I'm sorry, El," he stammered. Fear and grief overwhelmed him, as well as a deep sense of regret over the past. What could he have done differently back then to keep Ellie in his life? How had he failed her so much that she'd thought leaving was the only option?

And was he only going to fail her again now?

Even with all those thoughts pressing against him, he knew he'd need to keep his head. He had no right to touch her, no place in her life that made physical contact something that should be assumed.

"No, it's okay."

He'd surprised himself, not hesitating to touch her, and had to remind himself she wasn't his to be close to like that. Not anymore...even if their shared loss still hung between them.

"It won't happen again," he insisted, clearing his throat and hoping it was a promise he could keep. He'd already lost his sister, lost his relationship with Ellie and now someone was after him. Maybe both of them. How much grief, how much challenge could one person be expected to face?

"Where, um, where did you put the package?" she asked, drawing his attention back to the task at hand.

"In my closet. I've got a tiny attic space that's almost impossible to access, but I wanted to be extra careful, so I put it up there, inside an old suitcase."

Please let it be there.

He entered his small room and felt Ellie right behind him. It was...strange to have her so much in his space, in his house like this, but it wasn't his main focus right now. Instead he went to the closet, which had also clearly been disturbed by the intruders, and opened the attic.

There was the suitcase. He reached for it.

Inside was the package. It was a small manila envelope. Undisturbed. Relief flooded him.

"Is it there?" Ellie called from below.

"It's here." He climbed back down and held it out to her.

She shook her head and pushed it back in his direction. "No, it was sent to you. You open it."

He pulled it open, slid out a sheet of paper, ran his eyes over it and held it where Ellie could read, too.

Dear Seth,

If you're reading this, I'm afraid I was right. My life was in danger, and I'm no longer alive...

He stopped. Glanced down at the signature at the bottom of the page. Liz.

His heartbeat thudded in his ears, loud enough to drown every other emotion with the sound. She'd been his little sister and he'd failed her. Why had someone done this?

Would this letter tell him? Had Liz known?

He'd never felt so heavy that his shoulders sagged like this, never felt so overwhelmed.

He looked at Ellie, her eyes were as wide as his own, as though she could feel how shaken he was and understood.

"Not only does it have to do with Liz's death, but..." He trailed off.

"She wrote you a letter."

And whatever was in the letter was worth attacking him for. Which meant that yes, this was his chance to find Liz's killers. Bring them to justice, once and for all...even if that meant risking everything.

It wouldn't bring Liz back, his beloved sister, but maybe it would give him a chance to keep living in a way he realized he hadn't quite been able to. He glanced at Ellie. And maybe it would help, too.

Now all they had to do was catch the killers before they paid with their own lives...

FOUR

"Wait, wait…" Ellie spoke up. Seth glanced in her direction and saw that her eyes were squeezed shut and she was shaking her head. "Why now? Why are you just now getting this package?"

Valid question, but he'd have finished reading the letter before asking them. He glanced down at it. There was a chance she might explain.

She was Liz. Liz had written them a letter, had it sent by her lawyer posthumously. Dizziness struck Seth as he took a deep breath, remembering the sound of his sister's laugh, the emptiness of the last few years without her.

"Let's read it together first." He took a breath before he spoke but still heard the shakiness in his own voice. In last few hours, he'd been able to maintain some degree of composure, running on adrenaline maybe, but now he was losing that steadiness and could feel emotions threatening to crash like a rogue wave.

Ellie nodded and sank down, sitting with legs crossed on the floor, her back against the bed.

He joined her, and while her closeness overwhelmed him, it somehow also made him stronger. It had always been that way. Ellie was one of the strongest people he knew, and her fortitude was contagious. With her, he believed he could be the kind of hero she deserved. She made people believe in themselves.

But he knew firsthand that missing her had its own kind of power. Her absence was as strong as her presence and if she'd made him stronger when she was there, he'd felt the pieces of himself chip away, felt broken, like he'd been left with half of himself when she left.

Depending on her, needing her, was dangerous. Because she'd leave again, he knew that. And he'd be right back at broken.

He took a breath, summoning every bit of courage, and read aloud. "'Dear Seth, if you're reading this, I'm afraid I was right. *My life was in danger, and I'm no longer alive...*'

"'If Ellerie is okay—it's too much for me to consider she might not be, but I'm afraid if she started investigating and I'm dead, she might be, too—please read her this letter, also. Make sure she knows she was the best friend I could have asked for.'"

A sob broke out of Ellie's throat, and she cried quietly. He stopped reading, not sure how to comfort her, how much closeness she wanted. He finally reached for her hand, squeezed it and then lessened the pressure on it.

She didn't let go. He didn't, either.

Seth took another breath. "'I wanted to tell her and you my suspicions, but Aaron figured out I was wary of him, I think, and I never had much time alone with either of you. Aaron is involved in something bad. He's picking up some kind of smuggled goods—drugs, I think—north of Anchorage, somewhere along the Glenn

Highway. I've heard things in his phone conversations, enough to start to put pieces together, and I've found some emails of his to an address I don't recognize. I asked a computer friend for help, and he said they were sent from a computer on a network in a shopping mall in Raven Pass. One of the businesses in that strip mall is Raven Pass Expeditions, and they take regular trips from there to Eklutna, which is on the highway north of Anchorage. Maybe a front for the smuggling, right? Maybe a coincidence. I don't know. I know Aaron is involved. I know someone in that shopping mall is involved, at least at the time that I'm writing this. I'm going to seal this letter and ask my lawyer to mail it to you three years after my death, should I die unexpectedly. My thinking is this—three years should be enough time for someone in law enforcement, besides Ellerie, to figure this out and arrest these people. The only way I want either of you involved is if these people are still walking free in three years' time. Otherwise I'd never ask you to risk it. I dearly hope—'" now his voice broke "'—I dearly hope you never see this letter. I hope three years from this moment we are all sitting around a fire, camping somewhere, and I'm telling you about the crazy paranoia I had... But in case you see it, in case the worst happens, I love you. You were the best brother I could have asked for.'"

He finished, took a deep breath and let it out slowly, blinking tears away from his eyes.

His only sister. Only sibling. Reading the letter felt like losing her all over again, reminded him of all he'd lost.

He wanted to feel angry. Wanted to desire vengeance so much that he could crowd out all these other feelings with white-hot fury.

And he did want the men caught. Brought to justice and prosecuted to the fullest extent the law would allow.

But mostly he wanted Liz back. Wanted his old life back. Ellerie back.

And Liz was never coming back.

His old life was over.

And Ellerie had left. Changed her name and her life. Not the same as being dead, not the permanence, but not something he knew how to handle, either.

So. Much. Regret.

How did someone move past all this? Move through it?

Ellie squeezed Seth's hand harder, looked up at him.

Something flickered in her eyes, and she leaned closer. Just slightly, but as she did so, her head tilted up to his.

And then her arms were reaching for him. Slowly, she wrapped her hands behind his neck, tugged him closer to her.

So much time. So much between them.

And then she was kissing him, soft and warm and like she wanted to make it better, but they both knew that she couldn't. Still, for a minute he forgot everything else.

And then memories, the truth of their current situation, the fact that she'd left him, all slammed into him at once and he pulled back.

"Ellie…" He trailed off, clearing his throat.

"I shouldn't have…" She looked away. Scooted several inches from him.

"Listen, we're adults. You were trying to…" Well, what *had* she been trying to do just then? She'd kissed him, full on the lips, with more emotion than he'd imagined she could still feel toward them. Who left someone and then embraced them like that? Why?

"You were sad." She shrugged her shoulders and sniffled. It wasn't a pity kiss, they had too much of a past relationship for that. Rather it had been instant, a way to reach out and offer comfort.

All the years, her leaving, and they were still connected. Maybe they always would be. And that was what Seth was afraid of. This woman had always held such a large part of his heart, and when she'd left, he'd never gotten it back.

He didn't want to lose himself in the past, in regret, bitterness, any of it. So he took a deep breath, pushed the thoughts away. He nodded. "What's a kiss between—"

"Friends?" she asked like it was an offer. And it was. She'd broken his heart and left, and he'd not even known where she was until now.

Friends was a step up. And even if he was wary of trusting her again, he'd take it. For his sister's sake. Being friends didn't mean he had to let his guard down again, expect anything more. He could keep his guard up and still be amicable. Seth nodded. "Yeah," he said with a small smile. "Friends."

They sat for a minute, eyes locked, before Ellie looked away. "So...the letter."

"She had this sent to me three years after on purpose. She hoped that, if she died, the police would be able to solve the case. That's what the letter said." He was processing out loud, something he often did when he needed to think.

Ellie flinched. Had she taken that as some kind of indictment or insult? He hadn't meant it that way. She'd left the police department almost immediately after Liz's death, first with a leave of absence and then per-manently. Even though she'd never explained the decision—he'd had to find out about the leave from a friend of his at the department—he thought he understood. Trauma made people do inexplicable things... like breaking up with the man they intended to marry right after his sister died, and disappearing.

Or had that been because of something he'd done wrong? Seth had never known. And here she was. He could ask. But somehow, he didn't want to know. Not yet.

"I should have stayed," she muttered, taking his worries and making them true. "I should have tried harder to figure out—"

"No."

She looked at him. Frowned.

Seth shook his head. "Stop. No. You don't know if it would have helped, and you had to do what was best for you, too."

"But Liz..."

"She wouldn't have wanted you to blame yourself. You know that, don't you?"

She couldn't meet his eyes. Or wouldn't.

This was more than residual guilt. This was something much deeper, more serious. He'd try to bring it up later, but didn't see what else there was to do right now but let it go. Their own feelings, and shared past, didn't matter as much as getting justice for his sister. And he had to keep her safe, no matter the cost.

"We have to do something now," she stated, looking back at him. Or at least in his direction. She made just enough eye contact to be socially acceptable but kept glancing away, like being in such proximity to him was too much.

Then again, five minutes ago they'd been kissing

each other. So she might be right about the fact that proximity seemed to make them forget all the years that had passed since they'd been a couple…and how she'd hurt him.

It made him do stupid things like kiss her back. Risk her heart again. After that first betrayal, he should know better.

"I think we should go to the state troopers," he said.

She nodded. No argument at all.

"I'll…" He trailed off, realizing if he walked away from her now, he didn't know when he'd see her again. Where was she living? He knew it was somewhere in town, but he hadn't spent much time there lately. He didn't want to leave now and not see her again for years. "I'll go now, unless you want to come with me?"

He didn't expect her to, but she nodded. They stood up, and he held the letter tight in his hands as they walked to the front yard and his waiting pickup truck.

Hopefully in less than an hour law enforcement would be looking into this, and it would be out of his hands. Figuratively and literally.

Then he'd pray hard that the bad guys were brought to justice. For his sister's sake.

And he'd keep a close watch on the woman who'd been the one he'd intended to marry. Because if the murderers had made a link to him, it would only be a matter of time before they found Ellie.

For the first time in three years, Ellie felt something more than just guilt.

Sitting beside Seth in his truck as the road to town passed outside the window, she felt afraid. Whoever had attacked Seth would be back. She couldn't lose someone else she cared about again. Even though she'd gutted their relationship, left it with no chance for a future, she still cared about him.

He never needed to know. Either way she didn't want to lose him.

She felt hopeful. When years had passed and Liz's murder had remained unsolved, Ellie had started to assume it would always be that way. She hated it, wanted closure. Not just for herself but for Liz's family. She'd even reached out to her old chief to see if she could have the case files, but he'd refused, telling her that even if she was still an officer he wouldn't let her on the case because she'd been too close to it emotionally. She'd considered investigating without the notes, but it seemed…

Well, foolish. Like something doomed to fail before it started.

But now, with these new threads to tug, new leads to follow and Seth's help?

Maybe she could try. Maybe now after all these years, she could help bring that closure.

She felt…

Well, her heart was still pounding from that kiss. It was a foolish feeling, and even if it was stronger than anything she'd had these past few numb years, that didn't mean she needed to pay attention to it.

She watched him while he drove, found herself admiring the muscle in his upper arm as he held the wheel. Let her eyes travel to his face, to the stubble on his jaw. It was set firmly, like he was determined not to let anyone down. Oh, Seth. She wanted to run her hands along that stubble, tell him he'd never let her down, not once, that it was all her. She'd been the reason she left, her failures. Not his.

He knew that, right? That it hadn't been his fault?

Ellie wasn't brave enough to face that conversation yet. So instead she just kept watching him, struck by how familiar he still seemed, three years later.

How handsome. Her gaze wouldn't leave him. And she didn't want it to.

The truck slowed, and Ellie blinked, looking away from Seth and looking out the front window. They were pulling into the parking lot for the small clinic Raven Pass had.

"I need to get this checked out." He motioned to his side, smiling apologetically.

How could she have forgotten he was hurt?

"Of course. Do you want me to go in or, I guess..." She trailed off. Of course he didn't. He was an adult and she was just a friend.

His smile was gracious. "I'll be fine in the room alone. But come in the waiting room so you aren't alone in the car."

Ellie nodded. She should have thought of that. She was the one who had been law enforcement. She followed him inside and made herself comfortable in the waiting room. He was called back quickly and then back out to her faster than expected.

"Already?" she asked in surprise.

"Wasn't much they could do besides clean it and stitch it. I'm supposed to keep it clean." He shrugged. "Ready to go file our report?"

Ellie nodded. They drove to the Raven Pass trooper station. Since Liz's murder had been in Anchorage, it made more sense to go with the state agency that had jurisdiction both here and there, rather than the Raven Pass Police Department.

"I'm sorry," she apologized to Seth. "I was kind of lost in thought."

"Don't apologize."

And she heard more in the words than he meant, maybe. But her shoulders relaxed. None of it needed an apology. They somehow seemed to be okay, and that meant something to her.

He put the truck in Park. "Ready to do this?"

She nodded. As much as she'd ever be... She opened the truck door and stepped out, the cold hitting her in the face. Her cheeks stung almost instantly. But that wasn't why she shivered. That could only be attributed to the fact that in the parking lot she felt exposed, vulnerable to attack. She scanned the parking lot, lined with trees on the edges, some of them planted by a landscaper, some at one end a natural forest, the tall Sitka spruce seeming to reach almost to the sky.

It was deep and dark, providing the perfect cover for someone who wanted to watch them.

Or worse.

She shivered again.

"You all right?" Seth turned to her, always more perceptive than she wished he was.

"I'm fine." The words were automatic, not entirely true, but the way he raised his eyebrows and tilted his head to the side told her he saw through her facade.

"It's going to be okay."

But the words were empty to her ears. How could everything be okay when everything had been falling apart for the past three years? She'd felt like her heart had threatened to bleed out and die so she'd cauterized it to every kind of emotion. Then, she'd quit her job, the one she'd dreamed about since childhood when, instead of playing normal games with her dolls, she'd played police officer. She'd always wanted to be the rescuer, the one who righted wrongs.

Instead, when such an awful wrong had found her, she had run, unable to deal with her guilt and the darkness that had threatened to overwhelm her.

So she'd become another kind of rescuer. Saving lives through search and rescue work mattered to her. It just hadn't been her plan.

She took a deep breath in, let it out slowly and nodded. Maybe she didn't believe his reassurance, but it still meant something that he'd offered it. Perhaps he wasn't as indifferent to emotion as she was. She needed to remember that.

They walked together to the door of the trooper station.

"Can I help you?" A woman in her fifties, Ellie would guess, looked up at them from behind a sheet of glass. The whole building smelled like law enforcement and made her weirdly homesick. It was a mix of musty files and coffee, a smell with which she was familiar.

"We need to speak to a trooper."

"Do you need to file a report?"

Seth glanced at Ellie, and Ellie nodded back at him. A trooper joined them within minutes and motioned them toward the back. "You can come with me."

They sat down in an office with a desk and some chairs and spoke to the man behind the desk who introduced himself as Officer Patrick.

"I'm Seth Connors." Seth stuck out his hand and

shook the officer's with confidence. Ellie had always loved that about him.

"Can you tell me what happened?"

One more glance at her first, which Ellie felt to her bones, and Seth started talking. "I was out on a training run yesterday when I was attacked."

"By how many people?"

"Two, I think. Definitely more than one, but by the time the first one got to me and hit me on the head, details got a little fuzzy, so I can't be sure."

The trooper nodded, took notes. "Any description to give?"

"They were wearing face masks, the kind people wear in winter. Nothing that I'd note except they were both average height. I'd have noticed if one was especially short or tall."

He asked more questions, but Ellie found her mind wandering. Taking a statement was all so familiar to her, but it had been years since she'd done this. She missed it—but that part of her life was gone now.

She focused back in when she saw Seth pull out the letter from Liz.

"And this is from…" The trooper trailed off.

"It's from my sister. She was killed just over three years ago."

"Cause of death?"

Ellie spoke up. "She was shot. It looked like a drive-by shooting, and police eventually ruled it random, a wrong place, wrong time thing. But it wasn't."

"And your relation to the victim? The reason you know this?"

"I was her friend." Ellie hesitated. "At the time of her death, I worked at the Anchorage Police Department."

The officer nodded. "And you both think this incident is tied to her case."

Seth handed him the letter. They waited while Officer Patrick read it.

"I see what you mean. It does cast some suspicion on her death being an accident."

"More than some," Ellie commented. Office Patrick looked over at her, and she saw the apology in his eyes before he made it.

"Listen, Ms. Hardison, I see your point. And I will take this to my superiors. But while we will certainly make an effort to investigate the attack Mr. Connors sustained yesterday, it's highly unlikely we will investigate a cold case when the connection is tenuous."

Ellie felt angry, heat rushing to her forehead, and shoved her chair back. "Ten—"

Seth's hand on her arm stopped her. "Don't."

She stared, seething with frustration. Waited.

"I do understand." He shook his head again. "But you know how it is. This is a small department. We have to do what we can for many people, and reopening a cold case is not likely to be a high priority. I will talk to my boss and let you know. I just felt it was more respectful to be honest with you."

Ellie supposed she could understand and appreciated this. But she'd have preferred not to have bad news at all. Why hadn't she known this would be a likely outcome? In hindsight, she should have. Because everything he was saying was right. There was a connection, more than a small one, but nothing right now that a prosecuting attorney could argue was indisputable evidence to connect the attacks on Seth with Liz's death and this letter.

"Thanks for your time," Seth said and stood. Officer Patrick saw them both out of the building.

"That didn't go well," Ellie finally said once they'd walked back outside and were halfway across the parking lot.

"No. It didn't." His voice had darkened. Ellie exhaled a deep breath. She was going to have to come up with a plan to keep Seth in her sights, or at least close to it. She might not be an officer anymore, but she still had her training.

"You're going to have to be careful until they find out who is behind the attacks on you," she said aloud. He snorted.

Snorted?

"Ellie, they're not going to find anyone. If these incidents are connected, you really think people who were able to get away with murder are going to slip up enough in attacking me that they get caught? We have nothing. No fingerprints and no substantial crime scene since some messed-up snow doesn't really give investigators a whole lot to look at."

She glanced at him. He looked like he was bracing himself and then asked, "So…what's your plan?"

She turned to face him.

"I'm going to investigate on my own. Take a leave of absense."

She hadn't fully decided till she said the words aloud. She knew Seth wanted to find out who was behind this, also, but she had police connections she could use, maybe, and if not she still had her training.

Seth was a capable Alaskan, with talents that ranged from backcountry navigation to dog mushing to hunting. Back when Liz had been alive, he'd worked at a local outdoor company, guiding fishing and hunting trips. Nothing specifically qualified him to do something this close to police work.

But Ellie? She was qualified. And she was tired of letting this go unsolved. Tired of blaming herself for Liz's death. This wouldn't bring Liz back, but it would be doing *something*.

"El, I think we should—"

"What? Wait for the troopers?" She shook her head. "You heard them. They aren't going to be able to do anything. If I start looking into it myself, maybe more comes up."

"Let me help you."

Even though they'd discussed as much earlier, working together to figure this out, the idea made her recoil now. She trusted him, but he wasn't trained for this. She could ask him to put himself in danger.

"No," she said, already shaking her head, ready to list her reasons.

"Why?"

"Too dangerous. You're a civilian."

"As are you."

"With training." She frowned as she shot the words back at him.

Now he was the one shaking his head. "It's not your job to protect me from danger. Worst case scenario, I'm attacked again, but we get actual evidence."

Hearing him even put forth the idea of being used as bait made her feel like someone had stabbed her in the chest. "You can't do that."

"I can and I will. I want to help." She knew that voice. He was committed to this, and nothing she said was going to talk him out of it.

He unlocked the truck, and they both climbed in. When they'd shut the doors and Seth had started the engine, Ellie turned to him.

"Do you at least have a concrete plan to contribute to *my* investigation?"

He shook his head, grinned that sideways grin at her, and her heart skipped like it always used to. Ellie did her best to ignore her racing pulse. "No plan," he admitted. "Why, did you have ideas you wanted to share? I'd be willing to let you in on this investigation."

"*My* investigation," she insisted.

Just the word *investigation* made her heart beat in a way it shouldn't have. She shouldn't miss her old job this much. She *had* a fulfilling life, even now. There wasn't anything she was missing out on, careerwise. She wasn't defined by a job.

Right?

And yet, she couldn't talk herself out of trying to solve this case, go back to who she used to be, just for little while. Not because she wanted to investigate that badly—walking back into their past, thinking about Liz, all of that sounded hard. But if she was helping him, she'd be close to him. Able to keep him safe.

And yes, hopefully able to bring Liz's killers to justice.

No, she had to be honest with herself. It wasn't just about Seth. It was about her, too, about wanting back into her old life, her old job, even if just in this little way that couldn't last.

"So both of us? Working together? We're going to do this?" He was still grinning, and first thing she'd do in this investigation was lecture him on taking things more seriously.

But for now she nodded, her own face void of a smile, and said the words aloud. "Yes. We're doing this."

FIVE

The drive back to Seth's house was full of logistical discussions.

"Did you know Aaron well? The guy Liz was dating who was involved in whatever this was?"

Seth shook his head. "I met him once and didn't like him. Liz kept him away from me after that."

"Same." Ellie nodded. She pulled out her phone and googled his name. Aaron Richards.

"What are you doing?" Seth glanced over at her. She looked up.

"You're supposed to be driving. I'm googling Aaron since we know next to nothing about him. Not that there's much on Google. The guy has no social media. It looks like he works…for a home improvement store in Anchorage."

"Nothing else interesting?"

"Let me check another site. No court cases against him. Huh." She set the phone down. "Aaron Richards is extremely boring."

"If Liz suspected him, I still do," Seth insisted.

"I agree," Ellie found herself saying. "But I think

we're going to have to come at this from another angle to investigate."

Ellie kept going, asking him more questions she wanted his opinion on. Where would they start? Did they work under the assumption that the expedition company was involved in the smuggling or drug running or whatever it was, or did they keep open minds?

Seth didn't have answers for every question she asked, but his respect for her rose with each one she raised. He'd always known her mind worked a mile a minute, but it was still interesting to hear her talk it all out aloud, to see how she worked. She had been a good cop.

"I think," he said in answer to the most recent question she'd asked, "that we should start with Raven Pass Expeditions."

"You think Liz was right, and they're the ones doing something shady?"

He shook his head. "No." He said it aloud in case she wasn't looking at him. He glanced in her direction every now and then. "I don't think we can know that for sure. She had good reasons to think they were, and they may have been then. But three years is a lot of time. An employee could have been up to no good and left since then. But if we start with them, we can talk to them, see what they've seen, maybe even go on the route Liz thought was being used for drug smuggling."

This time he glanced her way a couple seconds.

She looked interested in the idea, something he took as a good sign. Seth chose to stay quiet and waited for her to respond.

"How would we go on the route? Do you mean ask for a tour, or sign up for one like we're undercover, or…"

Seth shook his head. "Not quite." He pulled into his driveway, waited until he'd put the truck in Park and then shifted in the seat to face her. "But you were right about the undercover part."

Her gaze didn't flinch, and he could almost see her thought process in her dark eyes, but she didn't say anything; she waited for him to go on. She'd never been one to jump to conclusions or demand explanations.

"I think we should apply for jobs at Raven Pass Expeditions."

"Doing what?"

He pulled out his phone. "I brought up the website earlier, just glanced at it for a minute."

"And what did you find?"

She was getting more curious.

"They're hiring dog mushers right now for an upcoming expedition. It starts in just under a week."

"So you think you have a chance of getting hired? But what about me? I don't like the idea of you doing that on your own while I work some other angle. It's too dangerous, even if we bring weapons, I don't want to be in a position to need to use them, and I'm the one with experience, and…"

This rant was an uncharacteristic-for-Ellie kind of speech, and Seth didn't know what to do with that. Why was she so passionate about him not going alone? Even if they managed to be friends, and this was strictly about Liz, he wouldn't have expected her to care that much.

Almost immediately, he realized he'd been wrong to think that way. If the shoe were on the other foot, wouldn't he be devastated if anything happened to her and encourage her not to take unnecessary risks?

"I think you should come with me."

Her eyes widened.

Seth took a breath, decided he'd try to lay it all out at once. "Yes. I think you should come with me," he continued. "We'll both apply for jobs as mushers after I teach you how. That will enable to us keep an eye on their operations just in case anyone is still involved or ever was, and it will give us a chance to talk to people there, see the route Liz described. You don't have to decide yet if you want to do it, but we need to take a break because I'm starving. Do you want waffles?" He reached for the door of the truck and climbed out.

If RPE didn't have anything to do with the drug running, if it was another business in that shopping complex as Liz had said it could be or if whoever had been involved had moved on in the three years since she'd written that letter, then they weren't risking too much. A week lost for the expedition, a few days lost before that training Ellie to mush…

Although that wouldn't be time wasted. He tried not to think too hard about how it had felt for her to stand in front of him on the runners of the dogsled, his arms on either side of her holding on to the handlebar of the sled. Their bodies close together. Spending time with her wouldn't be a problem, except that he'd have to keep reminding himself that what they'd had was over, and they didn't have a future.

"Go undercover as dog mushers," she stated from somewhere behind him as he unlocked the door to the house and they both went back inside.

"Yes." He set his keys down on the table near the front door and moved to the kitchen, where he began pulling out ingredients. Flour. Sugar.

"You think I can pull that off?"

Seth opened the fridge. Butter. Milk. Eggs. He shut the fridge door and turned to face Ellie. "Yes. I do."

She blinked a few times and then nodded. "Okay. Well, you're the one who'd have to teach me everything I'd need to know. If you think it can be done, I'm game."

That was what she was worried about? Whether or not she could learn enough to handle the job of being a musher guiding on the adventure? He'd have thought she'd have needed to consider the danger a bit more, but what had he been thinking? This was Ellie. She wasn't scared of anything.

Ellie watched Seth watch her and exhaled a breath of relief when he turned back to preparing the waffle ingredients.

This was a crazy plan he was concocting, just crazy enough that it might work, but full of more risk than she was comfortable with. For him, not her. No, she didn't know how to mush, and she was under no illusion that it would be easy. But the danger of going undercover…

In a way, she'd almost welcome it. She could well remember the way her body and mind had responded in the thick of an investigation when she'd been a police officer. She was ready for the sense of being one footstep away from the edge of a precipice, the way her heart raced and she fought to keep her breath steady when an investigation was going well. The way interrogating a suspect both invigorated and enlightened her as she got closer to the truth.

But the idea of Seth being in the line of fire was too much to consider. Her mind didn't even want to go there, but she forced it to. *Every* cost should be considered if they were going to do this.

She watched him as he worked, tried to reconcile the man she'd known with the idea that soon he might be acting in that undercover capacity. It was hard to imagine as he moved with ease through the kitchen, cooking her food like they were the picture of that domestic bliss. His hands were careful, gentle as he measured flour and added it to the bowl.

But she'd known him long enough to know that he wasn't all careful movements and methodical steps. She'd seen him blaze a trail through the wilderness, bold steps leading the way, watching him stand down a grizzly bear on a hike once and not even flinch while she'd been shaking in her hiking boots.

Seth could handle this just fine. The undercover work, the danger, all of it.

She was the one who was going to have a hard time.

"You're sure about this?" she asked, stepping closer almost without realizing it and then tensing up. The last thing they needed right now was to complicate this plan by adding any kid of romantic entanglement between the two of them. The kiss was a one-off thing. Well, not technically, since they'd kissed in the past. But for the present, it was an isolated incident, something that couldn't happen again. They needed to be alert in order to figure out who had been behind Liz's murder.

"I think it's our only option." He said it with a straight face, not in a dramatic manner at all, but Ellie still felt it like a punch to the stomach. She hadn't considered the idea that they didn't have other options. In her mind, it was still something they were choosing to do on purpose, to hopefully solve Liz's murder. But Seth had a point. If they didn't start being proactive and trying to figure out who had been behind all of it, then it was possible the attacks against Seth would continue. And it was also possible they'd start to target her, as well. This was what they had to do.

Her chest tightened a little at the idea, the enormity of it. What they were attempting was risky in a way that few things in her life had been. Ellie knew that, but still, she felt settled, and determination seemed to flow through every muscle group and fill her with a certainty that reassured her. "Okay," she said, agreeing again to help.

This time, though, Seth really seemed to hear her. He looked at her, like he was looking for something, his gaze curious. Searching. "So we'll eat and then get started?"

Learning to dog mush. Yesterday she'd been a search and rescue worker. Then, she'd rescued her ex-fiancé. Been shot at. Taken shelter in a cabin. Gone to the police. Asked for a leave of absence from her job. Decided to investigate. Agreed to make a plan to bring down murderers. Now, she would learn to mush.

The last twenty-four hours had been too overwhelming to put into words, but what else could she do but the right thing?

"I'm ready. Whatever you've got to teach me about dogs and mushing, I'm ready to learn. We also need a more solid plan."

"But first, waffles." He grinned at her, removed the first waffle from the iron, put it on a plate and handed it to her.

The food he'd made was delicious, and she enjoyed every bite, savoring the way he'd made them just the way she remembered: not too sweet, so she could flood them with syrup without being overwhelmed by sugar.

They ate in silence, and it felt right to Ellie. Familiar. It also gave her some mental space to process all the changes that had happened in such a short time span, which she appreciated. She'd always been an internal processor. Later, she was sure, he'd want to talk things out, and she would do her best to respect the fact that he needed that, but right now she was thankful for the quiet.

"As far as the plan," Ellie started, "how are we going to pull this off? I haven't mushed before so I don't have a résumé or anything. How am I going to get hired?"

"Just put normal references down that they can about work ethic and all of that. As far as mushing experience, a lot of mushers get jobs up here from recommendations. They won't question your qualifications if you seem like you know what you're doing."

She nodded, still thinking through everything else they'd needed. Liz had thought someone was smuggling drugs. Ellie had spent some time while she waited for Seth at the doctor researching the area, the companies in the strip mall she'd pointed out, and that research had turned up nothing. Even if it felt like they were flying blind, going undercover was their best way forward to gather more information, since what they were looking for was so vague.

"Okay, if that will work, then…let's get started." Ellie smiled.

"First things first, you need some gear," Seth said as he stood, pushing his chair back from the table. "And maybe more coffee. Would you like more coffee? I have travel mugs."

"Please." She didn't know how she was going to mush and drink coffee, but she'd only had half a cup so far. She was definitely going to need more if crazy things were going to keep happening like they had yesterday.

She took the travel mug when he offered it. "As far as gear, I've got all this." She motioned down to her snow pants and fleece sweater she had on.

He looked at her boots where they sat by the door and raised his eyebrows. "It's those I've got a problem with."

"What is wrong with my boots?" They were from a high-end outdoor brand, black synthetic material and rated to a trillion degrees below zero.

Not that far, obviously, but certainly they were made well enough he couldn't find fault with them.

"Nothing if you want to freeze an hour out on our run."

"You wouldn't let me freeze." She said it with a laugh, meaning it as a joke.

"I sure wouldn't." But Seth's voice was serious. His eyebrows were raised. Their eyes met and Ellie's breath caught in her chest. Somehow her teasing hadn't been met with the same. It felt like he'd taken what could have been casual flirtation and amped it up.

Seth cleared his throat. "Boots. Wait here. I've got some you can borrow."

"Our feet are not the same size," she said dubiously as she waited for him to return.

He came back carrying a pair of boots that looked like nothing she'd seen before. The bottoms were some kind of leather, the tops canvas, maybe, and long leather straps hung from them, but there were no holes for laces.

"And these are better than my REI boots, guaranteed to a thousand degrees below zero?" she asked him, eyebrows raised.

"For dog mushing, yes. If you try to wear those—" he jerked his head toward her boots "—you're going to freeze. Starting with your feet."

"Okay, fine, I will wear your strange boots. But what are you going to wear? And again, I'm not sure how I'm going to move in boots that are too big for me."

"I put some extra liners in them. The way they're made, you'll be fine."

"I'm going to look ridiculous."

"You could never look ridiculous to me."

There he went again, taking her teasing somewhere…well somewhere she wasn't quite sure she was brave enough to go. If she'd wondered if he still had feelings for her… It seemed like yes.

She was suddenly aware of how close to her he was sitting, the way he was leaning forward, their faces only a foot or so apart as he gave her directions about the boots. Not that she wanted to do anything with their proximity. One accidental kiss was enough for her. But knowing he was right there gave her a heady feeling, made her feel like she couldn't quite think straight.

"Thanks." She offered a small smile. "For the reassurance."

"Anytime." And the look in his eyes said he'd always be there. For anything she needed.

Ellie swallowed hard.

Boots. They were talking about boots. She reached for them, he handed them to her, and she pulled them on. It took some effort to get her feet into them, but she wiggled them in.

"Wrap them around. Yes, like that. Wrap them around your leg again, and one more time. Yes. Then tie them."

They looked like a cross between moccasins, winter boots and ballet shoes with long ribbons, and her feet had never been this warm in her entire life. They were a little roomy, even with the extra liners Seth had added, but she could see his point.

He was looking at her like he knew that already, face slightly amused, mouth quirked into a smile. He'd always taken care of her so well, anticipated what she'd need before she did. He had been the kind of fiancé who'd made sure the oil in her car was always changed, that her gas tank was full. She'd taken him for granted and it overwhelmed her now with regret. She blinked back tears.

He'd given her everything she'd ever wanted. And she'd walked away because of fear.

Seth had already stood, seeming this one time not to know exactly what she was thinking. Or maybe he did and he was giving her space.

Either way, he spoke up, breaking the moment.

"Now, grab your coat, and let's go make a dog musher out of you."

SIX

When they stepped outside, the yard came alive. His dogs had been curled up on top of their houses, or beside them—it wasn't nearly cold enough for them to want to be inside right now—until they saw him step out. Now they were all standing, barking in a crazy chorus, determined to make the most noise possible to assure that they got chosen for the team.

Seth looked around, uneasily considering the woods around his property.

A crack split the air.

"Get down!" he yelled, even as he searched for the location of the threat. It was broad daylight, and they weren't too far from town, but clearly whoever was after him had no qualms about attacking.

He looked beside him. Ellie was still standing.

"Ellie!" His heart pounded in his chest.

She shook her head. Pointed. "It was a tree, Seth. A tree fell."

Seth fought to calm his breathing, calling himself every kind of fool for overreacting. Nothing had been wrong.

But it could have been. And if there had been a threat…

Well, she hadn't gotten down when he'd said to. That didn't bode well.

"You need to be extremely careful. Listen to me and do what I say, even if it doesn't make sense."

"I have the boots on, don't I? I get that you're the dog mushing guy. I'll listen. But I saw the tree. I knew it was fine."

It was all he could do to keep going with this plan when he looked at her and saw everything he'd lost years ago. She'd only gotten more beautiful, though something about her seemed more fragile than it had back then. The awareness that life could change in a heartbeat had probably changed her. It added a layer of vulnerability. He hated that she'd experienced circumstances that had broken her—his sister's death had nearly broken him—but perhaps it had humbled her like it had him. Still, every change about her made her more attractive to him.

Her attractiveness had nothing to do with his concern about her and not wanting her to be hurt. That had much more to do with how much he enjoyed her company as a person. He'd somehow minimized it in the last few years, convinced himself that they hadn't been that close, that maybe what they had shared hadn't been real love.

He'd been wrong. No one had known him like Ellie Hardison, and he'd certainly never loved anyone the way he'd loved her.

Still loved her…despite the way she'd hurt him.

"Just keep an eye out, okay?" he tried again. "The woods, the open space…"

She nodded. "I know, Seth. Situational awareness was a topic at the police academy." Her words were gentle, but he'd needed the reminder that as fragile as she might look, she wasn't. She was trained for this. If anything, he should probably be worried about his safety.

But wasn't that what love did? Make you care about someone so much that you lost a bit of your capability for rational thought?

He didn't still love her, did he?

As soon as he wondered it, he knew the answer. He did still love her. With everything in his heart.

He looked over at her, dressed in her winter gear, ready to learn. He'd seen her in so many different circumstances, different roles, and she was just as beautiful to him in all of them.

How did a man ignore something like that? If he moved too fast, tried to get her back too quickly, he'd scare her away. She'd left for a reason and he still wasn't clear on what that was, didn't get the impression that she was ready to talk about it yet.

Seth took a breath. Reminded himself to go slow.

"First off, listen to that barking." He made himself focus on the lesson.

"I definitely hear the barking." She had to raise her voice to be heard above it.

"That's because they all want to run. Lesson number one is that the dogs love this, so don't let anyone tell you they don't. Look at them." He motioned toward the yard with his hand, took in the sights as she would be seeing them. Dogs standing up with wagging tails, excitedly jumping around, eyes alert, sparkling.

"I can definitely see that."

"Today we're going to run six dogs."

"Each? Or will I be by myself?"

"You're not quite there yet," he said with a smile, knowing that if she was like he had been, she might assume that six dogs weren't a very powerful team. When the guy who'd taught him had started Seth out with four, he'd been downright offended, and then he'd seen how fast those dogs could run. Seth wanted to be on the sled with her, partially because he'd almost lost his sled and dogs the first time he'd gone out alone, and partially because he didn't want the two of them separated quite yet. He'd been attacked only yesterday. And if this was about Liz, Ellie would be in as much danger as he was, since she was involved, too. The thought of someone attacking her…it made him want to put his fist through a wall. He wouldn't—*couldn't*—let anything happen to her. Maybe if nothing went wrong today and it looked like the danger had lessened somewhat, he'd be more comfortable with some space between them.

But right now, space was the last thing he wanted. He couldn't get close enough to her, couldn't spend enough time with her to make up for the emptiness in his life these last few years.

"So how does this work?" She'd walked over to his sled and had picked up the line, examining it.

"This is a gangline."

"Okay." She nodded, and he could almost see her brain filing the information, categorizing it for later. He loved how her mind worked, how methodical she was.

He pointed to the very end of the gangline, the end nearest the sled. "See these two long ropes?"

She nodded.

"These are tuglines. They attach to the harness, at the end. A couple feet that way are the necklines."

"The smaller ones attached to the gangline?"

He smiled and nodded. "Yes."

They worked on harnessing next, and while she fumbled with the first dog or two, by the time they were working with the next few, she'd gotten the hang of it.

By the time she was standing on the sled in front of him and he was ready to go, he was feeling confident about this plan.

"Keep your foot on the brake," he said to her, wrapping one arm around her as he held on to the handlebar. It was for practicality's sake only, he told himself. Nothing to do with enjoying the proximity to Ellie. He reached down and pulled the snow hook out of the ground that he'd been using to keep the team stopped in place.

"Ready? Foot off the brake, El. All right."

He'd given them permission to do what they'd been wanting—run. And run they did, down the packed trail, out of the dog yard and into the woods.

They were avoiding the trails he'd run yesterday, and staying much closer to town. He wasn't willing to risk a repeat of yesterday, especially with Ellie with him. Shadows of spruce trees, thickly wooded areas that he usually thought of as beautiful, made him tense now. Every movement of a branch and he wondered if a sniper was behind it, instead of a bird or maybe a moose. Seth was on full alert, desperate to keep Ellie out of danger.

She was quiet the first few minutes and then finally laughed, sounding a little breathless. "Wow, what a rush! I can't believe how loud they are and ready to go, and then all the sudden they're quiet like that?"

He smiled, even though she couldn't see him. One

of the best parts of mushing was that overwhelming quiet once the dogs focused on the job at hand and were happy to be working.

Maybe that was why he'd taken to mushing like he had. He'd walked away from his corporate job in Anchorage when Liz had died. The city had seemed empty without her. Overwhelming at the same time. He'd wanted space so he'd taken his savings and gone to Raven Pass. He made enough now with dog mushing sponsors and giving tours to tourists to feed himself and the dogs. Mushing gave him a focus, a purpose. Without it, he'd have been like an unoccupied husky—destructive.

"Gee," he called to the dogs, directing them to take a trail that veered off to the right. "Lean," he said to Ellie.

"Into the turn or the opposite?"

He'd never stopped to think about it. He just moved his body with the sled, like it and he and the dog team were one entity, running together. Now he had to pay attention to his body in order to give her the answer.

"You kind of shift into it, but not too much. Just be conscious of what you do with your weight, and try to work with the team instead of against them, but be ready to be a counterweight if the sled starts to tip."

She nodded. "Okay. What else are you going to teach me?"

"Shh." He smiled to himself. "You're learning right now. Just pay attention."

When he'd learned, it had driven him crazy that his mentor hadn't said much to him or the dogs. Seth had been desperate for more details, for some kind of how-to manual, but instead the man had just mushed on, with Seth with him. When situations arose—a dog got tangled, or there was a moose in the trail and they had to stop—he let Seth watch him handle the dogs and help him; without realizing it, Seth had learned.

Ellie, however, was so analytical that he knew she'd want more details later. Maybe they'd sit down and he'd write down some instructions for her to review. She'd need to learn fast; if they could get on to one of the expeditions Raven Pass Expeditions was leading, it would likely be soon. The snow season started to be unpredictable before long here, and they couldn't risk dog mushing being taken off the list of excursions. He wasn't sure what other options they'd have to go undercover that would serve so well.

Movement in the distance caught his eye and his body tensed. He stepped closer to Ellie, almost subconsciously, felt his arm muscles tense.

The shape moved and he blew out a breath. A moose. It was only a moose.

Still no sign of human danger. Seth kept scanning their surroundings, anyway.

"When we get back and get the dogs put away—" he spoke again, probably an hour into their mostly quiet ride "—I think we should go try to get the jobs."

"You think I can pass for a dog musher already?"

"You still have a lot to learn, but I think it's enough to get the job." At least, he hoped it was. They stayed quiet again, and Seth took his eyes off the trail just for a second to look at Ellie, leaning his head to the side to get a better view of the side of her face.

She was so focused, but she looked relaxed. She was special—he'd always known it—but he felt like today he just kept being reminded.

How could he have let this woman get away in the past? Or had her leaving had nothing to do with him?

Was it wrong to hope this could be some kind of second chance, that God was giving him a do-over? He could dream, couldn't he?

No, probably not. First, he hadn't seen much of God's involvement in his life lately. He wasn't going to say God had abandoned him but there was an absence he wasn't used to feeling.

Also, it wasn't like he had time to woo Ellie. Instead he'd be dragging her into tracking smugglers, going undercover to try to find some dangerous criminals. It was his idea to apply to RPE, so he felt he bore responsibility for the risks.

He hoped she wouldn't suffer because of his plan. Liz.

This had been brought on by the knowledge that they were all part of this, had been since Liz wrote that letter and mailed it off, referring to both him and Ellie. And Ellie had put herself in *more* danger by coming back into contact with him—to get justice for the woman they both missed.

Neither of them would be able to sleep without fear ever again if this threat weren't dealt with.

That's why he was willing to take this risk. Seth only hoped it would pay off.

Later, after Seth showed her how put the dogs away, they were walking toward the entrance to Raven Pass Expeditions. She'd gone home to shower and change and could only hope she looked the part enough to be convincing. What did dog mushers wear to ask for a job? Ellie didn't have the slightest clue. She should have asked Seth, but she hadn't and now it was too late.

Just thinking about him made her head feel fuzzy. Several times today she felt like they'd danced back over the "friends" line into something more. She had to tell herself it didn't matter, that it was natural that she'd have feelings for someone she was once engaged to. That didn't mean she deserved his love. If she'd taken the threats against Liz more seriously, he wouldn't have lost his sister. There was no way to spin this so she didn't have some fault in it, and she couldn't face his rejection once he fully realized that.

So she'd left before he could break up with her. And she needed to remember that.

Also, she was exhausted. She hadn't paid much attention this morning to what Seth did after a run, but now that she was supposed to be learning, she'd focused on every step of the process.

When he'd stopped the sled, he'd put the snow hook in the ground, then petted each individual dog on the head. He talked to them, too, and Ellie would have thought he'd be embarrassed that she was seeing him talk to dogs, but he acted like it was the most natural thing in the world. It just made her more attracted to him. He had no idea how sweet he was, how genuinely nice and how attractive those qualities were.

Then he'd fed a slice of frozen meat to each one. Watching the dogs lunge for the snacks had been entertaining. After that, he'd unharnessed the dogs and hooked them back up to their tethers. Some dogs he stood with for a minute and rubbed them down further with his hands, massaging the muscles they'd been using.

Ellie had watched him just long enough to learn the ropes and then had jumped in. She'd made a couple mistakes. Unharnessing took her forever as she kept putting the legs through the wrong holes at first. And one dog she'd hooked in the wrong place to a house that wasn't his, and Seth had had to correct her. But for the most part, she felt like she was learning. And working together with Seth, as part of a team, felt like what had been missing in her life. She'd missed being someone's other half. Someone's partner.

She'd missed Seth.

She was going to sleep better than ever tonight. The idea of doing this job for a multiday expedition was wearying. But she still thought this was their best chance, and she wanted to try. She'd do anything to find the men who'd harmed Liz.

"Sure you're up for it?" he asked her as he reached for the door to the RPE headquarters. His grin was casual and easy, but she could read the wariness in his clear blue eyes. He was concerned for her safety. She squared her shoulders and smiled back at him.

"I'm up for it."

Still, he hesitated. Ellie reached for the handle and pulled it open. A bell chimed.

"Hi, welcome to RPE. How can we help you adventure today?" a perky blonde woman behind the counter asked, her hair swinging in a ponytail.

Ellie had to school her features, keep them relaxed. The truth was, she was thrown off a little. She'd been braced for a place that reeked of having something to hide, if this adventure company was little more than a front for drug smuggling. But instead she had the opposite feeling. The room was decorated in kind of a trendy, outdoorsy style and had an energetic vibe.

Getting underneath RPE's friendly exterior was going to be a challenge. For half a second, Ellie wondered if Liz had been wrong, but her logic was sound. It was at the very least someone who worked in one of the businesses in this strip mall three years ago. But Ellie was also aware that appearances could be deceiving. And the idea of someone smuggling drugs on the exact route this company took people on adventures?

Well, Ellie didn't believe in coincidences.

"I'm Seth Calloway." Seth stuck out his hand and the blonde woman shook it, her eyebrows raised in interest. "And this is Ellie Hamilton."

Ellie hadn't realized he'd give false last names, but it made sense as a precaution.

"Nice to meet you both. How can I help?"

"I'm a local dog musher. I've heard about what you guys do here and wondered how to apply for a guiding position."

"Same here."

"You two know each other?" she asked.

They hadn't invented any kind of deep cover story, and yes, they obviously knew each other, so Ellie nodded. "He's the one who got me into mushing," she answered honestly.

"Well, you're in luck. A couple mushers we had lined up had to back out. Of course." She hesitated. "The trip we really needed mushers for is happening this weekend."

Ellie swallowed hard. It was already Wednesday, and she hadn't run a team by herself yet. She smiled, then looked over at Seth. "I don't know what Seth's schedule is like, but I could make this weekend work."

He nodded, also, though she thought she detected a flare of concern in his eyes. Oh, come on, she could learn to manage a dog team by the weekend.

Okay, yes, when she said it that way in her mind it sounded crazy to her, too. But they needed to find out who was behind this. Evidence pointed toward someone at RPE being involved and this was the best way to find corroboration. Too late to back out now. The woman's eyes had lit up with relief, and she was talking now about what fantastic timing this was. Ellie knew that they needed as much authenticity as possible on their side with something this risky, not just for their lives and safety—though that was weighing on her heavily— but for their investigation. If they were discovered, everything they'd planned to work on would have to be let go. Investigating people in person, trying to get a feel for who might have been involved, these were unorthodox ways to conduct an investigation, Ellie knew that. But it seemed like the best option to her.

The fact that it had worked out well enough—she literally thanked God for that—that they actually *needed* mushers for that very trip? Ellie couldn't have asked for better.

"It works for me, too." He kept his nod casual.

"Great, well if the two of you could come with me, the boss can ask you some questions, and we just may have a job for you." She motioned for them to follow her behind the counter and through a door to an office with the door open. The blonde woman knocked and then stuck her head around the wall. "Brandt? I have a solution to our musher problem." She turned back to them. "Brandt is the founder of our company."

The man in the office was behind a desk, Ellie could see now that they'd entered, and he was standing up and moving around it toward them.

"Brandt Bowker."

"Seth Calloway."

"Ellie Hamilton."

Ellie watched Brandt's face. He didn't react to their names at all.

"You two are both dog mushers?"

They nodded.

"Excellent! Two of our usual employees canceled this morning. Seems they fell in love on one of our trips and eloped." He raised his eyebrows and looked between the two of them. "So the two of you aren't at risk of that, are you?"

Ellie blinked, cleared her throat. "No, we, uh…" She looked in Seth's direction, then back at Brandt. "Just friends."

"Absolutely. Friends," Seth parroted in a way that did absolutely nothing to make their little protest more convincing.

Brandt smiled and waved a hand. "Listen, your romantic interests are your own business. I just need to know we can count on you for this weekend."

"It works for both of us," Seth answered for them.

"Great!" He nodded once. "Halley, can get you the paperwork they'll need to fill out, as well as our information packet for our partners."

"Do you work with a lot of different people? Dog mushers and other adventure providers?" Ellie asked, realizing the question might be useful for them.

"Oh, tons. Raven Pass Expeditions is an extremely large venture. We do everything the bigger companies do but better, and in smaller groups, which gives our tourists a better experience. And that's the goal, right? A good experience for everyone?"

His enthusiasm for his company seemed genuine, Ellie noted. But again, people could have dark sides. Things about them you didn't know. She'd seen it enough in her job when some of the people they'd had to arrest had been people who looked like pillars of the community.

"We'll be happy to get things filled out. And Friday is the day you need us?"

"Yes. You'll meet the clients right before the trip. They'll be arriving at three. Can you make it?" He seemed anxious, like he was anticipating them saying no and this whole thing disappearing.

It took all her restraint for Ellie not to elbow Seth in case he wasn't reading this right. They couldn't mess this up. If he wanted them there at three, that's what would happen.

"Three o'clock? We'll be there."

SEVEN

The moment they walked out of the office, Seth started to second-guess his plan. No, that wasn't true. He'd started to second-guess it the moment Ellie began talking, and she knew it, which was why she'd talked faster, dared him to speak up against her with that little sideways quirk of her head and her raised eyebrows. And he didn't have a problem with the idea of going undercover in general; it was still solid and by far the best option he had to investigate. But he shouldn't have let Ellie get involved. He ignored for a moment the fact that she was a former cop and this had been just as much her idea, and instead beat himself up, telling himself he should have said hello to her, done some catching up on old times and then let her leave. The farther she was from him, the better…and not just because he was heading into a potentially deadly situation. She was too important to him to risk her getting hurt. And too dangerous to his heart to risk getting close again.

At this point she might already have a target on her back from how much time they'd spent in proximity. Seth still had no way of knowing how the criminals knew he'd gotten that package. Had they been there when it was delivered? Followed it from the lawyer's office?

"The lawyer…" he mumbled under his breath. Then turned to Ellie. "When was that package postmarked?"

They were walking back to his truck, and there was no one around, not that he saw, but he kept his voice low, anyway.

"I don't remember. Why?"

"Wait. I don't know yet." He didn't want to say anything, to let his mind go there, if there was a chance he was wrong. Instead they climbed into the truck and drove the distance to his house in silence. Ellie had always been good at that, not filling up silence with words. Sometimes he wished she'd just talk aimlessly, because he loved hearing her voice and her thoughts about life, but today he was glad she tended to be quiet.

He hoped what he wondered was wrong.

They'd know soon enough.

He parked the truck, and they climbed out. The sled dogs greeted them with howls, and Cipher jumped down from where she'd been lying on the flat roof of her doghouse and nosed his hand.

"Hey, girl." He bent down and rubbed behind her ears. No doubt his dogs were picking up on the extra stress and anxiety he'd been feeling these last couple days. He needed to mitigate that as best he could, and showing them attention at times like this was one way.

"All right, let's see…" he said as he unlocked his front door.

"Going to tell me what you're thinking, yet?" Ellie asked.

He shook his head. "Not yet."

She followed him inside, and he was thankful he'd

managed to straighten up the mess the intruders had left in his house before. He locked the door behind them both, then walked to where he'd stored the box in his room.

Postmarked four days ago. And they'd come after him yesterday.

The criminals had had three days in between to discover the package was coming. Either because someone was looking out for his mail at the post office, though that seemed the least likely option. Or someone had been watching his house. Possible, but somewhat of a stretch.

Was someone watching his sister's lawyer? The man's name had been fairly public during the investigation, as a witness had reported seeing his sister come from his office earlier on the day she died, wiping tears from her eyes. Police had investigated and declared the lawyer innocent, and Seth, who had met the man, was inclined to believe him.

He'd liked the guy. Even though he hadn't had an answer for why his sister was crying. The lawyer had said she'd been fine inside the office.

And now he was afraid the lawyer might be dead… or about to be killed.

"Okay, you've really got to tell me. You're making a really bad face."

"I'm trying to figure out how these guys knew to watch me or knew this package mattered, and I wanted to see how many days passed from when it was sent to when I received it."

"Why?"

He reached for his cell phone. "To see how likely

it is that the police have already discovered that Liz's lawyer has been killed."

She blinked, jerked back. "You think…"

"Either they have been watching me this whole time, saw a suspicious package and acted, *or* they paid attention when Liz died, knew she'd been at her lawyer's, and have been watching where he sends packages. Or someone else at the office let them know a package was going out to Liz's brother. Any of those things would have flagged their attention, since both of us were connected to Liz."

Her eyes were still wide, and she only nodded. She didn't say anything, but what was there to say?

He dialed the number for a friend of his at the Anchorage Police Department. They'd been roommates for a while before his friend had gotten married and moved out.

"Hodges here."

"Hey, Hodge," he said. "It's Seth Connors. How are you?"

"Good, man, I'm good. Been a while since I've heard from you. You all right?" His friend's voice was cautious. And for good reason. Seth knew he had been hard to reach these last few years, appreciating that his friends checked on him via text now and then, but mostly replying in one-or two-word replies.

"I'm okay. Something's going on down here. Got attacked on a training run yesterday."

"You're kidding." He heard the frown in Hodges's voice. "That's an uncomfortable coincidence."

Dread sunk into the pit of his stomach. He'd had the suspicion, that's why he had called, but it sounded like he might have been right.

"Liz's lawyer? Mick Rogers?" he asked. "I got a package from him and just realized someone might have been watching his office. Is he…"

"Found him dead just off the Ship Creek trail downtown two days ago."

Seth looked down, took a breath and tried to absorb what felt like a punch to the gut. Suspecting it was one thing, being right was another. He hated that he man was dead, grieved for him. And at the same time realized that this meant the threat to himself and Ellie was all that much more real.

"You sure you're okay down there? These guys aren't messing him around. He was shot in the head, execution-style."

"We tried to get the troopers to look into Liz's death again…" He trailed off.

"But you think you came across more as a relative who can't let go and less like someone with actual evidence that it was necessary?"

Hodges had summed it up well. Seth nodded. "Yeah."

"I tried the same thing once over the past few years. My chief doesn't think there's enough to look at her specifically. That incident was written off as gang violence, wrong place, wrong time kinda stuff, but I'm with you, I think it's looking like a tangle. I'm looking into what I can. We're fully investigating the lawyer's death since he was clearly a target."

"Good." Not as good as it could be, but he'd take it. At least someone was looking somewhere. He hated that the lawyer had died, though. He'd been a good man, by all accounts. Seth's hands clenched into fists. His sister. Her lawyer. Too much death. No one else should have to die.

"I'll keep you in the loop as much as I can. Is that what you were calling about? Or is there something else?"

"Nothing else. I just want to know who is after me and El."

"Did you say El? As in Ellerie Hardison?"

He'd forgotten for a second that his former roommate was also good friends with Ellie, as they'd worked together back when she was an officer in the Anchorage Police Department.

Ellie turned to him at the sound of her name, head tilted a little, a question in her eyes. He shook his head. He'd explain when he was off the phone.

"Yeah. She's here."

"We miss her. I just thought of her the other day when someone made the coffee too strong. She was always doing that. She was a good officer, though."

"Yeah. I know. We're going to—" how did he put this in a way that didn't get his friend in trouble but to also ensure if anything happened, someone would at least know to look for them? "—look around some. Liz had some suspicions. Her lawyer had just sent me a package that she'd instructed to pass on three years after her death if she happened to die. Guess she was really worried, and she was right to be."

"What was in the package?"

"Her suspicions about—" he needed to stay vague "—some kind of smuggling operation she'd discovered. Look, Hodge, it was all suspicion, and while I know at least some things she was thinking had to be right, if her death wasn't enough to make law enforcement think she'd accidentally gotten tangled up in something, this won't be, either. Not yet, anyway."

"But she told you what she thought."

"Yes."

Hodges blew out a long breath. "You be careful. Keep me posted, okay? And don't do anything I wouldn't do. And make sure you keep Ellie close."

"I'm not going to let her get hurt." Seth lowered his voice as he said out loud the promise he'd already made to himself a hundred times in the last couple days.

The tension broke as Hodges laughed. "I didn't say that, man. I said, keep her close. I'm thinking if she's with you, I'm less worried about you getting hurt."

Seth smiled. "You have a point."

"All right, I'll keep you in the loop. Take care, man. Call me if you need me."

"Later." Seth hung up.

Ellie was looking at him, eyes wide. "Hodges? What's wrong? I could only hear enough to piece some of the conversation together."

He filled her in, including the fact that the lawyer was dead.

She listened. "We need to get started on the training then, because we can't afford to mess this up."

He wasn't sure he liked how determined she was, but he didn't have another option right now. So he talked to her about what she'd need to know to dog mush. They needed to go out again.

"El, about this undercover thing…"

"Yeah?" She looked wary. Seth shook his head.

"I'm not calling it off or anything like that."

Relief spread on her face.

"But I do think we need a solid plan. I didn't like how it felt to be winging things today."

She nodded. "Okay. That make sense." She yawned, covered her mouth. "Sorry."

"How do you think we should go about this?"

"Me? The undercover aspect was your idea," she reminded him.

Seth winced. "It was, but it was a little rash. You're the one with the experience, the training. How would you handle this?"

She seemed to be considering it. "I think we need to consider this a fact-finding mission. We need to watch the people who work for RPE closely and not just decide which of them is involved, if any of them are. We also need to see if the expedition lends itself to being a vehicle for smuggling, you know? See if groups split up, could one individual disappear for a drop and not be missed, those kinds of things. I also think it would be helpful to try to talk to the workers alone and get a feel for who they are and if we think they're involved."

Already she had more of a solid idea of what to do than he did. Seth would be lost without her in this investigation, and he'd never been more aware of that.

He smiled. "Nice."

"You think that'll work?" She sounded uncertain.

"Ellie, I think you're fantastic at this. It's an awesome plan. Nice job."

They talked a little longer, then when the light of the day started to fade, she stood up to head home. Seth offered to fix dinner for them, and while she could probably tell it was a ploy to keep her closer a little longer, she agreed. They sat down together at the table to a meal of moose steaks and mashed potatoes.

"You really should find someone to stay with during all of this, to keep yourself safe from these guys." Seth tried to keep his tone even, but his heart was pounding. He knew she couldn't stay here with him, it wouldn't look right, but he wanted her safe.

Instead of being understanding, she just raised her eyebrows and shook her head, looking at him with a tired expression. She was still beautiful, but she looked tired.

He wished he could fix that for her.

"Don't you understand?" she asked, shaking her head. "We are in danger because of Liz. Don't get me wrong, it's worth it to me, and I want to make sure her killers are brought to justice. But we are having to be careful right now because of our association with her. Which friend is it you want me to drag into this, knowing that someone could come after her next?"

Her look was pointed. She was right, and they both knew it, but he still wanted her safe even though it was selfish. He opened his mouth to offer his guest room, just in case, but she was already shaking her head.

"I am going home, Seth, later. If anything changes and that doesn't seem wise, I will consider other options. But right now, the only concrete thing that has happened to me is that someone shot at you while I was with you."

"They know you're involved, though, or will know soon."

"Maybe. Maybe not. Right now we have time and I'm going to appreciate that while I can." She smiled and shook her head. "You don't have to look so sad, okay? I was a cop, remember? I will be careful."

And he believed her, but if he could take all the risk away, or at least most of it, he still would. Maybe that's how it was when you cared about someone…still loved them, no matter what…

They ate the rest of their meal in quiet. She commented once on how good his moose steaks were, but that was the extent of their conversation for the rest of the night.

"So tomorrow, early?"

"Yes. I want to be able to go out and do a camping trip with you, a dry run. So we'll need to leave really early to make sure we have plenty of darkness to practice in."

She laughed. "As long as it stays dark right now, I think we'll be fine whenever we leave."

She wasn't wrong. In January, even though they were technically gaining daylight every day since the winter solstice and the nights were getting shorter, it was still dark for many hours. Alaska was called the Land of the Midnight Sun, but that was only in summer. Right now the sun was scarce, no matter what time of day it was.

Seth walked Ellie to the front door, watched her walk to her car. He'd give anything to call her back, press a kiss to the top of her head and tell her again to be careful. But like she'd reminded him, she was a cop. He had no right to be so involved in her life anymore, to care like he once had. They were only friends. Barely that. He missed being her fiancé. So much that he ventured a prayer as he watched her drive away, and asked God if maybe this could be his second chance after all.

And if God could keep them both alive long enough for that to be a possibility.

Ellie's second day of mushing training started earlier than she'd anticipated. When Seth had originally said "early," she'd been assuming seven, maybe six. But here she was, pulling into his driveway at three in the morning, per his instructions.

She'd slept at her own house the night before, contrary to Seth's urging to find a friend to stay with. He should have known that she wasn't going to endanger her friends, not with how much risk they found themselves taking on. She didn't want an innocent person in danger because of her. She didn't particularly relish the peril against her, either, but it felt right, walking back into this case. She'd let Liz down years ago and nothing could ever make that right. But if she could at least bring the men who had killed her friend to justice, she'd feel the smallest bit of redemption.

An unfamiliar feeling had crept over her as she'd considered Seth's suggestion last night and then realized the magnitude of what they were facing. When she'd been a police officer, walking into life-or-death situations had been something close to second nature. There was something less scary about it when she still had the illusion of control, when it had been assumed that she would be facing danger every day, when it was her literal job. Now, though, that control had been taken away from her, and she didn't know how to process the feeling that felt a lot like…

Well, fear.

How did she face an emotion she wasn't used to dealing with? Stuff it down? Listen too much to that lying voice?

She knew she should pray about it, seek God's face—seek to know Him better—and not just His answers. Or His reassurance. But fear's grip was too tight, and she felt frozen, unable to even pray or think through it. All she knew right now was that she was afraid.

She should walk up to Seth this morning, tell him thanks for trusting her to help him, but their plan was too dangerous. She could leave town and escape to Anchorage. Or maybe head farther south, onto the Kenai Peninsula and disappear into one of the little towns there. Homer, maybe. Or Moose Haven. At least that way maybe she could outrun the cold, hard knot of fear in her chest.

Or maybe not. She already knew, deep down, that running didn't solve any problems—it hadn't the first time, and it wouldn't now.

Would she ever feel normal again?

Not if she didn't face this. That was the truth, she felt it deep inside and recognized it as being the truth. So she stopped hesitating in the front seat of her car, took a deep breath and stepped out, heading for the house. She glanced quickly down at her fitness watch. Just after three. So she was a little late, but not very—

Suddenly, she heard something whiz past her. A gunshot, far wide of her ear, on her left.

They weren't shooting at Seth this time. He wasn't even with her. He was…where? Inside?

She ducked down, started to make her way to the other side of the car where she could shelter in place better. But…her eyes went to the dog yard, only for a second before she resumed scanning the dark, woodsy terrain where the shots had come from. She couldn't move closer to the dogs. She might have been a musher for only around twenty-four hours, but Seth had made it clear to her that you took care of the animals, and in return they took care of you. She couldn't bring harm to them. She hated the thought of it. Fear turned to anger now. How could anyone care so little about life that they'd kill several people and then come after more? Possibly endanger dogs?

Ellie was worried about them, but knew she couldn't be foolish about her own life, either. She had so much more she wanted to do…and that took precedence over both anger and fear.

Her body pressed against the cold snow, she crawled toward the house. Another gunshot echoed in the darkness.

Where was Seth?

There, now he was coming out of the door of his house. Silly man, running toward gunshots and not away, though she supposed she appreciated that he cared enough for that.

"Get inside," she hissed at him.

"Go around back," he yelled to her as he shook his head.

Wasn't the shooter *behind* the house somewhere? She didn't want to be even more at risk.

Should she listen to him? Or…wait, was he shaking his head at the danger? Or trying to throw off whoever was shooting at her and trick them into believing she was going behind the house?

Either way, the front was her best bet. She just needed to hurry. She army-crawled farther, the snow soaking through her clothes and chilling her front. She made her way around the corner of the house, feeling her shoulders relax as she approached the front door.

Almost there. Please, God, let her make it.

Another shot. Pain rocketed through the side of her left leg. She squeezed her eyes shut, pushed herself up off the ground with her bare hands, the hard snow cutting into them. If the shooter already knew exactly where she was, then moving slow like this was actually making her more of a target than if she just ran. And Ellie had no interest in being any more of a target.

She sprinted to the front door, her leg screaming at her, making her limp slightly, and turned the handle which Seth had thankfully let unlocked and dove inside.

Silence. No more gunshots. She lay on the floor, panting, her breath coming much faster than usual and keeping time with her pounding heart. Her leg still stung, but not enough that the wound could have been from a gunshot. She reached down.

Splinters of wood were stuck in her leg, in the outer part of her thigh, maybe from part of the deck that had exploded out like shrapnel when a shot hit it?

"Are you okay? Did he hit you?" Panic escalated in Seth's voice as he came toward her. She pulled her hand away from her leg and shook her head.

"No, no, he didn't hit me."

"I'll be right back."

"Seth!" she yelled but he ignored her, and went out the back door. She waited in the silence, breathing hard and wincing at the pain in her leg. *God, please let him be okay.*

The door creaked open and Seth came in, shaking his head. "No sign of him. The shots came from behind the house?"

Ellie nodded.

"He's gone. Let's look at that leg." He locked the door behind him and walked toward Ellie.

"You're bleeding." He motioned to her hand, which she'd held up in protest, but yes, she could see now it was dripping blood in several places. Probably not very reassuring. Her leg stung and throbbed; it needed some first aid, and she'd likely have a bruise, but it was nothing that would bench her. She was seeing this thing through now. If she hadn't decided before, she'd done so as soon as someone had made the mistake of actually shooting at her.

Seth knelt down next to her and looked at the wound.

"It's fine. Really."

"Would you be quiet and let me see it?"

"It's a few giant splinters. And, what, you got some kind of medical training since I knew you last?"

"Who do you think takes care of the sled dogs out on the trail if something happens?"

"So you're a vet?"

"Um, no, I'm a musher."

"And that qualifies you to look at my leg?" She tugged it away from him and forced a smile. "Really, I'm fine. I'll go in the bathroom in a sec and clean it up."

She couldn't afford to let him this close again. And if the kiss was evidence of anything, it was a sure sign that she did not have all her defenses up and firing when it came to Seth Connors.

His shoulders sank. "I'm sorry I wasn't there. I came back for this. I thought if I could see him—" He motioned toward the wall, where a shotgun stood propped against it. She hadn't seen him bring that in earlier; she'd been too distracted.

He wouldn't have been able to see anything in the inky blackness of the woods right now. Even if he'd been able to make out a muzzle flash, Ellie believed strongly in what she'd learned at the police academy: never shoot without positively identifying your target first. A firefight with an unknown target could be tragic for someone innocent who got in the way.

"You wouldn't have been able to see him and take him out," she reminded him without lecturing.

He shook his head. "I should have been able to do something." He stood back up and paced away from her. Ellie stood too and watched him. She could feel the tension coming off him, the frustration bred by powerlessness. She understood the feeling all too well.

"I'm fine." She stepped up next to him and put a hand on his biceps. It was toned and muscled, much more so than it had been when she'd known him before. She almost pulled her hand back in surprise, but took a deep breath, not wanting to be caught reacting.

"I need these guys caught."

"You think it's more than one?"

"Well, in the entire operation, yes. After us? I have no idea."

After *us*. He was right; that was one way this morning had changed things. They'd suspected that she might personally be in danger, but Ellie wasn't afraid to admit that she probably hadn't taken the threat seriously enough until now.

"I don't know if we should do this." Seth paced away from her again.

When he came back, she spoke. "Hey."

He stopped. Looked at her.

"If we don't do something, they're going to keep operating. Isn't the fact that they've attacked us both, or tried to, evidence that we are onto something, or they think we are? We can't stop now, Seth. It's too late for that."

He met her eyes, seemed to acknowledge that truth.

And then came the sound of something clattering behind the house. He ran toward the back door, grabbing his shotgun on the way. Ellie's heart jumped inside her. She'd never get used to seeing him run toward danger, would never be okay knowing that each time she saw him could be the last.

They had to solve this and she had to help him stay alive. Because even if she could handle walking away from him, for both their sakes, she couldn't handle losing him forever.

EIGHT

Nothing was present to indicate the cause of the clattering by the time Seth arrived. Once again, he was too late, unable to do anything to keep Ellie, or himself for that matter, safe. His shoulders sagged. Defeat tasted bitter.

He had tried not to let her see inside how shaken he was, but had probably failed at that, too. She'd always been able to read him too well. But the fact that she'd gotten hurt at all was unacceptable to him.

"Anything?" Ellie asked from inside as he stepped back in and locked the door.

He shook his head. It was like chasing a ghost. No, he wished that were true. It was more like being chased *by* a ghost. Seth wanted to hit something. But he wouldn't because Ellie was there and watching, and he wasn't about to put a hole in his wall or something equally stupid just because he was mad.

As much as Ellie looked at him like nothing had changed and he was the same guy he'd been before… well, it wasn't exactly true. He was starting to have the feeling he was going to have to tell her that one of these days. He had gotten into dog mushing and changed his life, yes, but only after he'd hit somewhere that had felt awfully close to rock bottom.

He'd like to think he was past that now. He'd left Anchorage and his job that was too fast-paced. He hadn't had a drink in over two years.

He'd tried so hard to be the kind of man Ellie deserved, while always wondering if she'd left him because she'd sensed somehow that he wasn't good enough for her. That his faith wasn't strong enough. Maybe that *he* wasn't strong enough.

Seth exhaled, tried to breathe out and expel all of the last thirty minutes, if such a thing were even possible. "Now will you be convinced that you need to stay with someone?"

"I don't know who I'd stay with." Her voice was even. Calm. Honest. But still somehow vulnerable. He couldn't quite categorize it, which reminded him of all the years that had passed since they'd been close. He'd once been able to tell most of what she was thinking on a fairly consistent basis.

They'd lost so much in the intervening years. And he needed to remember that unlike had been the case with him, the distance between them had been Ellie's choice. Some part of his mind kept thinking that maybe this was a second chance, that maybe they could start over.

She. Didn't. Want. That.

Seth had to focus on that, had to remind himself no matter how many times it took until he could get the information through his stubborn skull.

"Look." He took and breath and prayed that he was succeeding in keeping his voice casual. "I get that you can't stay here in the house with me. But I can sleep outside in a tent, in the dog yard. No one will be able to get close without the dogs sounding the alarm. Then I can hear and come back inside if you need me. You said yourself that you don't want to put anyone else in danger. You can't stay alone anymore without being foolish. At least here there's someone to call the police, who knows what's going on. There's the chance of having someone to help." Even if he hadn't been successful earlier, he felt the point was still valid.

She studied him. "You'd sleep outside in a tent?"

He nodded, not sure how to interpret her look. She looked…well, almost smitten, and he had to be reading that wrong. But she looked like she appreciated his chivalrous gesture. It made him feel like the king of the world instead of a guy who'd said he could give up his house for a couple days to keep a woman he'd loved for years safe.

"Okay, yes. We have, what, one day until the expedition starts? I can stay in your guest room until then."

He ran a hand through his hair, messing it up and shaking his head at the way their lives were turning out. Definitely nothing like he would have expected. And not in a good way.

"Are we still going out today?" she asked.

Seth hadn't figured that out yet. They needed to get some more training runs in if Ellie was going to pass for a dog musher, but without knowing where the person who had been shooting at her was, he wasn't eager to do that right now.

He thought about the trails he usually took, the ones he didn't, and made a decision.

"First I need to reach Raven Pass PD and tell them about the gunshots." Seth made the call and they promised to send an officer as soon as possible, though they said there would be a delay due to a bad accident on the highway.

Finally he turned back to Ellie to answer her question. "Let's wait for daylight and then back up and head out to some other trails."

"Around here?" she asked.

He shook his head. "No, we'll have to drive up toward Wasilla."

That was around a two-hour drive away, but he felt like it would be worth it. The likelihood of someone following them that far and neither Seth nor Ellie noticing wasn't high. It would be safer both for them and the dogs this way.

Besides, he could use the drive time to explain to Ellie some of the details of how to camp, to talk over how the cookstove worked, how to give the dogs a snack, things like that.

"All right, if that's what you think is best." Ellie yawned, barely managing to cover her mouth with her hand.

"Since we aren't leaving yet, do you want a quick nap?"

She looked hesitant, and her eyes were wide. He'd forgotten how much younger she always looked when she was tired. "Are you sure? We can get started now. I don't want to be what slows us down."

But already he could tell the decision had been made. Her adrenaline was crashing, and if they were going to go undercover, she needed to be well rested and able to hold it together under pressure. A nap would be the best course of action right now.

"I could use a little more rest," he said, knowing it was the truth but also that it was a reason to give her what she needed, one she wouldn't fight. Unless he was imagining things, she narrowed her eyes a little, like she saw straight through, but finally nodded. "Okay, yes, I'd love a nap if you can point me in the right direction."

"The guest room is this way." He led her down the narrow hallway, the floor creaking beneath their feet. He'd laughed at himself when he'd gotten this room ready because no one was likely to visit him. His parents were still living but had moved back to the East Coast after his sister had been killed. It was almost like they held it personally against Alaska that they'd lost a child there and had wanted nothing to do with the state ever since.

Now, here Ellie was, and he had a bed, fresh sheets on it like his mom had drilled into his head when he was younger, and he felt proud of himself, even though nothing was objectively impressive about the old creaky house, the room with the quilt on the bed or his life in the woods and running sled dogs.

But Ellie didn't say anything about the room or anything else. By the time they reached it, just a few steps down the hall, she was almost shaking with her adrenaline crash.

"When should I set my alarm for?" she asked as she climbed under the covers.

Seth blinked and looked away. She looked like she belonged here, in his house, and every feeling he'd thought he could ignore came back to the surface again like no time had passed.

"Don't worry about an alarm," he told her. "I'll wake you up. Just get some rest."

She was asleep before he finished talking. With a final look at her and a double check to confirm that the windows were securely locked, he stepped out of the room and into the hallway to give her some privacy, leaving the door open in case she needed anything.

They were in enough danger due to the people who were after them. And seeing Ellie sleeping in a house he'd more than once imagined her in, in daydreams where they'd gotten married and lived happily-ever-after, now Seth feared his heart was in danger, as well.

When Ellie opened her eyes, she took a minute to figure out where she was. Over the last three years, she'd slept in all kinds of places around her house, including the kitchen floor, because she'd developed a bit of insomnia and couldn't always fall asleep in her room. She wasn't completely disoriented, but she was puzzled about where she was.

Seth's house.

She remembered now. All of it.

Including how they hadn't ever actually talked about that kiss.

She threw back the covers, trying to finish waking up, blinking the sleep from her eyes. Not that they needed to discuss it. But shouldn't they have at least agreed it shouldn't have happened? No, it was better this way, to let it go. Move on.

They were moving on, right? Something in Seth's gaze when he'd told her to go to sleep had been too tender to be friendship. It made her feel like someone had tucked her in with her favorite blanket on the couch to watch one of her favorite Christmas movies.

She didn't dislike it. Or wouldn't if they were different people in another place. Yes, the feeling was nice; she could admit that to herself.

But she didn't deserve him. He liked this life—she could see that and appreciated it—but everything had changed, and it was because of her. Liz's death had wrecked her, wrecked all of them. And she was never going to be rid of the guilt from that.

A creak in the hallway alerted her to Seth's presence a second before she saw his head and shoulders around the door frame. "You're awake. Great, I just made moose stew if you want some."

He was taking care of her again, and Ellie didn't know if it was just because he was that kind of guy—nice, always looking out for others—or if…

Well, surely, he'd moved on. Forgotten about her in the years since. The kiss had been a fluke.

She needed to forget about that and focus on this undercover operation they'd gotten themselves into, or she was going to get one or both of them killed. In a time when distraction could be fatal, this was the last thing she needed.

"Um, yeah." She cleared her throat. "I am really hungry, so that would be great. I didn't meant to sleep so long." Her watch said it was after nine. She couldn't remember the last time she'd slept so late.

He nodded toward the kitchen and turned in that direction. She followed him, grateful he wasn't watching her. She was afraid all of her confused emotions were in her eyes right now and needed a minute to collect herself. He'd teasingly referred to her blank expression as her *game face* back when she was a police officer. Her friends at the department had teased her for the ability to completely mask her emotions, too, but she knew they had been impressed by it. It was a handy skill to have.

"You're sure your leg is okay?" he asked.

"It's fine." She hadn't even noticed it until he'd asked, and even now it was just a dull pain, nothing too distracting.

"I've been thinking about our trip up to Wasilla. You're sure you're up for it? I don't want to push you, El. Someone just shot at you this morning."

"Believe me, I do remember," she said as she took a seat at the table and he slid a bowl toward her. It looked like some kind of vegetable beef stew, and it smelled amazing.

She closed her eyes, prayed and then took a bite. "Mmm, what is this?"

"Moose and vegetables I grew in my garden last summer."

Her eyebrows rose. "Look at you turning into some kind of self-sufficient mountain man." She said it with a smile, hoped he knew it was a compliment.

"Thank you. But I'm not going to be distracted that easily from the question I asked."

"About if I'm up for the trip?" She shook her head dismissively and took another bite of stew. "I have to be. We don't have much time. Today is the last day I can learn anything before the expedition leaves tomorrow."

"Exactly."

Something in his voice.

She looked up at him. "Are you saying you don't want me with you?"

"No, that's not what I'm saying at all."

There was that look again, almost unreadable and yet somehow telling. Vulnerable. The fact that he didn't want her hurt wasn't surprising. He was a decent guy, and they'd been close, once.

But this seemed like more.

She'd hurt him too badly for a second chance, she reminded herself. And she'd left for good reasons. She kept her expression blank and did her best to maintain emotional distance.

"We have to solve this, Seth. And this is the only way."

He met her eyes, and this time she knew what she saw.

It *was* the only way. He knew it, too.

She took another bite of stew. "Let's eat and then let's go. I want to learn all I can before tomorrow."

For once, he didn't argue.

When they went outside, being in the open made her nervous at first. Her shoulders were unnaturally tense, and her gaze kept going to the woods without her meaning it to.

"You okay?" Seth asked. He'd noticed. She looked down, embarrassed.

"Yeah. Fine."

Was that what they called it? When fear felt like it had a tight grip on your throat and every move was distracted by a sense of overwhelming panic, when you couldn't forget about the scary thing that had happened once and your whole life was defined by it? Was that *fine*?

Ellie was pretty sure it wasn't. But she was equally sure she didn't know how to fix it; she could only push past it as best she could.

Was this the kind of thing Liz would have prayed about? Ellie never knew what to ask God for. She'd never felt like she understood how that was supposed to work. Liz had prayed often and casually, just little sentences here and there, but sincerely. Ellie?

She…

Didn't. At least not very often. She'd prayed lately here and there, asking God to keep Seth safe. And she believed in God. After talking to Liz she believed in the salvation God offered through Jesus. But she just… didn't quite know how to talk to God on a regular basis.

"You don't seem fine," he said as he laid out harnesses on the snow, making a sort of line.

"Do you put those on the dogs? I mean, do you want me to?"

"Let's just go slow here. No need to rush, okay?" His voice was easy and kind, the way it always was. Why couldn't they have lived happily-ever-after? Why couldn't Liz have lived?

Ellie took a breath, reminded herself that both reasons were the same. She raised her gaze uneasily to the trees, to the darkness of the woods. She'd let everyone down, and guilt had haunted her ever since.

Now someone out there wanted to end her life. And Ellie was left wondering how much of a life she still had. And desperately wanting a second chance to live it to the fullest again.

I don't want to die, God. Please help me, she prayed, then took a breath.

"Really. I'm fine. Now tell me how to dog mush." She looked at him with a small smile.

But she saw the concern in his eyes. She wasn't the only one who was afraid.

And maybe that scared her more.

NINE

Ellie was a natural; there was no other way to phrase it. The way he would have preferred to teach someone would have taken weeks, maybe months, of shadowing him, watching, just the way that Seth himself had learned. With that option not a possibility, they were rushed, and today he'd let her drive her own sled.

She'd been shaky at the start, pulling the quick release and then almost losing her balance as the team jerked forward, faster than she had probably expected. Her hands were tight around the handlebar, though, and she'd managed to keep the sled upright. He pulled his own quick release, then let the dogs have their way, as they ran behind her. He kept his heels turned in slightly, let his weight settle on the drag mat, the rubber rectangle that sat between the runners, dragging the snow. When he didn't need to slow the team down, he could take his weight off it, and it didn't create much resistance.

They'd parked in a little neighborhood at the edge of Wasilla, in a town called Knik, and now they were going down a groomed trail into the woods that was part of the historic Iditarod Trail. They'd mush for a few hours, then come back to where he'd left his truck, load the dogs and drive back to Raven Pass. It had been the best way Seth could think of to remove them from danger—to get out of town. That the Iditarod Trail was one of his favorite places to run dogs and train was just a bonus. That race—the Iditarod—started farther north these days, due to the unpredictable weather farther south, but it still made him happy to know they were mushing on a piece of that storied history. Running the Iditarod was a dream of his, one he didn't know if he'd ever attain, and somehow this made him feel closer to reaching it.

"I have no idea where I'm going!" Ellie yelled over her shoulder, her face a bit panicked. He'd told her to go first because he'd wanted to make sure she got started okay, but he'd known he'd need to pass her on the trail early on so he could lead the way. He tried to stop the smile at the corners of his mouth because she wouldn't appreciate being teased for being a little nervous, and honestly, she didn't deserve to be. She was impressive. He hadn't counted on how it would feel to be doing what he loved with the woman he loved. Seth felt happy, maybe for the first time fully since Ellie had left him.

"I'm going to pass."

"How does that work?"

"You've got to learn sometime. Just keep them on one side of the trail. They know how."

The pass went smoothly, and now Seth was in front. "Slowing down," he called over his shoulder to Ellie just as they reached a clearing.

"So hit my brakes?"

"Drag and then brake."

He came to a stop, and Ellie stopped behind him.

When he needed to slow them down without using the metal brake, which cut into the snow and made driving the sled a little more awkward, he could control their speed by putting his weight on the drag mat. Her lead dogs were a little closer to him than he'd have preferred, but it was pretty good for a first solo stop.

"So I'll stay in front to show you the trail," he said. "How does it feel?"

"Terrifying. Fun. Overwhelming." She shook her head. "I've got to be honest, when you said six dogs, I really didn't expect…" She trailed off.

"So much power?"

She nodded.

"It's a lot to learn at once." For the expedition, she'd start with ten or twelve, but he didn't feel the need to break that to her yet. She'd figure it out tomorrow.

"Ready to go again?"

"I'm ready." She grinned at him, like the brave woman she was, and Seth felt a rush of adrenaline.

And an overwhelming amount of love for this amazing woman who'd walked back into his life so unexpectedly.

They mushed across a power line, followed the woodsy trail down to a creek and skittered across on the ice. Behind him, he heard Ellie yell something that sounded a lot like *woo-hoo!*

He laughed and turned around.

"Did you feel that ice? It was like waterskiing!" she yelled over the noise of the swish of the snow on the runners. Seth laughed and kept going.

The trail took them into a swamp, partway between Knik and Big Lake, and it was some of the most gorgeous land Seth had ever seen. He didn't know if it would look this pretty on a regular hike, or if it was seeing it from the back of a dog sled that made it so special, but he loved it. Sharing it with Ellie was something else entirely.

Although he couldn't quite shake the sense of unease that had pressed against him for the last several days since all of this had started. He felt fairly confident they couldn't have been followed—this time, anyway. He'd been careful on the two-hour drive up to watch his rearview mirror for cars that he saw a little too often or that followed too close, but he'd noticed nothing. It was why he'd insisted they come up here to a trail so far from his home trails, but he couldn't help still feeling some of the anxiety over knowing that the safety of all his dogs and Ellie depended on him. He could still hear the gunshots reverberating in his memory, and the knowledge that they'd been directed at Ellie kept him focused on her safety at all costs.

Yet, at the same time, their safety required that they take this trip. He couldn't have let Ellie do the expedition tomorrow without this day of practice, not safely, anyway.

The woods looked and felt clear. His shoulders were more relaxed than they had been in days, and even though these weren't *his* woods or *his* trails, he was still out here with his dogs, in a place that soothed his soul, with a woman he…

Analyzing his feelings for her, or naming them, wasn't going to do either one of them any good, so he hit the brakes on that train of thought.

"Having fun?" he called behind him.

Her wide grin was answer enough. He turned back around and kept mushing.

If only this didn't feel eerily like the calm before the storm…

"That was amazing," Ellie said as she finally pulled up later, looking up at him, eyes shining and her cheeks flushed with windburn and sunshine.

The last half hour had only gotten better and better. Seth knew better than to let his guard down, but he'd still seen no signs of anything wrong. They'd passed no other people on the trail. No one was parked near their truck, here on the side of the little residential road, and while he was still watching, he still didn't see anything wrong…but that niggling feeling of danger still hadn't gone away.

Maybe this was going to work out. Maybe Ellie would do fantastic at the expedition, they'd figure out who had been behind his sister's murder and then…

What, live happily-ever-after?

It might be crazy, but right now it didn't seem entirely impossible.

"You were amazing," he let himself admit to her, even though it felt like opening his heart a little. He stepped closer, and she didn't move away. Instead, she blinked. Two times. Three. Her eyelashes were impossibly dark and long, and her lips were full.

She looked away and cleared her throat. "How do we, uh, how do we put them away into the truck so we can drive back to your house? That's probably something I should learn, too, huh?" She looked back at him and met his eyes with a small smile.

She wasn't pulling away, not entirely. Just redirecting their attention away from this particular moment.

"Yes, you need to learn. But it's really not difficult.

Unharness the dog, rub them down a bit and then put them back in one of the boxes in the dog trailer."

She was looking at the dog trailer. "I mean, I've seen them around, driving around Alaska for as long as I have, but I'm still impressed."

He tried to see the contraption he'd made with his own hands through her eyes. Some people had dog boxes on trailers, some put them in the bed of a truck. His was the trailer variety and looked kind of like a wooden horse trailer, but with twenty-four individual boxes. It had taken many hours of hard work, but he was proud of the end result. Working with his hands on something like this was something he'd discovered after Liz's death that he liked doing, and it wasn't just a passive joy. It seemed absolutely vital to his mental health to create things, and so he kept finding ways to do it that also benefited his life. The dog trailer was a prime example.

"Thanks. I'm happy with how it turned out."

She smiled up at him, and for half a second he let himself admit how much he loved that smile.

Yeah…*loved*…

This time he was the one who looked away and started boxing up dogs. The routine was so familiar to him that he was able to do it almost without thinking. He saw Ellie doing the same thing out of the corner of his eye, though it was taking her longer. She was handling it well, though, he noted as he moved to the next dog.

He heard Katya, his German shepherd, whine from the cab. He should have let her out to do her business when he first got back.

"Good girl. Sorry about that," he told her as he let her out and he went back to unharnessing.

He heard the thud first, then the muffled scream. And growls. Ellie. Katya.

Leaving the remaining dogs hooked up to the line, he ran to the other side of the trailer. A man was dragging Ellie away; they were already at least fifteen feet from the trailer. Seth's heart stuttered. He couldn't lose her.

"Hey!" he yelled, running toward them. Ellie managed to get one arm free, and as the man holding her was fighting to subdue her again, she used her head to slam back into his nose.

The man cried out in pain, and Katya, a retired police dog, used the opportunity to attack.

Apparently Ellie still remembered what she'd learned…and so did Katya.

Ellie's attacker let her go. Katya looked at him, then at Ellie and chose to guard Ellie.

Seth reluctantly left Ellie and pursued the still-fleeing attacker. But the other man had a head start and wasn't wearing as many layers of winter gear as Seth was. Seth only sprinted about thirty yards from Ellie when he realized that if he kept chasing, he was leaving her unprotected except for Katya.

He'd already thought there was more than one person after them, that there was some coordination in these ambushes. Being attacked like this all but proved it. No. He couldn't leave her alone at all right now.

Instead he closed the distance in a hurry.

"Are you okay?" he asked Ellie first.

"I'm okay," she said, but her voice was shaky. He looked her over, didn't see any obvious injuries. He'd come back to her but turned his attention to Katya for now. "Good girl. You're such a good girl."

"Did you see her attack him? She did such an amazing job." Ellie sounded like she was crying, and sure enough when he looked at her, tears streamed down her face.

"I saw." He ran his hands over Katya's long body, noting that she felt good. Not too tense. He saw blood, but only coming from her mouth, and he thought it was probably from the bite she'd given the attacker. Still, it was disconcerting.

Satisfied his dog was all right, he returned his attention to Ellie, who had propped her back against the truck.

"Are you sure you're okay?"

His heart pounded in his chest while he waited for her to answer him. He'd come so close to losing her just now, had done his best not to let down his guard and apparently had, anyway. That realization felt like a sucker punch to the stomach, coming a second after you had been tensed and ready for it but had just relaxed.

The admission that he'd failed her hurt. It hurt a lot. Losing her would have hurt worse.

God, please let her be okay. If this is a second chance, I don't want to lose her. And if You're giving me a second chance, well, I'll try not to mess it up this time.

"I'm okay," Ellie repeated again, as if saying the words over and over would convince not just a distraught Seth, who was still standing there with a look of intense concern on his face, but herself, as well.

"I'm okay." One more try. Ellie shook her head, then looked away from the pull of his dark blue eyes and petting the panting German shepherd beside her. Katya looked exceptionally proud of herself, Ellie noticed. "Your dog saved my life."

"You saved your own life by not panicking and fighting back. She just helped." Still, he reached over and petted the dog, too. Their hands brushed, and there was a small spark and a deep sense of warmth inside Ellie that felt like familiarity and comfort. And, well, home.

He kept talking. "You're amazing." Did his voice break on the last part? She thought it might have. "But we can't do this anymore," Seth continued.

"Dog mush?" She laughed or tried to. Her voice might not have been quite strong enough right now for a very genuine-sounding chuckle. Truth was, she was still shaken, even if she didn't want him to know it. When her attacker had pinned her arms to her sides, she'd felt helpless, and it was the first time since Liz's death that she'd felt genuinely powerless. Even in the depths of the fear she'd felt earlier that day—or had it been last night?—she hadn't felt completely helpless like she had during this attack.

Now she remembered why she had run away from Seth. She hated that feeling, hated the way it fueled her guilt. She *shouldn't* be powerless. She'd trained for this—repelling an assaulter—and for *that*, too, what happened three years ago. No, when she was in the police academy, she'd never have guessed that she'd ever be close to the investigation of her best friend. But she was supposed to be able to handle the fact that people committed awful crimes, that sometimes police could stop them and sometimes they couldn't.

And she still was supposed to have that sensibility...wasn't she?

She rubbed the soft fur behind Katya's ears. Leaned back against the side of the truck and exhaled. Slowly.

How could it have all happened so fast? Ellie tried to put the pieces together in her mind as she ran back over what had happened. Someone must have followed them up to Wasilla from Raven Pass, which up until now she'd admit she hadn't thought was possible.

Unless...

"Do you think someone saw us leave town and called someone else to follow us?" she asked Seth, who was still standing two feet away from her. For now, his presence was reassuring. She hated how scared she'd been and how weak it felt to know that another person's presence was so reassuring to her. But at the moment, she didn't have the emotional strength to fight it.

Any of it, she realized as she looked up at him while he talked. His warm blue eyes still contained those varied shades of glacier blue and deeper ocean blue that she'd always loved, even if time had framed them with some lines. His face didn't look older, not really. Just weathered, stronger.

He was stronger now than he'd been back them. He seemed sure of himself and what he wanted in life. Altogether, he'd come through the crisis they'd both experienced a better man, and she...

She'd barely made it out.

"Ellie? Did you hear me?"

She jerked her attention back to him, feeling her cheeks heat at the obvious answer. No, she hadn't heard him, she'd been lost in thought.

In his eyes...either one.

"Uh, no, sorry." She shook her head, like the physical motion would clear her confusion. "I didn't hear."

"I told you that I think you're right, there must be more than one individual." He looked away from her, frustration etched across his face in the tightness of his jaw, the frown knitting his eyebrows. "I was so sure we'd notice being followed."

"And we would have if one person had followed us," she told him. "You can't take responsibility for everything, okay? You couldn't have predicted this."

"Don't you see? I should be expecting *anything* at this point. This isn't safe, what we are doing. None of it is. They're always one step ahead. There are clearly more people than we thought paying attention. I don't know how I thought this was going to work, but I can't do it, El."

"Can't do what?" She was exhausted, overwhelmed, and truly didn't know what he was talking about.

The look he gave her seemed to say that she did know, she just didn't want to.

"I can't do this undercover investigation. Not with you, I can't risk your life."

He looked away again, and this time the tightness in his face seemed more like embarrassment than frustration. At being caught caring so much? She was flattered that he still cared.

But irritated. Because who was he to decide what amount of danger she could put herself in?

"You don't have a say in what risks I take."

"I do when it was my idea," he protested. "I'm the one who got you into this. Even though the investigation was your idea, it was finding me that dragged you back into this and I don't like that you have a target on your back. Or that you could be collateral damage because they're after me. Either way, you're in danger. The deal is off. We aren't doing it."

Ellie was lost in thought, only half listening. She was still working out how they'd been found. It would have been easy to follow them for one car, then to call someone else. There had to have been, what, at least three cars? She and Seth shouldn't have been surprised because if there was some kind of drug smuggling operation, more than one person had to have been involved...

"Wait, aren't doing what? The undercover op?" she asked.

"Yes."

"You can't stop me from doing it without you." The words were out before she considered them, because yes, he could stop her since she was going undercover as a musher and using one of his sleds and his dogs. But he shouldn't be able to. She was the one who'd wanted to investigate in the first place and despite the fact that he liked to ignore it, she had the qualifications to do so. Maybe not the credentials anymore, but she remembered what she'd learned. She could do this. She *had* to do this. For Liz. For herself.

"I'll tell RPE you don't have enough experience mushing."

Now he wasn't the only one feeling frustrated. Ellie knew this wasn't a time for her to give way to her emotions, but she was also tired of keeping such a tight grip on her feelings. And, well, tired physically.

"I can't believe you would try to stop me from this," she snapped, then stood up straight and looked him in the eye.

"Ellie..."

"No, seriously, I have every right to risk my life

doing whatever I want, and I don't appreciate…" She trailed off as he moved closer.

Their eyes were locked together now, and they were only a heartbeat apart. If she turned her head wrong, their noses would touch.

"I don't want to lose you again," he whispered. "I never did."

And then their lips met, again, for the second time since he'd come back into her life a mere forty-eight hours ago. She couldn't be doing this again, she thought as they kissed, slowly and with so much aching familiarity that she felt her shoulders relax and her anxious heart stop questioning it.

He pulled back first, and she was left blinking. At a loss.

Missing him.

And then the space between them sobered her like cold water on her face.

She'd left for a reason.

"Seth…" She'd let him down. Liz had reached out to her long before the day they were finally supposed to meet and asked if they could talk in person about some things Liz thought the police might need to know. It had been a busy time for Ellie, both at work and in her relationship with Seth, and she just hadn't made the time.

Until that day, when they had finally set up a meeting, and then just before Ellie arrived, Liz had been shot.

Too late. Too late on so many counts.

And far, far too late to salvage any sort of relationship with her dead best friend's very much living brother.

"Seth, I have to tell you something."

"Ellie…"

"It's why I left. Or it's… Anyway, Liz had wanted me to investigate earlier. I didn't, and I should have. And I'm sorry."

She shook her head.

"Don't, Ellie. Don't bring up the past right now. Please, can't we just—" he swallowed hard "—try again? Start over?"

Had he not heard her? Did he not understand that Liz's death was her fault? She couldn't say it again, didn't have the courage right now. But he wanted to *start over*?

If it were possible, she would do it. She'd never loved anyone like she'd loved him, knew she never would.

But life wasn't like that, and it didn't give real fresh starts. She could never tell him the reasons she'd left, about the crushing guilt she felt over Liz's death.

Which meant that starting over was impossible. She shook her head, walked away and climbed into the truck.

TEN

The drive from Wasilla back south to Raven Pass was made in silence, and not the companionable kind. If Seth hadn't already had hesitations about them going through with this undercover operation, he'd have them now. How were they supposed to work together in the wilderness for days, now that he'd ruined everything? She'd given no indication of wanting to start over, and yet that's exactly what he'd asked her for. He'd made an impossible request.

Except it hadn't felt like it, he admitted to himself as he followed the curves of the road around the tall cliffs of the Seward Highway. Maybe if he had really thought he was the only one who felt that way, he'd have been able to play it cool, not let his feelings show. But the way she'd looked at him, smiled at him...

He knew, deep down, that he was the only one who'd toyed with the idea of a second chance.

But it didn't matter now. She'd said no; that was the end of it.

Now they had to work together in what was already an incredibly tense situation. Much as he had tried to call the whole thing off, he knew Ellie would just find a way to investigate on her own, and that would be even more dangerous.

They were in too deep to stop now; the only way past this case was through it.

Seth just dreaded what the next few days could bring. More than once he'd closed his eyes to fall asleep and been tormented by images of what could happen to Ellie if she kept investigating. The thought of her life being taken from her was unbearable. Unacceptable.

But it was a risk that came with what they were getting themselves into. And Seth hated it.

"You feel ready for tomorrow?" He finally broke the silence as they turned off the Seward Highway onto the road to Raven Pass.

She nodded. "I do. I know there are things I don't know yet, probably things I don't even realize I know, but I think I know enough that I can fake it till I make it." She turned to him and smiled, but there wasn't as much joy behind it as there had been earlier.

Had he caused her to lose that happiness? Or was something else bothering her?

"We should pack up tonight so that tomorrow we aren't under so much pressure."

Ellie shrugged. "I thought we could look back at news reports from three years ago, see if they list anyone the police interviewed and things like that. Maybe make a list of names that keep popping up." It was grasping at straws, and they both knew it, but neither was sure how else to go about this. Seth had already looked into RPE online and tried to find police reports or anything else associated with them that implied they could be involved in something illegal, but had found nothing. When he'd mentioned that to Ellie she'd said she'd done the same, and also found nothing.

"Not a bad idea," he said. The letter from Liz had given them something to work with and had gotten them both thinking about the case again, but there hadn't been a lot of solid evidence.

Why had Liz been killed? For being a witness to someone specifically committing an illegal activity, or just a potential witness in general?

"So we'll start that in the morning?" he asked as he pulled up to his house.

She nodded. "Sure, sounds good. Do you want help putting the dogs away?"

He shook his head. "Nah, you know how that part works. You may as well start packing."

She nodded again. Headed inside.

And Seth sat in his truck with his head in his hands, wishing he could erase the last three hours.

Or go back and erase whatever had happened to derail their relationship three years ago.

By one in the morning, Ellie had created quite the list of things she would willingly do in order to have a good night's sleep. Clean toilets. Dust ceiling fans— her least favorite chore of all.

Anything short of tell Seth why she'd really pulled away from him. She'd come close earlier when she'd told him that Liz had told her about the threats sooner, but she hadn't spelled it out for him. He might not understand that she bore so much responsibility. And he certainly didn't understand that she couldn't face a lifetime of guilt. That felt too personal to share. She couldn't hurt him that way. Or let herself be hurt by his possible rejection. His defeated look earlier had half killed her and had definitely extinguished the tiny sparks of life she'd been feeling lately. Somehow she hadn't realized until now how little she'd really *lived* in the last few years. She'd cut herself off from the life she'd had before Liz's death and her breakup with Seth. Her friends on the search and rescue team, especially Adriana and Piper, had tried to talk to her multiple times. Adriana was always subtle, a listening ear. She had her own secrets, Ellie suspected. Piper was less subtle, steamrolling her way into Ellie's life, or trying, but Ellie hadn't shared much with either of them.

But yes, she'd been able to recognize from their prying questions that she probably held her cards really closely to the vest, lived too cautiously. A side effect of seeing life end far too quickly for her best friend, witnessing all her carefully crafted ideas for life shatter into pieces after that.

Being here with Seth again had felt like life suddenly bloomed into color, full and vibrant. Like the hottest late-June day of an Alaskan summer after a winter of snow and gray. And she wanted it, badly. She wanted Seth in her life again, wanted to walk down the hallway, tell him she'd never stopped loving him and let him wrap her in his arms and never let her go.

Ellie turned over again, flipped her pillow to the cool side and closed her eyes.

When she did that, though, she just saw Liz and her wide smile. *There* was someone who had lived life fully, even if her life had been short.

Why hadn't Ellie listened to her concerns? Would it have been so hard for her to take time out of her schedule sooner and listen to her friend?

She hated living with this constant awareness that she'd made a costly mistake. All she wanted was to rewind time. Why couldn't she? Why didn't it work that way?

God, please help. She squeezed her eyes tighter but sleep still refused to come. *God, can you help me fall asleep?*

Nothing was like it was supposed to be. Even this investigation wasn't going the way she'd thought it would. In her head she'd thought…well, maybe that things would go well, they'd learn who had killed Liz and they'd somehow find their footing as friends, she and Seth. She had certainly never thought it would feel like this, like having her heart pulled out of her chest, stomped on and then shoved back in.

And with the very real concern that they might do this undercover investigation, see it through and still *not* know who had killed Liz.

And possibly end up dead themselves.

Ellie threw back the covers and slid into her slippers. Between those, her black yoga pants and a hoodie, she was dressed for comfort, but it still wasn't helping. Her mind was a tortured tangle of *what if*s and *might have been*s. It was one of those times she knew in her head that God and her faith would be enough to see her through, but she struggled in her heart to *feel* like it was true. How much did feelings play into her relationship with God?

She wasn't sure. Liz had been far more knowledgeable about such things. Liz had grown up in church. Ellie hadn't even attended until she'd been living on her own as an adult and Liz had invited her. At church she'd learned that a God she'd always believed in but felt was distant actually cared about *her*, specifically. It had been obvious to Ellie that if God was willing to love her like that, she would be foolish not to love Him back and do her best to follow Him.

But she'd still been learning what all that meant when her friend had died. The last few years…she'd prayed and tried to read her Bible. She'd even tried to go to church once or twice, but it had reminded her so much of the few times she'd gone with Liz that she'd never gotten up the courage to go inside.

Most of the time she just felt alone.

And sometimes, late at night or out in the dark, she felt scared.

Even though she *knew* God cared.

Should she feel that way?

She padded down the hallway softly, careful to step lightly in the spots where she'd heard it creak earlier. When she reached the living room, she reached for a lamp and clicked it on.

Her phone rang. Ellie jumped. It was Seth's number.

"Hello? You okay out there?" He was sleeping in the yard in a tent, true to his word.

"I'm fine, it's you I'm worried about. I saw the light come on. Can't sleep?"

His voice was deep and caring, full of concern and it made her want to be honest with him about her questions about faith. He'd grown up in church like Liz. Maybe he'd have some of the answers she sought.

"I'm just thinking. Seth, does God really listen when we pray? And does he really want to know about all the little problems we have?"

She heard a noise than sounded like his sleeping bag shifting. "Mind if I come inside for this conversation?"

"Sure. That's fine." They hung up.

The door creaked open a few minutes later. "Hey."

She jumped at the sound of Seth's voice and immediately felt her cheeks heat. Did he know how hard she had to work not to betray every emotion when he was around? How could the sound of his voice affect her so much?

"Seth." Her voice escaped her mouth with more tenderness than she'd have preferred. Ellie cleared her throat. "Um, thanks for, you know, coming to talk. And answer my questions." She never fumbled for words this way, never seemed any less than put together, and they both knew it. If Seth wasn't aware already of her feelings for him, he would be soon if she didn't get a grip.

"So you're wondering about prayer?" He got right to the point. Ellie nodded, her shoulders sagging a little. She didn't like to be vulnerable and definitely didn't like to admit she didn't have all the answers.

"Hand me that Bible?" he asked, motioning to the side table beside where she sat. She hadn't noticed it there. She gave it to him, listening to the sound of the thin pages brushing past each other as he turned them.

"'Be careful for nothing; but in every thing by prayer and supplication with thanksgiving let your requests be made known unto God. And the peace of God, which passeth all understanding, shall keep your hearts and minds through Christ Jesus,'" he read aloud. "It's *Philippians* 4:6-7. God says to take everything to Him for prayer. Anything that makes you anxious you should turn into a prayer to Him."

"So big stuff or little stuff? All of it?"

Seth nodded. "All of it." He sighed. Let out a breath. "I'm glad you asked. I'd forgotten that lately. Faith has

always been so important to me, but since Liz died…
I had some hard questions I didn't feel like I got answered. It hasn't been quite the same."

"Do you have answers to your questions now?"

He shook his head. "No. But I have more peace about
not getting answers. Like that verse says, God's peace
comes when we pray about things. I'm working on trying to do that instead of worry."

Ellie nodded, then shivered. She rubbed her arms
and curled into herself, shoulders folding forward in
an effort to keep warm.

"Cold?"

"A little."

She smiled her thanks when he handed her a throw.

"One of Liz's," he said even as she'd recognized the
quilt as one her friend had made. Liz had been good
at crafty things like that, not like Ellie, who suspected
she didn't have one creative bone in her body. At least,
not one that didn't relate to solving cases or puzzles or
finding missing people. *Those* things, she was good at.
The quilt settled over her, at the same time familiar and
comforting and like a heavy weight she'd never be able
to shake. Would solving the case, figuring out who had
killed Liz, bring her some peace, even though it would
never bring Liz back?

She didn't know. Maybe that was the worst of it right
now, the nagging ache that kept her awake tonight. She
didn't know how any of this was going to turn out. If
she could just have some reassurance that the sleepless-
ness, the heartbreak of being around Seth, that all of
it was really going to turn out to be for her own good,
that would help.

"You okay?" His voice was soft. Reassuring.

She looked up and met his eyes. He'd always been one of the kindest people she'd ever known, and that hadn't changed, even after the way she'd left him without explanation. He cared about others to a fault, and to see the caring turned on her right now...

It mattered so much that it hurt.

"I don't know anymore. Haven't in a few years, I guess."

Honesty slipped out in the darkness, in the late hour. What could it hurt if he knew she was miserable? That wasn't a big secret.

Really, there were no secrets between them. No, this was less about keeping secrets and more about keeping a distance.

He reached for her hand.

She swallowed hard and let him take it.

"I'm sorry, El, about earlier. You've been clear that you want us to be..." He paused and she looked at him. Met his eyes. "Friends?" His voice rose, half question, half statement.

She nodded.

"I want to respect that."

She could feel the current between them, the chemistry that had existed as far back as she could remember.

"Thank you."

"Can we do this, work together?"

She nodded. She would do whatever it took, face any kind of heartache day after aching day, if it would bring them both some level of closure and keep them safe. "We can."

He squeezed her hand and let it go. That gesture felt so final she closed her eyes for a half a second, let herself absorb the impact of the loss.

Knowing it was right, that he deserved better, that she could never be honest with him about the guilt she felt; none of that helped right now. He was a gentleman. And Ellie knew beyond a shadow of a doubt that he wouldn't try to start anything between them again. He was too respectful for that.

Ellie let out a breath, decided they may as well talk about the case, since neither of them could sleep.

"Want to talk through some of what we know?" she asked.

Seth nodded. "Sure. What's on your mind about the case?"

"Well, you know how I told you we should make a list of people who the police looked at back then, all of that?"

"Yeah."

"Basically, that concept. I looked again at what Liz sent us."

"I was thinking of doing that later today." Seth smiled at her.

"She was convinced it was someone in that shopping center but didn't know for sure if it was Raven Pass Expeditions. So earlier I started working on making a list of all the people who worked in that area in one of those stores three years ago." Ellie reached for a notebook she'd set down on the floor earlier.

"How on earth could you do that?" Seth sounded impressed.

Ellie shrugged. "It's not comprehensive. I don't have all the entry-level employees for any of the places yet, but I am at least working on who was working in management in each place."

"Very impressive." Seth nodded.

"That's where I get stuck." Ellie blew out a breath. She knew she was good at conducting investigations. But she hadn't counted on how much more difficult it would be without police resources and a fellow officer as a partner.

"What would you do?" she asked him.

"I…" She trailed off. "I would start looking for connections with either Liz or her boyfriend at the time."

"Back to Aaron, huh?" They'd dismissed looking into him more earlier on when it became clear neither of them knew much about him, but that was another thread they could tug to investigate. Maybe it would help. Ellie wanted to believe it could.

And for a moment she felt hope sneak in, underneath the weight of darkness. Just a glimmer of it. But enough to make her think they might figure this out eventually after all.

ELEVEN

"So what have you found? Who's in charge of what places? Show me." Seth angled closer to Ellie, noting that she didn't shift away, but let them stay close.

"Well, the businesses in that shopping center are mostly the same but with some variation. There's Raven Pass Expeditions, next door to The Sandwich Shop."

"That's its name?" He laughed. "So much for creativity."

"Right?" She shook her head. "Beside The Sandwich Shop right now there's a small games store, Puzzle Craft."

"Like video games or board games?"

"Both, from what I could tell on their website."

"Huh. Interesting."

"But I don't think that store was there three years ago. I think three years ago it was a bakery, Sweet Savannah's. And the last in the lot is vacant right now. I'm having trouble figuring out what it was three years ago, too, since no one seems to remember. There's a lot of turnover, apparently."

"Interesting." He frowned a little. "So you think maybe that's the location where drug smugglers are working out of?"

"That's one obvious choice isn't it? But I don't know. I'm not sure. The information we found initially seemed to specifically implicate Raven Pass Expeditions."

"Let me see the names, and let's split them up and start researching…if you want to?"

"We should probably go back to sleep." She didn't want Seth to stay awake on her account. If he was actually able to get some sleep, he should.

"I can't sleep, so I can do these while you get some shut-eye if you want." Seth shrugged.

"Nah, I can't, either. I just didn't want to keep you awake."

"Let's split the names up."

They did so, and he started searching online. The first name he typed in was Brandt Bowker. The CEO from RPE.

And there was something interesting already. Surely it couldn't be that easy that he'd find a link at first try.

"Um, El…" He trailed off and held up his phone, showing her the captioned picture he'd found in an old newspaper article.

She read it out loud. "Brandt Bowker stands with sister, Robin Richards, at a charity event…" She frowned. "Richards… Aaron Richards? Liz's boyfriend, that was his name. Right? Is there a connection?"

He pulled up the second window he'd found, showed that to her, as well.

"So Bowker is Aaron's uncle. And runs Raven Pass Expeditions."

It did seem too easy.

But sometimes maybe life was like that?

"Let's keep looking." He pushed, just in case.

Nothing came up. Not a single suspicious, eye-catching thing about any other employee in that shopping center. The closest they got was to note a parking ticket Savannah from the bakery had gotten once, plus a reckless-driving charge for the owner of The Sandwich Shop. Neither had a record besides that.

"What if Aaron comes on this trip?" Ellie's face had sobered. "If he sees us…"

"He only met me that one time. I don't think he'd recognize me."

"He saw me a couple of times when he came to pick her up from our apartment."

"And you look different enough from then that even I didn't recognize you right away." He hesitated. Could he ask the next question, or would she shut him down? It felt like they were doing a delicate kind of dance, two steps forward, one back.

It was worth the risk, he decided. "Why did you change your appearance so much after leaving?"

She exhaled and seemed to be considering her answer—her eyes were focused on something on the wall, but it didn't look like that had her attention. Her gaze looked more like an aimless stare.

"I was afraid."

Not what he would have guessed. If someone had asked him tonight, right now, if Ellie had ever been afraid of anything, he probably would have said no. Sure, he knew she was human and had frailties because of that. But fear wasn't something he could imagine her struggling with.

"Of what?" he asked, feeling even more like he was stepping forward on just-frozen ice, waiting to see if he broke through.

"Everything." Her voice was little more than a whisper in the dark. "I was afraid of what had just happened. It was a worst nightmare come true, one I hadn't even known I had until it happened. And then for you. Your life. My life. That I'd let people down again."

"Let people down?"

She stood up. "I was just afraid. It's not a feeling I like, but if you've ever wrestled with fear before, you know it's a beast and a liar and will take over your life if you'll let it. I think I am sleepy, though. Maybe we can talk more tomorrow?"

The last line was more shutdown than invitation, but he nodded anyway and stood. "Sure. Tomorrow. I think I'm sleepy, too." He wasn't, but it was wishful thinking. And a desire to make her feel less awkward about whatever admission had chased her away.

Was she this upset she'd admitted to being afraid? He didn't think of Ellie as a prideful person, but she did appreciate being seen as tough and capable.

He watched her walk back down the darkened hallway and then decided to sit down again. He could sleep just as well in this chair, and he'd be closer to her room in case anything happened. Across the house, he felt too far away in case of an emergency.

What had she said just before she stood up? That she'd been afraid she'd let people down again?

But who had she let down? Him, by leaving town and abruptly ending their relationship? No matter how much he tried to stretch that idea to make it fit, it just didn't.

Ellie was hiding something, he was starting to see. Not just from him. Not even just from the past. But almost hiding from herself?

That didn't make any sense. She had nothing to hide.

Seth let out a breath, the deep exhalation not bringing

any real relaxation with it. Ellie was closer than she'd been in years but still further away. Someone wanted them both dead.

And tomorrow they were going to start an expedition that could go wrong so quickly.

At least he'd done enough research on the website to be fairly certain that Aaron Richards's uncle wouldn't be joining the excursion. The company had several staff members listed, so he assumed one or two would be joining them on the trip.

They'd see tomorrow.

And they'd start looking into Raven Pass Expeditions…and try not to draw the attention of a desperate killer.

Throughout the next morning, Ellie managed to keep herself on an even keel, despite the fact that she'd gotten very little sleep after returning to her room. She'd almost told Seth everything, in the accidental vulnerability that nighttime conversations bring. Keeping the secret inside her a little more every day, she never wanted him to look at her with pity or disgust—or if he took it even further than she had and literally blamed her for the death of his sister.

Ellie had run out of that room as quickly as she could. And she'd spent most of today eagerly packing what they'd need for the trip and then spending time with all of the dogs she'd be taking. Her premise was that the better she knew them, the more she'd seem like a legitimate musher.

But she wasn't sure Seth didn't see through that excuse for what it was—a reason to stay away from him.

By the time they were in his truck heading toward

RPE, she was exhausted from all the avoidance. Well, at least there would be no more of that. They'd be in physical proximity for the next few days out of necessity, but who knew if they'd get time to talk? Much as she'd been avoiding that very thing today, she did hope they'd be able to chat to each other a little. It would be useful for sorting out what they discovered on this trip.

"Any ideas for how we are going to talk?"

"Excuse me?" He glanced over at her, then back at the road.

Yeah, okay, so she'd asked for that, with her blatant avoidance of conversations today.

"How are we going to share anything we find while we are on the trip? I mean…" She tried to ignore the slight heaviness in her stomach. Dread. Anxiety. Whatever name you gave it, she hated it, hated feeling weak and like her emotions were all in control of her.

"I hadn't figured that out yet. A lot of it depends on what the situation looks like."

"But you agree we should try?"

"If at all possible. We need to be able to share observations and…"

"Narrow down the possibilities?" Ellie asked. She felt that with the solid connection between the CEO of Raven Pass Expeditions, a company with means to ship illegal product between their small town and the bigger city, they likely had their man to watch, if nothing else.

But…they both needed to remember that it was never over until it was over, and that everyone needed to be investigated.

At least, everyone on this trip. If Liz was right that someone from the company was smuggling drugs, whoever was behind it might not be on this trip. Ellie was expecting to wrap everything up after this undercover investigation. It was just the first step in getting to interact with the people at the company, see if any of them belonged on the suspect list.

"Exactly." He nodded.

"Who all is going?" She hadn't remembered to ask that before.

"You know, I didn't ask. I thought about it last night, and I'm assuming a couple workers from RPE, maybe a chef for excursions like this, as fancy as they are."

Ellie nodded. "I guess we'll see."

"I guess we will."

They pulled the truck into the parking lot of the shopping center where RPE was located and stared at the building for a second.

"You ready?" she asked him.

"I am." He met her eyes. "You?"

She nodded slowly, not wanting to break the connection between them. When they were undercover, they didn't have to pretend not to know each other or anything. Nothing was changing, not really, besides the fact that they were going deeper into this investigation.

Even though it felt like everything was.

They opened the doors and stepped out.

"You made it!" Brandt Bowker, the CEO, waved from the door. He was dressed in warm outdoor gear.

"Hi!" Ellie waved, turned to Seth slightly as she tucked her hair behind her ear. "I didn't expect he'd be coming," she said, voice lowered.

"Me, either."

"I can't tell you how much I appreciate that the two of you were willing to step in," he said, shaking both their hands once they'd reached the front of the store.

"And not eloping right before the trip." He laughed, and they did, too, but Ellie could tell Seth's laughter was as strained as hers.

"Anytime. More than happy to help."

"And you're punctual. Another good quality."

Brandt Bowker was full of enthusiasm and friendliness, and Ellie couldn't decide if she would automatically have assumed his demeanor was too much, were it not for his connection to Aaron. But with that connection in mind, his joy was overwhelming. She tried to keep her shoulders relaxed, but already the idea of being semiundercover grated on her. She didn't know why; her name was the same, she wasn't pretending not to know Seth and there were no intensely stressful or delicate elements like that.

But just knowing that she had a connection to the case she was investigating and that she had someone out there who already wanted her dead heightened the stakes for her a little. Right up to the line of what she was comfortable with.

She thought of her conversation with Seth last night. She'd been motivated by fear for so long, and she was tired of it but didn't want to be like that anymore.

"So orientation is first?" she asked, just to keep up the front of being able to have a decent conversation, something her real self barely felt capable of at the moment.

"Yes. Our three clients will be arriving—" Brandt checked his watch "—within the half hour, and we will meet with them inside in the Summit Room. Here, come in, I'll show you and explain how this works." He held the door open for both of them, and they stepped inside the lobby.

"Hello." The woman they'd met the other day—Halley, Ellie was pretty sure was her name—was standing at the front counter, also dressed in winter outdoor gear.

The entire company seemed like a larger outfit than just the two of them, but so far they'd not seen anyone else working there.

"Hello," Seth and Ellie said together.

"I'm taking them to the Summit Room to show them how we do things."

Halley nodded. "All right, I'll keep prepping. Have fun! It's going to be a great trip!"

They'd just reached the room when Ellie thought she heard the office phone ring, and then seconds later Halley stuck her head in.

"Sir, I'm sorry to interrupt."

"Can't interrupt what we haven't been able to start yet. Yes?" A flash of impatience crossed his features, and then his expression was neutral again. "I'm sorry, Halley, pretrip jitters. What did you need?"

Huh. Interesting that he'd apologized so quickly.

"Your nephew is on the phone."

Seth and Ellie looked at each other. Then looked away quickly. Ellie kept listening as the woman continued, "He says he was going to come visit this weekend but wants to know when you'll be back."

"I've explained this to him before. It depends on many variables about the trip." He shook his head and moved toward the door. "Excuse me, will you? I'll be right back."

They were left alone in the room, silence echoing around them, but Ellie didn't feel comfortable talking. Not inside the company's building, knowing there could be, well, listening devices. It sounded overdramatic to her ears, but if they were responsible for running a highly profitable and illegal drug operation that had already resulted in several deaths? Then no amount of drama would be past them, and Ellie and Seth needed to keep their guard up.

Still, Seth raised his eyebrows slightly. Ellie nodded. Then they looked down at the pile of equipment in the corner.

"That's a lot of gear," she commented.

"It's smart to be prepared for a trip like this. And customers of somewhere like RPE will be expecting a higher standard, like we talked about. They want things a certain way."

The door shut and echoed in the back. Ellie jumped.

"They certainly do, don't they?" Brandt reentered and laughed, his face looking more stressed than it had when he left. "I apologize for that interruption. But you're right, our clients do expect a certain standard."

"I've always been curious about businesses like this. How do you balance a genuine experience with the luxury clients want?" Ellie asked.

His eyebrows rose. "Insightful question. I like to think we accomplish that mostly by being prepared. We are taking risks with our clients. They know when they sign up that participation is potentially dangerous, but we also try to mitigate hazards. Each sled has a tracker, the kind many dog mushers use in races."

"I'm familiar with those. I've done some races." Seth nodded.

"And you?" Brandt asked Ellie.

Ellie felt her chest tighten and tried not to look accusingly at Seth. They'd have to stretch the truth here and there, for their safety and the investigation, but anything like this could be easily checked out. As soon as he checked her story, he'd see there was no record of her in the dog mushing world at all.

"I'm more of a recreational musher," she answered with a smile. "But I do know how trackers work."

He nodded, not asking for any more explanation than that, which relieved her. "Excellent. As I was about to say before we were interrupted…" Ellie got the impression he was trying to do his presentation from the beginning, like a businessman who was used to giving the same speech before every excursion.

"Raven Pass Expeditions was founded in 1988 out of a desire to bring more people to the backcountry…"

TWELVE

Seth was listening to Brandt's talk about starting his business from the ground up while simultaneously trying to sort out his thoughts on the man himself. Even with the connection to his sister's former boyfriend, it was too soon to mentally try the man, he knew that. But he wasn't sure he trusted Brandt, the way he talked so smoothly, like his program was rehearsed.

Halley was another question mark. She seemed loyal to her boss and the company, genuinely friendly. Seth knew, though, that first impressions weren't always right and that women could commit crimes, too. He tended to think of Liz's killer in terms of *he*, but he knew he might be wrong about that.

"So what staff go on the trips?" Ellie asked, and Seth tuned back in.

"It varies." Brandt shrugged. "Typically I go, as does Halley, sometimes Peter, my business partner, and then we have a chef join us, as well. Then it's the clients and the mushers."

"So three clients?" Seth asked.

"Three. We have one more musher joining us." He flipped his wrist to see his watch and frowned. "He should be here by now. Hopefully there are no more problems. I've had enough of those for one trip. Excuse me again while I make a call to him." He flashed a quick smile. "Feel free to peruse the brochures on the table—that's what the clients will see. They should start arriving in about ten minutes." He left the room.

"Not a lot of info for an orientation, huh?" Ellie said to Seth with a smile as she reached for a brochure. She seemed more relaxed now, and he wished he knew if it was because she was starting to feel like they could solve this case or for another reason.

"It could have been longer." That was for sure. He had guesses but still wasn't completely sure how the logistics were supposed to work. He assumed they would each have a client to assist. But he didn't know if they were expected to mush on the sleds with them, or hook up to a tag sled, or have the client in the sled bag... "I've got a few more questions I need to ask," he admitted.

"Me, too. But I figured we'll probably find out during the client orientation. Rolling with the unexpected is going to work better for me, I think." She nodded, and Seth recognized now that she was in cop mode. All that stressing on her part, the worry she had about letting people down—once she was back in that sort of work mode, she was fully capable of handling this.

That was something he'd like to tell her if they got a chance to talk on this trip. She was stronger than she thought she was. Whatever regrets she was carrying, whatever fears she'd alluded to, she was stronger than those.

He turned to her, trying to decide if he could put his thoughts into words, but was interrupted by the sound of the door.

"Seth, Ellie, this is Wade Randall, another musher who will be helping out this weekend."

Seth nodded, recognizing a man he'd seen at multiple races and talked to a couple of times. "We've met."

"And Ellie?" Brandt asked.

"Like I said," she said with a smile, not appearing rattled at all, "I stick to my home trails. Maybe I'll get into the race scene eventually. I'm Ellie Hamilton."

"Nice to meet you."

"The clients will be here soon. Wade has worked with us before so he knows all this, but we will have tag sleds for you to use hooked behind your sled. That's what we've found is the best way to give clients the experience of mushing without them having full responsibility for a team of dogs. We value the safety not just of our clients and staff but the dogs, too, who we view as another level of staff." He smiled again. "We have several clients this time, a man on his own fulfilling a bucket-list dream, he's in his forties, and a couple who are up here for their fortieth wedding anniversary. I figured that Wade, you'll take the bucket-list man. His name is Austin Kline. Ellie and Seth can take the couple, Darci and Todd Hanson."

Seth felt relief flood him. If they were assigned to a couple, chances were better their charges would both want to take breaks together, ride close together and overall give him a good reason to keep Ellie close to him. God was working this out in ways Seth hadn't thought to ask for, and he was grateful for that.

The clients arrived soon thereafter. Brandt told the three mushers to take a seat in the back of the room and listen. In addition to the clients, Halley had come into the room, as had Peter, Brandt's business partner.

There was also another man Seth thought he recognized as the owner of The Sandwich Shop, who would work as the chef.

All he knew was they might possibly be sitting in a room now with a killer. Someone who wanted them dead. Seth and Ellie might have suspicions, but they were operating under assumptions and guesses, not facts.

The people who were after him? They knew for sure what he looked like. And chances were good they knew what Ellie looked like, also—unless they'd just been shooting at her because of how often she was in proximity to him.

Either way, they weren't disguised. They were here, open and vulnerable targets, counting on the fact that surely not everyone in the party was guilty. The murderer, whoever it was, wouldn't want to kill them publicly.

That might keep them safe.

Or it might not… They were about to find out.

Ellie couldn't believe how much Wade looked like a stereotypical musher. He was probably ten years older than she and Seth were and had a mountain-man beard that no doubt many men would be jealous of; she wasn't sure why men had such a fascination with beards. Seth often had that layer of scruff, like the perpetual start of a beard, and she admitted to herself she might actually like it.

Still, it didn't have the same wild, mountain-man feeling as a full, inches-long beard. But while Wade might not have been her type, he certainly fit the trip well. He looked as though he'd been born outside in the wilds of Alaska and had been adventuring ever since. In contrast, Ellie felt she might still fit in pretty well on a ski slope near Anchorage. Her outdoor gear was top-notch but also had been bought with some degree of style in mind, and she hoped she didn't disappoint the client assigned to her by not fitting what she'd been expecting.

Worrying about clients, she reminded herself as she listened to Brandt, was only her job as far as it positioned her to investigate undercover. She needed to remember that her first priority was to find out who had killed Liz and hopefully get a better idea of why.

She was glad she and Seth had had time to talk last night, even if it had ended so badly. Researching the people associated with RPE had been helpful in her understanding of Liz's letter. She was still not sure about several of them, and while it was tempting to suspect everyone, all the way down to the chef that was part of the expedition, she knew that the likelihood of all of them being involved was slim.

Unless Raven Pass Expeditions really was entirely a front. But in that case, would clients be in on the smuggling, also? No, that all seemed too far-fetched for Ellie to give serious consideration to.

"Any questions?" Brandt was saying, clearly signaling the presentation was finishing up.

"Do we need to go hook up the dogs or anything? Are we supposed to be ready to leave right now?" Ellie should have paid closer attention, she knew, but she'd just been too distracted.

The corners of Seth's mouth tugged up, and she knew that he could tell she'd been distracted, too. He gave a slight shake of his head. "No, our clients want to have the entire authentic experience, so we will hook up with their help."

"What about the trail?" This time Seth asked Brandt the question.

"It's well marked. We always use the same trail. Mushers seem to stick together pretty well."

Seth frowned. He might be more comfortable with that, but Ellie didn't have much experience. He'd have preferred a map. "I really think…"

"I'll mention the maps to Halley and she'll get them to you. Excuse me, I have a few things I have to see to before we leave. But don't worry, the trail is very easy to find."

Had she really considered how difficult this was going to be? It was all in service of finding Liz's killer, though, and uncovering information to solve this case.

"Let's get started. Please find your musher and do what they tell you to. The RPE team will be packing your gear onto our snow machines, which will follow behind or go ahead during the trip, depending on trail conditions. Your adventure begins now."

Ellie wished she had the luxury for a regular adventure. Instead she was stuck in this investigation, in a place where it was safer to take risks than to sit around, waiting for danger to strike.

A woman in her midsixties, dressed in expensive gear from head to toe but with a warm smile, approached Ellie. "You must be Ellie. I'm Darci Hanson. I'm just so excited about all of this!"

The woman seemed genuine, and Ellie smiled at her. "Nice to meet you. Ready to get started?"

Her enthusiastic nod was the push Ellie needed. Resisting the urge to look over her shoulder for Seth, she started outside. She and Seth had talked about needing to stay close to each other if possible, to keep an eye out for threats, make sure the other was okay, but Ellie also knew that to do that too much would draw undue attention to them and could end up compromising their cover. Right now, while they were still in town, Ellie needed to make sure she kept her distance from Seth to a certain degree, so it wouldn't look like they were overly attached to each other.

"Is that nice young man your boyfriend?"

Then again, maybe it wouldn't be bad to have a reason for people to assume they sought out time to be together. Brandt had already figured as much, and their blushing faces had likely done little to change his assumption.

Ellie just smiled, not confirming or denying.

"Oh, that's so sweet! Love and dog mushing." The woman smiled. "That's why we're on this trip. We were looking for something to do for our anniversary, and I said to Todd, what could be more romantic?"

"I hope you have a fantastic time," Ellie told her genuinely. "Let's introduce you to the dogs, shall we?" As Ellie started prepping the droplines, guilt started settling over her. She hadn't considered the fact that their undercover investigation could endanger people, that the three innocent clients could become casualties of their need for justice. Not to mention whichever of the guides or workers on this trip could be innocent…

"Are you okay?"

Ellie hadn't realized she'd stopped walking until Darci asked her that. She shook her head, cleared her throat. Attempted a smile. "Fine, I'm fine." Her gaze went to Seth, who had come outside and was standing on the other side of the dog truck, but within view.

"You miss your honey, huh?" Darci grinned conspiratorially. "Don't worry, I'll make sure you still get plenty of time to see him this weekend."

This time Ellie's smile was more genuine. She appreciated having an ally, even if Darci didn't know exactly how much she was helping. And there was still her oppressive level of guilt to contend with.

But for right now, the best cure for the load of it she'd been carrying for years was just to solve this, finish it. And then move on.

Whatever that meant.

"This is Cipher." Ellie started with her favorite, a gorgeous girl whose coat was varying shades of brown. "And this is Spruce..." She continued through the list, introducing all twelve dogs that Seth was letting her use. Goofy. Willow. Marvel. Hawk. Bagel. Viking. Puzzle. Donut. Bacon. Captain.

She'd laughed at the names when he'd first told her, but he'd explained to her how sled-dog naming worked, that mushers usually did the whole litter at once, and they had to get creative. So then there were dogs like Bacon, who had once been part of a litter with names of breakfast foods.

Still, Darci chuckled when she heard the names, too. "I love them."

"Let's start hooking up."

Out of the corner of her eye, Ellie could see that everyone else was in a flurry of activity, too. Seth was hooking up his dogs, as was Wade, and the Raven Pass Expeditions staff was bringing out the tag sleds. Even with as little as she knew about mushing, she could tell that those sleds were expensive and well made. This was a company that prided themselves on the quality of its trips, for sure.

Would Brandt endanger the company he'd built by running drugs? Not unless smuggling was far more profitable; nothing in the way the business ran seemed to say *front for drug running.* If it was, why spend so much money on gear? And on personnel? The amount they were paying her and Seth just for a weekend would add a nice chunk to her savings account, which was good since she'd had to take a short leave of absence from her job on the SAR team in order to be part of this investigation.

Nothing appeared to add up, but wasn't life confusing sometimes? The facts seemed to argue with her and with each other, twisting into a convoluted mess.

Ellie felt uneasy. She almost felt like she needed to forget everything she knew so far and keep an open mind. See how she felt.

But that went against so much of the training she'd had. She'd been taught to gather evidence, prepare a solid case. In this particular situation, there hadn't been a lot of evidence to gather. The main crime had been committed three years ago. The perpetrators hadn't gotten away with it for lack of police investigating. They'd tried to discover who'd been responsible for Liz's death. That made Ellie think she did need to trust her gut here, be open to what they could find without a rock-solid strategy. But she was used to her strengths. Her training. And without that?

What did she have except a possibly hopeless desire for justice and her deep and overwhelming fear that she and Seth would be next?

THIRTEEN

Hooking up had taken longer than usual, Seth thought to himself, having to tell Todd about everything he was doing. The man wasn't incapable or anything, but he wasn't quite as quick a learner as Ellie had been, so it had been more of an effort to teach him. Now they were all out on the trail, and Seth was able to relax. At least, it was the part of the run where he usually felt like he could breathe for a minute.

Today that wasn't true. He appreciated how RPE had set up the whole excursion, down to the fact that their offices connected easily to the trail, and had appreciated their concern for safety. Attached to his sled handlebar was a high-tech tracker, similar to ones he'd used in races, but that also had a button on it that could supposedly alert local law enforcement with their location so they could bring help.

They'd thought of everything to keep their customers safe.

But did that mean they weren't part of a drug-running scheme? Or just that they were good at multitasking?

If it was up to Seth, if all that happened recently was just the attack on him, he'd give up this entire plan and just live with the threat for the rest of his life. He didn't want his sister's killer to walk free, but he also didn't want to sacrifice Ellie's life in order to bring a criminal to justice, and the farther from civilization they got with a group of people he couldn't trust, the more he was concerned that to continue was to do just that.

But it wasn't his choice anymore. He'd let her get involved—had asked her to, because he knew he needed her help—and now it was too late to put a stop to any of this.

But that didn't make him feel less worried about the situation.

"How are you doing back there?" he called over his shoulder to his tag-sledder when they were on a straight-away that let him take his attention off the trail for a minute.

"Great!" the man yelled back. Todd seemed like a nice enough guy. His wife, Ellie's passenger, also seemed delighted.

When he thought of Ellie, he looked back up the trail. Wade had volunteered to be the first dog team for this part, and his bucket-list passenger had a competitive streak and liked the idea of being in the front. Seth had suggested Ellie go next, preferring the idea of her being in between two other mushers and away from the support crew, who rode behind them on snow machines. The crew was made up of Brandt, Halley, Peter and Jared, The Sandwich Shop–guy-turned-chef for this expedition.

When Seth had researched to find out how much clients paid for something like this and he'd seen the amount, his eyes had almost fallen out of his head, but now he understood. They had four support staff and three mushers. Seven people working full-time to provide an adventure to three clients.

Yeah, he saw now why they charged so much.

It seemed like they made a good living. So why would they feel the need to run drugs? Pure greed?

Seth turned his attention back to the dogs. There wasn't a lot he could find out while they were running down the trail. Better to just try to enjoy the ride for now and make sure he paid close attention at dinner tonight. The times when they weren't mushing would probably yield the most information for the investigation.

An hour or so later they came to an open area, a treeless part of a pass essentially, and he saw that Wade and Ellie were already stopped up ahead. He pulled his team alongside Wade. "Press on your brake as you say *whoa*," he instructed Todd as he did the same. Like the others, they were arranged so that the musher's sled was directly hooked to the team. The client's sled was attached by a rope behind that sled so they got the feeling of dog mushing without being in full control of the team.

"Everything all right?" Seth asked Wade.

"Usually we stop here to give the dogs a snack. I realized they didn't go over stopping points with us this time, probably too chaotic today, so I figured we should go ahead and halt."

Seth nodded. Made sense to him. He instructed Todd on how to feed the dogs and then helped him, even as he kept half an eye on Ellie.

She was doing this like an old pro, and it made him smile to see how well she was able to look and act the part of a musher.

The dogs finished eating, and Seth was about to ask Wade if he thought they should wait for the support crew when he heard a buzzing behind them, like angry bees. That was always what the obnoxious noise of a snow machine made him think of when it shattered the quiet that was so easily enjoyed on the back of a dog sled.

"Sorry about that," Brandt said once all the machines had pulled in. "Peter had a family emergency and had to go back. It'll just be us." He motioned to Halley and Jared, each on their own machines and pulling a sled behind them loaded down with gear, but Jared seemed to have the most. Seth could see something sticking out of his sled that looked like the makings of a fancy kitchen. He half wondered if he had a kitchen sink in that sled.

"I hope Peter is okay." Ellie sounded concerned, and Seth wished he knew it was just because she was a kind person and worried about whatever emergency the other man was having, or if Ellie was scared about something else.

Not being able to talk to her anytime he wanted was something he wasn't used to yet, and honestly didn't want to get used to. He'd never expected to have her back in his life, and here she was and now he didn't want that to change.

Ever.

"He'll be all right. We will just have less staff on this trip, which means more food for you guys." He flashed a smile at the clients, always working, always trying to *shape good outdoor experiences*, as one of the brochures Seth had flipped through had said. "We have quite the plans for food this weekend, right, Jared?"

"Not to flatter myself, but it's going to be amazing." He spoke with the passion of a foodie, Seth noted. He only hoped the guy's plans for good grub involved actual food. He wasn't into fancy.

"Let's keep going," Brandt said to Wade, the de facto mushing leader.

"All right." His dogs took off at the command. Ellie followed and then Seth.

They mushed as the day turned to dark, and Seth clicked his headlamp on, hoping Ellie had done the same. He'd made sure she'd packed it in her sled bag, in a place where it was easily accessible, but still, he worried not being close enough to see her.

This distance between them wasn't working. At the moment they were all too spread out. His passenger was heavier than hers, and if she wasn't riding the drag mat some, slowing her team's speed down, she was going to stay too far ahead of them. He'd talk to her tonight, ask her to hold back a little so they stayed more in a group. That was better for a trip like this, anyway. And they all had SAT phones in case of emergencies.

After another hour or so, he saw lights in the distance, and as he approached he could see that an entire camp had already been set up. The support team was there already, so they must have taken a short cut trail to meet them. It was impressive seeing lights already strung on several trees like they were at some kind of fancy resort, and the smell of whatever Jared was cooking was good enough to make his stomach growl immediately.

"How was your trip?" Halley asked Seth as he pulled in.

"Good." He nodded at her, then looked away to set his snow hook.

"No problems?"

"No. Should we have had some?"

"It looks like your…" Halley trailed off, widening her eyes in an unspoken question. She almost seemed to be waiting for him to clarify their relationship. "Your girl-friend had some trouble finding the trail. So we weren't sure if you'd take the wrong way or not."

"No one called," he said as he slipped the SAT phone out of his pocket and checked it. "Nope."

"How long was she lost?" he asked. Halley's expression fell a little. So yeah, he might not have been imagining the slight interest in her eyes. Better that she know now that he wasn't available, though. Even if Ellie wasn't going to let him back into her life, he wasn't emotionally open to exploring another relationship right now.

"We just talked to her on the phone, and she's almost here," Halley said.

"Who was lost?" Todd's voice behind him held an edge of anxiety, and for the first time Seth remembered that it was his wife riding on Ellie's tag sled. And this was a very swanky, very expensive trip. He wouldn't have this job if he wasn't careful to play by the rules, and that included not making clients panic.

Fortunately, Halley was used to dealing with incidents like this, or seemed to be. She moved smoothly to where Todd was climbing off the tag sled. "Your wife's guide took a wrong turn, but they are fine. They called a minute ago and are almost here. About a mile out."

Todd started to pace. "I shouldn't have said yes to this crazy plan. Darci's always wanting more adventure, and I should have put my foot down…"

"Todd, they're both fine." Seth worked to keep his tone even despite the pounding in his chest. His heart was thudding double-maybe triple-time. He wasn't buying the *took a wrong turn* until he had a chance to talk to Ellie and confirm. It wasn't okay that they'd disappeared. And it wasn't okay that the mushers hadn't all been given detailed directions. Even though there were trail markers every so often for them to follow, it was easy for those to fall. Or for an inexperienced musher like Ellie to miss one if the snow had drifted over it. At the very least they should have had trail maps, but they hadn't been given those, either. He'd talk to Brandt before they went out in the morning and make sure all of them had what they needed tomorrow. But right now, in order to keep this job and keep their cover, he needed to stay relaxed.

"I just don't—"

"Want to help me with the dogs? We need to unhook the line that connects them to the tugline, but leave the neckline on."

"Okay. Sure. We'll do that and then they should be back, right? How long does a mile take?"

When you were waiting for someone you loved? Hours. Years.

"It should only take them a short time. Even if the dogs are tired, ten minutes would be a slow mile for them."

Todd nodded, and his face seemed to relax. Halley walked back to the support staff, seeming to be content with how he was handling the situation.

They got to work undoing one of the clips, and as he'd expected, by the time they were almost done there was a swoosh of runners, and there was Ellie.

She was okay, he saw from a quick assessment. Everything looked fine, dogs were fine, no evidence of the sled being broken. She was standing tall on the runners, but her jaw was tight. She looked...

Angry?

"I've got to go see my wife." Todd flashed him an apologetic look as he hurried away.

He didn't mind; it went faster when it was just him working, anyway. He worked his way through the dogs, rubbing them to check for muscle soreness. They all seemed happy.

Finally he started to walk toward Ellie, who was still standing on the sled. Her passenger had abandoned her and was sitting by the fire with her husband. The support staff was handing them food and probably planning to smooth over this incident to make sure the couple was still happy and having a good trip.

All Seth wanted to know was if Ellie was okay.

And what had *really* happened out there in the woods. Seth had tried to fool himself into thinking that he could protect her, even when they were mushing separately, but this proved that had been wishful thinking. Had someone sabotaged her? Caused her to lose the trail on purpose? The thought made his chest hurt, but he reminded himself that she was here, she was okay. He hadn't lost her.

Yet.

Ellie was still shaking too hard to be able to do anything with her dogs that required fine motor skills. Whether she trembled from fear or anger she wasn't sure, but one emotion was threatening to overwhelm her.

Maybe both of them.

They'd been following Wade closely, as Ellie wasn't completely confident in her trail-finding abilities. Brandt was right that the trail was visible in most places, but in some the wind had blown the snow in such a way that it was hard to distinguish the trail from open field.

She should have insisted on a map, but after Brandt had brushed Seth off, she hadn't wanted to push. And everything had gone fine for a while. She and Darci had been having a good run. Ellie had felt better on her own, without Seth, than she'd anticipated, as far as her skills with the dogs, but maybe she'd gotten too cocky.

Or maybe she'd been too focused on the job and hadn't remembered to be suspicious enough. They were here, doing this, because they were in danger. She'd let her guard down.

She'd taken a wrong turn after Wade had disappeared from sight because the false trail had been looking more recently taken than the new trail. She'd had her headlamp on, and while she didn't see Wade ahead, she knew he must not be too far because her team seemed to be maintaining a good pace.

The trail kept narrowing the farther they went. Ellie started to realize something wasn't right.

And that was when she'd started to feel watched. Chills had run up her arms, her spine. She'd have yelled for help but who would have heard? Instead she felt almost paralyzed, fear pressing in on her.

"Is everything all right?" Darci had asked when Ellie put her feet on the drag mat to slow them down, then took both feet off and encouraged the dogs verbally go to faster, while she kept checking in the woods.

She'd forgotten her client for a minute. She looked back and smiled. "Fine, just not sure about the trail. Sorry." Honesty was the best policy, she believed, so she didn't pretend she was sure she knew where she was going.

Darci was a good sport. Even when the trail disappeared altogether and they were trudging through the snow, pushing the weight of the sled to help the dogs as they struggled through the thick snow, she kept a good attitude. At one point she ran up to Ellie and asked if they were going to be okay. That was when Ellie stopped them, pulled out her SAT phone. She hadn't wanted to use it before because it felt like admitting defeat. But it was necessary. Brandt gave her directions based on the GPS location her tracker showed, and she got them back here.

They were fine.

Nothing had happened.

Except…the trail she'd taken had been wide and packed down. But after they turned around and reached the junction where it connected to the real trail, Ellie had felt like the snow got deeper. Like someone made a false trail but then covered its entrance with snow again so no one else would take it, so no one could find her, maybe.

But had Ellie imagined the feeling of being watched from the woods?

She didn't think so. It had been more than a quick impression. It had felt like a steadfast stare.

"Are you okay?" Seth asked her now, standing in front of her. He laid a hand on her arm, the familiar weight of it relaxing her shoulders, making her feel like she had permission to fall apart.

Permission didn't make it practical, though. Maybe the others around the fire would think she was crying from stress. Maybe that would be okay with them. Or maybe she and Seth would be fired and unable to look into any of the people they wanted to investigate. Brandt. Halley. Peter. Jared.

"I'm…" She shook her head. "I don't know."

"The trail?"

"I think it was intentional. The trail I took was fantastic, fresh and better than the correct one. Then it narrowed and disappeared. On my way back, though, it seemed like some of the snow had been moved back to hide my side trail. Maybe that's why you didn't take it."

"Do you think someone...what? Put a snow machine down it and then turned around?"

She shook her head. "I don't know. I'm not sure. But I am sure that it wasn't an accident."

"But to what purpose? Nothing happened, right?"

She set her snow hook and stepped off the sled runners, moved toward her sled back to get her dogs dinner. "I don't know."

Seth followed her, waiting for more, and Ellie didn't blame him for the look of confusion he wore on his face. She wasn't making much sense right now.

"I felt like someone was watching me," she finally admitted to him.

He stood there, inches from her, and she wished he'd do something, pull her in his arms, tell her it would be okay. But she knew she'd made it clear that she didn't want more than friendship with him. Seth would be careful not to do anything that could make her feel pressured.

So he stood there, arms at his sides, though she noticed his fists were clenched.

"But you're right," she said, trying to reassure both of them to ease the tension. "Nothing happened."

"That isn't nothing."

Ellie fed the last of her dogs and then started unhooking their tuglines, which connected to their harnesses. This, Seth had explained to her, gave them more room to move and lie down to rest, and signaled to them that they were taking a break. It was part of what they'd practiced on the run near Wasilla.

"Ellie, you're back. Everything all right?" Brandt was coming toward them.

"She had some trouble with trail finding."

She recognized that take-charge tone of Seth's and stood quickly. She didn't need him trying to handle this and getting both of them in trouble or drawing suspicion. "I lost the trail, as you know, but thanks for helping."

"My directions were good?"

She nodded. "Yes, thank you."

"Why did she get lost in the first place?" Seth asked. "We had that entire orientation, and you went over quite a bit of information, but giving the trail map to the mushers taking your clients on this trip wasn't a high priority? You said Halley would get them to us before we left."

"Seth…" Ellie started.

"No, he cares about you. I understand why he's upset." Brandt's face fell. "We usually do. I'm sorry. Wade is familiar with the trail, and so it seems that the maps were forgotten about."

"You *forgot* them? After I asked for a map?" Seth was still standing a few feet from the other man; Ellie had stopped worrying that he was going to blow their cover, but he was still fairy angry.

"Halley forgot to make the copies. The rest of the trail should be marked, though. And if it's not, Jared has offered to go ahead and make sure it is clearly marked. That would give him some extra time for setup, anyway. It wouldn't be the first time we've sent him ahead, since it does make it easier for him to do his job. We won't have this problem tomorrow. I'm truly sorry for the trouble."

He did seem distressed.

Had he or someone else meant to isolate and kill her? Had Darci's presence saved her somehow? Ellie thought back to when she'd been the most nervous and felt like someone could see her. It was right about that moment that Darci had come forward and stood beside her. They'd made the phone call together, then Darci had gone ahead to turn the dogs around, and Ellie had stayed on the sled. Then they'd been off.

What if someone had been waiting...a sniper...but didn't want to hit the wrong woman?

It wasn't outside the realm of possibility.

"Thanks. I'm glad it won't be a problem tomorrow." Ellie finally found the words, stuttered through them.

It seemed to be enough for Brandt, who nodded and walked away.

"You're sure you're okay?"

She nodded. "We have to join them now. Talk later?"

His eyes didn't like that, she found she could easily see. She didn't look away from him, blinked a couple of times. He hurt when she hurt, she was seeing now. He was more scared for her than she'd been for herself. Was that part of love? Not just being attracted to a person, not just wanting what was best for them, but caring about them to such a great degree?

She reached out for his hand. He raised his eyebrows but took it.

And they walked together, hand in hand, toward the fire.

FOURTEEN

If there was one thing Seth had learned from the expedition so far, it was that RPE knew how to run something like this. Dinner wasn't the typical campfire fare; instead, a salmon chowder and some of the best sourdough bread Seth had ever had. Dessert was some fancy chocolate cake with sea salt—not a combination he would have thought of, but it was incredible. The support staff was fed the same food as the clients, for which he was grateful. It would have been hard to eat a peanut butter sandwich, knowing what the guests were being treated to.

Ellie had let go of his hand when they'd taken seats on some of the chairs the support staff had hauled in, but she'd scooted her chair as close to his as she could. He still wasn't sure what had happened between them just then, or if it was just wishful thinking to believe that anything had. She hadn't said anything, and neither had he, but he thought he'd seen something shift in her eyes right before she took his hand.

Maybe it was a cover? She might just want it to seem like they were romantically involved so that if they sneaked into the woods to talk it wouldn't seem strange.

Or maybe it was real?

"I'm still not thrilled about today." Todd spoke up, frowning in Ellie's direction. "I can assume there will be no incidents tomorrow?"

She gave him a gracious smile and nodded. Seth looked away, realizing this was his chance to see how the other staff reacted to the conversation.

Halley looked sympathetic, both to Todd and Ellie, the way she kept glancing back and forth. Jared hadn't looked up from where he was cleaning the dishes. Brandt looked like he was forming a response, much like a startled politician looked at a press conference that wasn't going their way.

"I think they've worked out a way to ensure that it doesn't," Seth said.

Wade nodded his agreement, grunted a little. He wasn't a big talker. "What time are we heading out in the morning? I'm ready to get some sleep."

Seth glanced at his watch. Just past eight o'clock.

"We'll want to pull out of camp around eight in the morning, so let's plan for breakfast at seven to give us a nice leisurely amount of time." Brandt flashed a smile. Wade grunted again and lumbered over toward his sled, then set up a tent next to it. RPE loaned the mushers the kind that was easy to set up in about five minutes. Usually Seth would bring his own tent but had decided it was better to just use the equipment they were being lent.

One by one, people headed to sleep. The RPE staff were all in small pop-up tents, but the two client tents—the married couple was sharing one—were large, and the entrances were rimmed by twinkling lights.

Soon it was just Seth, Ellie and Jared by the fire.

"Can I trust you two to put the fire out? I usually handle it," Jared asked. "But I'm ready to turn in and you two look cozy."

Ellie had reached for Seth's hand again, and he was only too happy to hold hers. Even if there was no actual skin-on-skin contact, since they were both wearing gloves.

"We can do that." Ellie nodded.

Jared nodded his head in a kind of good-night gesture and wandered off into the darkness to where his tent was pitched near Halley's and Brandt's.

They were in three clusters. Client tents. Staff tents. Musher tents. Like a little city in the woods with space in between them. Seth couldn't begin to compare this to the mushing camping trips he was used to. The solitude and chance to be truly alone in the wilderness then were unparalleled, and this wasn't anything like that.

However, right now, he had Ellie with him. Maybe that made it worth it. Or it would, under better circumstances. As good as it felt to be holding her hand, all he could think about was the danger she was in. That they *both* were in. She could have been killed earlier, when she'd been isolated from the group. Murdered miles away from him, and he'd have been helpless to stop it. Seth swallowed hard.

"What are you thinking?" She laid her head on his shoulder, and he took a breath. She felt so right there, but he knew that this was largely practicality. Sound carried easily in the cold night air, and they needed to avoid being overheard. He wished they could just go talk in one of their tents, but though that would provide the illusion of privacy, it was probably just as easy to hear them there, and they wouldn't be able to see anyone standing close by the tent.

"I don't like any of this," he whispered.

"But who do you think…?" She trailed off.

"Any of them could. Brandt has the obvious connection to Aaron, plus he's in charge of the trips. Halley knows so much about the company and handles the operational details, she could be coordinating with someone. And she was the one who conveniently 'forgot' the maps. Jared isn't with the company, but if he goes on these trips, he could be responsible. Peter, we don't know much about, but he had to leave this trip at the last minute, which makes me wonder if that has something to do with a drug drop."

Ellie nodded. "My thoughts, too. At least my logical thoughts."

"And your gut instincts?"

She shook her head. "I stopped trusting those a long time ago."

"Maybe you shouldn't have."

The fire crackled as she appeared to absorb his words and then slowly nodded her head. "Maybe you're right."

He wanted to ask her about last night, about what emotion she was still so afraid of. He wanted to talk to her about his sister's death. She acted as though she were responsible, somehow, in the way she talked about it. But Seth had no idea why and wished he could make her see that she wasn't at fault, that she could keep on living her life. Liz wouldn't have wanted guilt to hold her back.

"Why the hand-holding?" he wanted to know.

"I can't…" She exhaled. "Maybe I shouldn't. I don't

know, being out here with you, seeing how scared you were when I was lost…"

"Yes?"

"It almost seemed like…" She trailed off, but he heard the unspoken words. It seemed like he loved her.

Because he did.

"I do."

"I'm not the same person I was back then," she said, tugging her hand away gently.

He didn't let go of it.

"Ellie?" he said, using her nickname not just because they were undercover but because that was who this new version of her was.

"Yeah?"

"I love you now just as much as I did then. All the stuff that happened? It didn't make me love you less. This person you are now? I love her, too."

He held his breath while he watched her expression, searched her eyes to see if she felt the same. He expected her to break eye contact. Maybe go back to her tent. Run again.

Instead she spoke. "And I love you." For once she didn't look away. Seth closed his eyes, letting the words soak in, feeling the impact of them as he relaxed.

She loved him, too.

He leaned close to her, eager to kiss her now that they were on the same page. He knew she wasn't going to pull away again, and neither of them was going to regret it.

A noise behind them grabbed his attention first. He stopped his forward motion, dropped her hand and looked behind him.

"Sorry to bother you." Brandt cleared his throat. "I

left some of the extra blankets out here in my sled..."
He was digging through the snow-machine bag. Pulled
a blanket out and held it up like a trophy. "Uh, carry
on. Just remember, no funny business until after this
trip." He laughed a little and headed back to his tent.

"You think he was listening?"

"I think if he was, he could only have been around
long enough to hear us talk about our feelings, which
doesn't incriminate us much, does it?"

Ellie smiled. "I guess you have a point." Her face
turned serious again. "But do you think he was trying
to eavesdrop?"

Seth considered it, moved closer to her, still wanting
that kiss. "I think it's very possible."

"If so, that could make him our guy."

"But if it's not, we could overlook who it really is.
And remember, we have to find evidence." He took a
deep breath, decided he wanted better than this. If this
really was a second chance, he wanted their next first
kiss to be stored, not something rushed in the shadows while they wondered who was watching. And who
wanted them dead. "We should get some sleep."

"I don't think I'll sleep at all, alone."

There was nothing he could do to help her, and nothing he could say that would change the truth. She should
be scared, because right now they both had more than
enough to be frightened of. But he'd always do everything in his power to keep her safe.

Ellie's heart pounded, and she fought to keep her
breathing even. She was tucked deep into her sleeping bag, inside a tent that was only ten feet away from
Seth's, and still she felt alone.

She had only become surer that her gut instincts from earlier were correct: she had been watched when she'd taken the wrong trail and slowed down in the woods. In retrospect, the more she ran the scene over in her head, she was almost positive. The way her shoulders had tensed and she hadn't known why, the way the darkness of the woods had seemed all-encompassing and unnerving when she usually found it familiar...

Besides her subjective feelings, Ellie knew there was evidence, if she had stayed longer to process the scene. The snow had been moved to recover the trail. Her police training in situational awareness had made her notice that on the way out. It had been an intentional trap.

Someone had been waiting, anticipating she'd take the wrong trail and planning to take advantage of that.

To kill her where she stood? It made sense. Or maybe drag her away and kill her somewhere else. She had no doubt that they wanted her dead, whoever *they* were.

She turned over again, every movement she made so loud in the quiet.

Her SAT phone vibrated.

You okay?

It was Seth's number. He'd insisted that they each get a SAT phone in case of emergencies or if they got separated. She should have called him on it when she'd gotten off-trail earlier, but with Darci standing right there, it had made more sense to call the people actually in charge of the expedition. If it happened again, she'd call Seth. He needed to know if anything else went wrong before anyone else knew.

Not just because they were working together, but because she loved him.

She felt herself smile just at the thought. She loved him. She still loved him and she'd told him and he still loved her.

If only circumstances were different, if this threat wasn't still hanging over them, she could bask in the knowledge that maybe it wasn't too late for them.

But fear unsettled her stomach. Someone had gotten too close earlier. Probably could have killed her. She couldn't let that happen again.

Fine.

She texted him back and waited.

Usually that's code for not fine.

See? He was a smart man.
She picked up the phone again.

I think someone was watching me when I was in the woods on the wrong path.

He texted back quickly. You mentioned that.

I'm more sure of it now. And I want to know who.

A few minutes passed. Then one more text came through.

Me, too.

While the trip had just started, it was only a few days long. Would they be able to find anything out in such a short amount of time?

Ellie had envisioned people sitting around the fire longer, getting to know the employees of Raven Pass Expeditions, but there hadn't been much time for aimless chatter, or for listening for it. Maybe tomorrow night would allow for more of that. At the moment she still didn't know what to think.

She wasn't sure she trusted any of them. Actually, scratch that. She was completely sure that she didn't.

Ellie stared at the phone for another minute, then decided to try again to get some sleep. She took a deep breath and laid her head down again.

She'd just drifted off, or at least it felt that way, when she woke up suddenly.

The night was cold and quiet. She frowned. Why had she woken up, then? Was she that tense?

Then she heard it. Something was moving outside. One of her dogs whined. Ellie sat up straight and swallowed against the knot of fear growing in her chest.

Footsteps on the snow. Slow. Deliberate.

Ellie reached for the zipper.

Stuck. Her zipper was stuck. Panic snapped in her brain, like electricity overloading. She'd had a friend in college play a practical joke on someone by zip-tying their tent shut once. But this was no joke, and unless she cut herself out of the tent she was stuck.

Was her knife in here with her? Or in the sled bag?

She thought it might be the latter.

Ellie heard something splash against the side of the tent. Smelled gasoline.

No. No. No.

Should she yell? If she yelled, would whoever was out there just shoot her?

She pressed the phone buttons quicker than she ever had.

Hoped Seth would see it.

Help.

Ellie's text came through, and panic surged in Seth's heart. He went for the zipper of his tent, found it wouldn't give and reached for the fixed-blade knife he kept in his vest pocket, then sliced it open. The noise it made, cutting through the vinyl, was loud and dramatic.

All at once his senses were overwhelmed. He heard the sound of footsteps running away, and as he pushed his way out of the hole in his tent, he saw a shadow moving far away in the woods.

Then came the overwhelming smell of gasoline. Smoke.

Ellie.

Her tent was on fire, flames just licking up the sides, her screams echoing in the night. Seth hurried to the tent, reached for the tent zipper.

It was zip-tied shut. Like his must have been, also. "Ellie!" he yelled.

"Hurry!" she screamed. Then coughed. Smoke inhalation was as real a danger as the flames. Either would be a horrible way to go. Seth reached in his pocket for a knife.

"Back up. I'm going to cut it."

"There's nowhere to back up. Seth, hurry!"

Seth grabbed his knife, sliced open the end, pulled

the tent fabric until the hole he'd made was big enough to climb through.

Ellie stumbled out, sobbing.

She was still in danger. They all were if this fire spread. Seth reached back inside his tent for the water bottle he kept in the bottom of his sleeping bag and threw it on the flames, then reached for loose snow and kept throwing and throwing it till the flames were more under control. Ellie joined him, throwing piles of fluffy powder. Then Seth grabbed a large water jug and poured it over the flames that were still licking at the fabric. They sizzled and died.

Ellie was sobbing and stepped outside. "I thought I was going to die."

He held his arms out, and she stepped into them. He pulled her tight and then let her go. "Let's get your things out." Much as he'd like to just stand there forever, being thankful that she was okay and calling himself every kind of idiot for not doing more to protect her, they needed to save what they could of her belongings.

He pulled her sleeping bag out, which was fine, and her backpack. The tent itself still smoldered, and the smell of gasoline had rendered it a loss. They'd pack it and throw it away.

Movement to their left drew Seth's attention. Wade was climbing out of his tent. It was not zip-tied. "What happened?"

"Someone set her tent on fire."

Wade's eyes widened. For a second, Seth wondered if they could have this all wrong. What if someone like Wade was running the drugs, in his sled bag, maybe, and had just used the Wi-Fi at RPE, and that was why

Liz's friend had given her that location for the computer messages?

"Is she okay?" He came closer.

He didn't smell at all like gasoline.

Would he have been able to douse her tent without
some part of him having the smell linger? Seth was inclined to say no.

"We're short a tent," Ellie said with a sniff. "But
I'm okay."

"I can bunk with Wade and you can have my tent,"
he told her, glancing at Wade for confirmation that was
okay with him. The other man was nodding, his expression guileless.

Ellie just continued to cry.

Had he ever heard her sob like that? They'd seen
each other once after Liz's death. Well, twice, but one
of the times, Ellie was breaking up with him and was so
much not like herself, completely guarded and careful,
that it hardly counted. The time he'd seen her was right
after and she had cried then, but it had been a silent cry.
This was not quiet. It was anguish, plain and simple.

Seth hated that he couldn't make her pain go away.

"I want this to be over," she whispered.

Seth looked up. Blinked as he realized that it could
be. If they could figure out which of the staff members
hadn't been in their tents at the time of the fire, they'd
know who had likely been responsible.

"Come with me." He grabbed her hand and moved
toward the tents. Brandt's first.

"Watch the other tents," he said to Ellie. "Brandt?"

Movement inside, like someone getting out of a
sleeping bag. But that could be easily faked.

"What happened?" He seemed to be taking in their

appearances, and as he did so, the look of concern on his face grew. "Is everyone okay? Do I smell smoke?"

Ellie opened her mouth to speak, but Seth could see she was about to blow their cover and end this.

They couldn't do that if this wasn't really over, not without giving up on solving the case.

"Someone set Ellie's tent on fire."

"Someone…" His frown deepened. He seemed to be trying to wake up and process what Seth had said. After a few seconds the frown turned to an expression of shock. Maybe anger. "Someone what?"

Seth walked him through the events of the last few minutes.

"Let me get the rest of the team." Brandt pulled his boots on and started out of the tent toward the other two support-staff tents.

He walked to the first one as Seth and Ellie watched. Halley came out, looking tired. The next tent. Jared came out of it.

So was Peter, the partner who had gone home, the one who had set the fire? But how, if he wasn't on-site? Had he stayed nearby to sabotage them, rather than returning home like he'd said?

Had one of these three people done it and managed to get back into their tent before Seth had realized he should investigate?

Or was someone here calling the shots and had told an outside party where they'd be? That made the most sense. It would be too risky for any of the support staff to do it themselves. But there was no reason one of them couldn't be working with someone else and providing locations.

"Someone set her tent on fire," he explained. "We'll

need to adjust our plans, shuffle sleeping arrangements around some for tomorrow night." He checked his watch. "And the rest of tonight apparently."

Seth glanced at his watch. Just past three in the morning. "She's using my tent for tonight. I'll stay awake just to keep an eye on everything."

"The clients are fine, correct?" Brandt looked like he'd aged ten years in the last few minutes, and the worry lines around his eyes and forehead seemed genuine. Could that be faked? Seth supposed so, but the man didn't seem to be manufacturing his anxiety over the entire situation. Still, Seth would think that as the CEO, Brandt'd want to cancel this expedition. Things were clearly not going smoothly and they could all be in danger. The fact that he didn't suggest this as an option raised Seth's suspicions. But he didn't want to suggest canceling. He hated that Ellie had been in danger, but some part of him hoped that meant they were getting closer.

If the trip ended now, how would they go about investigating? This was still their best option. Seth kept quiet about those thoughts, answered the question Brandt had asked instead.

"I didn't notice anything wrong over in their camp. And it's separated enough that no one woke up."

Brandt nodded, seeming to consider the situation. "Good, good."

"Should we call the police?" Halley asked, nervousness in her voice.

"No," Brandt cut her off so quickly that Seth's suspicions rose again. "No police right now. We can file a report when we get to town, but we need to finish this expedition." His eyes went to Ellie. "Is that all right with you? I assure you that I believe a report should be filed, but as the clients are innocent in this, I don't see the point in ruining their trip."

She looked at Seth. She considered it from his perspective and finally nodded slightly.

She looked back at Brandt. "We can wait. I would like a report filed when we get back to town, though."

"Of course, of course." The man seemed to be gathering his bearings and reminded Seth more of the person he'd met who had set up this trip. He was far more in control of the situation than he had been a minute ago. If he was acting, he had impressive skills. But Seth had been fooled by people before.

"We should look for footprints in the woods leading to my tent." Ellie spoke up, seeming to be getting her confidence back, also. "But they'll still be there in the morning. For now I think we all need to go to sleep." She glanced back at Seth.

They all nodded their agreement. One by one, they returned to their tents. Brandt stayed outside after the others had left.

"Are you sure you're okay?" He seemed uncomfortable. "I don't only pride myself on these trips being a good experience for our clients. I try to ensure that guides have an enriching experience outside, also, and this hasn't been that for you so far." He frowned. "This doesn't have to do with you getting lost, does it?"

"They don't seem obviously connected," Seth stated, because it was the truth, though he and Ellie knew they likely were.

As sincere as the CEO of RPE seemed, Seth wasn't ready to discount him as a suspect, not yet.

"You'll be okay?" he asked Ellie.

She nodded. "My throat hurts. But that's nothing compared to what could have happened."

Seth nodded. The flames incinerating the tent had irritated his throat, also. But thankfully neither of them had been burned.

"Try to get some sleep," he finally said and watched her as she climbed into the tent. His heart was still pounding hard due to awareness of the fact that he'd come so close to losing her.

He'd intended to stay awake keeping watch from inside Wade's tent. Instead he found himself walking toward the burned shell of Ellie's. The area around it was covered in footprints. His. Ellie's. Wade's. They'd destroyed any evidence of someone walking around it in the middle of the night to tamper with it.

But that didn't mean there wouldn't still be tracks in the woods. And Seth didn't want to wait till morning. Instead he walked into the woods himself, careful to look behind him and keep an eye on the camp. All seemed quiet.

There were no footprints.

Whoever had set Ellie's tent on fire had come through the camp. So either someone had been quiet enough not to wake the other staff—not hard to imagine since they all apparently slept hard enough that it had taken so long for Ellie's screams to wake them up.

Or one of the staff had done it, and then crept back to the safety of their tent.

The second option made his blood hot with anger. The concept that one of them could try to kill her in such a gruesome way and then pretend innocence...

It made him feel like they were facing more than danger here. They were facing evil.

FIFTEEN

Ellie slept harder that night than she had in days, even after everything that had happened. Or maybe because of it. The next morning, all of her was exhausted, from her tense shoulders to the muscles in her back. Anxiety felt like a heavy coat she didn't want to be wearing, but no matter how hard she tried to shrug it off, she couldn't quite do it.

Helpless. She'd been completely helpless last night. She'd needed Seth to save her and while she was grateful he had, she didn't like being someone who needed saving. That wasn't going to happen again. Maybe Ellie couldn't control her circumstances while investigating this case, but she could sure control her responses to them and her preparedness level. Game on.

Except it wasn't a game.

She blew out a breath as she checked her watch and saw it was almost time for her to start getting ready. Seth had entered his tent and was sitting by the door.

"You haven't been in here long, have you?" she asked, almost embarrassed if he'd been watching her sleep. There was something vulnerable about not being awake and in proximity to someone else. But it felt right with Seth. The admission that she loved him had broken down the last remnants of a wall between them.

He shook his head. "No, and I'm sorry if I shouldn't have come in. It's just I wanted to make sure you woke up on time. You slept really hard."

She nodded. "I did."

Seth gave a little nod also and then stood, backing out of the hole in the tent. "I'll fix this when we stop for the night tonight," he promised her. "So don't worry or anything."

"Okay. Let me finish getting ready and then we can look for footprints." She smiled. She was fully dressed, had dressed before she'd fallen asleep for the second time, so she was ready for the day, just needed to brush her teeth.

"I checked last night."

"Without me?" She felt a flicker of frustration but then realized Seth wasn't trying to take over. He'd just been trying to let her get much-needed rest. She was part of a team now, she needed to remember that. Ellie recovered quickly and asked, "What did you find?"

He shook his head. "Nothing good. There are no footprints from the woods to your tent. Nothing that stood out on the trail nearby. It was either someone from the camp, or someone sneaked right through the camp."

Ellie nodded slowly. She'd not held out much hope that footprints would tell them anything in this case, but it had been a hope. Now it was just a deadend.

"Thanks." She let out a sigh. "Let me brush my teeth and I'll join you outside."

He nodded, stepping back out of the tent.

Ellie brushed her teeth quickly and then pulled her boots on. Today was a new day. Seeing Seth this morning had bolstered her courage. She wasn't investigating alone. He had her back, she had his, and it felt like they were a team. And no, her situation hadn't changed, but she was ready to face it. Twice she'd been caught off guard. She couldn't afford for that to happen a third time. There could only be so many near misses before whoever was after her got lucky.

"Seth?" she called as she stepped out of the tent. The day was dark still; winter darkness tended to linger, and the air felt colder than it had the night before. She rubbed her arms to warm them.

He walked over from where he'd been doing something near the dog sleds. "Yes?"

She lowered her voice. "I don't think it's Brandt."

He nodded slowly. "Yeah."

"You agree?"

"I do. He seemed genuinely concerned last night, and not like a man who had something to lose in a criminal sort of way. He seemed actually bothered by how this was going to impact the trip for the clients and for you."

"Could be that he isn't used to one business endangering the other," she pointed out with her cynical side.

Seth seemed to consider that. "It's possible. But that's not the only reason I don't think it's him. He seemed to have been genuinely asleep last night. I think he was actually out cold when the fire was set. Either that or he's the best actor I've ever met."

Ellie didn't, either, which was why she'd told him her opinion in the first place. But if it wasn't Brandt...

She looked toward the fire, where Jared was already cooking something and Halley was laughing at something he'd said. Brandt wore a frown and was looking at something on his SAT phone.

Who else could it be, if not the CEO?

Clearly, they had options right in front of them. But neither Jared nor Halley was what she would have expected.

Then again, there was still Peter, the partner they'd only met briefly. Had he given up the trip because he saw them on it?

Or was it just a coincidence?

She wouldn't stake her life on any of her suspicions right now, but that was exactly what she was going to have to do eventually.

"I just don't know. I just hope today goes better. No incidents."

Seth put his hands on her arms, turned her toward him. "If the smallest thing happens, let me know. I'm not planning to let you out of my sight today."

She nodded, reassurance filling her at his words. "I'd feel better that way." She laughed. "Todd probably would, too. He wasn't very happy that his wife took a little detour yesterday. And he doesn't even know…" She trailed off. "You don't think I'm endangering her, do you? Staying on this trip?"

"Absolutely not." Seth shook his head. "Like you said, if someone had meant to harm you yesterday when you took the wrong trail, they didn't when they couldn't tell the two of you apart. So probably they're not willing to have any collateral damage."

Ellie nodded. It made sense. Still, she couldn't help the gnawing anxiety of knowing she could be putting someone else in danger. But not investigating would be putting more people in harm's way.

"You'll be okay," he told her, and she hoped that he believed it, too.

They ate breakfast with the rest of the support staff and the clients. No one mentioned last night's incident, and Ellie noticed that the burnt shell of her tent was gone. Someone had moved snow over the area, and while a slight sticky burnt smell hung in the air, it was faint. No one who hadn't been awake would notice it enough to ask what had happened.

"Did you…clean up my things?" she asked Seth quietly, hoping that the way she'd phrased it was vague enough that if the clients overheard they wouldn't know what she was specifically talking about.

He shook his head, nodded toward Brandt.

"You saw?"

"Yeah."

She nodded. Naturally he wouldn't want the tent there, as it would have scared the clients. Still, part of him was uncomfortable with the fact that he had removed the tent. She'd have liked to take it and examine it for any evidence they hadn't seen the night before in the midst of all the chaos.

Now they wouldn't know. Unless they asked for the tent back.

Seth was looking at her, and Ellie could almost feel him watching her internal debate. They'd talk about it later. It wasn't as if Brandt could get rid of the tent out here in the wilderness, so chances were good they had a couple of days to figure out if they wanted to ask for it for evidence or not. It wasn't worth asking for it now and arousing his suspicions. As far as he knew they were two dog mushers. There was no compelling reason for her to ask to have the tent back.

Wade stood up and excused himself from breakfast to get his dogs ready, and Seth and Ellie both followed not long after. As they went to see about their separate teams, Seth squeezed her hand one more time, and Ellie reluctantly released her grip on his fingers and let her own hand drop to her side.

"I'm not letting you out of my sight today. I'll do my best to keep up with you. Just use your drag and slow down some if I drop out of sight. I won't leave you on purpose," he promised. "It'll be okay."

Ellie nodded. She hoped it would be.

Hooking up the dogs went well, and soon she and Darci were off mushing.

Wade eventually mushed out of view, but when Ellie glanced over her shoulder, Seth was still there, following as he said he would be.

Still, she didn't relax, not today. Instead of just taking in the view, the way the trail had opened up in front of them in a clearing and the bright blue of the sky against the white snow on the mountains, she was looking in the distance at the trees and wondering what the woods could be hiding. And *who* could be hiding in them.

The trail narrowed again. Ellie looked behind her. Seth was behind her, a little farther back, but close enough still. As she heard the buzzing of a snow machine, she tensed. She'd need to figure out where they could safely pass her. Though they were in a woodsier section of the trial right now, it opened up again soon, and it looked like the kind of area where several trails might connect at something like an informal crossroads.

The buzzing whine of the engine grew louder. Ellie pressed her feet down on the brake. Slowed her speed some. Her heart fluttered in her chest, the stress overwhelming her. If only she could see where...

There, ahead and to her right, was a snow machine—

but coming straight toward her. As she'd thought, this was an area where multiple trails connected, but as Ellie looked around, she couldn't see how he was going to safely get around her and her team. Slow down? Speed up?

She took her feet off the drag and decided to speed up if they could. "Hike up," she told the team, who responded with enthusiasm, but the snow machine kept coming.

Ellie slammed her brake down, felt the tag sled behind her catch, which told her Darci had done the same.

At first, she was afraid the machine was going to hit her team, and visions of injured dogs almost made her cry out, but the machine hit her sled instead and sent her flying off.

As she hit the ground hard on her left side, Ellie tasted blood in her mouth. Had she bitten her lip? The buzzing was still close by. Leaving, or coming back to hit her again? Her side throbbed, but she had to ignore the pain. The danger hadn't passed yet.

She saw Seth's dog team out of the corner of her eye, turned her head the other way to see that Darci still had their team stopped. That was a relief at least.

Ellie's temples slowly started to throb, as did her left leg, the one she had fallen on. Someone had hit her sled with a snow machine. Deliberately. Of course she'd seen nothing identifying on the driver, just a person bundled in layers of warm gear.

"Ellie!" She heard running footsteps in the snow, kept blinking and trying to find the will to get up.

"I think I'm okay." She sat up, her head throbbing worse but not so badly that she couldn't keep going. They'd get through this the same way they'd gotten through the incident last night. They were one step closer to figuring out who was behind all this, she reminded herself to try to make it better.

A buzz of another snow machine in the distance made her start to shake, and her eyes widened.

"Are they back?"

Seth shook his head. "I called Brandt. They're coming to check on us."

Ellie watched as three machines pulled up. None of them was obviously recognizable. They'd all come from the same place. Had one of them been used to run her down only minutes before? It had happened too fast, she hadn't gotten any good visual identifiers of the snow machine or its driver. She'd been too busy trying to react appropriately and keep herself, Darci and the dogs safe. Brandt's face was serious. "What happened?"

Ellie felt vulnerable, for the second time in a short period of hours. She stood up, brushed the snow from her pants. And decided she was done pulling punches.

"I think someone just tried to kill me with a snow machine."

If Todd had been horrified when his wife had been late the night before, he was downright hysterical now, and Seth couldn't blame him. He felt the same way, the same anguish, about Ellie being hurt.

He'd watched the snow machine come toward her like it was in slow motion and had been stunned when it hadn't veered off. He'd thought, at worst, it was a plan to intimidate her.

And then the machine had hit, and she'd been thrown off. At least, it had collided with the sled. Seth didn't know if that was an accidental miscalculation. It seemed like if someone wanted to kill her for sure, they'd hit *her*, instead of the sled.

Unless, as they'd discussed, the person wanted to avoid collateral damage and didn't want to risk injuring Darci.

Someone who had a stake in the business and didn't want to see it harmed because of this?

Seth didn't know.

"Why would someone try to kill you?" Brandt finally asked. It seemed like he'd needed a minute to process Ellie's words.

Ellie looked at Seth. Seth shrugged. However much or little she wanted to tell them was up to her. At this point he thought he was done with the investigation. It was time to take her home, get her somewhere safe and, in the meantime, report to the troopers the things that had happened.

He should text Hodges at the Anchorage Police Department and let him know he'd be calling him soon to update him. He'd forgotten his promise to keep his friend in the loop, or he'd have gotten a message out last night.

"I didn't get a chance to ask them why. But they ran me down with a snow machine. Not unlike the ones the three of you are riding on," Ellie said, face void of any emotion, shoulders squared. Rather than make her timid, this attack had made her ready to fight, and Seth wanted to kiss her for it. *This* was the Ellie she'd been before. Fiery and full of emotion.

Brandt cleared his throat. "Let's see. I think for this next stretch while we work this out, could we have the two of you ride on the snow machines? Just while we check out and address some safety concerns." He addressed the words to both Todd and Darci, but Todd was the one to nod vigorously.

"Halley, would you get them situated? Thank you. I'll catch up."

In only a few minutes, Jared's and Halley's machines took off, each of them carrying a passenger that had been Seth's and Ellie's responsibility.

She still looked ready for a fight, but not like she'd realized their undercover trip was over. Seth knew, he'd seen it in Brandt's eyes as the other man considered a sort of quick cost/benefit analysis and risk assessment.

"I think you need to report this to the police," he told Ellie.

"We discussed that we would after the trip," she said, shoulders still back.

"Your trip is over. I don't know what you've gotten into or who is after you. But you are done here."

"Were all three of you together?" Ellie asked him. "Just now, did you see the other snow machines the entire trip?"

"The entire trip. Now that's enough, Miss Hamilton. The two of you have caused enough trouble on this trip and you're fired."

Her shoulders fell. Seth expected her to argue, but she just nodded. Though he understood why Brandt made the decision, Seth still asked, "You're going to fire us for her being in danger?" If only they'd had one more night around the fire to try to listen to conversations better, put more pieces together as far as what Brandt, Jared and Halley were like as people.

"I'm sorry, but I can't have my clients put at risk." His expression actually did seem to convey that he hated the decision he was being forced to make. But he seemed resolved about it. "This is the second incident, third if we consider the lost trail to have something to do with this. I don't know who is after you, Ellie, but you need to get this settled." He shook his head. "I regret that we can't continue the trip as planned. You have what you need to get home?"

They nodded.

"Just untie the tag sleds and leave them here. I'll handle those. You may keep the trackers until you get back if you'd like them for emergency purposes."

Ellie looked at him with questions in her eyes. Of course they wouldn't want the trackers with them...if Brandt was behind the attacks on her.

But since there *was* still a possibility Brandt could be behind this, they also didn't want to alert him that anything was wrong with that idea by refusing right now.

"Thank you," Ellie said instead, and then looked at Seth. Her body ached from the attack and emotionally she was spent. They'd failed in their undercover investigation, might not be any closer to finding who had killed Liz and attacked them.

But she couldn't give up yet. Ellie took a deep breath, reached down deep for the fight she knew she still had left.

They'd leave here with the trackers and then dump them somewhere so that whoever was threatening them couldn't find them. Got it. He smiled and gave a slight nod so she'd know he got the message. He'd always been so good at knowing what she was thinking. That connection was still alive as ever.

"I'm sorry to be losing you." Brandt looked between them. "But I have to do what is best for my company and my clients."

"All right, you okay to mush back?" Seth turned to Ellie, seeing that Brandt had no intentions of leaving until he'd seen them head back in the direction from which they had come. No reason to waste time here, anyway. The sooner they got back and talked to the police departments, the better.

She nodded. "I'm okay. You head out first, and I'll follow."

The trail might not be as well marked on the way back so her decision was a wise one. He stopped when he'd gotten back on his sled runners, and before he pulled the snow hook out, he pulled his phone from his pocket and texted Hodges a quick update.

Ellie in danger. Tent was set on fire, hit by snow machine while mushing. Turning back to Raven Pass now, will call sometime later.

He had just put his hands on the handlebar when he received a reply. Location?

Seth texted it out quickly. Eklutna Traverse. Not halfway. "Ready?" he asked the dogs and then pulled the snow hook. "All right."

And then took off again. He glanced back to see that Ellie was right behind him, was keeping much closer than he'd kept during their time earlier. Brandt was where they had left him, seemingly just watching them take off. Seth wondered how he was going to handle the rest of the trip, with only one musher to help three people have an adventure of a lifetime. Seth didn't like letting people down, but it wasn't possible to continue now. They'd been fired and left alone. Seth didn't know if he felt safer now or if he was less safe.

Whoever was behind all of this wasn't watching their every move in person anymore, but with the trackers, it wouldn't be difficult.

He still wanted to dump those but had a spot in mind farther down the trail. The last thing he wanted to do was to get rid of them too soon and arouse anyone's suspicions.

Probably, he should have just let Brandt take them earlier. What did it matter now if the RPE CEO thought they were paranoid? Even if he wasn't behind the attacks, he now knew they were happening. So nothing strange they did would have been without explanation.

Seth kept mushing, feeling his head start to pound with the tension that stretched from his jawline all the way into his head.

Nothing about this trip had gone the way he'd hoped. Except that he did feel like they were narrowing down a suspect list. No matter how much he tried to make Brandt fit, he did not think the CEO had been behind everything. Aaron being his nephew was too much of a coincidence to completely ignore, but just because Brandt was related to a criminal didn't necessarily mean he was involved. There was still a chance Aaron was using the business in some way without his uncle's permission, but Seth didn't think Brandt was complicit.

Peter was a logical choice, but maybe too much so. What kind of drug runner ran from his route, or whatever they called them, at the first sign of trouble? Wouldn't that be drawing more attention to himself than just staying and finishing out the trip would have been?

He turned back again to make sure Ellie was still behind him. Her face was lined with worry, and even from twenty or thirty feet away he could tell that she was still upset about the situation. Not only had she been hurt, but they'd lost the potential to find a lead this way. They hadn't even had much time to investigate.

Seth hated it, too. But the situation was what it was. They'd had an unlucky break.

They could really use something in this case going their way about now. Seth wanted to forget all about attackers and murder and let himself relax in the knowledge that Ellie loved him, but he couldn't. Not while there was still a threat against them. Against Ellie.

The case was far from finished. And he needed to make sure they both stayed alive.

SIXTEEN

They'd only been mushing back toward Raven Pass for about an hour by the time it started to snow. "I need a break," Ellie called ahead to Seth, who apparently heard her immediately. He put his feet on the drag, then the brake, and slowed his team, coming to a stop in a lovely section of woods.

"Thanks. I had planned to feed them about now." Ellie wanted to stick to her plan, because first of all, she liked plans, and second of all, it seemed right to do so when she'd been so proud of herself for putting together a strategy for how to take her runs and rests as one of the guides this weekend.

"Sure, fine with me," Seth said, giving her a tired smile. He looked exhausted. She felt the same way inside, worn through. Beaten down. The snow machine had rattled her in a way the other attacks hadn't, and if Ellie thought about it for too long, she feared she might crumble. That wasn't an option, so instead she pushed the feelings away, tried to stay focused.

"Listen…" She trailed off when he came closer to her. "When we get back…"

"Yeah?" he asked, stepping closer to her. It didn't

matter how long she'd known him; being so close to him always made her catch her breath just a little, and she hoped it always would.

If he gave her a chance, it would be *always*.

"When we get back," she started again, "I still want to be…" Now she felt her cheeks heat as she considered the fact that they hadn't really defined what they were, and now wasn't really the time or place. "I just mean that I don't want to lose you again," she finally offered as an explanation, shrugging her shoulders.

"I'm not planning on you losing me." His voice was lower than usual, rough with emotion. "For any reason. And I don't want to lose you, either."

Ellie nodded and felt herself blush. "Okay. Well, I'm not going anywhere."

He wrapped her in a hug and squeezed, finally releasing her. "Ready to head home?"

She nodded. *Home.* Why did she picture him when she thought of that word? Not Raven Pass, not her house. *Seth* was home. It felt as though she'd been away for years, avoiding the concept, avoiding him, but now she was back, and Ellie never wanted to leave.

"Yeah. Let's go home."

He pressed a kiss to her forehead and went back to his sled. Ellie climbed onto hers, and they started back down the trail.

The snow was falling faster now. Thankfully snow usually meant warmer temperatures, so at least Ellie wasn't as cold as she had been the day before. People tended to associate snow with cold, but once it fell down to single digit temperatures and below it rarely snowed. Today it must be in the twenties for powder to be falling like it was. Her hands, which had felt almost per-manently curled to the sled's handlebar the day before, were almost warm now.

But the snow made the trail almost disappear from view and blend in with the endless white around it. That was one thing Ellie liked about being deeper in the woods, like they would be later today; it was easier to tell where the trail went. Of course the forest had its disadvantages, too. Surrounded by a barrier of dark green winter spruce trees, Ellie and Seth would be boxed in, with nowhere to run or hide if someone was waiting for them along the trail.

Would there be? It was the question on her mind and probably on Seth's, too. On one hand, turning back had been an addition to the original plan. But they believed someone on the trip was calling the shots, and since Brandt would tell the others where the mushers had gone, it wasn't out of the question. Besides that, Ellie knew that at this point they should make a habit of expecting the unexpected.

Because nothing so far had gone according to plan.

She watched Seth up ahead, admired the way he mushed his team with so much confidence. She didn't know exactly what the difference was in how she did this versus how he did, but she could see it came with experience and showed in the ease of his movements.

The distance between them was like an accordion; sometimes she came close enough she had to use the drag mat to ease her team's speed so they didn't overtake him. Sometimes they both stopped to give the dogs a snack. And sometimes the distance between them stretched out. This was one of those times. Ellie could still see him, close enough to yell if she needed him, at least she thought so. But they were now farther apart than they had been.

Unease crept across her already-tense shoulders. The danger still hadn't passed, and as much as Ellie was trying to stay levelheaded, she couldn't ignore that. The fear was growing too big to shove aside.

"Haw," she called to the dogs as they reached the crossroads where Seth had turned left. They followed Seth as she shifted her weight, using the drag and her feet on it to help make the turn. It was a movement that had become familiar to her over the last couple of days, so she felt comfortable taking the corner faster than she usually did. She needed to close the distance between herself and Seth, and a faster turn would help.

This time, though, as the sled tipped to one side, she realized she had been too confident. She balanced her weight, tightening her muscles and trying to save herself from falling. Ellie tightened her grip on the handlebar, knowing that no matter what, she couldn't let go of the sled.

The sled flipped. She went down, hard into the snow, and dragged as the dogs kept running. She shoved one foot down to try to stand, but it only made her tangle worse in the snow. "Whoa!" she called in case they were inclined to stop. Sometimes the dogs would do that, and sometimes they just wanted to run, their instincts overriding their knowledge of the command.

They didn't stop, their drive to run strong, but slowed slightly, just enough for her to jam a heel into the snow and right herself in a kind of gymnastic-like move that she was surprised she'd been able to execute.

Breathing hard, Ellie got her feet comfortable on the runners again, took a deep breath. That could have gone worse. A sense of pride swept through her. She'd handled that well, but...

Where was Seth? He was out of view now, too far ahead for her to see. She squinted off into the snowy distance, brushing her face with one hand to try to clear the snowflakes out of her eyelashes. She'd had no idea until she'd started mushing how easy it was for snow to stick to them.

Ellie still didn't see him. She swallowed hard. *God, please help me not panic.* The prayer was almost instinctual, even though she hadn't talked to God much the last few days. She remembered Liz telling her that He cared about every aspect of a person's life, though, so this seemed like the kind of situation she should talk to Him about. It was worth a try anyway, in a situation like this.

Despite her prayer, her chest tightened. She breathed deep, held her breath and exhaled.

She could call him, but the SAT phone was buried in her sled bag. To get it out meant stopping, and that was the last thing she wanted to do right now. What if he was only a curve or two ahead of her and she could still catch up? Then stopping for the phone would have been a bad decision.

No, she wasn't sure enough that calling him was the best idea, not sure enough to use the time she would use up stopping and digging for the phone.

Her head cleared a little as she sorted out a plan. She needed to catch up to him, which meant no more riding the drag unless she absolutely had to. The thing she needed to keep in mind was that Seth had been glancing back now and then, so he'd probably do that soon enough and stop to wait for her.

She was okay, despite the fact that her heart was beating so fast it felt like it was going to run away.

She exhaled deeply, tried to keep all of her attention focused on the team in front of her. And did so, right up until the point that pain suddenly exploded in her head. She realized something hit her—a rock?

She didn't have time to wonder as she fell to the ground. She felt the cold sting of the snow against her cheek, then felt nothing at all.

Seth had lost her, and he didn't know when. After the turn? But how long after?

When he'd seen that she wasn't behind him, he'd slowed down a little, then finally stopped his team and waited. She'd never shown up. Turning a dog team around one hundred eighty degrees was a tricky proposition and hardly ever advised in any situation. The dogs got confused, started to lose confidence in their musher as a capable leader of the pack if you did something like that. He'd heard more than one story of a musher who'd gotten into a dicey situation that way, so he didn't want to do that. It was worse than a last resort.

He called her SAT phone. No answer, and now he was too concerned to stay and wait any longer. Instead he continued down the trail to where he knew there was an intersection of several trails, turned back around that way.

But she wasn't anywhere he'd found yet. Night had fallen half an hour or so ago, and it was dark. The snow had turned into almost a full blizzard, and visibility was low enough that Seth wasn't sure that if she was just off the trail that he wouldn't have mushed straight past her.

I don't know where she is, but You do.

It felt like an incomplete prayer, like he should verbally ask for help, or at least ask God in his head, but
if God knew all his thoughts, didn't He know that was
what Seth needed? Help?

*You do know, God. That's what I need. Help. I keep
trying to do this on my own, but You are on my side.
Please help me find her. Please keep her safe.*

He felt some of the tension leave his jaw.

Seth blew out a breath, hoped that God would answer his prayer. And kept searching.

Hurt. Her head hurt. Ellie blinked her eyes open.
Shut them again.

When she opened her eyes again, it was dark. She
reached her arm out, trying to stretch in the hopes it
would help her wake up. She was stuck. Inside…inside
her sled bag? She felt around, reached to the top, where
she found a zipper just as she'd expected to. Fumbling,
Ellie unzipped it, climbed out. She'd been mushing, everything had been okay. Then pain in her head.

And this.

Someone had attacked her?

That realization didn't hurt as much as the one that
met her when she pushed out of the sled bag. She had
to blink a few times to adjust her eyes to the dark, but
when she did so, she saw that she was alone. Just her
and the sled.

She turned back to the sled bag. The SAT phone.
Was it still there?

She dug through the sled bag and came up empty.
Whoever had attacked her had removed the phone, as
well as the handgun she'd brought. She had nothing.

The dogs had been unhooked from the sled, were out

there somewhere running as a team with no sled behind them. Best-case scenario.

Ellie choked back a sob. She'd love to sit here and cry, over her head, over her lost team. Over Seth. Because, where was he? If he hadn't come to find her, then something had happened to him. Everything had gone so very wrong, and worst of all, they were no closer to figuring out who had been behind the drug ring. Actually, if she were honest, they hadn't found any evidence there *was* a drug ring.

She opened her mouth to call out for Seth and then realized if he was close enough to hear, she'd probably see him. Yelling would only alert whoever had attacked her that she was still alive. She could figure things out; if she had been left here without her dogs, especially in the sled bag, whoever had hit her with the rock had expected her to die out here. Maybe not from the strike to her head, but they'd expected her to die of hypothermia. Because, yes, out here without her team, she was hopeless.

More than she ever had, Ellie understood all those things Seth had taught her about how important it was to take care of the dogs, because they took care of the musher, too. And Ellie had done that, but she'd not understood just how much she'd needed them.

And here she was. Alone.

She stood silent in the darkness, breathing in the cold air, breathing out. Think. She had to think. Ellie had been a runner before, but she wasn't running this time. Partially because she didn't have a choice—it was fight or die.

And partially because she was tired of giving up. She was wondering about what might have been. Yes, she'd let Liz down when she hadn't investigated as thoroughly as she could have. But she hadn't done anything negligent intentionally. Liz hadn't filed a police report; she'd just been talking to a friend. Ellie couldn't have known how seriously she needed to take the claim.

Which meant…maybe Liz's death wasn't her fault? Maybe she hadn't failed her friend, however this turned out.

Even with that knowledge washing the guilt from her mind, Ellie wasn't ready to quit. This was about more than redemption. It was about justice. She wasn't done fighting for that.

This time it wasn't over until it was over. Ellie would give her last breath to see this through.

But she prayed she wouldn't have to.

God, I'm not ready. Please help.

She heard something, just off in the distance. She stopped, lifted her head, like looking up would help her hear. A dog? Was that a dog whining?

Then, through the trees, she heard a bark.

She closed her eyes and smiled.

God, was that You? Did You really help me?

"I'm coming," she whispered into the darkness and started off through the snow. Her feet were warm, and she was thankful for the boots she wore. Seth had done a good job preparing her for this trip as much as possible. Of course, none of his preparations had included her trekking through the snow, alone without her team. The trail had been fairly packed down from when they'd traveled this way yesterday, but another six inches had fallen when she was unconscious; she could tell by the fact that she didn't see dog tracks anywhere.

Ellie continued on, realizing as she did that whoever

knocked her unconscious could have taken her off a side trail. She really didn't know where she was.

As she walked she listened, and every time she heard one of the dogs bark or whine, Ellie changed her course to go that direction. Then finally, through the snow and in the darkness, she caught a glimpse of white. Moving near a tree.

"Bagel?"

The shape barked in return, and Ellie grinned, would have laughed out loud if it weren't for her dire situation. She ran that direction and was relieved to see all twelve dogs. They'd curled up in the snow, were happily sleeping. Except for Bagel, who had gotten one of her lines tangled around a small tree's branches.

"You silly girl." Ellie worked to untwist the lines. "You guys okay?" She looked over them, hands tight on the tugline. They all seemed fine.

She took a deep breath. Here was the tricky part. "Okay, ready to go for a nice twelve-dog walk with me helping?" She winced. How this could go anything but badly she wasn't sure.

Ellie put herself in lead-dog position, at the front of the line, and started to walk through the snow. The snow coming down worked to her advantage, she realized, as the powder slowed down the dogs some. Still, her arm muscles screamed in protest as she fought to keep them under control. Finally, she made it back to where she'd left the sled, out of breath, sore. It was the middle of the night. She had Seth's tent in her bag. She could set it up, rest until the snow eased some. Snow was falling hard enough now that it was covering the dogs' tracks already. They couldn't start off in this.

She hooked the team back to the sled and reached into the bag for the tent.

A gunshot shattered the night.

The dog's ears perked up, and Spruce whined. Something was wrong. And they knew it.

Seth?

"Change of plans. We have to find him." She put the tent back, zipped the sled bag and headed straight for where she thought the shot may have come from.

Please let him be okay, she prayed, finding it more and more natural every time she tried.

Ellie just hoped she hadn't waited too long to try to find her way back to God. *Please keep me safe. And Seth, too.*

SEVENTEEN

He'd heard a snow machine and turned to look behind him. The vehicle roared up, too close, then rammed into the back of his runners. The sickening crunch of wood hit him first, and then it hit against his leg. It had barely clipped him, but it hurt, and Seth flew off the sled.

"Whoa!" His dogs stopped running as he scrambled to his feet. Dismounting from the machine and approaching, his attacker hit him in the side of the face, and Seth stumbled backward, shoved the person when he came close again. He couldn't see a face—the person was wearing a mask—but the frame looked like a man's build.

Seth had just taken a breath when he heard a gunshot, felt something rip into his side.

Fire exploded in Seth's lungs with every breath he took. He had never been shot, but he'd broken a rib before, after a four-wheeler accident when he was a teenager. This felt like that, but with dynamite.

Pain and exhaustion overwhelmed him suddenly, and he fell down, unable to fight off his attacker anymore.

He heard laughter.

And then a snow machine driving away.

Ellie. He had to wake up, had to get up. Had to find Ellie. He couldn't let anything happen to her.

The fire deepened to an icy burn. Until it hurt so badly Seth couldn't keep his eyes open anymore. He let his head fall back into the snow.

God, be with her.

How long did you hold on to hope before giving up? Ellie's face stung against the snowflakes. It had been more than half an hour since she'd heard the shot. She had to be going the wrong direction. But where to turn around?

A small indent in the snow caught her eye, right where an alternate trail split off to the right.

"Gee," she told the dogs, hoping she was seeing signs that Seth had come this way and not something irrelevant. She had only heard the one gunshot, and she didn't know for sure if that was good news or bad.

She squinted in the dark, focusing on the trail the glow of her headlamp made. Were those tracks in the snow ahead? She thought they were.

"Find them, okay?" she whispered.

Minutes passed. Then Ellie felt the dogs speed up. She felt her shoulders tense. Hope mixed with a sinking feeling of impending doom. She wanted to find Seth, but at the same time, she couldn't forget she'd heard a gunshot. Finding him would not necessarily be good news.

Her mind almost couldn't process it. Yes, this entire time she'd been desperate to keep him safe, not let anything happen to him, but had she really thought she could? Had she let herself fully acknowledge what it would do to her if he wasn't okay? Losing her friend had been hard enough, wondering if she could have done more, beating herself up.

To lose the man she'd loved because she was too late would be unbearable.

I've already lost one friend. God, please don't let me lose another.

That was his sled. His dogs were still there, but she didn't see Seth. He wasn't standing behind the sled on the runners. The little hope she'd had mixed with the doom was suffocated.

And then she saw him, crumpled on the snow. Her breath caught and she forgot to take another breath for a full three seconds. He couldn't be dead. He couldn't…. She let her dogs run closer to his, then stopped them about ten feet behind his sled, hit the brake and set her snow hook.

"Seth." She ran toward him, put her hands on his shoulders to roll him onto his back. His face had been pressed down in the snow. Could he breathe that way?

Was he still breathing at all?

He groaned. He groaned! He was alive.

Thank You, Lord.

But the snow underneath him was stained dark. Her headlamp shone on the area when she moved her face to look at it. Blood. A lot of blood.

"Oh, Seth." She brushed a hand across his forehead, swallowed hard against a sob and then shook her head. He wasn't dead yet. She wasn't giving up. Wasn't running.

Was. Not. Quitting. Not leaving him—not again. Never again.

"All right." She put her hands on his shoulder. "Wake up. I can't do this on my own. Wake up."

Couldn't he see she needed him? She'd run after Liz's death, not just because of the guilt but because she'd doubted her abilities to find the killer. She felt she'd let her best friend down by being late that day, felt like she was inadequate.

Yes. So much of her life had been spent feeling that way. Liz's murder, the way it had happened, the blame that Ellie had placed on herself…all of it confirmed her shortcomings.

And here she was. Alone. No help…but she wouldn't let that stop her.

You aren't alone.

Ellie took a deep breath. She wasn't alone. God was with her. God had made her, given her strengths.

Once upon a time, one of those strengths had been police work. Conducting investigations. She was a trained search and rescue worker and EMT, too. She could handle this situation.

She reached into the sled bag, found a flashlight to shine on him and enough gear to make a makeshift bandage. Then she unzipped his jacket, pressed the bandage against Seth's wound. Then did her best to wrap it with an ACE bandage she'd found in the sled. She zipped the jacket back up and prayed she'd done enough. Then Ellie felt his forehead. Normal temperature so far, best she could tell. There was a fancy first-aid kit in the bag somewhere, but nothing that prepared for the contingency of someone getting shot, so she didn't bother to drag it out.

When she was sure she'd done the best she could, she pondered her next steps. They needed to get out of here.

Ellie took a deep breath, faced the fact that he wasn't waking up, not right now, and stood up, grabbing both of his feet. She dragged him toward her sled bag. He wasn't going to wake up in time? Fine. She'd hook his team to hers and mush them both back this way. It wasn't ideal. But it was what she could do.

She shoved her gear down into the bottom of her sled bag, pausing now and then to look up and around. She didn't want to be caught off guard, and she had no idea if whoever had shot Seth was still around. Finally when she felt she'd made enough room for him to fit inside—there was a bit of a size disparity between them, so even though she'd been inside the bag earlier she was fairly certain he wasn't going to fit without some adjustments—she grabbed his shoulders again.

"One more chance to wake up and help me," she said and then braced herself against the sled and heaved him into the bag. She couldn't do it without jostling, and she winced when she saw the side of the sled bag hit his wounded side, but it was what had to be done. She needed to get him out of here and back to Raven Pass.

Hooking the two teams together once she'd situated Seth proved challenging, but she managed.

"Ready?" she asked out of habit, as it was how Seth always started mushing. But this time it felt less like she was asking the dogs and more like she was asking herself. Was she ready?

Yes. She was. Ready to be who she was, without regrets or might have beens. Ready to be brave.

God, let me not be ruled by fear anymore. I'm tired of living that way.

"All right," she and the dogs took off. Twenty-four dogs, even dogs who had been in a blizzard and working hard, ran substantially faster than twelve. Ellie had to use every ounce of focus to hold on to the sled. She found her way back to what she was fairly certain was the main trail.

How far were they now? She didn't know.

She exhaled and kept mushing, kept praying and kept hoping that this was almost over.

The woods grew more and more familiar until Ellie recognized the trails as some she'd driven around while searching for Seth the other day. So much had happened since then, more than she would have ever thought possible. She dropped her eyes to the sled bag. Was he even alive?

A light in the distance caught her attention. Then a whir. A buzzing.

Snow machine engine.

She closed her eyes for a second. *I need You. Please help me*, she prayed.

And Ellie was not afraid.

Not when the machine drew closer. Not when they pulled directly in front of them, cutting her off from escape. The dogs stopped abruptly, not wanting to hit the machine, and Ellie almost lost her balance.

Then she focused her attention and her headlamp on the man in front of her—whom she recognized.

"Jared?"

He shook his head, any sort of friendliness gone from his face. "You had to keep pushing, huh? Warning you off wasn't enough, just like it wasn't for your friend. You had to keep pushing. Just like her."

He didn't know how much of a compliment that was. Ellie was proud to be anything like Liz.

"We don't know anything. Not really, we don't have any proof," she admitted. He hadn't said anything incriminating, and even if he left them alone right now as witnesses, they had nothing conclusive that would stand up against him in court.

He laughed. "You have enough. You have that package she sent you, don't you?"

"There was hardly anything in it. It was a letter. She was just speculating, also."

Something crossed his face; Ellie couldn't quite explain it. Regret? Did he wish he hadn't acted so rashly in killing Liz? He probably thought it was too late to turn back now, and in some ways it was. If Ellie lived through this, she'd see to it that he went to jail for murder and attempted murder on multiple counts.

But what she was saying was true. There was no proof. He could let her live.

"You know enough. And she did, too." His face hardened. "She had to die."

"You killed her?" Ellie had to know.

"Her boyfriend wouldn't. So yeah." He shrugged and something inside her screamed. Her best friend had died, her and Seth's lives had changed forever, and he shrugged.

"He should have, as soon as she found out about the drug running. She started asking him questions, started noticing he had more money than a guy with his job should have had. And then she started turning up at places she shouldn't have been. Like she was trying to catch him in something." He shook his head. "She should have stayed out of it. That lawyer, too. He kept poking around, asking questions, and then he sent that letter to him." He jerked his head toward Seth.

Ellie frowned. "How did you…?"

"Administrative assistants don't make as much as they're worth, it seems. Didn't take much convincing to pay the lawyer's admin to let me know if he communicated with Liz's friend or her brother. Now. We're done here."

He held a gun up, level at Ellie.

"She didn't suspect you, you know." Ellie hoped to keep him talking. Gut instinct told her to. She had never faced this sort of situation when she was a police officer, but something told her to try this route. Maybe she'd just watched too many movies where the bad guy's downfall came when he wouldn't be quiet. But it seemed worth a chance.

"Oh, yeah?"

"No, she was sure it was someone who worked directly for Raven Pass Expeditions, not someone who worked with them."

His grin was evil. "Brilliant, right? They do the trips, plan the stops and shoulder all that load, and I just get to cook and move product. Aaron told me his uncle was clueless. He was right." He shrugged again. "It's brilliant."

Evil. It was the only word she could think of.

She opened her mouth to ask another question, any question. But he was pulling back the hammer on the large revolver that he suddenly had in his hands.

Something shook Ellie. She looked down. Seth?

He sat up. "I wouldn't do that," he said to Jared, his voice tight with tension and pain.

"Shoot you? Why is that? I've done it once."

Ellie waited, held her breath. What was stopping him from killing them right now?

"For one thing, you're not the only one with a gun." Seth was holding up his revolver. Apparently his attackers hadn't found it where he'd hidden it in his jacket. His muscles, usually strong, were quivering under the weight of the gun because of how much blood he'd lost. He couldn't hold it up for long. But he'd known he had to try this when he'd heard them talking. Seth had lain there for a minute, formulating his plan. First, he'd pressed his emergency tracker, which was in his jacket pocket. He'd planned to ditch it on the trip back, so he'd taken it out of the sled and kept it close. If what RPE had bragged about during the safety meeting was true, it should bring a law-enforcement officer almost immediately.

He'd also pulled up his phone, called Hodges and put the phone on speaker after whispering to him what was going on and to be quiet.

Then he'd felt the solid mass of the gun pressing against his side. Remembered he'd put it on under his jacket this morning rather than leaving it in his sled bag because of the threat against them escalating. And he'd heard Jared threaten Ellie.

"Yeah, but if I shoot you first, she won't have time to get the gun," Jared argued. His voice was growing more reckless by the second.

Seth nodded. "True. But even if you do that, the police are almost here."

Jared laughed. "Nice. Good try."

"I still have my tracker." Seth kept his eyes on the man, hatred growing inside him. This was the man who had killed his sister. Who had tried to kill him and Ellie. Anger rose inside him, and mentally he dared the man to move. Give him a reason to shoot.

The sound of snow machines in the distance grabbed

everyone's attention. Two of them. Jared glanced behind him. He kept his hands tight on the gun's grip.

So did Seth.

"Alaska State Troopers! Lower your weapons."

Seth stared. Lowered it down, set it by his side. Relief and disappointment fought inside him. He'd been ready to kill the man who'd killed his sister. Had wanted to. But that wasn't his place, wasn't what needed to be done. *God, help me. I don't know that I'm ready to forgive him, but help me not be ruled by hate.*

Relief swept through him. If it had been self-defense, it would have been justifiable, but he always would have wondered how much had been motivated by revenge. "Sounds like they're going to take over investigating this case," Seth heard Hodges say on the phone. He held the gun with one hand and shoved the phone in his pocket. He'd finish filling him in later, but he needed to focus.

Jared raised his revolver again, pointed it straight at Seth. Seth fumbled for the gun he'd set down. Self-defense was a different story.

A gunshot rang out from another direction, and Jared fell off his machine and onto the snow. One of the troopers had shot him.

It was over. Seth closed his eyes. Took a full, deep breath.

The troopers both approached him.

"Still breathing."

Seth set the gun back down in the sled bag, turned to Ellie. "Are you okay?"

Her eyes were wide and beautiful. But not afraid. She seemed different somehow, since the last time he'd seen her.

"I'm all right. You? You've lost a lot of blood."

He blinked. "I should probably see a doctor."

One of the troopers was loading an unconscious but moaning Jared onto his snow machine.

"My friend needs a doctor," Ellie said, sounding desperate to get him help. One of the troopers loaded him onto the machine. Her feelings for him were clear in her voice. No more walls between them, no more running or hiding. They'd both changed, this time for the better. For the first time in years, hope filled him.

"Take care of the dogs," Seth said to her as his eyes started to close again. "I need to know you'll take care of them."

"I'll take care of them. But you're okay, Seth. You have to be. I'll be there as fast as I can."

He nodded, overwhelmed with love for her, then felt himself slipping away.

EIGHTEEN

Ellie mushed back to Seth's house the same way they'd gone the other day. Past the public-use cabin with the shattered window. Past the same trees. So much hand changed in such a short amount of time.

She took a breath, let it out slowly. She could relax now…at least regarding the case. It was over. Jared's confession to the two of them might be enough to hold up in court, but the troopers had seen him there holding the gun, knew Seth had been shot. There were several things the man could be charged for, and maybe all of the charges wouldn't stick, but enough of them would that Ellie felt fairly certain he'd be in jail for a long time.

They were finally free, both her and Seth…so long as he got better.

She needed to talk to him, she told herself as she went through the process of unhooking dogs, putting them back on their tethers at their houses and then watering all of them. She needed to tell Seth why she'd run. And maybe a hospital wasn't an ideal place to have that conversation, but as soon as she'd taken care of the dogs as promised, Ellie would go over there and talk to him.

When she'd finished with the dogs, she started toward her car. She smelled like camping trip and animals, but she wanted to be there with Seth. Once, she'd been too late. She didn't want to be too late again.

Tires crunching on the gravel made her look up. A light green Subaru was pulling into the driveway.

"I thought you'd want a ride to the hospital. I know I wouldn't want to drive in your condition." Halley's usually cheery face was etched with pain, and Ellie appreciated the empathy. Everything had happened so fast, and then someone had to take care of the dogs. It was true, she'd rather not drive herself.

She was a little surprised to see Halley back in town, but Ellie figured if Jared had left the RPE expedition and they had no one to cook, they'd probably had to call the whole thing off.

"Thanks." She brushed her hands on her snow pants. "I can… I can run inside and change quickly if you don't want the stink in your car. I smell a little like dog." She shrugged apologetically.

"You're okay, just get in. Let's go."

Was her voice impatient? Ellie didn't know. She was exhausted. Emotionally, physically, every way someone could be exhausted. She climbed into the car and shut the door. Halley put it in Reverse, hit the gas a little too quickly.

And Ellie had to stop herself from a sharp intake of breath.

Had Jared said he hadn't worked with anyone from Raven Pass Expeditions? Was that why he'd seemed so upset by what they knew, even though all they'd known to do was suspect someone who worked at the company?

But not Halley. Surely not. She was all pretty blond hair and helpful cheeriness.

Ellie glanced sideways, careful to keep her expression blank.

But Halley was watching her, too.

"So. Thanks for the ride." Ellie tried to keep up the pretense, even as fear crept over her again.

"Let's drop the pretense. We both know you're not getting a ride there. With any luck he's already dead, and I've only got one of you to take care of."

Heaviness settled in Ellie's stomach. "Halley…"

"Don't." She gripped the wheel tighter. "Don't say anything to me. I don't want to hear it. You don't know what it's like. I worked for years to build this business, to take care of these clients…"

"At RPE?" Ellie still held out some small hope that maybe she'd misunderstood, and they were heading to the hospital after all, and she hadn't climbed straight into the car with a crazy woman who wanted her dead.

"Did you think Jared did all this? That *Jared* was smart enough?" Again, that laugh. Void of actual humor, like a scratch on an old chalkboard. "And Aaron certainly isn't." She pressed the gas harder. "*They* were supposed to handle things like this."

"Aaron. Of course. Aaron set my tent on fire." He must have also been the one who shot at them, too. It made sense. They'd known he was involved, thanks to Liz, but with no proof, the man still walked free.

"A lot of good that did," Halley mumbled. "You're still here, aren't you?"

Ellie frowned. "What about Brandt? The clients? You didn't…"

"You can't seriously think I'd hurt any of them?"

She glanced Ellie's way. "I don't think you understand. To do that would be to admit defeat. To be desperate. Maybe Jared got that way. But I'm calling the shots, and I am not desperate. I left him alive because I need Aaron's overly optimistic uncle to keep running this business, keep being so focused on his ideals of adventures in the outdoors that he doesn't notice anything going on behind the scenes."

"Like drug running."

Halley rolled her eyes. "*Moving product*. You're so dated with your terminology. What is this, a cheesy cop movie?" She jerked the wheel to the right, down a gravel road that Ellie had explored.

That didn't seem to bode well. Gravel roads in the middle of nowhere when someone was being held hostage rarely did.

"You haven't actually hurt anyone yet, then. It's not too late for you." Ellie's heart pounded. How much could one person take? Hadn't she just done this earlier?

She wanted to go back in time and yell at herself. And Seth. Why hadn't they considered that it could be *two* of the people on the trip? Or maybe they had and she'd just forgotten. But when Jared had shown up, seemed to take credit, she'd thought it was over. And then Seth had gotten hurt and she'd been distracted.

"It's really not too late."

"Oh." She turned to Ellie. Stared her down. And then looked straight ahead and hit the gas. "It really is."

"See, we will have an accident. Not a bad one. Just bad enough to bang up the car and explain any injuries you have. And then you'll die of those wounds, which I'll help with, by the way. And I will eventually heal and go free."

All the sweetness, all the perkiness, covered up some of the worst evil she had ever seen.

Ellie took a deep breath. Prayed. *God, help me know what to do when.*

Her attention focused on the steering wheel. If she grabbed that, yanked it the other direction... Could she unsettle the other woman enough to gain control of the car?

Yes. It was the only choice she had.

"Sorry you didn't get your happily-ever-after."

Ellie looked ahead of them. Nothing but woods. She was going to drive them straight into the trees? Her attention was fixed straight forward. Her eyes unnaturally wide.

Now.

Ellie grabbed the wheel.

Halley screamed and fought her.

"No. You don't get to decide how this ends. And your product-moving days are over."

The car came to a juddering halt, and Halley threw the door open and started to run. Ellie took a deep breath, knowing she was at a disadvantage in boots. This, she knew, she had trained for. At the academy and in real life.

She might not be a police officer anymore. But God had given her the skills she needed for this moment. And though fear could have overwhelmed her, instead all she felt was confidence.

Thank You. She prayed as she ran. Her boots pounded against the snow as she gained on Halley. Fifteen feet away. Thirteen. Nine. Five. Three.

Ellie threw herself forward, arms out, and tackled the other woman to the ground. Pinning Halley down, she finally managed to wrestle the criminal's hands behind her back.

She pulled a neckline out of her pocket, one of the ropes used to hook dogs up to the gangline that attached to the sled, and tied it around Halley's narrow wrists.

"My best friend died because of you," Ellie said out loud. Heard the words sink deep into her heart.

She'd carried the guilt for all those years. Should have been early. Should have listened sooner. Should have…should have…

It was time to stop accepting blame that wasn't hers.

It was time to really live.

"But you did not kill me. You didn't kill her memory." And hopefully she hadn't killed her brother. Ellie swallowed hard. She still needed to see Seth. *Please, God, let him be okay.*

"Oh, shut up."

Ellie sat down on top of the woman's back, pulled her phone out of her pocket and waited for the police to arrive.

When an officer did, she told him everything as he loaded Halley into his vehicle.

"Do you need a ride?" he asked Ellie, looking at the car and then back at her.

"Yes, that's her car. Could you take me to the hospital?"

The ride was quiet. The officer in the front seat was a man Ellie didn't know, and she didn't have anything else to say after pouring out the whole story for him earlier. Instead they rode in silence to the small local hospital, and Ellie stepped out of the car.

"I need you to come by the station later, go over your statement with me and make sure I got it all right."

Ellie nodded. "Thanks."

The police car pulled away, and Ellie stood there looking at the building where Seth was supposed to be. He'd lost so much blood.

She didn't want to lose him again.

She took a deep breath, fought against fear one more time for the day and then walked inside.

No one knew where Ellie was. Seth had called his next-door neighbors to ask them to let him know when she arrived, and he'd just gotten a text from them that her car was there, the dogs were there, but that she wasn't.

Please let her be all right, he prayed.

He'd woken up on the ride to the hospital and thankfully stayed conscious since. The bullet had gone through, he learned when the doctor examined him, and there wasn't a need for surgery, though he had needed a blood transfusion. He felt woozy and exhausted, but he was alive, and he needed to see that Ellie was, too.

Because something had been nagging at him. Even though they'd gotten the head of the organization—Jared—he could still have other people out there willing to do his dirty work for him, like someone had done the night Ellie's tent had been set on fire.

"Seth."

He heard her voice, and he smiled, relief and love flooding through him. "You're here."

"You're alive." She moved toward him and took a seat in the chair beside his bed.

"Are you okay? I realized you might not be safe, still. We have to be careful in case anyone else—"

"It's over." Ellie shook her head. "The person calling the shots is in jail."

"Even with Jared—"

She shook her head. "Not Jared."

His eyes widened, and fear threatened to choke him, but Ellie was sitting here next to him, clearly okay, so he needed to calm down. "Who?"

"Halley. She came to the house."

"Where is she now?"

"The police have her. Apparently she came to tie up loose ends, and I was one."

"But you're okay."

Ellie laughed. "I'm right here, aren't I?"

He wasn't ready to laugh yet. This had been the longest nightmare of his life, stretching over years, and he wasn't taking any more chances. If he'd been fully conscious and cognizant earlier, he never would have let Ellie go off on her own.

"She started naming names the second we got in the car. No one we know besides Jared and Aaron. I think most of her workforce, if you will, is in Anchorage. But she decided if she was going down she wasn't going alone. The police are rounding those people up now. We are really free, Seth. I mean, besides the trial and the testifying." She made a face. Then smiled a little. "It's over."

He pushed himself up against the mattress to try to sit up.

"No, keep resting. Do you need anything?"

"Just…" Should he have this conversation in a hospital bed? Seth wanted to wait, for his pride, but he'd lost this woman once, and he had no intention of losing her again. Ever, if he had a choice in the matter. "Could we talk?"

She nodded. "Yeah. We can."

"It's about this." He motioned between the two of them. "Are we... Could we... I was thinking maybe we could...just see where life took us?" He was fumbling through this, badly. But as she stared at him with those incredible eyes, he realized they were alive, no one was trying to kill them, and second chances at life and love didn't come along every day.

"Are you asking me to...date you? Try again?" Ellie looked serious. "Seth, I left you. I shouldn't have, and I'm sorry, but I don't know if you should trust me again." She made a face. "I felt guilty for Liz's death. I know I didn't cause it, but she'd wanted to get together in the days before she was killed, and I just didn't have time... And then that last night, I was late—and then she was gone. I just... What if..."

"Ellie, I'm asking you to stay this time. I don't blame you for her death. Please don't leave. The past is the past. Let's just leave it there."

He did sit up this time. He couldn't properly kiss her lying down but held her close.

"I don't think I'll ever get tired of kissing you. So yes, let's leave the past where it belongs." Ellie grinned at him, bent down and brushed her lips against his one more time. "I'll stay here in this hospital till you're out, and then I'm thinking we should seriously consider reinstating our engagement."

"Oh, yeah?" Seth smiled.

Ellie met his eyes and whispered, "Yeah." Then she leaned back and shrugged. "Mainly because I know the dogs miss me, and I can't live out there with them until you and I get married."

Seth laughed, or started to until his side hurt. He put his hand there.

"You rest, Seth. I promise. This time I'm not going anywhere." She took his hand in hers. He squeezed it. Smiled up into her eyes and thanked God for second chances.

It had been fun enough falling in love with this woman once. Twice? He was a blessed man. And Seth planned to spend the rest of his life remembering it and making sure that Ellie knew she was the reason.

"I think you have a good idea." He teased her even though he'd already planned to ask. "Marry me? Want to try this again? I love you, Ellie Hardison."

"It just so happens I love you, Seth Connors. So yes, I think we should get married."

"Today?"

She laughed. Full and musical. And Seth knew he could listen to that sound for the rest of his life and never get tired of it.

Blessed indeed.

* * * * *

Elizabeth Goddard is the award-winning author of more than thirty novels and novellas. A 2011 Carol Award winner, she was a double finalist in the 2016 Daphne du Maurier Award for Excellence in Mystery/Suspense and a 2016 Carol Award finalist. Elizabeth graduated with a computer science degree and worked in high-level software sales before retiring to write full-time.

COVERT COVER-UP

Elizabeth Goddard

When thou passest through the waters,
I will be with thee; and through the rivers,
they shall not overflow thee: when thou
walkest through the fire, thou shalt not be burned;
neither shall the flame kindle upon thee.
—*Isaiah* 43:2

To my only daughter, Rachel.
God is always with you.

Acknowledgments

Thank you to all my writing friends and family who encourage and tolerate me along this amazing publishing journey!

ONE

Katelyn Bradley stood at the curb and stared at the dark home. No lights were on. Not even a porch light. No surprise since it was after midnight.

Here goes nothing.

The streetlights were few and far between in the neighborhood and shed little light. No dogs barked that might alert her to danger, but she would stay cautious. Shoving aside her fears, she crept forward while remaining aware of her surroundings. She swatted a mosquito that buzzed her ear.

Everything was probably all right.

Bushes edged the porch and the windows around the house. She hoped no one was hiding in the foliage as she continued up the steps and onto the porch. She peered into the shadows around her, but couldn't see a thing. Katelyn knocked on the door, then turned her back to the house and looked around the yard, also glancing at the neighbors on each side and the houses across the street. In her peripheral vision she could see that next door, Clara remained on her own porch watching Katelyn's every move.

After she got no response, she turned to the door

again. "Beck, it's Katelyn. Your neighbor. Clara told me she was concerned. She sent me to check on you."

A few more moments passed.

This time of night, he was probably in a deep sleep. He might be furious at her for waking up his son, too. Regardless, she wished he would turn on the porch light and chase away the shadows. She wished he would answer and let her know that he and Oliver were okay.

Clara had informed Katelyn that she'd seen someone creeping around the house. She was a caring elderly woman whom some considered too nosy. Katelyn thought of Clara in different terms—the woman was simply concerned. More neighborhoods needed watchdogs like Clara.

While she waited, Katelyn palmed the gun she kept hidden and tried to decide her next step. Was this another one of Clara's false alarms? Clara had called the police on too many occasions.

Katelyn had moved into the house next to Clara six months ago. Since Katelyn ran a private investigations and security partnership with her brother Ryan's fiancée, Tori Peterson, Clara had turned to asking Katelyn to check on neighborhood anomalies when they occurred, instead of phoning the police.

After too many times knocking and ringing the doorbell, concern tightened her chest. Though she again palmed her weapon, she reminded herself that she was no longer a police officer. The last thing she wanted to do was unnecessarily frighten Beck or his young son, Oliver.

The distinct sound of shattering glass erupted inside the home.

Katelyn tensed. Clara had been right. Unless, of

course, it was only Beck knocking over a lamp as he walked in a groggy state to respond to her untimely knocking. But her instincts told her Beck was in trouble.

"Who's in there? Open up!" She paused. "Clara?" she called over her shoulder.

"Yes, dear. I'm watching from my porch."

"Call the police." In the town and county seat of Rainey, the Maynor County Sheriff's Department served that role.

"Are you sure?"

"Tell them Katelyn Bradley requested help."

Still, the police wouldn't get to the home in time and Beck had a child—Katelyn couldn't wait. The struggle inside continued. She tried the doorknob and it turned, which both surprised and relieved her. Holding her weapon at the ready, she entered the home as if she was in her old job as a cop.

She wanted to shout "Police!"

That could stop whatever chaos reigned inside, but then she would be impersonating a cop.

Even now, she wondered who she thought she was, going in to save the day when she'd failed so spectacularly before.

Katelyn focused her thoughts on the moment. Grunts and groans came from somewhere in the home. Clinking and clattering, too. Her eyes adjusted to what little light filtered through the mini blinds from outside. Following the sounds, she rushed into the large comfortable living room, then down a long hallway decorated with framed family photographs and a child's artwork. All this she took in as she prepared for what she might encounter.

"Beck? Are you okay?"

Sirens rang out in the distance. Still, much too far away. Every second counted. Katelyn would continue to search until she found him. She prayed he would be safe, but her gut clenched as dread took hold.

Entering a spacious library, more light spilled in from a neighbor's security light. She spotted an overturned chair and froze. Shards of colored glass from a Tiffany lamp were spread across the wood floor.

And a body... Beck was on the floor.

At the sight, her heart stuttered. Gasping, she rushed forward. "Beck!"

He groaned.

Before she could drop to her knees next to him, a bulky form grabbed her from behind. Katelyn used defensive techniques to free herself, but in the process, the hulking invader disarmed her. Panic engulfed her. He was gaining the upper hand and she had to get back the advantage. Gulping for breath, she knocked the gun from his hand and freed herself, then whirled to face off with the masked man.

When he lunged for her, she kicked him in the throat. As he stumbled back, she tore off his mask. The light spilling into the room lit up his face, and she memorized the details. Katelyn didn't miss the threatening, murderous look in his eyes. Eyes she would never forget.

A display of red and blue lights flashed in the windows and reflected on the walls. Sirens blared.

The now unmasked face scowled. Her attacker swung his massive fist toward her. Katelyn dodged, but he kicked his leg out, too, and she lost her balance, falling to the floor as he fled the room. Katelyn glanced at Beck. Unmoving, he was awake and gave her a pensive gaze as he pushed to sit up.

Deputies rushed into the home. Lights flooded the library.

Guns were aimed at her and Beck as they remained on the floor. Squinting, she held up her identification— her PI credentials. "*I* called *you*."

"I'm the homeowner." Beck shifted to his knees. "The attacker fled the house. Maybe someone should look for him."

Unlike Beck, Katelyn made no movements until the deputies lowered their weapons.

"Katelyn Bradley." Deputy Clemmons, one of her detective brother's friends, helped her to her feet. "What happened here?"

"I walked in on an assailant who had attacked Beck." Katelyn waited for Beck to take the lead.

He held her gaze a moment, then looked at Deputy Clemmons. "I dropped my son off at his grandparents' and when I came home, I walked in on a burglar. He attacked me. Then Katelyn entered just in time." He sent her an odd look.

Clara hadn't mentioned that Beck had just gotten home. She'd only said she'd seen someone creeping around the house. Had that been Beck she'd seen, checking out his home? Not that it mattered at this point.

"Do you need a paramedic? You look kind of beat-up."

Beck's face reddened. He was a fit guy. Worked at some rock-climbing facility. Clara had said he'd once been a world-class rock climber—no doubt he was strong.

"I'm fine." His voice projected confidence. "I was caught off guard."

By someone strong enough to take down Beck Goodwin. Katelyn was glad the law showed up when they had.

Deputy Clemmons started taking their statements

and filling out the paperwork for the report stating that Beck had walked in on a burglary and had tried to restrain the thief. Inserting herself into the incident, PI and neighbor Katelyn Bradley had walked into the home and eventually the library, where she found and engaged the assailant, who fled upon the arrival of law enforcement.

"Ah, whose weapon?" Deputy Clemmons asked as he eyed the gun on the floor by a chair.

Now it was Katelyn's turn to be embarrassed. "That's mine."

Clemmons reached down and grabbed it, then handed it over. "Might want to hang on to it." He leaned closer. "I won't tell your brother."

Great. Now he would hold that over her—he'd wanted a date with her since forever ago. Not happening.

"Well, folks, I think we've seen enough. You startled a burglar. Good thing no one was shot." Clemmons's tone had turned more serious as he held her gaze. He studied Katelyn. "You saw his face."

"Yeah. I got a good look."

"What about you?" Clemmons asked Beck.

"No."

Clemmons acted like he questioned Beck's response, but then focused on Katelyn. "Can you come in tomorrow to look at mug shots? Maybe he has a record."

She nodded. "Of course."

"See you tomorrow then. I'm sure Mr. Goodwin here is grateful to have such a skilled neighbor, but… Katelyn, please wait for us to arrive next time." His last words held a scolding tone.

Of course he would say that. Maybe she deserved that reprimand, but what about Beck's life? Plus, in her mind things weren't adding up. If the attacker had only been a burglar, why had he stayed until the moment the deputies arrived? Why fight Beck and then Katelyn? Why not flee the scene as soon as his presence was discovered in the home?

The deputies cleared out, and Katelyn turned to look at Beck. She should leave, too, but she wanted to make sure he was truly okay. Her heart had beat a little faster the few times she'd interacted with him, which hadn't been many. She lived two houses down from him—on the other side of Clara.

His gray eyes took her in. "I would thank you for barging into my home to play the hero but you could have been hurt. I had it under control. I almost had the burglar."

Seriously? She stifled a laugh. Well, of all the ungrateful attitudes. "You were on the floor when I found you."

"You could have been killed."

A knot grew in her throat. Rather than continue the conversation, she turned and marched home. Two county vehicles were still parked at the curb. One deputy stood at his vehicle and talked on the radio. Were they out looking for the burglar? Or lingering only to make sure he'd fled the neighborhood for good?

Whatever. She didn't have to stick around and listen to Beck's criticism when he should have been thanking her instead. That's what she got for trying to help. The man didn't appreciate it. If she hadn't intervened he could have been killed. He could be dead right now.

She took a shortcut and crossed Clara's lawn rather than using the sidewalk. The woman was nowhere to be seen. Good. Katelyn would be hard-pressed to produce a smile at the moment. Ryan would hear about her involvement tonight sooner or later. Detective Ryan Bradley was her twin, but could be annoyingly over-protective, which was especially true after what he'd been through months ago when he'd almost lost Tori Peterson, the woman of his dreams, now his fiancée. Tori had become Katelyn's partner in her private in-vestigations and security services business—Peterson Bradley Investigations.

Let them find out in good time. She wouldn't bother either of them at this hour. Her brother and Tori were getting married this coming weekend and Katelyn wouldn't throw a wrench into that event, especially since it seemed that some obstacle was always getting in the way. She was happy they had both found each other. She'd thought she'd found love once but had been betrayed. Katelyn wouldn't give away her heart again.

Home and in bed, Katelyn tossed and turned, fear-ing that she would fall asleep and dream again of her failure to protect her partner when she'd been a cop on the Shasta PD. Then she finally gave in to exhaustion…

This was it. She was going to drown in the lake if she didn't do something. But what could she do? Death loomed large and much too near. Her lungs burned as she gasped for oxygen. For air. She had to get to the surface, away from the darkness. Away from the death.

She kicked and…

Katelyn flung her arms, her lungs screaming. She was wide-awake now. This wasn't a dream. Someone was pressing a pillow over her face.

With both hands, Beck gripped the shoulders of the big man and yanked him from where he was hovering over Katelyn and smothering her with a pillow. Beck had broken the man's hold. The formidable attacker cursed, and before Beck could tackle him, the man whipped out a gun and aimed at Beck's head.

Katelyn screamed, "No!"

Beck knocked away the weapon as it fired, the shot deafening. The attacker kicked him in the gut. Pain ignited as Beck fell against the dresser and landed in the corner.

The guy fled the room, just as he'd left the library earlier that evening.

Beck scrambled up and started after him. He chased him through the dimly lit home, knocking items from a table as he moved past.

"Wait. Come back. Who are you? What do you want?" Beck called after him.

In the laundry room, the man escaped out an open window.

Beck caught himself and bent over his thighs. What was he thinking? Like he really wanted the man to come back and shoot him in the head. But Beck was desperate for answers.

Still, as desperate as he was, he wouldn't chase the guy down. Not when Katelyn could be injured.

He needed to go back and check on her, but first he peered through the window and watched the man disappear across the back alley and into the shadows. Even if he tried, he would never find him now. If the man had any brains, he would leave the vicinity. Should have already left with the recent police presence in the neighborhood.

Dawn would be breaking soon and there would be more eyes to witness his crimes. Beck shut the window and locked it. Had she left her alarm system disarmed? The window unlocked?

Beck left the laundry room and headed into the kitchen to get back to Katelyn. Before he crossed the space, he spotted her. She stood at the hall entrance, staring at him with wide eyes—those big blue-green eyes that had caught his attention the first time he'd met her.

Katelyn trembled—with rage or fear, he couldn't tell.

Though he'd wanted to chase after the man and get the answers he sought, he'd been right to stay behind.

He closed the distance and reached a hand out to touch her, but held back. "Are you okay?"

"I'm fine." She turned her back to him.

He followed as she marched down the hallway to her bedroom, where she flipped on the lights. She stared at her bed and the pillow her attacker had used.

An ache coursed through Beck. "No, you're not. You're in shock."

"Go after him. Go get him," she shouted, tears in her eyes.

"No." Beck stood his ground. He wanted to take her in his arms, but he instinctively knew that would be a big mistake. He was attracted to this woman without even fully knowing her and should steer clear. "You're not all right."

He owed her. He'd been too harsh on her earlier— she'd probably saved his life. But he wished she hadn't gotten involved. "Sit down and I'll get you some water."

He guided her to a plush chair in the corner of her room. He flipped on the small table-side lamp next to the chair and noticed the Bible was open. Before he got the water, he did another check around the home to make sure their attacker hadn't decided to come back. Beck double-checked that all the doors and windows had been locked. Sure, he should probably wait in case investigators wanted to dust for prints. But while he hoped they would look for evidence, he thought it more important to ensure Katelyn's safety. The man had tried to kill her. Even though he'd worn a mask, Beck was sure it was the same guy. Same big shoulders he'd encountered in his own home. He'd locked horns with him twice in one night.

The house secured, he got the water from the kitchen sink, and when he turned Katelyn was standing in his path again. Only this time she held a gun at her side.

"I want to know what's going on right now. Why were you here and able to…?" She choked on the words.

Beck handed her the glass. She set it on the counter. Fine. He took it and gulped it down, aware of every second her eyes remained on him. Then he finished and set down the glass. Her eyes had never left him.

"I was watching your home tonight," he said.

"Why?"

See, this was why he wished she hadn't tried to save him tonight. "I was afraid he would try to kill you."

TWO

A shiver raced up her spine. Still gripping her pistol, Katelyn rubbed her arms. She'd grabbed the gun before coming into the kitchen in search of Beck. What did she even know about her handsome neighbor? Well, except that his form was toned and fit and he didn't appear to have an ounce of fat on his body. That should be good for rock-climbing. Or was it because he was a climber that he had no fat? What was she even doing thinking about his toned physique?

"I should call the police." Again.

The last thing she wanted was for Tori and Ryan to worry about her as they approached the biggest event of their lives. The most important day of all—their wedding. Could be there was nothing to worry about.

If only.

She'd left her cell back in her room and debated leaving Beck alone in the kitchen while she retrieved it.

Beck paced her kitchen and filled the space with his presence. Edgy like a tiger, he prowled around. Counter. Sink. Refrigerator. Counter. Sink. Refrigerator. She instinctively knew the image of this well-tuned athletic guy with his sun-bleached shaggy hair and broad shoulders pacing, as if anxious to escape, would forever remain in her head.

But she wouldn't let that distract her from getting answers.

"I want to hear the truth from you. Why did you think he would try to kill me?"

He stopped pacing to stare at her. Instead his jaw took up the movement and worked back and forth. "I would think that would be obvious." Beck began his incessant prowling again.

"No, I'm sorry, but it's not obvious. What's obvious is that you know something you're not telling me. You didn't tell Deputy Clemmons everything, either."

Beck stopped again, his eyes shifting to her and settling on her face. The disturbed look in them shook her insides.

"What's obvious is that you pulled his mask off tonight. You saw his face. You're the one who can identify him. I couldn't see him because you were standing in the way. Don't you get that?"

Katelyn couldn't voice her thoughts as she absorbed his words. She waited for more information from him. She also waited for him to avert his gaze before she did. She had to stay strong and not back off. Finally, Beck the tiger went back to his feral movements. Ran both hands through his hair.

"I thought he would try to kill you because you saw him. I couldn't know for sure. Call it paranoia." Beck suddenly stopped in front of her and took a step closer. "But I couldn't take that risk that he would hurt you. So… So I waited in the shadows and watched your house."

That lump in her throat again. She struggled to breathe as the memory of a pillow covering her face flashed through her mind. And now she couldn't breathe again for far different reasons. Katelyn gasped but she could get no air.

"Hey, hey. It's okay. I'm here." Beck's voice was soothing as he led her to a chair at the table. He urged her to sit, and she did. All she cared about was getting air. Calming her heart. Composing herself.

At the table, she gripped the white tiled top. Ran her hands over the cold, smooth surface until her heart rate slowed. That she'd so easily allowed him to guide and comfort her was disturbing.

"I guess I should thank you." She guessed? Oh, she should definitely thank him, but the way he'd treated her earlier still stung.

He slid into the chair across from her and dipped his chin as if those gray eyes of his could search her deepest thoughts. Her soul. "But you don't want to because of the way I thanked you at my house earlier."

Well. He *had* searched her soul.

When she said nothing, he continued, "I don't blame you."

Beck Goodwin had to be one of the best-looking men she'd ever met. Not that looks should matter too much, but here he was sitting at her kitchen table being all sensitive, too. Her vision blurred. She couldn't afford to get distracted. "You haven't told me what's going on. Who is this person who broke into your home and is clearly much more than a simple burglar, Beck? You owe me the truth."

"I wish I knew what was going on."

"That answer is not going to cut it. You know something you're not telling me. You're hiding something."

"What makes you say that?"

"Just a feeling I got while I was at your house. That so-called burglar was prepared to stay and fight until the police got there. That isn't the reaction of a typical burglar."

He scraped a hand across his scruffy face. Katelyn wondered what those whiskers would feel like against her cheeks, then quickly banished the thought. She hoped he didn't notice the sudden rush of heat to her cheeks.

"I honestly don't know who he is. But I've been considering hiring a private investigator."

She arched an eyebrow.

"I'm only going to share the *reason* for that consideration with the PI after signing a contract."

"Why not go to the police?"

"With what?" He gave a half smirk. "I don't know anything."

"This conversation seems circular and I'm getting tired. It's late. Or early." She rose. "I'm calling the police to report the incident."

Katelyn was almost surprised that Beck didn't try to stop her.

Fifteen minutes later a county vehicle pulled into her driveway. Deputy Clemmons again.

He eyed Beck and then Katelyn, as if he believed there must be something going on between them. Katelyn explained the events in detail.

"Mr. Goodwin, what *aren't* you telling me?" Clemmons asked.

Beck remained stone-faced and shrugged. "I honestly don't know who the man is or why he was in my home."

"But you decided to watch Katelyn's home in case

he came for her because you didn't know anything."
Deputy Clemmons let his sarcasm drag out as he scribbled in his tablet.

"And...he wants to hire a private investigator," Katelyn added.

Beck frowned and glanced her way, almost looking a little hurt, as if she'd shared something he'd told her in confidence.

"Is that so?" Clemmons crossed his arms, the tablet dangling from his hand. His gaze slid from Beck to Katelyn. "What time are you coming in to look at those mug shots? I'll put in for a forensic artist if you don't identify anyone. In the meantime, I suspect this will get passed to a detective." He eyed Beck.

Ryan. *No, please.* See what she got for calling the local law? But she couldn't *not* call them.

"Mr. Goodwin, I suspect we'll have more questions for you. Please stay in town." Deputy Clemmons tucked away his pad. "Katelyn, I'm off duty in an hour. I can come sit here at the curb if you want to feel safe."

"Thanks. I can take care of myself." She would get an earful from her brother—she was sure. "Please don't make a big deal about this to Ryan. He's getting married in a few days, and I don't want him worrying about me when he should be focused on that. Understand?"

Clemmons grew taller, as if he was reading some meaning into her request—like his cooperating would get him on her good side. Maybe after this was over, she could have Ryan have a word with Deputy Clemmons. Katelyn wasn't the girl for him.

Or anyone, after Tony's betrayal. Trusting men wasn't on her radar.

Beck had already crossed the sidewalk in front of

Ollie meant everything to Beck, but he'd been consumed with finding answers to Mia's death and had left him with his parents. Beck trusted them entirely and had gotten lost in the happenings of the previous night and this morning. He was stumped as to how to respond, which told him his mind was still much too distracted.

What do I do about Ollie? How do I keep him safe? Staying with Beck was not safe for Ollie right now.

"I thought perhaps we could just meet you there at the park. If you want to bring the chips, I'll bring the sandwiches. Oh, and I baked my million-dollar cookies."

Squeezing his eyes, he pinched the bridge of his nose. *Let me think. Let me think.*

How was he going to solve this while keeping both Ollie and his parents safe? He couldn't turn the clock back to close the box he'd opened that had led to the burglary and now two murder attempts on Katelyn's life.

Detective Bradley and Katelyn's partner, Ms. Peterson—soon to be Mrs. Bradley—stepped from the room. They hovered near Katelyn as if protecting her, and both gave him a severe look as they ushered her down the hallway, like they would take her to safety and far away from Beck. He hadn't officially hired her as a private investigator—no binding paperwork had been signed—and it looked like he was on his own, after all.

He preferred it that way and it was probably for the best, but on the other hand, did she realize she was still in danger? Had he convinced her the accident was no accident?

"Your breathing sounds funny, son." Dad now. "Are you okay? Your mother handed me the phone. You really should think about stopping that climbing business and join me at the hardware store. That door is always open."

"I know, Dad, and thanks."

"Daddy!" It sounded like Ollie had wrestled Mom's cell away. "Dad, let's go on that picnic. I helped Mimi bake the cookies and make sandwiches."

Beck's heart melted with love and he couldn't help but smile even in the middle of this nightmare. He couldn't deny his son anything. "Okay. Put Mimi back on the phone."

"Mom?"

"Yes, Beck."

"I'll meet you at the park at one thirty. It will mean a late lunch. Is that okay?"

"Perfect. We'll see you there."

Time with his family would ground him, and he definitely needed clarity. Maybe he could pay for a cruise to Alaska for them and get them far from town while he figured this out. He scratched his head. A woman cleared her throat.

He turned and found Katelyn dangling keys. "Tori is letting me borrow her car."

"I... Uh..." He thought she had left with her protective brother and friend.

She arched an eyebrow. "I don't think I've seen you speechless until this moment. I haven't decided if I like it or not." Katelyn turned and walked down the hallway, seemingly expecting him to join her. With the way she held herself, confident and strong, no one passing her in the hallway would ever know she'd just been in a car accident. Was that an act? Beck had been in the same car, and he was sure he appeared frazzled. He hadn't lost consciousness, so didn't need to be examined like Katelyn.

He caught up with her, still scrambling to shift his plans again.

"So who are we meeting at the park?" she asked.

"Honestly, I thought you were long gone by now."

She stopped and turned on him. Fisted her hands on her hips. "Gone? Where would I be going? I have a new case to solve."

"Yeah, about that…"

"You look indecisive about something. You can tell me about that on the way to the office to sign the PI paperwork."

"As I was saying, about that…" Was Katelyn better off getting back to her life? Maybe her attacker would back off if he had nothing to fear from Katelyn. Except she wouldn't let go. She was the only witness and had planned to look at mug shots.

Katelyn stepped closer and got in his face. Her pretty expression sobered. "Remember, I'm already in this and I'll be investigating with or without you. I told my brother and future sister-in-law nothing you've said to me. And about the accident you believe was deliberate, I'm willing to go with you on that. I'm here for you, Beck."

Beck hated to admit that he'd forgotten her earlier threat, but she'd acted on this new offer to help him as if she cared… And as if it was more than business. He had to be reading more into it. He hoped he was reading more into it, because Beck wasn't entirely sure he could resist this woman, even with his resolve that he wouldn't trust again.

"Now, tell me where we're going," she said.

Beck returned her smile. "To sign the PI paperwork and then to the park to eat sandwiches and chocolate-chip cookies and celebrate our new partnership."

"I love picnics." Katelyn offered a soft smile and laughed. "You're full of surprises, Beck Goodwin."

As are you, Katelyn. As are you.

He enjoyed the lyrical tones of her laughter entirely too much, especially with the danger breathing down their necks.

FIVE

A breeze whipped around her, tossing her hair into her eyes as she hiked through the grass next to Beck toward the picnic tables. A playground with a slide and swings was situated a few yards from the tables. Even though she'd grown up in this region of the country, she'd never actually been to this state park near the aptly named Castle Crags—the rocks jutting out of the spiking, lofty mountain looked exactly like a "craggy castle."

As she and Beck approached the tables and playground, an older couple stood. Katelyn recognized Oliver on the swing. He jumped and flew from the swing, landing on his feet. Without a break in his rhythm, he sprinted over to Beck.

The man picked him up and swung him around. "Hey, buddy. How you doing?"

Oliver giggled as Beck set him on the ground and shifted to tickling him. The boy's giggles sent warmth spreading out like a pebble dropped in a pond.

"Stop it!" He pulled away but kept laughing.

"Let's go try some of this grub you made." Beck pulled Oliver to him and knuckle-rubbed his head.

Oliver slipped out from his arm again and nearly tackled his father to the ground.

Myriad emotions surged through Katelyn. She couldn't pull her eyes from the pair. At the same time, her heart ached for their loss—Beck's wife and Oliver's mother—only a year ago.

Was it an accident or something much more nefarious, like Beck believed? Obviously, he had good reason to be suspicious of the past. If she let her thoughts go there, Katelyn could still feel that pillow pressed hard against her face so that she couldn't get any air. With a young boy in the mix, there was so much more at stake. Katelyn suddenly became aware of Beck's parents— she assumed—staring at her, questions in their eyes.

"Oh, excuse me." She thrust out her hand. "I'm Katelyn Bradley."

"It's nice to meet you, Katelyn. What a lovely name. I'm Marilyn Goodwin, Beck's mother, and this is my husband, Rayce."

Mr. Goodwin gave Katelyn a power shake. "Beck's dad. It's nice to meet you."

As if Katelyn wouldn't have recognized those same piercing eyes and strong jaw in Beck's father.

Mrs. Goodwin smiled and shook her head. "Beck never brings girls around. You're the first in quite some time."

Grief briefly flashed in the woman's eyes. Of course, Beck would grieve his wife. The mourning period was different for everyone, she'd heard. Some took months and others years. What would it take for Beck to get over the loss? Would he marry again soon for Oliver's sake, so he could have a mother, too? The boy was happy with his father—Beck was a good father, no doubt there.

Katelyn realized that Mrs. Goodwin was still waiting for an explanation from her. Beck's mother had the wrong idea about Katelyn's presence. She needed to set his parents straight, but she had no idea how much he'd told them about what was going on. Did they need to know she was a private investigator? Katelyn should have discussed this with Beck, during the drive over.

They had gone by the office space she shared with Tori for their private-investigations business. She'd snatched the paperwork from the printer just as Ryan called. While she talked, they'd gotten back into Beck's vehicle and headed straight for the park so they wouldn't be late.

Beck had that sense of urgency—a man on a mission to protect his son.

During the drive, Ryan had kept her on the phone, apprising her of the situation. They could return to their homes this afternoon. No evidence had been discovered so far. Then Ryan had started interrogating her about Beck and if she planned to work for him.

Katelyn hoped that Beck hadn't heard Ryan's side of the conversation. Ryan had advised her against working with Beck.

Yada. Yada. Who did her brother think he was, anyway? Katelyn had suspicions of her own, but she didn't want to share them with Ryan.

So she'd quickly changed the subject before the conversation got out of hand. "You sound like you have the wedding jitters, as some call it. Are you getting cold feet?"

"Of course not. I've loved Tori as long as I've known

her. You know that. How could you even suggest such a thing?"

Ryan had protested too much, in Katelyn's opinion, and she figured she'd hit the mark, but that was his issue to process. At least Katelyn had successfully redirected the conversation with Beck listening in.

The next thing she knew Beck was pulling his vehicle into the state park.

He still hadn't signed the documents because her call had taken entirely too long.

"How long have you known our Beck?" Mr. Goodwin asked, bringing Katelyn back. How on earth would she set them straight?

Beck released Oliver and his eyes found hers and held her gaze. He'd heard his mother's question.

Rescue me! She hoped he could see the pleading in her eyes.

"How long have I known Beck?" she asked, stalling, as she moved toward him, hoping he would be the one to answer. "Well, we're neighbors and—"

"Katelyn was in a car wreck today." He put it out there so bluntly, Katelyn's mouth dropped open.

His mother and father both gasped.

"Oh, you poor girl," Mrs. Goodwin said.

"And I was only doing the neighborly thing by inviting her to our picnic." The way his eyes crinkled at the corners when he grinned, and those huge dimples around that great smile, made Katelyn's heart tumble against her rib cage.

"Well, you have to come to the table and sit down. I take it you weren't terribly hurt." Mrs. Goodwin eyed Katelyn's forehead as she led them back to the picnic table. "Is that from the wreck? I didn't want to stare or be rude and ask about it."

The moment of the crash rushed over Katelyn as she eased onto the bench at the picnic table. Maybe she had pushed herself too soon to come here with Beck, but she would make up for it later. Find a safe place to rest.

She touched her head and winced. "Yes. I think my head hit the mirror or the airbag. I can't be sure."

"Oh, dear. You have a concussion?"

"I don't think so. I don't have a headache. I blacked out, though." Katelyn thought back to the moment she woke up in Beck's arms and wished she hadn't remembered—everyone was watching, including Beck. Was he thinking back, too?

Mr. Goodwin's expression showed his concern. "What happened?"

"Dad." Beck shook his head. He might have brought up the wreck as a means of explaining Katelyn's presence, but it was clear he didn't want to discuss the wreck in front of Oliver.

"Which sandwiches did you make, Ollie?" Beck asked.

"I'm sure Mimi's are better." Oliver laughed as he pointed at the bread. "I left fingerprints."

"Those are the best kind." Beck snatched two fingerprinted sandwiches and handed one over to Katelyn. "Eat up. This guy is going to be a famous chef one day."

Oliver howled with laughter. Katelyn noticed Beck called him "Ollie" instead of Oliver.

Katelyn had to hand it to Beck. The man was under tremendous stress, but his son, his family, would never know it. She understood that. Beck wanted to protect Ollie—not just his physical well-being, but Beck didn't want his son to have any reason to be afraid. Admiration for him filled her. He put on a great show, for his family's sake, and yet, she knew that fear and anxiety hovered just beneath the surface. His gaze flicked to her briefly and she saw the hint of a warning there.

She hoped he knew that she would never give away his secret.

This time with his family, with his son, was too precious. But she worried that danger was quickly encroaching.

"I like Katelyn, Dad. I'm glad you brought her along. Is this a date?" Ollie moved to the end of the picnic table and grabbed three cookies before his grandmother could swat away his hands.

"Um, Katelyn is our neighbor, Ollie. Remember? And we're friends. She's your friend, too." Beck popped the rest of his sandwich in his mouth and winked at Katelyn.

She couldn't help but smile. She accepted the cookie Oliver offered and took a bite. After chewing, she said, "Yum, these are awesome. Did you make these, too?"

"I helped. Mimi's the cook. Dad knows there's no hope of me being a cook. But my momma was amazing." His expression soured as though he wished he hadn't thought of his mother.

Katelyn thought her heart might break.

"Mimi" lovingly swatted Oliver away from the cookies again. "That's enough for now. You go swing. I'll clean up."

Oliver headed for the swing set. Mrs. Goodwin eyed Beck, her face filled with love and concern for her son. "Beck, why don't you go for a walk with Katelyn. Your father and I'll clean up this mess. Then I suspect we should talk."

thing different about her. She was on edge. I couldn't help but feel like she was hiding something. We were so close and I knew something was wrong. She wouldn't tell me. I loved her so much and I didn't want to smother her or stifle her. I didn't want to act like a possessive and jealous jerk."

Katelyn eyed him. "But you did, anyway."

"I didn't think I was, but she accused me of those things. She accused me of being paranoid."

"Do you ever think you might have been just that? Paranoid? That you're being paranoid even now?"

He heard the insinuation in her tone—and her unspoken suggestion he should see a doctor. "There's nothing wrong with getting help so I agreed to see a marriage counselor, only Mia was the one to refuse. Still, even without counseling, everything improved for a while, but then she lied to me. I followed her and spotted her meeting with someone."

"Meeting. What does that mean? She could have been meeting someone for any number of reasons. Did something happen between them?"

"Not then. Not that I saw, but it shook me up pretty bad. It was then that I became a crazed jealous husband, at least on the inside. I kept it all to myself…for Ollie's sake. For our family's sake."

"From what I've seen of your interaction with your family today, I believe you could actually pull that off."

"I watched her. I found…a gun. She had a gun she never told me about." He covered his face for a moment, then dropped his hands when he remembered his family was watching. "I started to suspect that she was a federal agent."

"What? You mean…undercover?"

"Undercover or more like a spy. When Ollie was five, she started traveling for her job."

"Wait. What did she do other than climb rocks?"

"She worked for an outdoors company, then became a buyer and traveled. At least that's what she told me. I confronted her one night when she returned from a trip. I'd—I'd had enough. But she had this power over me—"

"You mean love. She loved you and you loved her."

He nodded. "I gave in and as she held me, she whispered in my ear that she would tell me everything."

Katelyn shifted to cross her legs, her eyes riveted to him as he told the story. He could hardly believe he was telling anyone all of this. Just laying it all out there to this woman who he didn't know that well. A stranger, for all practical purposes.

"The next day I'd come down from a training session and I found a note in my locker—Mia would meet me for dinner at our favorite restaurant. She was going to tell me everything. She had arranged for my parents to watch Ollie for the evening. She was so secretive and on edge—but I knew—" he held Katelyn's gaze "—I knew that she loved me, and that she was somehow in trouble and had been protecting me and Ollie the whole time."

Beck didn't say more but watched Katelyn. Was she tracking with him? Believing him? He couldn't understand why her opinion, her belief in him, was so important to him at this moment. His throat grew dry, making it hard to form his next words.

He squeezed his eyes to block the emotions that suddenly rolled through him—he remembered that night as if it had happened mere seconds before.

"I'd arrived at the restaurant anxious to see her. I wanted to help her with whatever this was that she'd gotten herself into. I wanted to stop it from coming between us." He released a ragged breath. "I spotted her car as it crossed a short bridge over a river. An oncoming truck was going slowly and it suddenly sped up and crashed into her car, crumpling it before my eyes. If that wasn't enough, it continued forward and pushed her vehicle through the guardrail and into the river."

Katelyn pressed her hand over his, and he soaked up the comfort she offered. "I'm so sorry, Beck. So sorry."

To her credit, she didn't interrupt him with questions, but gave him the space to process through the emotions. Somehow, she seemed to sense how much was roiling around inside him.

"I jumped into the river after her. Swam down to try to free—" He caught himself as his voice choked. He couldn't speak with those traumatic images in his mind.

After a few moments, he regained his composure. "I told the police what I'd seen and that the vehicle had intentionally sped up. That someone had deliberately rammed her and then driven away. I told them she was about to tell me the truth, but I'm sure you can imagine how they interpreted things. For a while, they even suspected me of hiring someone to kill her because I was a jealous husband who suspected her of having an affair."

He hung his head, hating to relive everything, but now was the moment when he had to share it all, and he thanked God that Katelyn was kindhearted and understanding, and the person to help him.

"For a while, I had to put it all behind me for Ollie's sake. He'd lost his mother at only seven. He needed normalcy, not a crazy paranoid father. So I told myself the police were right and Mia's accusations were right—I was too possessive and had become jealous."

"But deep inside you knew differently." Her tone was gentle and reassuring.

"After six months had passed, I allowed myself to review everything and I knew I was right all along. Besides, Mia loved me, and she wasn't going to break off our marriage that night. I've been making a few phone calls here and there. Tried to talk to someone from her company to find out more about her job and travels."

"And?"

"That company never existed."

SIX

His words knocked the breath from Katelyn, and she drew in air. More than anything, she wanted to believe him on every account. The Beck she'd come to know in a short time was full of love and self-control. Mia had been a fortunate woman to have found a man like him. But she suspected there was much more to this story and Katelyn decided that she was in this with Beck for the long haul, however long it took.

"Tell me what you found in your house, Beck."

"I suspected that Mia could have hidden something in our home. We lived in an apartment, and then when she became pregnant we bought a home to fill with love." He was quiet for a few heartbeats, then said, "When we first moved in, I worked to remodel, renovating and upgrading, like anyone does in an old home, but then when I became suspicious of her, I used that as an excuse to search for anything she could have hidden. I thought I was probably grasping at straws or losing it, but I had to try. It was the only way to keep me—" He cleared his throat. "To keep my sanity."

He gave her a look that seemed to beg her not to think him crazy.

Katelyn pressed her hand over his to reassure him and sat taller. "You found something in the house?"

He subtly nodded. "After she died, I kept working, again, to keep my sanity. Two nights ago, I found a safe behind a wall in the basement. I hadn't worked on remodeling down there, but had focused on the main floor. The wall had been painted in such a way so it would look old and match the rest of the basement. Once I looked close enough, I could tell it was new and had been installed since we'd moved in—right under my nose! We'd been living in the home for years. So it wasn't that hard. When I found the safe, I knew it must contain information Mia wanted hidden. Kept secret from others including me, her husband. Or maybe she would have shared everything—including the fact she'd had a safe installed in our home—that night if she hadn't been murdered."

He hung his head.

Katelyn gave him the time he needed.

"I took Ollie to stay with my parents the next day after school. To keep up the ruse that everything was normal, I had to stay for dinner, and then played a few video games with Ollie. I stopped by a hardware store to get a variety of tools I might need to open the safe. Just in case. When I got home I heard noises down in the basement. I found someone down there. He fought me and fled, and then I chased him back up and fought with him. I wanted to know who he was and get answers. I'm embarrassed that he got the best of me."

"And I stepped in to save the day." She offered him a grin. "I know you didn't want me involved, but, Beck, if what you're telling me is the correct interpretation of the events, then that burglar could have killed you."

He shrugged. "He came for the safe. I don't think he was going to kill me initially, but then after I chased him and we ended up in the library, I think he made his decision to get rid of me. I know I didn't act like I appreciated what you did, but I do. You probably saved my life last night."

"You're welcome. Thank you for saving mine, too."

"I guess that makes us even." He stared at her as though he might chuckle, but none of it was funny. "It took me too long to figure out that someone must have planted bugs or cameras in the house after Mia died, waiting for the moment when I would discover whatever Mia had hidden. Once I did, he came in to retrieve the items from the safe. Once those items were gone, I would have nothing to back up my claims that Mia had been murdered." He sighed. "Once again I would look like a paranoid fool if I tried to go to the police."

"Except that didn't happen, Beck. I was there and I saw the guy. Things have obviously escalated, with the attack on me. Since I've seen the man's face, I still need to go in to look at those mug shots, but I don't hold out any hope he's in them—I mean, if this is really cloak-and-dagger spy stuff." She tried not to make it sound like she was making a joke. "And in that case, I can meet with a sketch artist, but first I want to see that safe."

He nodded and pushed to his feet, offering Katelyn his hand. She didn't want to become addicted to the feel of his grip, or even that surge of energy that shot through her at his touch. She had a feeling that was exactly what would happen. Beck stirred longings in her heart, and she thought she had more control over those feelings. So she pushed to her feet without his help.

She eyed Beck's family, still at the picnic table. Ollie was on the slide. "What now?" This was his show, after all.

"Now, we go back to the table. You swing my son for me while I talk to my parents. I'll only tell them enough to let them know to be wary of strangers or danger. Mom suspects something already. She's always been able to read me."

Katelyn walked with Beck back to the picnic table, only this time they didn't hold hands—his parents noticed, but said nothing.

Mrs. Goodwin rose and smiled at them both. "There's a few more cookies left. Please eat them up so I don't need to pack them." She opened the plastic container and offered the cookies. "Everything okay?"

"I'm going to hang out with Ollie." Katelyn smiled, then left Beck to speak with his parents.

She approached the playground. Ollie had lost interest in the slide and was now crouching and playing with a stick.

"What are you looking at?" She squatted next to him.

"Oh, just a cricket."

"Mind if I hang out with you? We could swing."

"I guess so." Ollie left the cricket to return to its business and raced to beat her to the swings.

He scrambled on and started rocking back and forth until he propelled his swing so high she was afraid he would fall out.

She was slower to get into the swing next to him, barely fitting her rear into it. She smiled at Ollie and started kicking her way to swinging high like him— something she used to do as a kid. But her insides went queasy now. She glanced at Beck and noted the serious expression on his face. His parents had their backs to

Katelyn and Ollie so she couldn't see if their faces reflected his somber appearance.

Ollie slowed his swing, then flew out of it, landing on his feet.

"Ollie, wait!" Katelyn hoped to prevent him from interrupting Beck's conversation, but she was too late. He took off to the picnic table.

Beck smiled and wrapped his arm around Ollie. Katelyn watched as she made her way toward them. Ollie frowned and shrugged. What was that about? Everyone rose from the table as she approached.

"What's going on?"

Beck's intense gray eyes held her gaze. "Ollie's going camping with Mom and Dad."

The kid didn't appear all that excited about the news. Katelyn guessed he wanted to come home and spend more time with his dad, and she so got that. Beck was a special kind of guy. She'd have to be an idiot not to see that.

"Baseball just ended, Ollie. This is the perfect time for you to hang out with Pops and Mimi."

"But you're not going to be there."

Beck ruffled Ollie's dark hair—he must take after his mother, Mia, in that department. "I know, but I have to work. And I promise once I finish, if I can, I'll join you at the campsite."

Ollie jerked his head to Katelyn. "Will our new friend come, too?"

Beck's chuckle sounded forced as he glanced at her. "I don't know, Ollie."

"I need to get my fishing pole and my DS."

"You don't need electronics." The man looked to his mother for help.

Mrs. Goodwin rose from the table. "Come on, Ollie. We have enough clothes for you. You don't need to make a trip home. Pops has an extra fishing pole or we can buy one. We plan on heading out as soon as possible."

Mrs. Goodwin hugged Beck and kissed him on both cheeks. "You be careful now."

She eyed Katelyn and smiled, then shook her hand, pressing it between both of hers. "I'm so glad you're here for Beck."

Katelyn tried to absorb the heartfelt thanks and maybe with it she could get a sense of just what Beck might have told his mother. A lot? Or very little?

Ollie trudged off with his grandparents, leaving Katelyn more than curious. "Just what *did* you tell them?"

"Everything."

Katelyn felt her jaw drop again. She'd thought Beck had intended to hold something back. "Wait. Everything?"

"Yes."

"But why?"

"I realized they weren't going to settle for half truths."

Beck frowned as he watched them get into their SUV and quickly drive away. He waved at his son as the SUV headed around the park to the exit, then turned his full attention on Katelyn.

"What did they say?" she asked. "How did they respond?"

"They think I need help."

Back in town, Beck took Katelyn to the county sheriff's offices. He waited while she sat at a desk in the corner and looked through stacks of mug shots. Katelyn didn't see the intruder in the photographs. Beck hadn't thought she would, but they'd needed to get that out of the way. The county forensic artist was recovering from surgery, so it would be next week before Katelyn would meet with him.

Then it was on to the moment they had both been waiting for—when Beck would show Katelyn the safe. He parked his vehicle at the curb down the street from his house instead of in the driveway, or even in front.

"Why are you parking here?"

"Just want to hang back and see if anyone is lurking about."

Katelyn said nothing to that, but he knew she had more she wanted to say. She had kept quiet during the drive back and he appreciated her sensitivity. He tried to rise above how profoundly his parents' reaction affected him. They hadn't exactly come out and said they didn't believe him, but he saw it plain as day in their eyes. Mom had asked him several times about seeing her counselor friend. She and Dad both thought that Beck had suffered some sort of emotional break with reality since Mia's death. His biggest fear where they were concerned was that they could possibly try to take Ollie away from him—but then again, his parents knew that Ollie would have none of that. Beck was good for Ollie, and he loved his son dearly.

Still, it broke his heart when at the table today his mother had reached over, taken his hand and said, "For your son's sake, Beck, please, can't you see this is only going to make things worse?"

He released a long and heavy sigh that Katelyn couldn't have missed, but she didn't comment. Now he was curious about what she was thinking. But he could wait her out. He didn't trust himself to speak just yet, anyway.

Katelyn shifted to look at him. "Okay, well, under normal circumstances this would be the moment I should say thank you for an interesting day. Then I would get out and head home. But I want to see what all the fuss is about, and what someone has tried to kill me twice over."

He turned to face her. Took in her lovely features. Soft smile, and amazing eyes. That hair. *Careful, Beck.* "Thanks for that, Katelyn."

"To some degree, I know what you're going through—I mean, how hard it is when others don't believe in you. You begin to second-guess everything. To doubt yourself." Katelyn gazed off into the distance like she was far from him as she spoke.

"Sometime, I'd like to hear *your* story."

"My story?" She jerked her gaze to him.

"What happened to you before that helps you to understand what I'm going through right now."

Her smile was tenuous. "I can't truly understand, but I'm trying."

"You have no idea how much that means to me," Beck said. "Now let me sign those papers and we'll go look at the safe."

The private-investigator contract signed, they hiked down the street and tromped up the front walk. Would Clara be watching? At the front door, Katelyn brandished her weapon. "Let's make sure it's safe inside the house and no one is waiting for us."

"I have my own gun." Beck tugged his gun from the small holster at his waist. Carrying a concealed weapon was a new and necessary habit for him. "But you're the ex-cop who knows more about how to wield a deadly weapon. You first then." He gestured for her to take the lead because he knew she wanted that. She appeared to be in her element and he wouldn't take the moment from her.

She was definitely a take-charge woman and he loved that about her.

Once they were sure no one was in the home, Beck tucked his gun away. "He doesn't need to be here in the house to hear us and see us."

"You mean the bugs."

"I do."

"Let's exterminate them. You take that side of the house, I'll take this side."

"Um, I don't exactly have a lot of experience with this. What am I looking for?"

"I know a little about it." Her shrug was cute. "I don't use bugs or cameras in the PI business, don't get the wrong idea." She explained what he should look for and they each scoured the home.

Katelyn found a small camera in the living room. "That was it."

"I found a listening device in my bedroom. Guess the police weren't exactly looking for bugs and cameras. Just prints and any DNA left behind by the intruder."

"Right. And there could still be more that *we* missed," she said.

"I figure that we have limited time before someone else shows up here. The doors are locked and the alarm is armed."

Katelyn shoved back her hair and twisted it into a ponytail. "Okay, so show me the safe."

Beck led her down a hallway and into the basement.

He hadn't found any bugs or cameras down here, but that didn't mean anything. What difference did it make at this juncture, since the safe had already been discovered? He feared that the contents had already been stolen. At the wall, he removed the Sheetrock that he'd put back in place to hide the safe.

"Now that we're looking at it, any chance you know how to open it?"

"I've tried birth dates and anniversaries." He frowned. "Any suggestions?"

"We could hire someone to open it," she said.

"That would be my last choice."

"It might be your only choice." Katelyn glanced around the basement. "Let's do a little research about this kind of safe and how we could break it open."

He chuckled.

"People learn how to build bombs on the internet. I wouldn't be surprised if we could learn how to open this safe without the combination."

"The internet connection isn't so great down here. Let's go upstairs. I'm parched. We can get a drink while we research." Once upstairs, Beck shut all the mini blinds. "Don't want anyone looking in."

Katelyn glanced through a slat in one of the blinds. "I don't see any suspicious vehicles out there. The sooner we get this over with, the better."

Beck poured a glass of milk and offered it to her.

Katelyn frowned. "Got any chocolate syrup?"

"I have an eight-year-old." He grabbed the syrup and handed it to Katelyn. "Of course I do."

He watched her pour syrup into her milk and then laughed. "You're as bad as Ollie. I have to do it or he abuses the privilege."

She smiled and winked, then drank from the glass, her eyes never leaving his. He downed his milk and wiped away the residual moustache. *Time to get busy.* While Katelyn used her cell phone to search for information, he focused on his laptop, which was open at the kitchen counter. He was very aware of Katelyn Bradley's every move. Every breath. Every twitch of her nose. Every pucker of her lips.

Katelyn Bradley was quickly getting under his skin.

He reminded himself that Mia, whether for the right reasons or the wrong reasons, had lied to him and acted duplicitously. No one could ever truly be trusted, including Beck. He hoped that Katelyn knew she shouldn't trust him.

Lost in his thoughts about Katelyn, he didn't realize she'd moved from her position until she hovered much too near and looked over his shoulder. "So I have a question. What happens if we open the safe and we find...nothing?"

He whirled in the chair. "What do you mean if we find nothing?"

"You're hinging everything on what's in the safe, Beck. What if there's nothing—nothing in the safe? Then what?"

He frowned. "It could mean that someone already got to the safe and took everything."

"Or it could mean there was nothing in there to begin with. Who owned this house before you? Could be it belonged to someone else and the information wasn't passed along to you by the Realtor or the previous owner."

"The safe and its hiding spot are all new. I explained that." And he thought she believed him.

"Is there any chance you could be wrong about that? Even the slightest chance?"

"Nope."

"Okay, so what happens if we open the safe and you find something…incriminating? Or even something to prove that Mia was a government agent. Then what?"

"I don't know."

"I do. We need to give the information to the authorities."

"You mean the police."

"I'm sorry, but yes. What else can you do with it? You're trying to prove that someone killed Mia. You can't do that on your own."

"I'm not doing it on my own. I hired you, remember?"

Her ponytail sagging, Katelyn weaved her fingers through her hair. "Beck, I'm not the police. I can investigate but at the end of the day the information—especially incriminating information—will need to be handed over."

"Don't forget, I tried telling the police before."

"Before you had any actual evidence. I'm just trying to establish some game rules here. Or rather ground rules. We find something. We turn it over."

"You mean to your brother." Beck shoved from the counter and paced his kitchen, loathing that he seemed to be doing that an awful lot lately. "I thought we'd already addressed this and you were on board with it. Katelyn, you're in danger. You've already experienced that. Each person you tell will then be in danger."

"You told your parents."

"Because they need to know in order to keep Ollie safe." He rubbed his temples. "We need to get into that safe. In the meantime, act normal. Like everything's normal. Even to your brother."

"How am I supposed to ask questions and investigate? That's why you hired me, remember?"

Beck pressed his palms against the counter and leaned forward, hanging his head.

"Beck." She touched his back. "Why don't you just move and leave the safe, leave it all behind?"

He turned to face her. He couldn't help it. He gently grabbed her shoulders. "Whoever was behind killing my wife, whoever was behind the attack in my home and on you, will keep coming. Don't you get it? I have to know what's inside that safe. I have to know the truth in order to protect those I care about."

With the words, Beck knew that he cared deeply about Katelyn, deeper than he had a right to. With the shimmer in her gaze, Katelyn knew that, too.

She slowly nodded. "For everyone's sake, I want you to know the truth, too. Let's go break into that safe."

SEVEN

With growing exasperation, Katelyn pressed her head against the safe and groaned. She'd tried to find the combination, using the techniques she'd read about, but it remained locked. She dropped her hands and growled, then marched away from the stupid safe.

"I don't get it! I've tried this ten times and I still can't open it. It shouldn't be this hard. What am I doing wrong?" She stretched out her arm and opened up her palm. "I think we should hire someone. We're wasting time trying to do this ourselves."

Beck's face remained stone, but a scowl brewed behind his gaze. "I'll give it a try."

She knew he didn't want to hire someone, but this was ridiculous. "You've already tried, remember? We're done. This is taking too long, Beck."

He approached the safe and stared at it.

"So it's in the wall, but is it heavy to lift?" she asked.

"Why do you ask?"

"We can move it out of here. Take it somewhere to get it open." She threw her arms up and let them drop. "I don't know."

Katelyn understood why Beck couldn't trust anyone else with this. Trusting could be both dangerous to Katelyn and Beck, as well as to the person charged with opening the safe. She didn't need him to tell her again that getting the police involved at this juncture would only muddy the waters.

She was with him—they had to find some hard evidence, no matter how small, to support Beck's theories about Mia. That would help them stop the madness... and keep them safe. But, honestly, she was more worried about Ollie.

At some point, she feared this would come back to him—the most precious person in Beck's life. But she kept those words to herself. No doubt, he had already considered that even sending Ollie away wouldn't stop someone who was determined. In fact, with that thought in mind, she could almost wish that whoever was after the contents of the safe had already retrieved them. Maybe the danger would be over for them.

Beck had pressed his ear against the safe again. He was going to try figuring out the combination.

While he worked on the safe, she pressed her back against the wall and rubbed the tension in her shoulders.

She could hardly believe any of this was happening. If she told Ryan, he would insist she back away and drop the case. Ryan trusted her, but only to a point. He was protective, and she got that. He definitely wouldn't want her getting involved in something so cloak-and-dagger. And that was just it; Katelyn wanted to believe Beck with everything inside her. Sure, she'd been attacked in her own home, but that could be for the simple reason she'd seen the man behind the mask. That did not necessarily mean that car accident was something more.

It didn't mean that attacker was after the safe, or that Mia was a spy and someone had killed her.

Admittedly, all that could be in Beck's imagination. Beck believed it, and for now, that was good enough for Katelyn. She would work alongside him and push away the doubt.

But what if she was wrong? What if Beck was actually suffering from mental illness and he was clinically paranoid? She had to consider that reality. The Beck she'd spent the last day with appeared as lucid as anyone she'd ever met. He was strong and trustworthy. Loved his family. But was her heart simply wishing what he said was true because she'd been so hurt in the past?

She sighed. She was no professional if she allowed the events of her past to color her work so spectacularly. Regardless of professionalism, it was because of that hurt that she would do well to ignore her attraction to him—that strong emotional connection that bordered on being overwhelming, as well as that ping of energy that zinged through her every time she got too close. The attraction was nearly impossible to ignore.

But all things were possible with God, and—*God, help me*—with His help, she could resist Beck Goodwin.

An alarm sounded somewhere, only it was muffled. Was that coming from outside? Some other house?

Katelyn stiffened. "Beck, you hear that?"

"Quiet," he barked. "You know I can't do this if you're going to talk."

She doubted he could do it, anyway. They had both tried. They would never succeed in the safe-cracking business.

Katelyn headed for the steps out of the basement and as she neared the door, a pungent odor slammed her.

"Smoke, I smell smoke! Beck—it's the smoke alarms!"

He stumbled away from the safe, a deer-in-the-headlights look in his eyes. "Let's get out of here!"

Katelyn grabbed the knob and twisted.

The door was locked!

Beck's insides twisted into a tangled, painful knot. He could smell the smoke, too.

Please let it not be my house that's burning. Though wishing that on someone else wasn't something Beck wanted, either.

Katelyn stepped aside. Beck grabbed the doorknob and twisted. Stupid, stupid! He shook the knob until his hands ached. Frustration boiled up and he pounded on the door as if someone was on the other side and would come and help them. As if the person who had locked them inside would quickly unlock the door because Beck wanted out.

"What happened? Why won't it open?"

He ground his molars to keep from blurting out what he thought should be obvious to Katelyn, but maybe she didn't want to admit it and was hoping he would offer up another explanation for why they were locked in the basement. If he told her what he thought, he would only sound paranoid. He wanted Katelyn to come to her own conclusions, or at least be the first one to say what they were both thinking.

The only explanation was that they had been locked down here deliberately. Whoever locked them in had also set the house on fire.

"Beck, why don't you answer me? What are we going to do?" Katelyn's panicked voice yanked back his focus.

"Give me a second."

He pressed the heels of his palms into his eyes. Why was this happening? If the attacker couldn't get at the safe, then he didn't want anyone else getting into it, either, and discovering the contents. That had to be it. But again, if he said those words out loud he would sound like he'd lost his grip on reality...even to himself.

None of that mattered at this moment. Fear swelled in his chest and he glanced at Katelyn. He couldn't stand to see that same fear reflected in her eyes.

"It's going to be okay. We're going to get out of here." He projected a confidence he didn't feel as he bounded down the steps.

"Oh, yeah? How?" Katelyn was right behind him.

He searched through the construction materials. Plywood and tools. Hammers, nails, screwdrivers. Power tools. Brooms, mops and rakes clustered together in a corner.

That was it.

He stepped over boxes and a power saw and searched the random tools for one in particular.

An ax. The was the tool of firemen. Beck gripped the old rusty thing he'd found in the basement when he'd cleaned it out, grateful he hadn't tossed it yet, thinking it had no value for him.

Beck lifted the ax and stared at the rusted head. "This should work."

Alarms continued to sound in the house. He hoped the fire department was already here and dousing the place with water, and that firemen were already working their way through the house to see if any unfortunate soul had been caught inside and was unconscious on the floor.

He glanced at beautiful Katelyn. He would not wait

in hopes they would be found in time. He couldn't trust that the fire department had been called at all. Clara, the neighborhood watchdog, could be visiting her son, out for dinner with friends, or running an errand.

Katelyn's eyes widened when he lifted the ax and turned toward her.

"Move out of the way."

She quickly moved out of his path as he ran back up the steps. The door was at a landing at the bottom of another set of stairs. "I'll try to hack open the door, but we can't be sure we'll find a way out."

There, he'd told her the truth. He hadn't sugarcoated their options.

"Okay. You do that. I'll try to break open one of the windows and call for help since our cells are useless down here."

Creating an escape window, bringing all the windows to code, had been on his to-do list. This older home had no such window.

Sweat beaded at his temples as he lifted the ax and drove the rusty blade into the thick wood, glad this door wasn't galvanized steel like his front door. The ax landed in the wood, the action jolting him all the way up his arms to his shoulders. He'd splintered a portion of the door.

He lifted the ax and continued hacking at the door, creating some cracks. The blare of the smoke alarm, no longer muffled, now emphasized their treacherous predicament.

Now that he thought about it, he hadn't closed the door while they were down here, and he didn't think Katelyn had, either. The idea that someone had crept through the house and down the steps to shut the basement door—and lock it—without them even being aware chilled him to the core. Ignited his fury.

He wouldn't let whoever was after this safe hurt Katelyn.

Beck chopped, chopped, chopped at the door. Wood splintered everywhere, but he kept chopping.

"Beck. Beck… Beck!" Katelyn's voice broke through the chaos in his mind.

Panting for breath, he dropped the ax at his feet on the top step, along with pieces of wood.

"The door is dead," she said. "No need to keep hacking."

He stared through the hole he'd opened up in the door at the glowing landing. "I'm not sure we can get out this way."

There were no good options.

Beck needed to pray. He was angry and hurt, and he didn't feel like he could face the Almighty in that condition, but now he was also desperate.

Lord, please help me save her!

"Help! Can someone hear me? Help us!" Katelyn was still at the window. She shouted through the opening that was much too small to escape out of.

But how could anyone help them, even if they heard her cries? Beck was done deliberating about what to do next. It was time for action, so he went back down the steps.

"We have to face the flames, Katelyn. It's the only way. I'll go up and check it out first."

Katelyn grabbed his arm. "No. You can't."

"I can't let you die here."

EIGHT

Beck shrugged out of her grip. Katelyn watched, dis-
believing, as he clomped up the steps toward the hacked
open door. He carefully stepped through the jagged,
splintered opening.

"Beck, wait! Please don't go up there."

He glanced over his shoulder and peeked back
through the opening, looking as if he didn't expect to
see her again. Then he continued rising up the stairs
until he disappeared into the smoke-filled, glowing,
crackling house.

"Are you crazy?" she shouted.

The words had slipped out before she'd caught them.
But he was definitely crazy. Still, they had no choice
but to try to escape.

Katelyn had no idea if this was the way to go about
it, nor did she have the time needed to figure it out. The
fire was eating away at the house and getting closer to
taking their lives. If they stayed in the basement, eventually the roof above would cave in on top of them—that
is, depending on how out of control the fire had gotten.

If the fact that she was already drenched in sweat

was any indicator, she might only have a few more moments to live. And in that case, she would die trying.

Here goes nothing. Or everything.

Katelyn took one step forward.

Lord, You say when I pass through the waters, You will be with me. When I pass through the rivers they won't sweep over me. So now when I pass through the fire, I will not be burned. The flames will not set me ablaze. Let that be true right now. Please protect us!

She took another step. Then another, repeating the verses in her head to give her strength.

Smoke had engulfed the stairwell up to the first floor, and she stepped through the splintered door, into the thick layer of toxic, noxious air.

"Beck!"

Katelyn coughed, but fear choked her even more. Her knees shook. She couldn't go any farther. To do so would mean her death. Beck... Was he already dead?

Pain exploded in her heart at the thought. Why had he gone up there? To try to save her? Beck had tried to save them both, but he couldn't have survived.

Katelyn's knees shook and she couldn't breathe.

Oh, Lord... When I pass—

Just as she thought she would crumple, a blanketed form rushed out of nowhere toward her. The blanket lifted.

Beck. The strong mountain-climbing man had returned. He yanked the blanket from his body, revealing another blanket underneath, and wrapped her in it before she could protest. The blanket was cool and wet. He kept the other one over himself.

Still, she tried. "Wait! What are you doing?" Coughs racked through her again. No more words could come from her raw, hoarse throat. Beck coughed, too. Neither of them could talk about this until they were out of here.

Wrapped like this, she wasn't going anywhere, so she stopped fighting. He'd wrapped her before she had a chance to comprehend what he was doing and act on it.

Beneath the wet blanket over his head, he'd covered his mouth and nose with a scarf, and his gaze pierced hers. Fear boiled behind his gray eyes. Fear and determination.

If anyone could get them out of this, Beck was the one person to do it. Beck covered her face, then grabbed her up into his arms and held her against his chest as he climbed back up the stairs. She was wrapped in a cold, wet cocoon.

She buried her face in the blanket and squeezed her eyes shut. Willing Beck to get them out. Willing them to be okay. Willing strength into his limbs and breath into his lungs.

Thank You, God. Beck is the one You sent to walk us through the fires.

She pushed down the panic and calmed her breathing. He was risking his life for her to get her out of here. Pops and cracks filled her ears and closed in on her from every side. Even the cold, wet blanket grew warmer as Beck held her tight against his lean, strong physique, grunting and groaning and coughing. She sensed the tension and anguish rippling through him as he tried to find them a way out.

Fear engulfed her—were they doomed from the start?

Suddenly Beck seemed to stumble. Katelyn braced herself for crashing against a flame-lit wall, but Beck rushed forward. Glass shattered and he tumbled to the ground, then rolled to protect Katelyn. Still, they hit the ground hard and pain ignited through her body as the limited air in her lungs rushed away.

But it was nothing—relief filled her. They were out of the house. Out of the fire and certain death.

Beside her, Beck coughed and hacked.

Her eyes burned and she couldn't open them. She wanted to see him. To see that he was okay and not burned or injured. But she was powerless to unwrap herself. Katelyn drew in the fresh air. Though it smelled smoky, it was certainly not toxic, like what they'd encountered in the house.

"A little help here?" She croaked out the words, sounding weak and feeble.

Rough hands dragged her away from the heat, and as she struggled, a fireman assisted her out of the blanket. He offered his hand and helped her to her feet.

"Ma'am." He tried to place an oxygen mask over her, but she pushed it away.

"Beck. Where is he?"

"Who?"

"The man who saved my life. He got me out of there."

The fireman shook his head. "I don't know. Someone had to have brought you out. You were wrapped like a burrito."

"Could he have gone back inside?" Concern overwhelmed her. Where had he gone?

"Is someone else in the house?" the fireman asked.

Water from a hose rained down on the house. "Not that I know of. I mean, his son is staying somewhere else…"

It hit Katelyn that she didn't know this man in the fireman gear. Maybe he wanted information. Now she was thinking like Beck—completely paranoid and suspicious.

Katelyn scrambled farther away and stared at the house engulfed in flames. Tears streamed down her cheeks.

"Are you okay?" The face asking the question didn't register. Then finally she realized her brother was the one shaking her shoulders. He'd replaced the fireman. "Katelyn, are you okay?"

"No. I mean, yes. But, Beck… He saved me. We think he might have gone back inside."

Apprehension carved deeper lines into Ryan's features, then a scowl formed. "Why would he do that?"

The safe…

But she kept that to herself. Telling Ryan wouldn't help either of them right now. What did any of it matter if Beck went back inside that house and died tonight?

Katelyn dropped to her knees and watched the flames amid the water spilling onto the disintegrating structure. An explosion boomed and light flashed. Ryan dropped to the ground next to her and held her. Together they watched the roof collapse.

The sky flashed, and she thought it was another explosion, but thunder rumbled. Drops of water hit Katelyn's forehead. She looked up, expecting to see a hose flying in the wrong direction.

"It's raining. Yes, it's raining, Katelyn." Ryan pumped his fist. "We haven't had rain in much too long. Thank You, God!"

She covered her eyes. "He saved me, Lord…" *He can't be dead. He just can't be dead.*

Arms gathered her against a broad chest and Katelyn let the rain join her tears.

"Katelyn, it's okay."

That voice. His voice. She pushed back from that chest to look up into Beck's gray eyes, rivulets of rain washing down his face.

She had thought Ryan was comforting her. She glanced around and spotted him now talking to a fireman. She focused back on Beck. "I—I thought you were dead. If you didn't go back into that house, then where did you go?"

He cupped her face and stared into her eyes, oblivious to the rain. The dying fire lit his drenched hair and face. Katelyn didn't care that others watched the two of them. At this moment in time, she only cared about Beck. She held the connection as long as she could. Life could be snatched away in milliseconds, and tragically. Or someone could give their life to save another's.

Katelyn had thought she'd lost Beck.

"I'm sorry I left you, Katelyn." He rubbed his thumb against her cheek. Emotion flared in his warm, searching gaze, which seemed to sweep through her soul. "Firemen had arrived. I knew you were safe. I skirted the houses to watch for myself."

She nodded. "You mean you were looking for the person who deliberately locked us in the basement and set fire to the house."

His lips smiled as a laugh burst from his chest. "Yes."

"You were worried I wouldn't track with you."

He nodded.

"And you wanted to hear me say it first."

He nodded and pressed his forehead against hers. Emotion welled in her heart—but from the near-death experience? From almost losing him? Or should she listen to the alarms going off in her head warning her that Beck Goodwin was eroding her protective walls?

A blaze consumed his home. Firemen doused the flames. Rain drenched them. Neighbors gathered. But none of it mattered. All of the events surrounding him seemed far away and down a long tunnel.

Heart pounding, he kept his head pressed against Katelyn's. Time seemed to stand still as Beck held on to the connection he had with this woman.

I could have lost her tonight.

She meant much more to him than just a hired private investigator. More to him than a neighbor or a close friend. Yes, she was a friend, a good, close friend, like he'd told Ollie. But more than that, Beck and Katelyn were kindred spirits, and more than anything he wanted to know her so much better. Why did he feel such a strong emotional connection with her? Why was he constantly dodging the magnetic attraction to her?

If only he could trust her with his heart. He wished he could get over his inability to trust, but Mia—even if unintentionally—had destroyed that part of him.

Suddenly the world around them crashed through the moment and broke them apart. He grabbed her hand and pulled her even farther away from the sizzling house and down the street where he'd parked. Beck tucked her into his vehicle, where she would be safe and warm. He reached for the door to shut it but she pulled him to her.

"Beck, I forgot to thank you. Thank you for saving my life. For saving us." Her hold on him drew him closer. He found himself millimeters from her face, from her lips that he knew would be supple, and fought the need to have them. He hesitated, wanting to know...

Then she met him halfway, and her soft lips pressed against his mouth. He wrapped his arms around her and savored her warmth, her beauty, both inside and out. She was everything he wanted but couldn't have.

A throat cleared.

Beck slowly released her, but he held her gaze. He was keenly aware her brother stood behind him. When he dropped his arms, she slid all the way into the truck and he closed the door. There. Now she was safe and warm.

He ignored Ryan's glare and jogged around to the other side of the truck. Ryan gripped his arm and whirled Beck to face him. "Where do you think you're going?"

Beck scraped his arm across his face to wipe the rain out of his eyes. "Trying to get warm, that's all. What's your problem?"

"You have a lot to answer for tonight. Your house just burned down. How do you explain that?"

"I can't explain it. Someone will have to investigate," Beck said. No way was he going to offer up his theories only to have them trampled, or be accused of being crazy again.

He could already hear that conversation in his head now.

It would go something like this:

"Why would someone try to kill you?"

"Because they think I'm going to discover what my wife was hiding. That she was a federal agent. Maybe CIA."

"Uh… Huh. And why do you think your wife was a spy?"

"She acted funny. Strange. I saw her with someone."

"Uh… Huh."

"I found a safe. She was hiding her secrets inside."

"Uh… Huh."

No, thank you very much. He'd tried with the police. If he was on the right track, he would find something to validate his suspicions and then the hard part would come—finding whom he could trust with the information to investigate Mia's death.

And right now…

His son. He had to think of Ollie. He had to keep his son safe.

And Katelyn.

Shame engulfed him. She was in this now and he couldn't help but blame himself.

"Believe me, someone is going to investigate." Ryan's tone was threatening.

"Ryan!" Katelyn had exited the truck and stepped between the two of them. "Beck saved my life tonight. He risked his own life to save mine."

"To be fair, we were both going to die," Beck added.

"Do we have to discuss this in the rain?" She shivered and wrapped her arms around herself, glaring at both of them.

Beck and Ryan both instinctively reached for her to wrap their arms around her, but collided. Beck pulled back and Ryan took the protective stance toward his sister.

Katelyn shrugged away. "Will you stop this, Ryan? I'm not a child."

"What were you doing in the house?"

Katelyn's eyes remained on Ryan's. She flinched but didn't glance at Beck, which would telegraph they held a secret between them. He didn't want Ryan asking too many questions.

"Back off, Ryan. The fire chief will investigate and then we'll know something."

He literally took a step back.

"Don't you have a date with your future wife tonight?" Katelyn asked. "Now, I'm cold and tired and shaken." She stepped close to Beck and wrapped her arms around him as if letting Ryan know they had a thing going, which they didn't, and yet, they did. Beck was getting confused, and he needed to avoid that confusion at all cost. But he understood that she was doing this to push Ryan away from their investigation.

Her brother lifted his hands in surrender and started to walk away, but gave Beck a warning look before he left.

Beck was duly warned—but not because he was afraid of Ryan.

No. He was more afraid of himself and how being with Katelyn affected him.

Still, that came second to keeping them alive so they could discover the truth.

NINE

Katelyn took in the scene and was stunned to see the protectiveness in Beck's eyes—protectiveness equal to her twin brother's. How could that be? She couldn't process it. Beck remained a statue, rain pelting him and dripping off him as if he was stone, while he watched her brother stalking away.

Time to redirect. She grabbed Beck's shoulders and turned him to face her. Turned his attention back to her. "Never mind him. Let's get in your vehicle and out of the rain."

She held his gaze until he seemed to shake off whatever darkness consumed him. "Right," he said. "Let's do that."

He ushered her around to the passenger side and opened the door for her. Not that he needed to, but Beck was a gentleman and Katelyn didn't want to stand in the way of that.

At some point, Beck had shifted from being not just her client, but a man bent on protecting her. Katelyn wasn't sure how she should handle that, but it wasn't like she could turn him down—he'd saved her life back there. And a few minutes ago she'd sent away her brother—her brother, who also wanted to protect her. She shook off the guilt. Ryan had meant well, but she didn't need the stay-away-from-her, big-brother act from him.

And… She hoped as she and Beck dug deeper into this mystery that she wouldn't need her brothers'—all of them—assistance.

Or Tori's. She and Ryan needed their wedding day to go off without a hitch.

Katelyn shuddered. *God, please don't let me be the weak link here. Just…let them get married.* She'd done her part to keep Tori in town so they could have another chance. The last thing she wanted was to be the obstacle in their path.

Beck opened the door, climbed in and slammed it. They were both soaking wet, and even though it was the end of the summer, it was chilly out. He turned on the vehicle and cranked up the heat. Beck reached into the back seat and grabbed a fleece hoodie. "Here, use this."

She shook her head. "No, it's yours. You're cold, too."

He ignored her suggestion and blanketed the hoodie over her. "We need to get out of here. Get somewhere safe. Except—" he shook his head and growled "—I want to get back into what's left of my house to get that safe. I can't believe after all this, we still don't have it or the contents inside."

"You can't go back in."

"Don't you think I know that?" He huffed. "I know I can't go looking around until they're done investigating."

"And not until the embers have cooled." She wanted to reach for him, but that was becoming much too comfortable. Katelyn was getting out of her depth with him. Crossing the lines she'd set. Instead, she wrapped her arms around herself beneath the fleece hoodie he'd thrown over her. "I'm so sorry, Beck. I don't know what else to say or think."

As the heat warmed them, they watched the flow of water from the fire truck hose finally stop, and the flames finally die out. Between the firemen's work and the skies opening up, the dragon had been slayed, and the fire destroyed. Charred remnants, blackened pillars and wet ash was all that remained.

Even the last of the neighbors who'd stayed out in the rain to watch finally returned to their homes.

Katelyn's heart ached at the sight, her emotions reeling from the roller-coaster ride. First fear, then relief, and now pain so deep she couldn't describe it. But they were alive, and for that she was also grateful.

"What am I going to tell Ollie?" The defeat in Beck's voice nearly broke Katelyn.

She made no attempt to answer his question.

If that wasn't enough, in the midst of the tragedy and loss, and the attempt on their lives, the intimate kiss they had shared fought for space in her mind and heart. The emotions had overwhelmed her. Maybe she'd always had a thing for him, deep inside, which had developed from the few times she'd interacted with him in the past.

But the question of her heart—could she love someone like Beck? After the kiss, she knew without a doubt that he was someone she could fall for. He was a good man, but right now they both had serious, life-threatening issues facing them.

But at the end of the day, even if they didn't, all she

had to do was picture Tony as she took those pictures for a husband who had hired her to find out who his wife was cheating with, and her stomach would instantly turn.

Reflexively, she leaned closer to the door and away from Beck. She couldn't trust anyone again, so would fight to keep her heart in check.

"Stay here," Beck said. "I'll go check with the firemen again to make sure it's okay for us to leave."

Katelyn should go, but it was Beck's house and she didn't want to face her brother. She hoped he had gone to his dinner date with Tori. Tomorrow night was the rehearsal dinner, and Katelyn would not ruin that for them. She would not be the reason for interruptions in their wedding plans.

Beck got back in the vehicle. "The rain helped the situation, but the house is still destroyed."

"What did they say?"

"They suspect arson. I could be a suspect. The fact that I was still in the home and saved you is in my favor, though. But they'll have to process through that. Someone will call me as soon as the fire chief has completed his investigation."

"In the meantime, we need to stay somewhere safe, Beck."

"I hope you're not suggesting your house, Katelyn. You've been attacked in your home, and it's only two houses away. I wouldn't consider that safe."

"Then where?" Because if Beck was right and Mia had been with an agency—like the CIA—then whoever they were battling could have resources, and in that case, nowhere was safe. Even staying at a hotel could signal their whereabouts to anyone who knew how to look.

But there was one place…

She snapped her fingers. "I know where we can go. We have a family lake house up by Shasta Lake. No one will be there. Why didn't I think of it before?"

"That's still connected to your family, Katelyn."

"Do you have a better idea? Because right now, I don't." She sighed. "Look, it's safe for now, even if only for a few hours, and will give us a chance to regroup."

Frowning, he subtly shook his head.

"I'm going to grab some dry clothes at my house," she said. "No one is going to bother us there. Too much going on in this neighborhood tonight." Katelyn hesitated, then said, "Oh, I'm sorry. What about you? You need dry clothes, too."

How could she be so insensitive?

Then his right cheek hitched with a dimple. "I've always got extras in the truck. With the climbing, I never know when I'm going to need a change of clothes. Well, that's not true. I usually always need a change of clothes."

"Yeah, well, you're going to need something nice enough to attend a rehearsal dinner tomorrow night for Tori and Ryan's wedding. I can't miss that, and I don't want…"

"Yeah?" He watched her, waiting for her to finish what she was going to say.

She had a feeling he already knew because this was becoming a thing with him—he wanted her to say the words.

"Okay, um… I don't want you to leave my side. And not for the reasons you think."

"What would those be?"

Her throat tightened. What was he going to think about her take on things? He might think it was all twisted up. "I'm protective of you, Beck."

There, she'd said it—only her words were the complete opposite of the truth. She wanted—needed—his protection.

As Beck parked in the driveway of the dark home by the lake, his protective instincts kicked up a thousand notches. He'd hired Katelyn partially under duress, and while she was an ex-cop and had all the skills, she had no idea how protective of her he'd become. He didn't want her putting herself on the line or in harm's way for him. If she hadn't done that to begin with, he would be in this alone.

That's where he should be. In this alone.

That would be safer for her, and safer for Beck—he felt the connection he had with her growing stronger each moment he was with her, despite his attempt to keep his heart stone-cold.

As he killed the lights on his truck, he turned to Katelyn. "Wait here. I'm going to check the perimeter."

She laughed.

"What's so funny?"

"I was the cop. I still have those skills, believe it or not, so let me do this."

"We'll do it together." He got out and walked toward the two-story home with a rocked front and a blue door. He figured the back was filled with windows for an amazing view of Shasta Lake. The family had some bucks somewhere, or maybe the home had just been in the family for a long time. Laughter echoed across the lake.

Above the evergreens, a few stars could be seen beyond the clouds moving out after having dumped their load on a dry Northern California.

Insect noises filled the night as he and Katelyn crept forward.

They both brandished weapons, and he hoped no one spotted them. Neighbors could misconstrue them as a threat to the homeowners. If the police were called, that could give them away to the assailant from whom they were hiding.

The home breaker. The killer. The arsonist.

His cell phone buzzed in his pocket. Retrieving it, he recognized the caller. "Mom, everything okay?"

"Yes. Ollie wanted to say good-night."

Ollie's voice burst through the cell. He said good-night to his son, his heart aching. He had no idea how he would break the news to Ollie about their home, or to his parents, either. Since they were camping through the weekend, he hoped this would all be resolved and he could tell them before they saw it on TV. He also hoped that the news he gave them would include letting them know the bad guy, Mia's murderer, was behind bars.

He ended the call and jogged to catch up to Katelyn. "I'm not sure this was such a great idea anymore."

"Neither am I, but we're here." She lifted a brick and found a key.

"You live in a family of cops and you guys keep an extra key under a brick?"

Without answering, she unlocked the door, then quickly moved to disarm the security system. At least they had one. He felt a little better.

She flipped on the lights and together they checked the house to determine if it was safe. No security breaches here. No walking into a break-in.

"I'll grab our bags." He plodded out to his truck, images of the fire chasing him. Thoughts of Katelyn in his arms, depending on him for their lives...and all because of that stupid safe.

And here he was, no better off for their efforts. Somehow he had to get his hands on the contents of that safe before someone else did. He couldn't be sure no one else had. And he couldn't be sure the safe was "fire safe," as most claimed.

When he returned, Katelyn was making coffee and grilled-cheese sandwiches. She flipped a blackened sandwich, scrambling to save it, and smiled up at him. Then her focus went back to salvaging the sandwiches. They were charred and he pushed images of his house out of his mind—easy enough, when he looked at her smile.

But he could tell the smile was forced. Her eyes lacked that sparkle, that I'm-every-woman determination that he admired so much. Her smile and the sandwiches were meant to offset the heaviness. They both needed levity. Too much had happened in a very short time.

He dropped their duffel bags on the plush sofa and looked around, admiring the spacious room, wood floors and brick fireplace. Cozy furniture. And beyond those big windows, he knew a big deck looked out over the water. He'd seen it on their perimeter check.

"I told you the place was stocked. I could have made something else, but this was quick and easy. Someone must have stayed here last weekend. The block of cheese was new and the milk was still good. Bread, too. So I'm making dinner. Oops—" she dropped the hot sandwiches on plates "—that was close. Sure they're a little burnt, but at least you don't have to eat on the floor."

"At least." In that moment, he found her utterly irresistible.

His stomach growled and she laughed.

She set the plates on the counter. Pushed a glass of milk toward him. "At least I know you like milk. I hope the sandwiches will do."

"This is great." He couldn't help his frown.

She arched an eyebrow.

"Sorry. I'm…" Something about sitting here and eating sandwiches felt all wrong. Beck should be doing something, but he couldn't exactly figure out what.

She rushed around to him. "You're in shock, Beck. You lost your home tonight."

"Someone tried to kill you again." He couldn't help himself—all the pressure of the last few days closed in on him from all sides, so he pulled her to him. He drew reassurance from her. He couldn't reconcile his emotions—the frustration that she was involved in this, and how grateful he was that she was involved in this.

He finally released her. "I don't know what came over me. Earlier tonight, I shouldn't have…" *Kissed you.*

"I get it. I shouldn't have, either."

She understood him then. It was uncanny how well she read him.

"Let's eat," she said. "Then you can take the loft upstairs and I'll keep watch."

"Wait a minute. I didn't hire you to protect me. I hired you to help me investigate."

"And so far, you're not letting me do much."

"You have to admit, we haven't exactly had a chance. Someone keeps trying to stop us." He stared at the black-crusted "grilled" cheese.

She scooted onto a stool and inhaled her food, oblivious to the blackened bread. If she could do it, then he could, too, and he finished, then chased it down with milk.

"As I was saying," she said. "Pick a room, I'll keep watch. It doesn't have to be the loft."

"We'll take turns then."

She frowned. "Okay. Arguing with you will just waste time. I'll take the first shift."

"You couldn't wait to get cleaned up and change into something dry and warm, remember?" He winked. "I'll take the first shift."

She'd been in a hurry and hadn't changed at home when she'd stopped to grab a few things. The small duffel she'd packed in hand, she headed down the hallway. She'd flipped on most of the lights when they'd cleared the home and now went through and turned half of them off. The house remained well-lit.

For a few moments, maybe even for the entire night, Beck could actually catch his breath.

A half an hour later, Katelyn had said good-night and chosen a bedroom near the living area so she wouldn't be too far in case he needed her.

Beck crept quietly around the home, checking windows again and again.

If he listened hard enough, he could still hear the party going on somewhere across the lake.

He hoped the raucousness was the only reason edginess skated across his nerves.

TEN

Katelyn bolted awake. Darkness surrounded her. No light shining in from under the door. She'd purposefully left on half the lights in the house so she should have seen at least a glimmer.

A chill crept over her that had nothing to do with the temperature. She couldn't see her hand in front of her face. Had Beck turned out all the lights?

She doubted it.

Had the electricity gone off?

Or was the worst-case scenario unfolding for them—had someone deliberately cut the power?

Katelyn hesitated. If she got out of bed, the sound could give her away. On the other hand, staying in bed didn't seem like a good idea, either. Fearing someone could be in the room with her already, she waited and listened, then tensed, ready to flee or pounce as necessary.

Then she heard a subtle breath. Panic spiked through her. She slowly eased the cover away to make her move.

"Beck?" she whispered.

"Yes." His reply was barely audible.

She sensed when he approached the bed. Heat emanated from his body—all that fat-burning metabolism, she supposed. Katelyn reached for her gun on the side table, then completely escaped the blankets. Beck found her hand and squeezed. She held onto him so they wouldn't get separated in the darkness. The clouds must have covered the moon. Absolutely no light leaked through the windows.

Katelyn bit back her need to ask if Beck had seen or heard something. But his actions should confirm her suspicions—the power had been deliberately shut off.

The attacker had found them here at her family lake house. Followed or tracked them somehow—but he was here with them now *in* the house. She fought the shudder that rippled over her.

Was her would-be killer wearing night-vision goggles so he could see them while they walked around blind?

A thousand thoughts raced through her mind. What had the man after them planned for them? Still gripping her hand, Beck started to head out of the bedroom, but she pulled him back in and quietly shut the door. She tugged him to the far corner of the room near the window and leaned close. "No, Beck. We're walking blind out there. He'll see us before we see him."

"Flashlights?"

"He would follow the light."

"What's your plan then?"

Her voice trembled. "I don't know. We could climb out the window instead of going through the house."

"Someone could be out there watching for our escape. Someone could be out there *and* someone could be in the house." His warm breath fanned her cheeks.

"I'm calling 911."

"Go ahead," he said, "but you didn't wait for the police to arrive before bursting into my home."

"Because they wouldn't get there in time." Katelyn bit her lip. She would call for help but they had to rely on themselves to survive.

"Exactly."

"Then let's go out the window. We'll take our chances outside." She felt her way forward and prayed the moon would come out. "You go first, Beck. I'll have your back if he comes into this bedroom."

"It's a risk either way you look at it. You're going out the window first. Just be quick about it." He quietly opened the window, then removed the screen, which unfortunately creaked.

They both froze.

Three muffled gunshots fired through the door. Katelyn stifled her scream.

Beck and Katelyn returned fire.

"Go, go, go!" he shouted and practically tossed her through the window.

Someone kicked the door open as she fell into the bushes.

Bullets flying, Beck dove through the window and rolled through the bushes. Pain ignited like fire as a branch scraped across his back, arms and legs.

Or had that been bullets? Probably not, or he'd feel much worse if he survived at all.

"Beck! Let's go." Katelyn gripped his arms and pulled him to his feet. He stumbled against her, then found his legs and ran.

"Run!" She spoke in hushed tones, but if there had been anyone outside watching the house for their escape, they were dead. He hoped they'd made the right decision.

They were about to find out.

A sliver of moon had broken through the gathering clouds, exposing them and yet lighting their way. They headed for the shadows in the trees that edged the north side of the house.

Her gun ready to use, Katelyn took the lead—she knew the area and Beck didn't. All that mattered was that they got away from the house and the bullets. But neither did they want to run right into someone else who might be watching and waiting.

So far, their attacker seemed to be working alone. But he doubted that with all that was going on, it was a one-man job.

"Whoa." Gasping for breath, Katelyn skidded to a stop. "The lake. I thought we had a few more yards."

Beck gasped for breath and tugged her behind a tree. The moon reflected off the water and he could see the breadth of Shasta Lake, mountains all around. Lights flickered from houses all along the edges of the lake and in the hills. "And I thought we were headed for the woods, not the lake."

Water lapped and he heard it over and over again in his mind. Remembered diving into the water after Mia's vehicle. He had to think about their current life-and-death situation. Stay away from that part of the nightmare from the past.

"I think we should make that 911 call now," he whispered.

"Yeah, about that. I grabbed my gun. Not my phone."

He inwardly groaned. "I dropped mine in the bushes." Weren't they a promising team?

"Then let's head to a neighbor's house and call."

"And away from the water. The neighbor lives away from the water, right?" He should never have agreed to come to a lake house.

"Wait." She tugged him to the ground. "I see him. He's heading this way. I'm going to sneak around behind him. It doesn't look like he's wearing night-vision goggles so he won't be able to see me if I stay hidden."

"And what are you going to do after you sneak around behind him?"

"Apprehend him."

She made to move away and he gripped her wrist. "Katelyn, you're not a cop anymore."

"I can make a citizen's arrest."

He ground his molars as he forced the words out, hoping she would hear the warning in his tone. "You're not going to get that far. He's... He's a trained assassin." *And you might have been a cop at some point, but that was before and now you're a private investigator who is unprepared to face off with an assassin.* The words were truth, but they might hurt her, so he kept them to himself for the moment.

He pressed her down into the grass. Both of them were flat against the cold wet ground. Water sloshed near his feet. The man crept around the edges of the yard, his silhouette barely visible. The moon disappeared behind the clouds again. The security light from the nearest neighbor's house was like a distant twinkling star and offered no real illumination other than to reveal the stalking silhouette.

"He's getting closer." Katelyn's whisper was hard to hear. "He'll see us if we try to get away now. But... I have an idea."

He had a feeling he wasn't going to like it.

"We can slowly slide into the water and hide there. We could quietly swim our way to safety."

Water. *God, please, not that.*

"If we're going to do this without him hearing, we have to do it now. Time is running out."

Grass rustled behind Beck, drawing his attention. Katelyn was already sliding toward the water. It sloshed up against his ankle, cold and wet.

Oh. His chest constricted. He couldn't catch his breath. Then, he heard no sound other than the lake water lapping against the shore or the grass, wherever it touched.

Katelyn had been right to submerge herself in the water. Would the assassin think to look for them there? It seemed their only choice, but fear kept him paralyzed. He was an idiot. A real idiot.

He could climb mountains and hang on to rocks hundreds of feet from the ground without ropes or gear, completely free-handed, and he was going to let some dark, black-as-night water scare him?

It wasn't as much fear as it was that terror reigned in the depths. Mia... She'd been alive when he got to her, but she'd drowned before he could get her out of her car. She'd been pinned.

He hadn't told Katelyn that part. She'd been murdered, but Beck had been the one to fail her. To let her die.

No one but him, and God knew the truth. His throat grew dry. Now wasn't the time to panic. The slightest movement drew his attention.

He glanced up and could no longer see the skulking silhouette of their pursuer.

The hair on his neck rose. Instinct kicked in and he rolled. Two muffled gunshots sounded at the same moment bullets pumped into the earth. Bullets meant for him.

Beck dove forward, slamming into the assailant, and knocked the gun from him. The man was lightning-fast and punched Beck, knocking him back, and he splashed into the inky black water. Before he could right himself and pull his head up to breathe again, the man was on him, pushing his torso, his face, into the water that could kill. The water that had killed his wife, in the end.

This wasn't the same man he'd fought in his home, or pulled from attempting to smother Katelyn. This man's body was taut and lean. He was more agile. Beck fought for purchase. Anything. His lungs were on fire. One suck on water and he would be gone.

Ollie… Oliver. His baby. His son… He had to live for Ollie.

Water. Blackness. Death surrounded him. His lungs screamed.

Air rushed from his lungs. His body writhed, fighting for air, but he fought back.

If he breathed he would drown.

ELEVEN

Treading water, Katelyn turned around when she sensed Beck wasn't following and peered at the darkness—where the water met the grassy shore was completely black. She thought they'd been in agreement that slipping into the lake was their next move. But she had thought wrong. Beck had been acting funny about the lake—was he afraid of water? Nah, that couldn't be it.

She'd willed him to follow her out, but instead the thumping sound of bullets that erupted from a suppressor had her swimming back for Beck.

The lake remained choppy and her muscles screamed with the effort to swim back to him. Now closer to the house, she spotted the dark shape of a man. His form and movements told her this man wasn't Beck—it was the assassin. He was in the water and was trying to drown Beck. His arms were thrusting into the water and he rocked, fighting to win.

Beck! Her heart stuttered. She had to draw the man's attention.

"Hey! Hey, you! Over here!" she shouted and gasped for breath as she continued swimming for him. *God, please help me make it in time!*

Her feet touched the bottom and she sloshed closer and lifted her weapon. "Stop, or I'll shoot."

Images accosted her. Tony with a gun to his head. Katelyn should have taken the shot. Tony could have died. Someone else, another officer, had taken the shot because Katelyn had been a coward.

Beck would die…

Katelyn fired a warning shot. "The next shot will be in the center of your chest! Let him go. Raise your hands in the air so I can see them."

Though if the man moved she wasn't sure she would be able to see him, dressed in black, as he was on this dark night.

The man lifted his hands. Beck rose from the water, dragging in breath.

And the attacker dove into the inky black water. She couldn't see him. Katelyn aimed her weapon all around. "Hey! Come back here. You're under arrest!"

Then she spotted his form cutting through the dark lake until finally he made the shore and sprinted away.

How long would it be before he came back? As much as she hated to admit it, she'd have to deal with him later. He wasn't going to go away into the night never to return. Katelyn splashed through the water, her shoes heavy and weighed down, shoving as fast as she could until she found Beck. She plopped down next to him and grabbed him in a fierce hug. His body shivered and tensed, the anger pulsing through him.

She gasped for breath, as did he. *I could have lost you tonight.* "Let's get you out of the water and somewhere safe. Somewhere dry."

He shook his head. "He's probably searching for his gun. Let's get out of here before he takes us out this time. Your first plan—to swim to safety—was the best. I—I shouldn't have hesitated."

He started swimming, and Katelyn didn't waste time. She followed, but her limbs were already growing tired. The water this time of year wasn't too cold so at least they had that going for them. Katelyn swam behind Beck. She twisted to float on her back and then continued swimming on her back. But her arms ached. She didn't know how much farther she could go.

"Beck," she called. "Beck!"

When he didn't answer her heart rate kicked up. She tried swimming on her belly again.

"You okay?" he asked. She'd thought he'd left her behind.

"No. Let's head for the neighbor's pier. I'm not going to make it farther." Together they swam toward the nearest neighbor's home.

Heading in that direction was a risk. They could run in to their assailant there. The assassin could guess that was their next stop because they couldn't swim farther. She certainly couldn't. Though Beck hadn't wanted to take this route, he was a strong swimmer and could apparently outswim her.

As they approached the pier, she tried to search the yard and the shadows in the trees. A security light offered illumination. Maybe the man had given up for tonight.

Please let it be so. Please let it be so. God, please let him just go away.

She continued to repeat the silent prayer while she focused on keeping her pace and just getting to that pier.

Her family had spent many summers—reunions and spontaneous get-togethers—at their Shasta Lake house. Katelyn loved water sports, and before tonight, had thought herself a decent swimmer. But it had been a while and she was out of shape. Water skiing didn't require her to be able to swim across the lake.

Her muscles grew sore and tired until she had no more strength.

Katelyn slipped beneath the water.

The pier was a mere twenty yards ahead of them. Only a little bit farther. They were almost there. They were going to make it.

Beck had that weird sense that something was wrong. He paused to listen. The gentle splashing of Katelyn swimming behind him had stopped. He whirled around.

She'd been right there. Now she was nowhere.

"No, God, help me!" He swam quickly to the last place he'd seen her, sucked in a breath and dove for her. Once again, he couldn't see a thing. He waved his arms back and forth and…

There. He felt something. Skin. An arm. A hand? But it disappeared.

Mia's face came into his mind. Her eyes had been filled with fear as he attempted to free her. He'd let her down.

He focused on Katelyn and propelled his body in that direction, diving deeper and waving his hand around until he found purchase, then he gripped a hand.

I've got you, Katelyn. Don't let go.

He had her. He kicked until he surfaced with Katelyn. Beck didn't stop there. He didn't wait to have a conversation or a vote on what they should do next, and instead swam with her toward the pier.

Heart pounding, he gave a few good last kicks. Almost there…

Finally they gripped the pier's edge. Beck pushed Katelyn up, hyperaware that their pursuer could be waiting to take the next shot. But their options were few and the worst-case scenarios—drown or be killed by a bullet—didn't change that.

He joined her on the pier and tugged her to him, but his body had no warmth to give her. Together they rose and carried each other onto the grass and into the yard toward the neighbor's home. More security lights suddenly lit up the entire backyard.

They were an easy target.

Then again, the light chased away the shadows and potential hiding places for the man after them.

At the sliding glass door at the back, Katelyn pounded. A window treatment blocked them from seeing inside the home.

"Help. We need help!" she shouted.

"Are you sure this isn't just a vacation home, empty like yours?" He kept his back to the house, watching their surroundings.

"If it's the same neighbor who's lived here for years, she should be home." Katelyn pounded again. "Mrs. Kowalski, please, it's Katelyn. I need your help."

A gray-haired woman pulled back the curtain and opened the sliding glass door. "Why, Katelyn, what in the world? Come here. Come inside." She urged them in, patting them on the shoulders as they passed. "What's going on?"

"Thank you so much for your help." Long hair soaking wet and body dripping water on the tile, Katelyn stood in the room and hugged herself. "I need to use your phone so we can call the police."

Without more questions, the woman handed Katelyn a landline. Katelyn started to punch in the numbers. "Um… Mrs. Kowalski, there's no dial tone."

Katelyn shared a look with Beck.

"Can I use your cell?" he asked.

Mrs. Kowalski disappeared for a few moments, then returned. She handed her cell phone over to Beck. A crease deepened between her eyebrows. "What's this about?"

Limiting her answers, Katelyn explained the possible danger, while Beck called 911. How he appreciated his neighbor Clara's watchful eyes. The police would already be here by now if any of this was happening in their own neighborhood. Except Clara's watchdog approach wasn't a foolproof protection plan, since his home had been turned to ash.

He kept Dispatch on the line and spoke to Katelyn. "Let's find a safe place to wait in the house until the police get here. I'm concerned if the phone line was cut, the power will be—"

The house went dark.

Mrs. Kowalski yelped.

"It's going to be okay." Beck suspected that Katelyn's words were meant for herself as much as for Mrs. Kowalski. "Do you have a safe room?"

"Are you kidding me?"

"Unfortunately, I'm not."

His eyes adjusted and he realized a small light was shining from a plug in the corner.

Mrs. Kowalski noticed his glance. "In case the power goes out."

"Smart."

"You get her somewhere safe, Katelyn."

He braced himself for her counter-argument, but she

said nothing. He figured she probably felt a measure of guilt for bringing the danger to her neighbor's door.

But this was all on Beck, and he would end it.

"We'll head for the closet in the back bedroom," Katelyn said. "I used to hide in there with your kids when we were little."

The woman followed Katelyn as she ushered her away.

Now, Beck needed a weapon. He grabbed a butcher knife from the block.

He would be bringing a knife to a gun party, as the saying went. His only advantage would be one of surprise.

Beck chose a position in the shadows behind a large leafy plant. Waited. Watched and listened.

He had no idea how long it would take before law enforcement arrived, but a lot of harm could be done in ten seconds or less, so he would not wait for them to save the day. He hadn't waited for them to "save the day" for a year now. Nor had he wanted to involve them now, except this time bullets could be retrieved. There was at least proof that someone was trying to get to him, and now, Katelyn.

Even so, the cogs of an investigation would move much too slowly, and he would continue to retain Katelyn's services to get to the bottom of this.

Red and blue lights flashed in the windows as sirens rang out. They'd come faster than he would have thought, for which he was grateful.

Someone pounded on the door. "Police! Please open the door."

Beck stepped from his hiding place, dropping the knife in the plant, then opened the door.

Ryan Bradley scowled at him.

TWELVE

Katelyn tossed and turned in the comfy bed. She couldn't remember the last time she had been so utterly exhausted. She was in the extra bedroom at Tori's home—the house that had once belonged to Tori's deceased sister, Sarah. After giving their statements in separate rooms at the sheriff's offices in the county seat of Rainey, Beck and Katelyn had been released to go.

They had tried to avoid this scenario—bringing others into the mix—but they'd failed on that count. Still, Katelyn planned to be all about damage control. She and Beck could continue their investigation without giving away too much information.

Tori had insisted that Katelyn spend the night with her, while Ryan had said Beck could stay at his house. At least they had somewhere to go, but she worried about Ryan and Tori's safety. Sheriff's deputies had been assigned to each house to make sure anyone with harmful intent stayed away. Katelyn worried about those deputies, too, though.

Like Beck said, this person was an assassin, though if he'd been at the top of his murderous game, they would already be dead. She was honestly surprised that she and Beck had survived this long.

The very last thing she'd wanted was to pull her family into this and put them in danger. But there had been no choice except to call the police last night...and Ryan hadn't been far. He'd been shadowing them. Following them long enough to know she had chosen to stay at the lake house. Unfortunately he hadn't clued into their more dangerous shadow. But Ryan had remained close and that had saved them, and probably Mrs. Kowalski's home, from a few bullets. Maybe even saved her life.

While she was glad for Ryan's help, she felt bad at the same time. He'd canceled his date with Tori—because of Katelyn. She rubbed her eyes. Now they were all in this and she didn't know how to get them out. She had every intention of following through with her responsibility to Beck, regardless of an active police investigation, and despite the fact that Ryan had asked her to stay out of it.

He wasn't the detective in charge, anyway.

Oh, God, show me what to do. I don't know what to do.

A soft knock came at the door. "Can I come in?" Tori asked.

"Sure." Katelyn started to rise, but then dropped back against the pillow. She so did not want to get up to face this day.

Holding a breakfast tray, Tori entered.

Katelyn propped up on her elbows. "What are you doing? Trying to make me feel guilty?"

Tori sat on the edge of the bed and put down the tray as Katelyn fluffed her pillows and pushed up to a sitting position.

"Of course not." Tori scrunched her face. "You've had a rough go of it." Then her frown deepened. "I'm worried about you."

Katelyn shifted in the bed. She wasn't ready to talk about any of it, so she redirected. "Tori, please. If anything, I should be bringing *you* breakfast in bed. You're getting married soon. Your rehearsal dinner is tonight." The wedding wasn't for another two days, but schedules being what they were, the dinner to practice had to be tonight. "I'm so sorry about everything."

"There's nothing to apologize for, Katelyn. This isn't your fault. Evil happens. Bad guys will always exist. That won't stop just because Ryan and I are getting married."

Katelyn sipped on the orange juice. "Well, I had hoped you would have a small reprieve—time away from the evil in this world, ya know? At least you need time to put some distance between you and crime investigations." Katelyn released a heavy sigh and stared at the breakfast Tori had made. Pancakes, bacon and eggs. She'd gone out of her way. "I've not only taken on a case, but now it's encroaching into all our lives."

"Yes, it is." Tori scrutinized Katelyn. "I wish you would have told me about this from the start."

Guilt again. Katelyn sent her friend and partner a sheepish glance. "I hope you understand why I kept it from you. I want you and Ryan to focus on your wedding and not worry about me."

"Well, maybe we can resolve this together so that we won't have to worry. I know that you would never retract your agreement with Mr. Goodwin, nor would I ask you to. I understand that you're a witness to the crimes, so even retracting the agreement wouldn't change your involvement in this… Whatever it is." Tori stood, then leaned in to hug Katelyn. "Take your time. You're my maid of honor. We're going to retrieve your dress and accessories from your house today to make sure that it's all safe, and then we head to the spa."

Tori fisted her hands on her hips as if daring Katelyn to refuse a day away from the chaos.

"Hey." Katelyn threw her legs over the bed. "I'm the one who is supposed to be treating *you* to this." Tears threatened. "I had planned—"

"Don't beat yourself up, Katelyn. I know how it is. You're obsessed with your job. You're zeroed in on getting the bad guys. Crime doesn't wait for us to have a spa day." Tori smiled. "You can be real with me, remember? That's why we're so close. That, and well, you're my future sister-in-law. Don't worry about whatever you thought you wanted to do for today. The best-laid plans usually get sidetracked, anyway. We're going to have the best spa day we can, and then if we get a call about something pertaining to Beck Goodwin's case, we'll handle that as it comes. But for now, he's with Ryan, so you don't need to worry."

"That's exactly why I need to worry. You know Ryan and Beck won't be having a spa day together. Ryan will not be treating Beck to anything but glares and lectures."

After a shower, Beck dressed in the clothes that Ryan had grabbed from his own closet and shared with him. Though they were a little tight on Beck, he had just lost everything he owned when his home burned. All the memories—the photographs lining the hallway and in the many albums Mia had kept of family times and

Ollie. Any keepsakes she'd kept that he hadn't gone through yet because he had wanted to leave the house as it was when she'd passed. He'd been such a coward not to try harder. Not to face all of this sooner.

But last night when the fire erupted, he'd had the courage to keep them alive. Keeping Katelyn safe had driven him, allowed him to push aside the reality of his painful losses long enough to get them through. But now she was in someone else's hands and the roar of the fire razing his home echoed in his mind. At the moment, he was no longer distracted by the need to survive, so the images accosted him.

He sank onto the edge of the bed. Elbows on his knees, he covered his face. Any moment and dry sobs might rock through him. Who knew, maybe he would shed actual tears.

He had thought himself strong but the mystery behind Mia's death, the search for answers, was more brutal than he could have imagined. Somehow he had to pull himself together. He was responsible for starting this search for the truth, which in turn had disturbed the dragon's lair. Beck would not be denied the truth and he would see this through. It had cost him Mia and now his home. What more would it cost him?

The floor creaked, which made him pull his thoughts to the present. The last place he wanted to be at the moment was Ryan Bradley's home. The man knocked on the door once, then opened it.

Arms crossed, he stood in the doorway. "You look the worse for wear."

Beck huffed, but remained where he sat. He hadn't mustered the energy to face off with Katelyn's brother, who was also a detective. He needed the man on his side, at least, at some point.

Finally, Beck rose to look Katelyn's twin brother in the eyes. Ryan was concerned about his sister and Beck couldn't fault him for that. "Look, I appreciate you letting me stay in your home last night." More like insisted that Beck stay, and since he had nowhere else to go, especially since he needed to keep his connection with Katelyn, he had agreed. "But I should get going now."

"Where would you even go?"

"What does that matter to you?"

"It matters because you're in danger and you dragged my sister into this. As much as I don't want to admit it, I think she might have a thing for you. Even if she didn't, I can't let something happen to you. So unless you have a good, safe place to go, you can just stay here at my house."

Beck had been afraid the man would say that. Ryan didn't have a lawful right to keep him here in his home, but he wasn't using that angle. He was using Katelyn. Beck would have done the same thing. He *was* doing the same thing, as it were.

"Fine. But I need to do something. I can't just sit around. It's a waste of time." Beck started doing his incessant pacing in the small room. He hated it was here rather than in his own kitchen. The kitchen where he made Ollie's Mickey Mouse pancakes every Saturday morning. The kitchen where he and Mia had spent evenings cooking together—Beck had enjoyed letting Mia teach him how to cook. The living room where Ollie had taken his first steps. And on and on. The memories could crush him.

Ryan cleared his throat. "I promise, this won't be a waste of time."

Beck allowed Ryan's voice to bring him back to the present. He needed to live in this moment and not the past. Later he could think about what he'd lost, but he still had Ollie to protect, as well as others.

"Aren't you getting married today or something?"

Ryan smirked. "In two days. Tonight's the rehearsal dinner. Katelyn is the maid of honor. She is going to be at that dinner tonight. Tori is going to see to it. And I'm going to make sure you're there, too."

"Me? What have I got to do with it?" Though Katelyn had insisted that he attend with her. That was before they'd been separated, like children.

"Look, just work with me here, okay? I don't want to have to worry about my sister or my future wife. If you're there, then I won't have to worry."

Beck thought about throwing out "What's in it for me?" but that wouldn't be wise. He wanted Katelyn to be safe, too. He and Ryan were on the same team.

"Aren't you concerned for Katelyn's safety if I'm there? Or even if I'm not? Someone tried to kill her and not just once."

"We have law enforcement on the houses, and they'll be at the dinner *and* the wedding."

"Can you afford that kind of contingency? Don't you have a big county to cover?"

"As far as I know, you're the only two people who have allegedly been attacked."

"There you go, using police speak again." And it sounded an awful lot like the past, when he couldn't convince them his wife had been murdered.

"So please humor us all and come to the rehearsal."

Ryan dipped his chin, leveling his gaze on Beck. "For Katelyn's sake."

There he was using Katelyn again, knowing full well that Beck would comply. Beck shouldn't go. He should get back to the house and try to get to the safe before someone beat him to it. Maybe lead the assassin away from Katelyn, but the truth was, he couldn't do this alone.

"And just so you know," Ryan said, "Katelyn has two more brothers. Also in law enforcement. Reece is a special agent with the National Park Services ISB. The Investigative Services Branch. Then there's Ben, who was military police and is now a US Marshal."

"Is that a threat?"

"No. The point is that we have ample protection." Then Ryan smirked. "But you can take it as a threat if you want. Be ready to go in fifteen minutes."

"Where are we going?"

"I thought I'd make it my business to torture you today." Ryan sighed. "That wasn't fair. Sorry. You seem to think that's what I want, but honestly, I just want to help. Your house burned down. You need clothes and… much more."

Ryan sounded sincere, like he wanted to help Beck, but he was getting married. Starting a life with the woman he loved. Beck wouldn't get in the way of that. He wouldn't cause more trouble than he already had, even if indirectly.

"And it sounds like I need a decent suit to wear tonight."

THIRTEEN

Since Ryan had insisted a deputy accompany them today, Katelyn would try and relax a little. After all, it was broad daylight. They should be relatively safe. She watched Tori peel the cucumbers off her eyes.

Tori turned to stare at Katelyn, a funny look on her face. "I always wondered what this kind of pampering felt like. I decided that I'd try it because, hey, I'm getting married."

"Yeah. It was never my thing, either." Katelyn laughed. "Oh, I'm sorry. Were you saying it *is* your thing now and I misunderstood?"

"You didn't misunderstand." Tori snorted a laugh. "So… You can't stop thinking about him, can you?"

Tori sat up and began wiping the mud from her face.

"What are you talking about?" Katelyn rubbed a big white towel over her own face, though maybe she was supposed to use a wipe or something. Oops. She hoped she didn't mess up their towels. But what did she know? Nothing. Nada.

"Beck Goodwin. I'm talking about your neighbor. He's a looker. Kindhearted. Athletic. Seems to care about you."

Katelyn dropped the towel. "My only concern about him is regarding the case he hired me to help him investigate. I'm concerned that he has an assassin after him."

"I don't think this guy is an assassin."

Katelyn followed Tori to the showers and dressing rooms. "Why do you say that?"

"I mean, if he were actually an 'assassin'—" she used finger quotes "—you'd be dead, wouldn't you?"

"What do you take me for? I'm an ex-cop. And Beck—"

"Beck is what? He isn't trained as a cop. He wasn't military, was he? So how have you guys escaped this threat going on, what, four attempts now? I'm not buying that this man is a trained assassin."

"Well, I don't need you to buy it, Tori. I need you to stop thinking about my case and focus on my brother, okay?"

Tori approached Katelyn. "I want to focus on Ryan. It's my dream to think only of him, but you're in trouble."

"What are you going to do? Take me on your honeymoon with you?"

Katelyn's cell rang, jarring her. She snatched it from the counter without even glancing at the image. "Katelyn speaking."

"We heard from the fire chief," Ryan said. "We're good to go in and look for Beck's safe. And yes, he told me about it. I'm giving you a courtesy call on this. Detective Manning is still working it."

"Is—is—?"

"Yes. Beck's with me. He'll be there. Tell Tori I'll stop by and pick you up on the way to the house. She doesn't need to be involved."

Tori snatched the cell from her. "If you're going to be there, I'll be there."

Katelyn backed off. This had turned into her worst-case scenario. Her involvement was getting in the way of their wedding. She snatched back the cell.

"Ryan, let Manning handle this. You and Tori focus on each other. I don't want to be the reason you aren't, and I'll never forgive you if you make me that reason." Frowning, she was unsure if she was making any sense.

"Don't worry, sis. Both Ben and Reece will be here this afternoon. Tell Tori I love her, and I'll see her tonight."

He ended the call.

Katelyn looked at Tori. "Not sure if you heard that, but Ben and Reece will be here this afternoon and Ryan is handing me off to Manning and my other brothers, for lack of a better way to put it. He said he will see you tonight and that he loves you."

Tori twisted her lips into an uncharacteristic pout.

What would it be like to hear those words from someone she loved, and to truly be able to trust them? Would Katelyn ever know?

"Let's get back to your house so I can be ready. I promise I'll be back in time to help you dress for the rehearsal dinner. It'll be all right, Tori. I'll be all right."

Two hours later, Katelyn climbed from Ryan's county vehicle. Reece and Ben had been running late, so Ryan hadn't yet handed her off as promised, but Tori had been kept in the dark on that point. Just as well. "You shouldn't be working this week. You should take the entire week off." She was beginning to sound like a broken record and her brother wasn't listening.

He slid his gaze to her and said nothing. Just walked across the lawn to the charred remains, where Detective Manning and Beck waited on the edge of the burned-down home.

At the sight of Beck her heart pinged around inside. His build seemed to dwarf the detective's, but his demeanor revealed his anguish. He appeared defeated. Her heart ached at the sight. She wanted to rush up to him and hug him, but not with all the professionals looking on. She was supposed to be a professional, too, after all. He'd hired her as a private investigator, and look where that had taken them.

"Watch it. There are still a few hot spots. You can recognize them with the spirals of smoke." Detective Manning stood on the southwest corner at the back. "Mr. Goodwin tells me the safe should be right here."

"This is where I remember it," she said.

"Oh, so you saw it, too."

"Yes. I tried to break into it to help Beck."

He gave her a severe look. Yeah, maybe they had been messing with evidence. Actually, they were trying to get evidence enough to convince the police there was even a case.

"The house collapsed inward, most of it turned to ash. But from here, we can see down into the basement. We can see what's left of that wall." Manning marched around to the opposite side and everyone followed. "We'll get our guys in here to dig around, but..."

The detective hopped down.

"Watch out!" Ryan yelled.

A board snapped with Manning's weight. He was an older detective and an ornery know-it-all, and thought he knew what he was doing. Maybe he did. Katelyn was too exhausted to argue. She wanted to talk about all of it with Beck.

Alone.

Her mind was reeling with chaotic thoughts about

everything that had happened, and her heart ached for reasons that went beyond explanation.

Manning used a rod he'd lifted to move stuff around. Very scientific and evidence-preserving of him.

"Nothing. See? Here's the spot you say it should be."

Ryan crouched as he looked down into the exposed basement. "You can see the cutout in the wall where a safe would fit. The hole is blackened, but it's still there and… Empty."

Katelyn's heart pounded in her ears. She glanced to Beck.

His tanned skin seemed pale. "Someone took it in the night. Someone took it because you weren't watching the house. I told you to watch the house. I told you that someone was after that safe. And just like always, you didn't believe me."

"Look. I believe you," Manning said.

Ryan nodded. "We believe you, Goodwin."

"It's too late," Beck said. "The answers were in that safe. Your so-called help only made things worse."

"Beck," Katelyn said through gently clenched teeth. She approached him slowly. Per usual, he was a tiger waiting to pounce. She'd had that feeling before about him. He was wound too tight, and anger was getting the best of him. She peered up at his gray eyes, grown dark now, and saw the storm brewing there.

She spoke in low tones, so only he could hear her.

"I gave you the benefit of the doubt from the start. Now I need you to believe me. Don't worry. I'm here and we'll find the answers. But you can't take it out on these guys. You need them on your side." Katelyn held his gaze, pleading with him to dial down the tension, as if she had the power over him to control that.

"Well, now that they have what they want," Manning said, "maybe that means you're safe."

Katelyn still held Beck's gaze, and she saw in his eyes what she also suspected—they weren't safe now and depending on the contents of that safe, they could possibly be in even more danger.

That evening, Beck waited with Ryan at a fancy Italian restaurant in a private room where the rehearsal dinner was being held. Ryan and his family had participated in the wedding rehearsal earlier that evening. Upset over the loss of the safe, Beck had begged off and fortunately Ryan had acquiesced to his need for some alone time. He'd stayed at Ryan's house, a deputy guarding the place, while the wedding practice ensued. But Ryan had returned in an hour to get Beck for the dinner. Ryan insisted Beck couldn't miss that—Katelyn was expecting him there.

So here he sat, waiting for the rest of the wedding party to arrive. Apparently Tori had also wanted to change before dinner.

So he waited next to her detective groom-to-be, wondering how he found himself in this situation. Beck had once thought that if only the police would believe him and take him seriously, then his circumstances would greatly improve. Now they believed him, and that belief had changed nothing. He still had no answers, and Katelyn was still in danger.

Who was he kidding? He was still in danger, too.

A deputy had taken Tori and Katelyn home, and then would be escorting them to the restaurant. That let Beck know that Ryan didn't go along with his detective coworker's assessment that Katelyn was out of danger now that the safe had been taken. Ryan wouldn't leave his bride-to-be and sister unprotected.

Smart man.

Any other time, Beck thought he and Ryan could have been friends, but the man still didn't trust Beck. Two men approached the table where Ryan and Beck waited, and Ryan introduced him to his and Katelyn's brothers, Reece and Ben. Both sharp-looking men. Just how much of what was going on had Ryan shared with his brothers? By the expressions on their faces, everything.

He could tell by the looks they gave him that neither approved of Beck's presence in Katelyn's life. How did she operate successfully as a private investigator when they were in her business like this?

The next thing Beck knew the room began filling with way too many people—members of both families. Tori Peterson's parents, along with the Bradley family. Katelyn's parents, too. Beck tried to shove away the idea that he was "meeting the parents" of a woman for whom he had long-term intentions. Thankfully he didn't get the sense from Katelyn's parents they had been clued in to the goings-on with his case and the potential for danger. The law-enforcement presence could even be here without the danger Beck brought to the proverbial table.

Suddenly Ryan's guarded eyes shimmered and a smile erupted. His brothers' faces shined, too.

That could only mean one thing—the ladies had arrived.

Beck instinctively knew that he would *react* to seeing Katelyn; seeing her all dressed up could most definitely heighten his awareness. He braced himself and turned.

He contained what should have been an audible gasp. She was already beautiful in every way, and he had never seen her dressed in her Sunday best. In this case, rehearsal-dinner best.

Ryan approached Tori to kiss her, and Beck wanted, more than anything, to also approach Katelyn, who stood behind Tori. Katelyn wore a flattering turquoise dress that emphasized her amazing blue-green almond-shaped eyes. He thought he'd prepared himself to see her like this—her gorgeous hair up in a messy bun, exposing her long delicate neck, some wisps of dark hair hanging down to frame her lovely face—but he hadn't realized the strong effect seeing her all soft and feminine would have on him. Katelyn was all woman, and he'd known that from the beginning. Now he knew it in a deep and painful way.

He approached her without realizing that he had, and this close, he now saw that she was wearing a light sheen of makeup that accentuated her eyes and lips.

Those lips that he'd kissed when he shouldn't have.

Those lips he wanted to kiss even now.

Someone bumped his shoulder, and still he couldn't move away. Reece leaned in. "Pull yourself together, man."

Right. He smiled at Katelyn and closed the short distance between them, floating as if she walked on air. Yeah. He definitely needed to pull himself together. She drew up next to him as everyone found their assigned seats—Beck had been a last-minute addition, but he was taking the place of someone who had to cancel.

"You look beautiful," he said. The compliment came from somewhere deep in his heart, and he tapped down the rising emotions.

"You don't look so bad yourself." She winked. "That one of Ryan's suits?"

"Nah. He took me to get it today. It needs some tailoring, but it'll do for tonight."

Her lips parted as though she was speechless.

"Hey, you two," someone teased and others chuckled. "Sit down so we can focus on the *engaged* couple here."

Heat ignited his neck and cheeks, and he found his seat next to her, avoiding the curious looks of Katelyn's family. They all had the wrong idea, no doubt there.

He listened to small talk and engaged in it, but was still in a daze, as if he was floating outside of his body and not sitting next to Katelyn at all. His heart rate had kicked up, just sitting next to her. He never thought anyone could make him feel this way again, after Mia died. He definitely didn't want to feel this way again after what he'd gone through with Mia. Her lies, his inability to protect her when it became clear she was in trouble and in danger, and she hadn't wanted to lie to him. He wanted to believe that about her—and that's one more reason it was so important to learn the truth about what happened. He needed to prove that she wanted to share the truth with him, but she had been killed.

If he could do that, then maybe he could be free to love again.

But not yet.

Not yet.

"Where are you, Beck? You seem a million miles from here." Katelyn's voice was soft and her warm breath fanned his skin.

He glanced at her, knowing he couldn't tell her where his thoughts had gone. Fortunately, Ryan's best man, his oldest brother, Reece, drew everyone's attention by clinking his glass, interrupting Beck's attempt at hiding from Katelyn his desperate need to be away from her.

FOURTEEN

Reece concluded his toast, then dessert was served. Katelyn remained hyperaware of big, strong rock-climbing Beck sitting next to her in a suit and tie. Her heart had jumped to her throat the moment she'd seen him. Why had she insisted he come to this dinner? Why had Ryan taken him shopping to get a suit? That electricity that sparked when they touched seemed to be buzzing between them and they weren't even touching now. She wasn't rubbing shoulders with him or bumping him and yet the sensation was there. She could almost forget the whole reason why he was there to begin with. She could almost forget their business together. The danger they were in.

That Beck Goodwin was here at the rehearsal dinner was all kinds of strange to begin with. But she had wanted him at her side until the danger was over. She was more protective of Beck than she had a right to be. His safety was much more to her than simply business.

His safety had become personal. Deeply personal.

Gritting her teeth, Katelyn focused on the variety of desserts served. She had chosen the black-tie cheesecake, but maybe the caramel apple pie would have been good, too. She plastered on a beaming smile. She truly was happy for her brother and Tori, and wished this Beck Goodwin business had happened at another time.

With another private investigator.

Next to her, the timbre of Beck's chuckle vibrated through her. In her peripheral vision she caught his chiseled profile—the kind of profile that was carved into stone statues in some Mediterranean countries. Oddly enough, it wasn't his good looks that drew her to him, but his kindness. That tough, lean and muscular frame housed a sensitive and caring man. Who could resist that?

Until she met Beck, her plan to avoid emotional entanglements had worked perfectly.

All she'd ever had to do was think about Tony's betrayal.

In a matter of a couple of days with Beck, she was already becoming willing to let go of what happened before, so she could forge a new future.

But she wasn't there yet, so there was still hope that she could keep her resolve of never trusting a man with her heart. She hoped they would finish up their investigation and Beck could get back to his life and Ollie— which would include finding a new home somewhere, she was sure—and she could get back to hers.

Friends and family began rising from their chairs, and that signaled to Katelyn the rehearsal dinner was finally over.

She hugged Tori. "I'm so happy for the two of you."

Tori's face beamed with love for Ryan. "You were the one to make this possible."

"What do you mean?"

"Don't think for a minute I didn't see through your scheme to get me to stay here."

"You knew?"

"I just never said anything. But now that it's really going to happen, I owe you a debt of gratitude." Tori winked. "And I'm warning you to be careful with the man for whom you seem so captivated."

Katelyn knew she appeared stunned to Tori. She had hoped she kept her emotions in check; after all, she'd worked hard on that all evening. "Oh, I'm so sorry, Tori. I hope I didn't come across as, um… What's the word?"

"Preoccupied." Tori laughed. "It's okay. Believe me, my thoughts were on Ryan most of the evening. But a person would have to be on another planet to miss the static charges flying between you and Beck. I just don't want to see you hurt—physically, because of the danger. Or…emotionally."

Katelyn hugged her friend again. "I'll be careful. I promise."

Ryan interrupted Katelyn and took Tori's hand. "Mind if I get a few minutes with Tori before you two head home?"

Katelyn nodded. "Of course. Go ahead."

Beck sidled next to her. He held her gaze, then quickly looked away. What was that about? Unfortunately, she thought she knew—this atmosphere was all kinds of awkward for the two of them.

"Well, what next?" he finally asked. "The safe is gone and now we have nothing. No leads."

Her purse vibrated. Katelyn opened the small black special-occasions purse and found her cell. A couple of text messages had come through from Clara. "Oh, we've got something all right. Clara texted me. She got the license plate of a stranger's vehicle on the street early this morning."

"Why didn't she call the police first?"

"Clara has been in the habit of telling me first for a while now. She has a history of—"

"Being a nosy neighbor. I get it. But what do we do with that information?"

"We're going to run the plates and find out who was sitting near your house. Maybe there is a connection."

"The police are involved in this now, though, so isn't this *their* investigation?"

"Yes and no. I'm still your contracted private investigator and I'm working the case, too. I'll tell Clara to be sure and let Detective Manning know about the suspicious vehicle tomorrow, and then I will also instruct her to go stay with her sister in Spokane," she said. "But I'm not going to wait on Clara or the detective. Now, I need to figure out how to tell Tori that I won't be staying with her tonight."

"I don't think you should go home yet. I'm not so sure you're out of danger."

"Who said anything about going home? After we change, we're going to the office and we're going to find who that car belongs to. It might not be the arsonist, then again, we could find ourselves on a stakeout. If this is our man, I'll call for backup." *As if I'm a cop.* Letting go of her training had been more difficult than she would have thought. Still, if this lead panned out, the cops would make the arrest.

Beck's frustrated demeanor shifted, and half his cheek lifted in a grin as admiration swelled in his eyes.

Oh, Katelyn could get used to that. And that was exactly why she had to wrap up this investigation and get far from Beck Goodwin.

* * *

Beck climbed into his truck and waited for Katelyn. She rushed out of the Peterson Bradley Investigations office, then hopped into the passenger side.

"I'll just punch the address into your GPS and we're good to go."

Katelyn had informed Tori she was going to stay at her own home, and she believed she was no longer in danger. Still, Ryan had assigned a deputy outside her house. In the meantime, Beck had thanked Ryan for his hospitality, and for taking him to get new clothes and a suit, but he had a son and family to check on at a campground. That was true, and he did call and check on them. He'd changed out of the suit, and with his new freedom, he planned to see this through with Katelyn's help.

God, please let us finish this tonight. Find out what we need to know tonight.

Katelyn had then snuck out of her own house and joined him in his truck, which was parked the next street over. While the police were actively investigating the shooting at her family lake house, the house fire and the stolen safe, they wouldn't move as fast as he and Katelyn could.

He had the distinct impression that even though the safe was gone, he and Katelyn were still in lethal danger. Would they always be looking over their shoulders? They had to get to the man and the safe he had stolen before it was too late—which it could very well be already.

GPS directed him and he found himself steering out of town along a stretch of lonely country road, and then finally up a winding mountain road.

Katelyn peered at her tablet—the light as a bit of distraction as he drove in the dark. Finally, she said, "This guy's name is Curtis Hunley."

"And you don't think the vehicle is stolen? Wouldn't a guy committing a crime use a stolen vehicle?"

"In the movies, sure, but most of the time the license-plate number leads us directly to the criminal."

"Regular everyday stupid criminals, you mean."

"There is that aspect. If the people behind Mia's death and the attacks on us are related to some sort of agency, say the CIA, that isn't typical, and we could be looking at a stolen vehicle. Then again, you and I weren't staying there—obviously your house was burned down—so maybe the arsonist took a risk and used his own vehicle."

"I'll guess we'll find out soon enough."

"I thought it best to head to the address. Knowing if he had a criminal background could also tell us something, but running a complete background check would take time we might not have."

"I agree. I think getting a look at him is a good start."

"Right. It will tell if he was the man to break into your house to begin with. The man who tried to smother me."

"When I fought with the guy at the lake house, I got the sense he was a different guy. He wasn't as broad-shouldered or bulky. He was lithe and agile. Also, he carried a gun with a suppressor. A different breed of killer altogether."

"So we're dealing with at least two people."

"Probably more." Beck released a heavy sigh. Was he doing the right thing by keeping her involved? After tonight, if this didn't pan out, he would release her of any obligation to this case. He would fire her.

He'd been selfish to keep her working with him. He'd used the excuse that she had threatened to investigate, anyway. While that could potentially be true, he would bring her brothers in on it to make sure she was occupied elsewhere.

With the thoughts, guilt infused him to his deepest core. If anything happened to Katelyn, how could he live with himself?

But he had to think of Ollie, and since he had opened this door by finding the safe, he couldn't stop now.

"Even if he's not the man we fought with on three occasions now, watching his activities could tell us something. That's why I wanted to do this stakeout before Detective Manning scared the guy off with a visit to his home to ask questions."

"Makes sense to me."

GPS let them know their destination was coming up on the right.

"Keep driving," Katelyn said. "We don't want to make the same mistake they did and park anywhere on the street where they might spot us. We'll hike in and hide in the trees. I've got a couple of pair of binoculars and a good private-investigator, high-quality camera." She held it up for effect. "Plus, we have our weapons."

Beck turned off the GPS so he wouldn't have to hear the voice repeatedly rerouting him. Then he steered around in the mountain neighborhood and parked one street over. "Our target might not see our vehicle, but someone could see us walking down the street."

"Everything is packed in a hiking backpack. This is mountain country. I doubt anyone will think twice about us. But we'll keep to the shadows without acting like we're hiding." She glanced up at him. "You can do that, can't you? Act normal at the same time you're trying to be invisible?"

He winked. "I'll follow your example. Lead on."

Katelyn strapped on the backpack, then handed one to him. "We need to both be hikers."

"In the middle of the night."

She shrugged. "We had a rough day today. Got lost and we're just getting back."

Katelyn looked like a hiker in the hiking pants and shirt, backpack and a camera hanging across her body. For a moment, he allowed himself to picture her in the turquoise dress from earlier this evening. She had since wiped off the makeup yet appeared equally beautiful.

God, please let us find the men responsible for murder and attempted murder tonight. Let it be over tonight.

Because he couldn't stand this sensation churning in his gut and growing stronger by the hour—he had a feeling they were walking toward certain death.

FIFTEEN

The heavily wooded neighborhood worked in their favor as they kept to the shadows. No dogs barked, which was also good. No one would be alerted to look out the window and spot two strangers lurking in the dark.

Though this was risky and dangerous, a thrill shot through her. When she'd been a cop, her true dream had been to eventually work for the FBI and maybe even work undercover. But she'd failed so royally at her job that she'd had to let go of that dream.

Was Katelyn putting both their lives at risk by insisting they conduct a stakeout on what could be a dangerous assassin—or two or three—hired by some nebulous government agency to keep Mia's secrets? Even thinking that way sounded utterly ridiculous. And that's exactly why they were on their own tonight.

She approached a wide pine tree and dropped her pack. "We'll stop here." She kept her voice to a whisper. "With these binoculars, I can look at the house directly ahead and see inside. We'll start with this, and then move if necessary."

Beck said nothing, understanding silence was best,

and dropped his pack to the ground. She pulled out a dark blanket and laid it near the base of the tree. At his funny look, she simply shrugged.

Why suffer against the cold wet ground if she didn't have to?

Katelyn handed binoculars to Beck and grabbed her camera. She could get an equally good zoom with the telephoto lens. She peered through at the home. Lights were on, but most of the windows were dark, covered with mini blinds or drapes. However, the kitchen window allowed her to see into the dimly lit home. A small light over the sink had been left on.

Was Mr. Hunley in bed already? Or was he brainstorming with his partners-in-crime?

If he was home, then at some point he would go to the kitchen to dump his coffee mug or get a glass of water or milk. Something. The kitchen was the hub.

A shadow caught her attention.

"Movement," she whispered. "Get your binoculars and look at the kitchen window."

A man stood in plain view, but had his back to the window. Dark hair and a sweater or a hoodie. His body language indicated he was speaking to someone either on the phone or in person. He suddenly turned and focused on the kitchen sink.

Katelyn took pictures. Her pulse skyrocketed. Blood roared in her ears and she could hardly breathe. The sensation of the pillow over her face, blocking her ability to breathe, rammed her.

"It's…"

She tried to suck in air, but her throat constricted.

Beck lowered the camera and gripped her. "You're okay. Breathe, Katelyn, breathe."

She nodded and listened to his words. Drew in a breath. And then another. Slower and longer now. She could do this. She could rise above the stupid panic attacks.

"It was him," she said as she peered through the camera. He had disappeared from the window now. She lowered the camera.

"I saw him," Beck said. "It's the same man who tried to…"

Smother me. Beck had held back probably because he didn't want her to start hyperventilating again.

"Stay here." Beck started to rise. "I'm going to face him and get answers."

"Beck!" She held on to him. He'd have to drag her. "No, you can't go. Let's watch him a little longer to see what he does before he is questioned. After he is questioned by the police, everything he planned to do will change. We need to know who he is working with. What he did to the safe. I'll have to call this in now, but give me a few more minutes."

Beck shrugged free. "Call it in. Do your job. I'm doing mine and that is finding out the truth."

Wait? What about Ollie? She wanted to ask him, but she knew that ultimately he did this for his son's protection. Mia's past, if that's what this was all about, could come back to haunt them all.

"Hold it right there." The raspy voice came out of nowhere.

And so did the muzzle of a gun at the back of her head.

Beck froze in his tracks. Fear curdled in his gut. Images of Mia's car crash and her vehicle going over the bridge and plunging into the water—it all slammed into him.

Not again, Lord. Please not again. Please keep Katelyn safe.

Beck slowly turned around to face this new threat. A man held a gun at the back of Katelyn's head, but not too close. She had dropped her weapon. The man's menacing eyes glared at Beck as he directed his next words to him. "Toss the gun. Move too fast or try anything and I'll kill her."

Chances were this jerk would kill her, anyway, if they didn't somehow gain the upper hand. But right now the man with the gun was in charge and used Katelyn for leverage. Beck and Katelyn had to work this right or they would both end up dead.

Slowly, Beck pulled his gun from the holster and stretched out his arm. He let the gun dangle from his fingers.

"I said toss it!"

Beck tossed the weapon off to the side, but not too far, his mind scrambling for a possible way out. Presumably someone would come along and retrieve their weapons later. But not this man. This man remained focused on the two of them.

By his build, Beck suspected he was the man he'd fought with at the lake last night, but he couldn't know for sure.

"Now walk to the house."

Beck turned back toward the house and did as he was told. He couldn't look at Katelyn's face. He didn't want to see the fear there. Or the disappointment. Instead of letting his anger get the best of him so that he'd begun to stalk off toward the house, he should have remained by her side. He should have stayed with her and remained on alert. Beck should have protected her. Then they wouldn't be in this no-way-out situation.

When "free" rock climbing, in which he used no equipment to help him climb, he had to have an idea of the path he should take before he even started because he needed handholds in the rock. Footholds, too. But there had been times he had found himself faced with no way up the mountain, which meant going back down to take another path and trying again. If he failed a pitch, then he could return using the rope, the only equipment, and plan a different route.

Failure wasn't an option in this situation. They would not be allowed to try this again. His mind burst with possible ways up the "mountain" of trouble.

And if he couldn't find a way out of this for them, at the very least, he intended to get answers before he died.

But… Katelyn.

Beck needed to survive this for Ollie and his family, and for Katelyn. But how? Anguish could crush him. Though he had no idea what to do next, he would trust God and take one step at a time. One excruciating breath at a time. Sweat trickled down his back as he strode toward the house looking for a way out, or a distraction to pull away the gunman's attention.

But no such distraction came. Another man opened the back door, his big silhouette filling the doorjamb as light poured from the house.

Hunley?

"Ah. Mr. Goodwin. We meet again."

Beck didn't know what to say to that. Had they been introduced other than to tackle each other? He said nothing as the man moved from the doorway and they were escorted inside the typical home, decorated as if Hunley had a wife. Maybe he did and Hunley's wife was clueless to his nefarious activities, like Beck had been about Mia.

"Have a seat." The gunman waved them toward the chairs around a small kitchen table, so they sat. He'd grabbed their packs and tossed them against the wall.

The safe rested in the middle of the table and had been opened. Beck noticed that Katelyn stared at the contents, which were spread out. Maybe she understood more about what she was seeing than Beck did. He'd have to get a closer look and be allowed time to figure it all out. Time he wouldn't get.

"Now that we're face-to-face," Beck said, "maybe you can tell me what this is all about. Maybe you can tell me why my wife was murdered."

Hunley smirked. "You're too smart for your own good. That's why you're here. Except on that count, bringing the woman into this was stupid. Now she has to die, too."

Fear flicked across Katelyn's features. The man was right. Beck had been stupid to hire her. Idiot. "Look, you killed Mia. That doesn't mean you have to keep killing. So…what? Was Mia some sort of agent?"

The gunman kept his gun trained on them, while Hunley eased onto a chair opposite the two of them.

Beck was surprised they hadn't been bound and gagged, but that could only mean their lives were about to end. These men wouldn't waste the time and energy to tie them up when they were only going to kill them in mere moments.

His pulse raced and he fought to listen to the man's droning words.

"Yes. Your wife—Michaela—was an agent. In the safe she had stashed her alternative identification documents for her aliases, along with incriminating evidence about someone else. I was hired to retrieve the information and kill her. I had to complete my task before I could get paid. That meant watching and waiting for the moment when someone would find where she had hidden it."

Just like he thought, Beck's discovery of the safe had triggered the attacks.

"I slipped into the house and would have gotten into the safe, in and out, without your knowledge, had you not come home too early and encountered my presence. And still, I might have gotten what I needed if your girlfriend hadn't come to your rescue. But she saw my face. That's when the dominoes began to fall." He huffed a laugh. "I can't believe you've survived this long, even after I hired an assassin to take you down while I went for the safe."

Hunley rose.

And Beck tensed, expecting to die at his hands.

He waved his gun around. "I'm guessing that you found your way here because of my license plate."

Beck didn't respond and neither did Katelyn. If Detective Manning got the information and could make his way there to ask questions in the morning, they didn't want to warn off this man so he would leave, and the truth about their deaths would never come out.

Hunley sat again and fidgeted with his gun. He wanted them to think he wasn't worried, but Beck saw through the man's nervous twitches. "I had a reason to park my car on that street," Hunley said. "I've maneuvered my way into a woman's life. So if the cops come here, that's what I'll tell them. I decided to drop by to visit my friend. As for you, I can't kill you here." He lifted the backpacks. "But you can die a tragic death in the mountains when you fall."

Beck thought he could hear Katelyn's heart pounding. He hoped Clara hadn't waited until morning to call the detective with the news, after all, and that she would have called immediately. Then again, Detective Manning might not act on it until the morning. He would knock on Hunley's door and be greeted by a surprised man, who would hide that he was a murderer.

The window exploded with gunfire.

Blood splattered and the assassin crashed to the ground. Beck shoved Katelyn down as Hunley grabbed his midsection, then slumped in his chair before falling dead on the kitchen floor.

SIXTEEN

Beck shielded her against the bullets, his body covering her on the floor without weighing on her. Katelyn gasped. Fought for breath. Blood. There was blood all around her. Was that a SWAT team outside, taking down their captors? She should feel relief, except she knew in her gut that it probably wasn't law enforcement that had taken out the two men, and it was likely that she and Beck were next. Whoever shot and killed the men might want to question Katelyn and Beck first, so had left them alive for the moment. But they were not going to wait to meet the killer.

"Move. Let's move." Beck urged them over behind a wall and away from the kitchen window. But was that enough?

Breathing hard, she struggled to speak. "We have no idea if someone could shoot us from any of these other windows. We don't know how many of them are out there."

Before she could change her mind or Beck could drag her in another direction, she darted forward and snatched the contents of the safe, then dashed back around to the wall. Another round of gunfire.

"What are you doing?" He ground out the words through gritted teeth.

"I'm getting us what proof we need. Now let's get out of here before it's too late." The gunman had dropped their backpacks within reach. Remaining behind the wall, she slid her arm forward and snatched at least one of them.

Beck was crawling down the hallway. "Katelyn, come on!"

"We could use what's in the pack." Another gun along with hiking gear to verify their story if needed. She shoved Mia's spy stuff inside the pack and put it on her back, then hurried after Beck.

"How are we going to get out of here without the killer knowing?"

A sound from the kitchen let them know the shooter was coming through the back door.

"Hurry," she whispered urgently. This was déjà vu. They'd been through a similar scenario before.

She unlocked the window and pushed out the screen, then jumped through. Beck followed. There was no time to discuss who would go first. They were working as a team, as if they had practiced for this for many years. Katelyn slipped behind a tree, then watched and waited.

Beck held another gun.

"Where'd you get that?" she whispered.

"It's mine. It was on the ground where I tossed it." Oh.

She pulled the additional gun from the backpack. When it appeared that they were alone, they kept to the darkest of shadows and moved quietly and quickly through the woods. She remained aware of their surroundings, and thought of the possibility the new assassin had not been working alone. With their two main attackers gone, Katelyn was at her wit's end to know who was after them now.

"Let's not go back on the street, but keep to the trees until we get to your vehicle," she said.

He nodded and together they stealthily jogged, then crossed the street at a point farthest away from a streetlamp. Finally at his vehicle, Beck unlocked the doors, and she tossed in the pack, then got in.

Beck was already in. He started the ignition, then they sped away.

"I hope nobody followed us this time. Or for that matter has planted a bomb in your truck."

"Or a tracker."

"Listen to us," she said. "See, this is why I needed to grab this stuff so we have proof."

"I don't care about proving that I'm not crazy and that my wife was a spy. I only wanted to know the truth about what happened to her. Now we know."

"Only what Hunley told us. There could be more. We still need to look at the contents to see why someone would want this so much. The incriminating evidence and such. There could be more than what he told us."

Katelyn had to report the bodies and she called Detective Manning instead of 911. She didn't want some unprepared patrol unit stumbling in on that or the new assassin. She got Manning's voice mail and explained the events of the night. Hunley was dead in his home along with another man, but there was still an assassin out there. And because of that, she and Beck would remain in hiding. She warned Manning to be careful. Guilt suffused her, but she'd done all she could do. They were so close to finding the truth now, and she and Beck would finally get to see the contents of that safe.

Beck drove in silence for a few minutes, glancing in his rearview mirror almost more than he looked at the road. Then he suddenly swerved from the road and pulled over. "We should stop and make sure there aren't any trackers on us."

They both hopped out, and, using flashlights, looked under the truck, in the wheel wells, every place one might possibly stash a tracker. They found nothing. Fortunately, no one had spotted Beck's truck. The shooter had come for Hunley and his assassin, and hadn't expected to see Katelyn and Beck. Maybe that's why they weren't immediate targets.

"Well, that's as good as we can do," he said. "Let's go."

"Where are we going?"

"Some place we can regroup and look through what we've found. I want to see what was in the safe—like you said, there could be much more than what Hunley told us—and then, and only then, we can turn it over to the authorities."

Katelyn said nothing more and figured Beck needed time to process what he'd learned about his wife tonight. Confirming his suspicions might be the one thing he'd desperately needed.

When he drove up an unpaved mountain road, she decided it was time to break the silence. "Please tell me where you're taking us."

"A friend has an old cabin up this drive. We used to come out here and hang out and climb. I had forgotten about it until tonight when we drove up that road to Hunley's house. Something about it reminded me about this place. Chances are nobody is here, so we should be safe for tonight. We'll have a chance to look at the stuff you grabbed."

He turned onto an even narrower road. Branches scraped the window as the vehicle bobbed with the bumps in the road. Finally, he stopped in front of a dark cabin.

Did it even have electricity?

He shifted toward her. "Thank you for that, by the way. For getting Mia's documents and the contents of that safe."

Their connection had shifted now and she couldn't put her finger on it, but with their lives on their line, repeatedly it seemed, their emotions had been scraped raw.

Katelyn wasn't sure she had a wall left around her heart. Not one single stone. "You're welcome. It was important to you." She swallowed against the tightness building in her throat. "To our investigation."

Beck dug around the rocks in the bushes and couldn't find the key. It had been a while since he and his buddy had met at the cabin. He dragged a hand through his hair.

"No key?" Katelyn crossed her arms.

"No key." This would be embarrassing if he cared about what anyone thought of him.

He marched up the porch and tried the knob. Locked. So he simply kicked in the door. He'd have to fix it later.

Katelyn remained on the porch. "Are you sure your friend still owns this place?"

He shook his head. He wasn't sure about anything anymore. When he flipped the switch, at least the lights came on.

Katelyn brought in the backpack and dropped it on

the table, disturbing the dust. Beck opened the fridge and found a few bottles of water. The place was dusty and hadn't been used in a few weeks, but someone could definitely show up. This didn't look like Patrick's style. Except… Wait a minute.

Beck spotted a photograph on the wall. Patrick and a woman. Two young girls. Twins. That made sense. He'd kept the place, but his wife had upgraded the decor.

"I get the feeling we shouldn't get too comfortable here," she said.

"Right. Let's look." Though Beck and Patrick had used this as a getaway, he might not be welcome anymore. He and Katelyn wouldn't stay long.

Katelyn pulled the items from the backpack—passports, papers and documents of various sizes—and spread them on the table like Hunley had.

"Hey, what's this?" She handed an envelope with his name scrawled on the front over to him.

Beck held the envelope and frowned. She'd left him a letter? Mia had suspected this day would come then. He opened it and pulled out the missive written in her handwriting.

Reading the letter to himself, he tried to absorb the information as he held back the sobs. He glanced over to see that Katelyn was examining one of Mia's alias passports. She deserved to know what was in the letter.

So he read it out loud.

My dearest Beck,
If you're reading this it can only mean one thing. That I didn't get the chance to tell you in person. To answer all your questions. I'm sorry I've kept you in the dark for so long, but please know that

I only did so because you and Ollie are my life. I love you both so much.

When I met you during the world climbing tour, I was working for the CIA. I was a plant in the group so that I could easily go in and out of certain countries. My main task was to uncover a terrorist plot by a foreign entity. I was able to provide sufficient intel to stop the plot. But by then I was in love with you. I'd had enough and wanted out of the CIA. I thought that since I'd succeeded with my task, that a real life should be my reward.

But my handler, Henry Cooley, had other plans. He wouldn't allow me to leave and threatened my life, if I chose to leave. For a while I secretly worked for them even after we married, but I knew my duplicity was wreaking havoc on our relationship. I also knew I wasn't free to leave with Cooley's threats. Instead of living in fear, of looking over my shoulder, I extracted incriminating evidence against him and used it as leverage to gain my freedom. If you're reading this letter, then you have also gotten into the safe. The evidence is with this letter. Please take it to a man who goes by the name Barr. You'll find his contact information is all there, too. My plan was to deliver the information to Barr myself, after I told you the truth. In case something happened to me, I wanted you to know. He is the only person I could trust that wouldn't throw me under the bus when facing off with Cooley. I've been searching for someone trustworthy for much too long and finally found Barr. Maybe I took too long.

If Barr can't be reached, then I advise you to

run and never look back. Go underground and never admit to anything. They have eyes and ears everywhere.

You and Ollie build a new life far from here. I've included new IDs for you and Ollie, Mimi and Pops, too.

I loved you with all that was in me, but now I realize that loving you was selfish of me. You didn't ask for a secret agent wife. You never asked for a wife who was so deep undercover she could never reveal her secrets, or that she and her loved ones would be targeted.

That's what they loved about me. I had no one else.

That was, until I fell in love with you, Beck. You're the strongest person I know and at the same time the gentlest. Please find someone else to love. Someone who will be a good mother to Ollie and wife to you.

A tear dropped on the paper. Beck wiped at his eyes. "So, she was going to tell me that night. She wanted to tell me before she tried to get the information to Barr, but she was killed."

"Oh, Beck," Katelyn whispered as she hugged him.

Beck let the letter drop and turned to hug Katelyn to him. He had no more strength to fight the current running between them, and for the moment he absorbed the comfort she offered.

He finally released her, and cupped her face. His emotions were raw and his guard was down. He should feel completely empty, but emotions he didn't want to unpack filled him when he was with Katelyn.

"I thought finding the contents of the safe, finding the truth, would end this."

She chewed on her lip. "But instead now we're only in deeper."

As if it would help her solve a problem, she shoved her hair on top of her head with both hands, her fingers weaving through the silky mane.

Beck looked through the rest of the documents and found contact information for the Barr person mentioned. He also found fake IDs and passports. Four of them, just like Mia had said in her letter.

What kind of life would it be to run and hide? To always be looking over one's shoulder? He couldn't do that to Ollie or his family.

Katelyn was in this now. He couldn't do this to her.

"We have to get a hold of Barr. Give him everything and pray he can shut Cooley down before he gets to us."

SEVENTEEN

Katelyn shifted on the comfy sofa that someone had purchased with sleeping in mind. Beck had secured the door he'd broken open in order to gain entrance and had also been able to contact his friend and ask permission to use the cabin, but for how long he wasn't exactly sure. How long would it take for their pursuer, whom she assumed was this Cooley guy, to find them?

She had a wedding to attend. She was maid of honor and couldn't miss it.

She wanted to tell her brothers what they had found in the safe, but it was the worst kind of information. Would telling them only get them killed? Would anyone who knew die in an "accident" like Beck's wife? She couldn't live with that guilt. And yet, not going to them seemed like all kinds of wrong.

I don't think the local law can help us or protect you. Katelyn thought back to Beck's words to her when this had all started. It seemed like a lifetime ago. He'd been right in his assessment that what was going on went beyond the locals. The sheriff's office would be hard-pressed to investigate or protect, but likely this was out of their jurisdiction. She hadn't looked at the incriminating information Mia had gathered on Cooley, but suspected it would include federal crimes.

She shivered under the throw blanket. Somehow she had to fight the fear wrapping around her.

"Wake up, sleepyhead." Beck gently shook her.

What? She hadn't thought she would ever fall asleep. She'd been too scared. Her panic attacks had been replaced with nightmares about the man after them kicking down the door like Beck had.

She pushed to sit on the sofa. "You made breakfast? Where did you—?"

"I hiked down to the little store on the corner and bought eggs and bacon. Orange juice, too."

"You what? Don't you think that was too risky?"

"I hiked through the back country. The store clerks are used to seeing all sorts. Hikers. Hunters. You name it. No one else was even there. We need food if we're going to keep going."

"I hope you used cash."

"I did, but I'm going to run out soon. Going to an ATM is out of the question."

She finger-combed her hair. "Yeah. This guy is probably plugged in enough to find us through those cameras." She pushed from the sofa, headed to the table and reached for her cell fully expecting a hundred texts from Detective Manning and her family, as well. Ugh. She dreaded answering all the questions to which she had no answers. Not yet, Manning. Not yet. But then she remembered she had turned off her cell phone so the signal could not be pinged and they couldn't be tracked. Beck had done the same.

"We're not going to run out of money, Beck, because we're going to call Barr this morning. And somehow

I need to communicate with my family about what is going on. Communicate in such a way that they are not put in danger."

She slid the chair out at the table and plopped down to the breakfast Beck had made her, hoping she would have control over the threatening tears before she lifted her head. Beck was right. They were burning up energy and brain cells and needed to refuel before they could think clearly.

"Thank you for this. It was thoughtful."

He poured her orange juice and hovered close enough that she thought he might kiss her on the forehead, if not the lips.

"You're welcome, but I wasn't going for thoughtful. I was going for smart." His cheeks dimpled as he sat and dug into his eggs.

She crunched on bacon and guzzled the juice. They ate in silence, each burdened by the fear of what could happen next. After breakfast, Katelyn busied herself washing the dishes in the sink. She'd have to remember to write a thank-you note to Beck's friend when this was all over. She dried off the orange-juice glass. And this *would* all be over and everything would go back to normal.

Who was she kidding? This wasn't going to end well.

The glass slipped from her fingers and shattered on the floor.

The sound jarred Beck away from Mia's letter, which he'd been rereading. He rushed to Katelyn. "You okay?"

"Yeah. The glass slipped from my hands. I'll make sure to replace it. I'm sorry."

She bent to pick up the pieces.

He joined her. "Let me do it."

"I've got it." Her voice was strained.

"No, it's okay," he said. "I should have been cleaning the mess I made as I cooked breakfast."

"You cooked breakfast. I can clean it up." She rose.

Beck stood, too. "Listen to us arguing."

"And look, while we fought over who would clean it up, we've picked it up."

He would sweep later for good measure, but wouldn't bring that up or another discussion might ensue about who would sweep. That Katelyn was upset was easy to see. Her hands trembled slightly. He slipped his palm into hers and weaved their fingers together, then led her to the sofa. She sat and he released her hand to plop on the other end.

"What—what are you doing? We should be calling Barr now that we've had breakfast."

Beck had to work up the courage to get through this day. Part of him wished they could stay here and be safe and warm and dry, and away from the real world. Their real world included being shot at by assassins from the spy world.

"Beck, what's wrong?"

He choked a chuckle.

"Sorry, that was a stupid question."

"No, it's not. I was rereading Mia's letter earlier. I wanted to make sure I understood everything. Or see if there was some nuance that we missed."

"As if being attacked and nearly killed multiple times wasn't enough," she said, "this is all so hard for you."

He steadied his breaths. Slowed his heart. "I was thinking about the past. About when I first met Mia. If I had known that she was working as an agent in that capacity, would I have still married her? I was so young and idealistic, I was sure that love could overcome anything at all. I was a world-class climber. I was getting ready to sign on with major advertising campaigns. Mia was a climber, but she wanted no part of the limelight. I gave it all up to marry her. To be with her."

"Beck, don't do this to yourself. Risk is always out there, even when we fall for people who aren't connected to the spy world and assassins."

He hung his head. "You're right. It's always a risk." He angled his head to look at her. "So what's your story?"

"Pardon me?"

"You're beautiful and strong. I can't believe there isn't someone. You know. A boyfriend. A husband."

"Oh." Her turn to huff a chuckle.

He half expected her to counter with "How do you know?" To which he would have responded with something along the lines of how she'd kissed him. He was relieved her response was far from what he expected.

She curled her legs under her in the corner of the sofa.

She definitely looked snuggle-worthy, and he fought the need to wrap himself around her and join her in that corner. Funny that they were having this conversation as if danger wasn't facing them at every turn. Maybe neither of them was ready for what came next.

He definitely needed to take a moment to evaluate his life and his choices—as if any of that could change the unknown future.

"Well, I was a cop in Shasta. My partner, Tony, and I grew about as close as anyone. We worked well together."

"And?"

"We ended up chasing after a dangerous criminal. It quickly turned into a life-threatening situation when he got the best of Tony and held a gun to his head, using him as a hostage. I had my gun aimed at him, and I should have taken that shot. I hadn't been able to pull the trigger—an essential requirement for the job. Another cop took the shot. The criminal fired, too, and the bullet went through Tony's shoulder. He was seriously injured."

"Sounds to me like no one should have taken the shot."

"There was a moment that I could have shot the guy before he had his weapon on Tony. I let that opportunity pass me. My hesitation could have cost his life." Katelyn paused, then said, "I saw the counselor and worked through whatever fear I had that stopped me, but at night I had nightmares. Panic attacks. It was always about that moment when I should have taken that guy out. That is, until recently. Now my dreams are filled with the new terror."

Beck bit back his comments. He wanted to hear the whole story.

"And Tony? You two were close?"

"He never blamed me. I resigned. What else could I do? Tony came over that night with flowers. He kissed me, and that gave me hope that maybe my resignation, the loss of my dream to be an undercover agent..." She gasped and glanced his way. "FBI—that sort of thing. Not...a spy. Not like..."

"It's okay, Katelyn. Please continue."

"He gave me hope because now that I wasn't with the force, we could date. I thought I'd finally found happiness. I even… I even imagined myself married to Tony. I know that sounds silly."

"Not at all. Most people fall in love and dream of romantic bliss." He pushed back the ache inside at how horribly his dream had ended. He couldn't let himself dream like that again. But he could encourage Katelyn.

"Tony cared and I thought we loved each other. That we were going somewhere. I started working as a PI and moonlighting as security around the area. Banks, the hospital. That sort of thing. Someone hired me to follow his cheating spouse. It's not glamorous work, but that's the kind of thing that takes up most of a private investigator's time, which is so sad."

"I agree." He had a feeling where this was going, and he wished he hadn't asked her to share because she was reliving that past. He could hear the pain in her voice.

"I did the work. Followed the woman. Got the picture. She was cheating on her husband with Tony."

Beck ached for the pain Katelyn had experienced. Though different than what Beck had gone through with Mia, it was no less crushing. He reached for her fingers and gently touched them, bracing himself for the current that ran between them.

Somehow, that current had grown stronger and more dangerous.

EIGHTEEN

Choked with tears, Katelyn's throat almost closed up completely. What was the matter with her? Beck's fingers barely touched hers and she knew exactly what that was about. One small spark between them could ignite the hope of a future with this man, and with that thought, she knew that she was well and truly over Tony.

She absolutely wouldn't cry in front of Beck, at least with respect to Tony. Even though she was over the guy, she wasn't over what he'd done to her and the pain he'd caused her—even the mere memory ignited inside her. Good thing she was talking about Tony because it served as a reminder that she couldn't give her heart away no matter how much she wanted to give it to Beck.

But he wasn't asking for her heart. If anything Beck had been severely emotionally wounded by his wife, so Katelyn could forget about her struggle where Beck was concerned. It didn't matter. She leaned forward and pressed her elbows on her thighs, then rested her chin in her hands. "We're procrastinating, aren't we?"

"You got me. I'm a procrastinator." Beck's arm relaxed across the top of the sofa and his gaze held hers. Emotion welled in his gray irises and the current between them suddenly jumped from him and surged up her arms, around her heart and into her belly.

"Beck…" She breathed out his name, and was certain he heard everything that one word on her lips could mean. Her heart was a traitor.

He rose, breaking the current. "I guess we should contact Barr now. I'll get the information."

Katelyn couldn't get enough oxygen. It was like she was on Everest or someplace where the oxygen was limited.

Breathe in. Breathe out.

This was the same panic that overwhelmed her when she had to shoot to save Tony and failed.

It's going to be okay. It's going to be okay. We're going to get a hold of this Barr guy and he'll take the information and get rid of that guy after us. Then I can go to the wedding tomorrow night, and Beck can go pick up Ollie and go buy a new house.

So much remained to work out, and it was all so complicated.

Beck sat at the table. "Why don't you join me? I'll put him on speakerphone. We can talk through what we have and Mia's instructions. I—I need you. I can't do this alone."

Was Katelyn showing that much weakness that Beck needed to beg? "Of course."

She just hadn't wanted to overstep. This was, admittedly, over her head.

Katelyn slid out a chair and sat at the table. Morning light spilled into the cabin and chased away the shadows and the overwhelming fear of danger, and certain death. She could almost pretend that the last few days had never happened.

But then, she wouldn't have gotten to know Beck Goodwin.

He set his cell on the table and turned it on. That in itself was a risk. "Good thing there's a decent cell signal up here."

Katelyn nodded and stared at the phone, wishing there was another way out of this, but they had to make this call. "Go ahead and call him."

Beck punched in the numbers and hit the speaker button. An answering machine came on. He glanced her way. "Not voice mail, but an old answering machine."

Katelyn shrugged. "Maybe voice mail can be hacked and this is more secure?"

He ended the call.

"What are you doing?" she asked.

"What am I supposed to say into an answering machine? 'Mr. Barr, Mia's dead and we're on the run. People are trying to kill us. Please call me or stop by and see me?'"

"Okay, okay. How about you try the number again."

"What for?"

"Come on. Just one more time."

Beck redialed the number. Together they listened as the phone rang.

"Hello?" A woman answered.

"Uh, hello! Hi, my name is Katelyn—" she knew this would sound better coming from her so had jumped in "—and I need to speak with Barr."

"Why? Who are you?"

"Um… Who am I speaking with?" Moisture bloomed on her palms.

"That's none of your concern. Why are you calling?"

"I'm so sorry, I only feel comfortable speaking to Barr. A friend told me to call if... If I was in trouble."

A sob cracked over the other end of the line. "I'm sorry, but he can't help you. He's dead."

"Dead?" Full-on panic swelled in her chest. "How? When? What happened?"

"It's been a year now. I didn't have the heart to change his number in case... In case someone ever called. But now that someone has, I realize there's nothing I can do. It's time to drop this number."

"No, wait!"

"I'm sorry, there's nothing anyone can do for you if you needed Barr."

"But who are you? Are you sure there's no one else?"

The line went dead.

That fear that kept threatening her, that she kept rising above, now snaked around her throat like a boa constrictor and tightened.

A painful silence filled the cabin with the terror of an unknown future. Beck shoved from the table and paced. Nothing was good when he had to resort to pacing.

A chair squeaked, letting him know that Katelyn had risen, too. "Well, Beck, I think it's clear what we have to do next."

"Yeah, what's that?" He kept his head down and his back to her as he paced. "We're out of road here, Katelyn. I don't know where to go."

"But I do."

He wanted to punch the wall and slammed his fist forward, stopping millimeters from even touching it. He needed to climb. That's what he needed to do. Climbing would purge every foul thought from his brain. From his soul.

Then once he stood at the top of the mountain, he could see as far as his eyes could see. He could take it all in and he would know what to do.

When Katelyn said nothing more, he stopped moving and lifted his face.

Waiting for him, she studied him.

"Well?" he asked.

"Mia's letter said to run and hide. Pretend that you know nothing. That's what we have to do now."

"You can't be serious."

"Whatever it takes to keep our families safe." Her brilliant blue-green eyes welled with tears.

Beck would give anything—*anything*—if Katelyn hadn't moved in to that house six months ago. If she hadn't come to check on him that night. Then one way or another this could all be over and Katelyn wouldn't be involved.

Beck might be dead, or he might not have the safe, but it would be over.

He took two steps forward and wrapped his arms around her. Held her long and hard. Close and tight. They fit perfectly together—from the way he could feel her heart beating, sense the emotions pouring from her, to the way her head rested just beneath his chin.

Holding her was almost like climbing the mountain and standing on the top. He had a great view of the vistas, and right now he knew what he had to do.

She stepped back and turned away. Her turn to pace. "Mia knew what she was talking about," she said. "She knew more than we know even now. If she told you to run and hide that must mean there's no other way. I'm not saying any of this because I'm scared. Yes, I'm scared, but sometimes a little fear is a good thing. Don't you agree if there was another way she would have said so in that letter? She loved you and Ollie. I know she did. I could feel it in her words."

He raised his hands, gesturing for her to slow down. "Okay, stop. Just stop."

She continued, rushing on with more words to persuade him.

"Will you stop?"

Katelyn whirled. "Well, then, what's your big plan? To pace this room? Huh? What has that ever gotten you?"

She rushed out of the cabin.

Well, that's just great.

He'd let her sit out there a while until she calmed down. Clearly their emotions were running too high. He grabbed some of the juice from the fridge, leaving enough for her to have another glass. He hadn't planned for them to stay even this long.

Okay. It had been long enough. He left the cabin and found Katelyn sitting on the porch. He plopped next to her.

"I just needed some fresh air. I'm sorry about that."

"It's okay. You were right. Pacing doesn't do much. But I need to expend energy. If I can't climb, then I pace."

That elicited a rare laugh, and he loved the sound. Her laugh sounded natural and joined the birdsong. He lifted her hand and weaved his fingers with hers. "I wish that I would have invited you to grill hamburgers when you first moved to the neighborhood."

Her cheeks turned pink. "I would have liked that."

She'd said "would have," so she was tracking with his thoughts on this. They wouldn't have a future together, and even if they survived this, each of them had too much baggage.

"I wish we could have gotten to know each other in the normal fashion."

"You mean…? You mean as in dating?" A smile curled the edges of her lips, but not fully.

"Yeah. Like dating. I wish that I didn't have this mess for a past, and maybe that Tony hadn't hurt you so much."

Beck released her hand, but he remained close. "Katelyn, you know that running won't solve this. It won't keep your family safe. Our families safe. In fact, it could only put them in more danger. And there's just no way we can pretend we know nothing, or that we left no one behind. There's no way my family is going with me using fake IDs."

She sighed. "You're right. Even if we left, I couldn't just leave without telling my family what's going on. And telling them would put them in danger. It's like my greatest fear is happening no matter what I do. No matter how hard I try to steer clear. I've always been so afraid of putting someone I care about in danger, and that due to my own ineptness. That happened with Tony, but I thought I was past that. And now here I am."

"Your being here is only because you have skills, and because you cared enough to come into my house and chase away a bad guy. You were smart enough to get a look at his face."

She shook her head and looked away. He wasn't making any headway with her. She'd have to process through it on her own.

"But the good news is that I know what to do now."
Maybe that would get her attention.

When she raised her eyes to him, admiration lingered
there. "I knew you would figure it out."

"We're going to take all this to the highest office in
the CIA. Drive or fly across the country. Walk in and
hand it over."

She snorted a laugh. "What makes you think you
can do that?"

"I have to try. If we have to face off with Mia's handler, this Cooley guy, then so be it, but only if it comes
to that."

He didn't tell her about the worst part yet, because
she really wasn't going to like it.

She was right. He was a procrastinator.

NINETEEN

They had downed protein bars and straightened up the cabin, then grabbed the backpacks, along with the contents of the safe. Katelyn followed Beck out of the cabin. For a short time, it had been a reprieve and she almost regretted having to leave. But it was already growing late in the afternoon. They needed to get on the road and get out of here. A pang went through her heart.

"Okay, well, then. I'm the maid of honor at Tori and Ryan's wedding. I don't know what I'm going to do. The worst thing I could do is bring danger to the wedding. What if men showed up and started shooting?" She searched Beck's gray eyes for answers, even though she knew he had none. "I guess I have to tell them I can't be there, but I can't tell them why, which will only hurt them."

"Shh." Beck approached, his eyes never leaving hers.

He grabbed her hands and cupped them against his chest. She felt his heart pounding, slow, steady and strong.

"It's going to be all right. You're going to be okay."

"How can you say that?"

"Just trust me. Now, let's get out of here."

Katelyn climbed into Beck's vehicle and watched as he hammered nails into a board that he'd placed across the door and to the adjoining wall, securing it in place. Beck had apologized about the door and promised to send some cash for the fix. He hiked down the path and then got into the driver's seat, glancing her way before he buckled up.

He was asking her to trust him, but he hadn't exactly laid out his plans.

Katelyn had briefly turned on her phone because they were leaving, anyway. She'd received several texts from Tori and her brothers. Mom, too, to which Katelyn had replied that she was working a case. That was totally true.

Beck steered them down the rough mountain road in silence, which was fine with Katelyn. She prayed silently as she thought of how to tell Tori that she had to miss the wedding. How to tell her brother. What could she possibly say that would make any sense?

Maybe she was losing it, really losing it. She now understood how Beck felt when people thought he was being paranoid. But she had lived through several attempts on her life. Maybe that could make a person lose their grip with reality.

She had been a cop once. She'd been strong enough to take on that role, despite her failure at the end.

Beck steered them into Rainey and Katelyn sat up. "Where are we going? I thought we were driving across the country?"

He said nothing, then finally parked in front of Ryan's home.

"Are you kidding me?" Anger boiled in her gut. "Beck, what are you doing?"

He shifted in his seat. "I'm firing you."

Her mouth opened but no words came out.

"I can't protect you but your family can. You're better off with them. I have to do this alone."

"No fair. I know what you're doing. You're trying to draw the danger to yourself. To lead them away. You're making my decisions for me, too, and I don't appreciate it."

He got out of his vehicle and came around to open the door for her, then gestured for her to get out.

"Please," he said. "I couldn't bear it if something happened to you. You talked about failing on your job. Well, I failed before, too. I failed to protect my wife and she's dead now. I can't risk not protecting you. I can't risk failure. Don't make this harder than it already is."

"Beck, you need me." The fury that burned inside was quickly overcome with the ache of failure. She couldn't protect Beck, either. "We worked well together. Didn't I have your back out there? Don't do this."

Regret and fear fought in his gray eyes. She dropped from the seat and stood much too close to him. *I don't want to leave you...* Could he read that in her eyes? Would it make a difference?

"Why do you want to stick around so badly?" His voice sounded husky.

She leaned into him, feeling the draw of everything about him. "I don't know when it happened, but I haven't been in this with you because you hired me, or because we're both running from danger and trying to find answers. I'm here because I care about you...as a friend." Oh, lame. So lame. What a liar.

He acted as if he would reach for her hand but he didn't follow through. "And I care about you, too, Katelyn. That's why you have to stay. I've already contacted your brother to tell him I'm dropping you off."

Katelyn risked a glance at the house and spotted Reece standing at the door.

"Yes, I know this is the day before Ryan's wedding, but no one is more invested in you than your brothers, your family. I have to go now, so I can lead the killer away."

He tugged her forward and she thought he would kiss her, but he stopped short and instead kissed her on the forehead. When he released her, he gripped her shoulders and leveled his gaze on her. "Stay safe, Katelyn. Go live a happy productive life in a career you love. Get married and have kids. Make your dreams come true."

Beck released her and stepped away.

Reece had made his way to the vehicle and he grabbed Katelyn into a big protective brotherly hug. Beck climbed into his vehicle, and without another look at her, drove away.

Excruciating pain throbbed through his chest. But he'd done the right thing. He had no choice. He couldn't be selfish anymore. Beck forced himself to stare at the road ahead of him and not look back at Katelyn. Metaphorically speaking, the road ahead he must travel alone.

He didn't think he meant that much to her, more than that he was a client, but there'd been a brokenness in her features, a sadness in her eyes. Beck had put that there and it crushed him. For not the first time he second-guessed his decision to leave her behind. Earlier, he'd had no choice because of her threat to continue to investigate. But now she had a wedding to attend and three brothers to contend with.

Still, he questioned himself.

Am I doing the right thing? Will she really be safer with them?

Beck had the contents of the safe—the incriminating information from the safe. So someone had to be following him, and not Katelyn. Surrounded by law enforcement, she wouldn't be an easy target.

Beck would be easier. This had to be the right thing to do.

He wanted to see Ollie before he left, but he feared that would only lead Cooley to his son and his camping location. No matter which way he looked at it, there was no good answer. He had a long journey ahead of him, and he wasn't entirely sure how he was going to make it.

Maybe he should convince his family to leave and use the fake IDs, after all.

He swerved and turned onto the street where he lived before his house had been obliterated. One last time he would hike through the ashes, through the memories of the life he'd lived and loved. Remember what he'd once had with Mia. The good and the bad.

He parked next to the curb. Clara's car was in her driveway so he assumed she hadn't left for Spokane like Katelyn had suggested. He prayed just this once that Clara wouldn't look out her window and see him. Even if she did, he hoped she kept to herself. He was in no mood to have a friendly conversation or be patient. Besides, anyone who got near him was either in danger or ended up dead.

That's why he'd had to leave Katelyn behind.

The wind picked up. Clouds built in the distance, easily seen when lightning brightened inside them. What was with this sudden onslaught of storms in a usually dry climate? The thoughts morphed into much darker questions.

Would Mia still be alive if he hadn't pressured her to tell him the truth? If he hadn't been so suspicious? Was the domino effect Hunley had mentioned truly due to Beck's continued search and ultimate discovery of the safe?

Thunder rumbled, the sound getting louder as the storms moved closer.

As he walked through the rubble and stood in the middle of the burned-out home, he kicked a few pieces of unrecognizable lumps he guessed used to be furniture, and let dry sobs build in his chest. He should let the tears fall if they came. No one could see him except God, who saw everything, even the hidden tears in his heart.

"What should I do?" he whispered.

Did he actually believe he could make it to Langley? And with incriminating evidence and a CIA operative on his heels? Unfortunately, he didn't. But how did he get the truth into the right person's hands, if Mia and Barr had both been killed over this? How was Beck, with no real operative training, to survive when they couldn't?

That was it then, he would need to go undercover and on the run—with his family—while he made his way to hand over the information.

He would go as Travis Hinckley, the ID that Mia had supplied.

I'm sorry, Katelyn. He thought she might have held

an ounce of hope that he would come back to town and all would be well. They could be "friends."

Beck hung his head. He plodded over to Ollie's room. How did he tell his son about his room? Ollie wasn't so shallow that his material things would matter that much to him, but still, he was just a kid. This would be so hard.

Then he spotted a Pokémon tin. Really? That had survived? He smiled. He had at least one item he could return to his son... It was something.

His cell rang with a number he didn't recognize. Sweat bloomed on his palms—instinctively he knew this call wasn't a wrong number. Dread coiled around his spine.

"Beck speaking."

"You have something I want."

"Who is this?"

"You know who it is."

Cooley. "I'm afraid I don't. I'm going to hang up—"

"Not if you want to see your son again."

TWENTY

All the blood drained out of him and his heart stopped. Had he understood the man correctly? Was Beck's unimaginable nightmare happening? He squeezed the phone in his hands, might have been crushing it, but he caught himself.

"What do you want?"

"You know what I want. But so there won't be any mistake, everything that was in the safe you took."

"Look, I don't have everything. Some junk I threw away. So tell me what you're really after."

A few heartbeats thumped by and for a moment, Beck thought he'd lost the signal. But he wouldn't be the first to speak. Somehow, for Ollie's sake, he had to get the upper hand.

Right. The guy had him, and he knew it.

Beck wanted to ask about his parents, too. He hadn't heard from them, so they could be bound or...

No. He wouldn't think the worst about them. He would crumple if he did and he had to be strong for Ollie.

"Bring what you have. If what I'm looking for isn't there, you can say goodbye to your son."

"How do I know Ollie is with you?"

He heard a shuffling, then... "Dad?" Fear quaked in Ollie's voice.

"Ollie!"

"Now you know."

"Don't hurt him, do you hear me? Don't hurt him or I'll—"

"Or you'll what?"

"I'll hunt you down and make you wish you were dead."

Silence was all he heard in response. His hands sweated profusely until he thought he would drop the phone. He swiped each palm on his pants, as he stood in the middle of his razed home, the scent of wet ash filling his nostrils. Eyes squeezed shut, he pressed the cell against his ears and fisted his free hand.

Hold it together. For Ollie, just hold it together.

"Tell me where you want to meet so I can get my son back. I don't care about anything else. You can have it all." *I just want Ollie back safe and sound. I'm so sorry, son. So, so sorry.* If only he had left well enough alone!

"If you tell anyone—call the police or share with your girlfriend at any point now or later—your son's life will be snatched from him. You know we can do this. You've seen it with your own eyes."

Mia...

"Do you understand?"

"Yes."

"I hear in your voice that you do, in fact, understand. You saw how quickly your wife died when she tried to share what she knew. Remember her."

"I understand." He fisted his free hand, imagining that hand around this man's throat and squeezing,

squeezing, squeezing. He could hardly bark out the next question. "Where do we meet?"

"The place you know best."

Beck scratched his head. "My house is gone."

"Your work."

"What? You mean—"

"Castle Crags. Head that way. I'll call you with more information in half an hour. I can see a long distance from where I'm standing. Don't believe you can bring anyone with you. Come alone."

The call ended.

Beck fought the anguish, the mad rushing tears. Once again he resisted crushing the phone he held in his hand. His knees buckled, and he dropped.

"I'm here with you, Beck. I'm going with you."

Katelyn.

A fist squeezed Katelyn's heart. Seeing him like this crushed her. She rushed to where he'd dropped to his knees in the ashes of his burned home.

He looked up at her and she saw the shimmering moisture in his eyes.

Oh, Beck. She couldn't bear seeing him like this. This ordeal had broken this strong resilient man into a thousand pieces. And yet, she knew he wouldn't break under this pressure, but would only be made stronger. He would pull himself together for his son's sake. If Katelyn knew anything, she knew that about this man.

"What. Are. You. Doing here?" He scrambled to his feet. Gripped her shoulders and shook her. "What are you doing? I don't want to have to worry about you, too."

"Okay. You're angry. I get that. But you have to worry about Ollie. Friends don't leave friends."

"Did you come to your house and spot me here? Did Clara see me and call you?"

"Nothing so covert. I—I thought you might come here first, looking for answers. Or to say goodbye."

His expression softened. "You know me that well? I didn't even know I was coming here."

She gave a one-shoulder shrug. "I wasn't sure I'd find you here. But I did, and I overheard your conversation. At least your side of it and it's enough for me to know that he took Ollie. Cooley took Ollie. It has to be him. He's the one who took out Hunley and the other assassin."

"I'm supposed to come alone."

"As far as he knows, you will be. I'll be in the truck with you. I'll hide. Now let's not waste time arguing about it. I can make my own choices, Beck. I know where you're going. I overheard that part, too."

"If I bring someone I could risk Ollie's life, Katelyn!"

She grabbed his hands and spoke gently, hoping he would listen to reason. "If you go alone you risk both your lives."

Beck dipped his chin, contemplated for several moments, and then finally said, "Let's go then."

They rushed to his truck and got in. He started the ignition and raced down the street. "So you have to tell me just how did you get away from your family? I thought you'd never escape your three law-enforcement brothers."

No doubt about it—her brothers would be furious. Tori would be worried. But they wouldn't find out until it was too late.

"I wasn't a prisoner, Beck."

"So you snuck out like a teenager."

"Nope. Instead of a bachelor or bachelorette party, Tori and Ryan were attending a small party given by close friends. I was invited, but they knew I was exhausted and heartbroken." She couldn't help the grin. "I stayed behind when they left, and then I simply slipped away. I'll text Tori later that I went home to go to bed. She'll understand."

He shook his head. "I don't get you. I gave you an out. I don't understand why you came back."

"I told you. Friends don't leave friends." And with the words, she knew what she'd tried to ignore since getting into this. What she felt for Beck was so much more than platonic.

None of that mattered when Ollie's life was in danger.

"What about your parents?" Katelyn asked.

"I didn't ask about them. I was afraid to bring them up. But I should call them now. It's just that… I don't think I'm going to get an answer." He steered with one hand and tugged his cell out of his pocket with the other. Made the call. The longer he went without getting an answer, the deeper his frown grew. Finally, he said, "It's Beck. Call me immediately."

He focused on the road and glanced at his cell. "Calling Mom this time."

Again, he waited, then, "Mom, this is Beck. Please call me as soon as you get this message."

He ended the call and gripped the steering wheel with both hands. He didn't have to say anything for Katelyn to know he was in anguish.

"I'm so sorry."

"I can only worry about one person at a time."

She understood. He worried about his parents but his focus was on Ollie. "You don't need to worry about me or expend energy. I'm here to help. I'm not your hired PI, but I am a former cop. I'll help you get Ollie back."

He was taking the corners at crazy speeds.

"You should watch out so you don't get pulled over and delayed."

"Right. You're right." He slowed down the vehicle. "So let's think about this. He's going to call me and re-direct. We can't know where the end will be. Somehow you need to slip out without him knowing and get into position so you can grab Ollie."

"Let's agree on something up front," she said. "And that is that you're not going to do anything stupid and get yourself killed."

"I wouldn't dream of it. And what I want to agree on up front is your one job is to grab Ollie. Nothing else matters. That's your only task. I'll distract Cooley with the contents of the safe, and you protect my son. I'm trusting you to do this one thing, so I'm begging you."

He was asking her to do the one thing she'd failed at before—save someone being used as a hostage.

TWENTY-ONE

Beck tried to focus as he drove toward Castle Crags, but all he could think about was poor Ollie. His little boy hadn't asked for any of this. Didn't deserve it—as if anyone deserved this to happen. But Ollie deserved better than this. Beck owed his little boy safety and security. That he and Mia had had lived their lives in an illusion for almost the entire time they were married shattered Beck.

Oh, Mia...

Why did she have to fall in love with Beck? Why couldn't she gain her freedom? Beck wished he had never searched for that safe and didn't know that Mia had left incriminating secrets against her old boss. Now the man would kill Beck and his son. He harbored no hope that he—or Katelyn—would be kept alive if Cooley somehow got the upper hand.

So together, they had to make their way out of this. Their release would not depend on Cooley, especially after what he'd done to Mia. There was no way the man could be trusted.

Beck hadn't had time to argue with Katelyn about coming with him, but she was fully aware that she could be sacrificing her own life now. She was going to help him get Ollie back.

She was right. She'd been right all along. He needed her. But so help him, he hadn't wanted to need her.

She'd said she'd come to him as a friend. *Friends don't leave friends...* But what he felt for her went beyond friendship, and she knew that.

But they had both drawn their own invisible lines they each refused to cross—both of them suffering with severe trust issues. Even though they danced around those lines, he knew that when this was over, if they survived, he would have to break both their hearts.

Best not to think about any of it considering they might not survive this. Beck forced his focus back to the curvy mountain roads as he steered through the Castle Crags Wilderness in Shasta-Trinity National Forest on his approach.

"Don't forget, I need to get out of this vehicle while I have the chance," she said.

"I can't risk him calling and directing me somewhere else, and then what? Just crunch down in the seat."

"If he has any kind of special vision detector, like night-vision goggles or heat-sensing equipment, he might see my heat signature. What about Ollie, Beck? Just let me get out right now and right here. It can't be much farther, can it? Worst case is you can come back and pick me up."

Ollie was already dead whether or not Katelyn had come, and in fact, she was their only hope. He didn't want to tell her that he was thinking that way. He didn't want to put that burden on her. Slowing the vehicle, he glanced at his watch. The call should have come through fifteen minutes ago.

He looked at his cell. He had a signal, though only a bar.

Katelyn had climbed into the back seat and scrunched onto the floorboard to hide.

He pounded the steering wheel and stopped.

"What's going on?" she whispered.

"I don't know. He was supposed to call me in half an hour."

"Maybe that had been a simple generalization."

"Maybe. Okay. Maybe." He started forward again. *Come on, and call. Call me!*

"What if you just call him back? His number is on your phone, isn't it?"

"Maybe he wants me to sweat. To be worried about my son, and I am worried." Fear curdled in his gut.

He continued urging the truck slowly forward, watching the woods around them. They'd escaped the approaching storm but it would soon catch up to them. The sun had already dropped behind the mountains and dusk would create deep shadows in this forest much too soon. He still didn't have his Ollie back yet. *God, please let Ollie be all right. Please... Just let him get away.*

Beck thought about Ollie's smile that looked so much like Mia's. His giggle and wit and amazing sense of humor. No father could ask for a better son. Beck had spent all his spare time with Ollie and he had even taught him to climb here at Castle Crags. Mia had joined in on that family activity.

His breath hitched. Ollie had climbed the mountains with him here. Ollie both knew his way around this forest and how to climb those granite spirals—if he could just get away he could make it to safety all on his own. *God, please let him get away.* Ollie was smart. Still, the thought sent fear through him—Cooley could shoot him for his efforts.

Besides, his little boy was probably scared to death. Much too scared to act on his knowledge of this area, which was exactly how Beck was feeling at the moment. Paralysis was slowly taking hold of him, as if he'd ingested a paralytic poison. Cooley had mentioned the place that Beck knew well. Breath whooshed from him at the realization.

Cooley likely also knew that Ollie could climb.

Once again he glanced at his cell. "He called. He called and my phone didn't ring."

Beck slammed on the brakes and put his vehicle in Park. He returned the call. It went to voice mail. He ended the call, fearing he would say the wrong thing. "No, no, no! I didn't hear the cell, you idiot."

He recalled the number at the same time his cell indicated he had an incoming call.

"Relax, Beck. Slow and easy," he said, coaching himself.

He took a slow calming breath and tried to make his big, clumsy shaking fingers receive the call, and answered, "Beck."

"I told you to come alone."

Katelyn remained frozen in place as she listened to the voice echoing over the cell phone through the cab of the vehicle.

Cooley knew she was here? Her gut clenched. Squeezing her eyes shut, she prayed for Ollie...

Oh, God, please, please, keep him safe.

"You want the evidence, then give me my boy." Beck's tone was forceful. Threatening.

Through all of this, she had never heard or seen this

side of him. He'd been crushed and the pieces of his soul thrown to the wind, but now it was as if the strong rock-climbing man she'd known—all of him had coalesced and was ready for this one moment. The energy built up inside the tiger who was ready to pounce and unleash his anger.

"I'll expect you to bring the private investigator with you to our meeting."

"No."

"No? What was your plan, Goodwin? To let her come up behind? You distract me and then she'll grab your son?"

"Nothing so elaborate."

"Remember, I call the shots for a living. Even your wife, another of my operatives, wasn't able to outmaneuver me."

Katelyn's heart pounded. How were they going to get out of this alive? She had to think of something, except Beck had given her one job. One task. And this time, she wouldn't—couldn't—fail, or Ollie would die.

"I'll remember," Beck said. "Now where are we meeting?"

"Keep driving another six hundred yards, then stop."

The line went dead and the vehicle started forward.

She hated asking him, but she couldn't read him so well right now. She wanted to make sure they were tracking the same. "What do you want me to do now, Beck?"

"You might as well get into the front seat. You were right—he was able to detect you were inside the truck. Your heat signature or something. Whatever. Somehow he knew."

Katelyn climbed into the front seat as he suggested. "I'm sorry. I didn't mean to complicate things. I only wanted to help. And I will help, if you'll just tell me what you're planning."

"You've put yourself at risk, Katelyn. I'm the one who is sorry. I shouldn't have let you do it. I tried to stop you. I think… I think there's still a chance that you can help save Ollie."

Beck slowed as he approached the six-hundred-yard point. "I didn't want to tell you this before. To put this pressure on you, but I think you just might be the only hope Ollie has."

Beck suddenly stopped, then turned. Cupped her cheeks and pulled her to him. He gave her a long, thorough kiss. Raw and desperate. She felt the rush of fear and emotion swirling out of him and rushing into her. Her heart quivered—she was anxious about what was to come. Torn about what she could lose if he was putting it all on her. He kissed her as if it was goodbye. As if he would never kiss her, or anyone, again. He'd never get the chance.

Oh, Lord… When I walk through the water… I'm about to get overwhelmed here. Help me!

Beck released her, then started the vehicle moving forward again. She understood they didn't have time to work out their lives when Ollie's was on the line.

"Understand me, Katelyn. I'm going to cause a distraction. I don't know what or how, but you'll know when you see it. Your job, your *only* job, is to get him to safety. Don't worry about me. I can take care of myself. Ollie is depending on us both. Do you understand?"

"Beck, I—"

"Do. You. Understand?"

"Yes…" She choked out the word. "You're going to give your life for his."

"If it comes to that, then yes, of course. If my life will give him a chance to live, then I'm expendable."

TWENTY-TWO

Beck parked his vehicle in the middle of the forest road. Heart pounding, he opened the door a crack. "This is it."

Thunder sounded. The storm would be on top of them soon. Trees rustled as the wind whipped.

Ollie would be so scared. He'd always been scared of the lightning. Mia would sometimes hold him at night during a rare thunderstorm until it passed or he fell asleep.

Beck wasn't sure if he should wait in the truck for another phone call or not, but he would get out and see what happened. He hopped from the vehicle, then slammed the door to announce his arrival.

Katelyn shut her door and walked to the front of the vehicle, where Beck joined her.

"Okay. I'm here," he shouted. "I want my son."

Standing in the middle of the road lined with evergreen forest on each side, Beck realized this was a setup for an ambush if he'd ever seen one.

"Daddy?" Ollie's shaky voice sounded small.

"Ollie! Ollie, where are you?" Beck whirled and let his eyes search the darkening forest.

Katelyn tugged on his arm. He followed where she pointed.

Cooley stepped onto the road about fifteen feet in front of them.

"Daddy?" Ollie tried to run but Cooley gripped the back of his jacket. He lifted his gun and pointed it at Ollie's temple.

Grief exploded inside Beck. He kept his chin up. His act together. His son needed to see that his father was confident that he would free them both. Beck hoped his demeanor and false confidence would replace the dread curdling in his gut.

"Let him go, Cooley." Beck hoped he sounded more forceful than he felt.

"Did you bring it?" The man growled the question.

"Beck, he could kill us all and take it from the vehicle." Katelyn ground out the words in a low tone.

Beck offered a subtle nod, letting her know that he understood.

The man yanked Ollie so that he cried out.

"How do I know you won't just kill us once you have what you want?"

"You don't." The man laughed.

Of all the… Beck would play a game of his own. It was all he had. "That's why I only brought most of it."

"You'd risk your son's life?"

"Absolutely not. You don't hand him over now, you won't see anything."

He heard the barely audible intake of breath from Katelyn. He could imagine her question.

What are you doing?

Beck had to overcome this mountain. He had to master it. To climb it. He saw Cooley as a potentially deadly spike of granite and Beck. Would. Master. Him. He would keep telling himself the same words he used when tackling a new climb. Let Cooley see in Beck a man not to be trifled with.

He tried to remain calm, but his heart pounded as he waited a few breaths for Cooley to respond.

"All right," Cooley said. "Bring it forward. Then you can find out if I like what I see."

"Katelyn…get the box."

In his peripheral vision, he saw her jerk her head to him.

"Just…get the Pokémon box."

Katelyn returned and handed over the tin box. Her eyes drilled into him but she said nothing. She knew like he knew that it only contained Pokémon cards. Ridiculous they survived the fire. She also knew what he required of her.

She subtly shook her head.

"You're wasting time," Cooley said. "You have ten seconds to walk this way and hand over the goods or I'm going to shoot him execution-style."

Cooley shoved Ollie to the ground. "On your knees." He pointed the weapon at the back of Ollie's head.

Katelyn gasped next to him. Beck's heart almost stopped and he stumbled as he walked forward, showing his weakness and fear.

To his credit, Ollie said nothing. He didn't cry out. This experience would change him forever, and Beck felt the strength he somehow gathered in these last few moments quickly fading.

Was he doing the right thing? Was he risking Ollie's life?

After all, what did he care if Cooley had the information? Except, they would all be killed if he gave over his last bargaining chip, so he hadn't even brought it. He'd buried it beneath the ash of what remained of the house he'd shared with Mia and Ollie.

Stunned, Katelyn forced her shaking legs to walk alongside Beck. Wind gusted and blew her hair into her face and she shoved it away. Beck had not brought the items that would save his son's life. She still couldn't grasp that move on his part.

But Beck was thinking far ahead—Cooley wouldn't allow them to live. Beck knew this was his last and only chance to save his son. And then to keep them safe in the future, he would deliver the information to some higher-up at Langley. Somehow. Some way.

But to have the confidence, the nerve, to go through with it blew her away. She was trained law enforcement but Beck was showing his true grit by standing up to this guy. Beck was a rock. A master at tackling challenges, and she hadn't seen that coming.

Nor had she expected the rest to unfold the way it had.

She tried to remain completely aware of her surroundings and stay alert and ready for the "distraction" Beck had mentioned. She suspected he didn't know what it was yet, so couldn't tell her, but he would know when to act. She had to be ready.

She could do this. She could save Ollie. *Oh, Lord, please save us all!*

She had to remain strong through this. Katelyn thought back to all her police-academy and on-the-job training, but nothing in real life ever went according to the training.

When Tony had been overcome by a criminal with

a gun, the unexpected had happened. Katelyn had to be prepared for the unexpected right now.

How did one prepare for the unknown?

Still on his knees, Ollie lifted his head to stare at his father. Hope and fear warred in his gaze. His eyes soon dropped to what Beck carried.

"What's in the Pokémon box, Dad?"

Oh, no. Ollie spotted his Pokémon box. Surely he didn't care if the cards were traded for his life.

"Ollie, it's going to be okay."

"I want to know what you're giving him in exchange for me? What's so important? Is it money? Am I being ransomed?"

"Your mom left some things behind. I found them in a safe. They're secret things that this man wants. He used to work with her, and he is forcing me to give them to him."

"Not Mom's stuff!" Ollie was in a full-on panic now. Tears and anger spilled from him.

"Relax, son."

Cooley yanked on his hair and pressed the gun barrel into his temple, deeper, harder. This time Ollie cried out.

"Stop it!" Katelyn yelled. "How dare you terrify a little boy."

"You can stop right there." Cooley gestured at the ground with the gun. "Set the box down. Then back away. I'll come forward and look. I'll decide if you deserve to live."

"I brought what you asked. Keep your end of the deal."

"You said you only brought part of it, and I can appreciate you're trying to use it for leverage. I'll give you that."

"How generous."

Katelyn tried to get Ollie's attention and hold his eyes. She hoped he could read in hers that he should run to her. They should run together when Beck distracted Cooley.

When was that going to happen?

They were running out of time. It would have to be soon. She tried to think ahead. When Cooley bent over for the box, that moment when his gun wasn't trained on Ollie—in that one single split moment in time, Beck would have to draw Cooley's attention.

Katelyn would have to save Ollie.

Her pulse raged in her ears as the storm increased. The wind picked up and a few big drops of rain hit her in the face.

Beck set the Pokémon tin on the ground and stepped back.

"Keep going until I say stop."

"No. You bring Ollie forward. You get the box when I get Ollie."

"I could just shoot you here and take it."

"And risk not getting everything you wanted? I don't think so."

Oh, Beck. Katelyn had no idea from what pocket Beck pulled his boldness.

"No. You can't take Mom's stuff." Ollie suddenly burst away from Cooley, dashed forward and dove for the box.

Cooley aimed to shoot him. Ollie rolled away.

"No!" Beck rammed into Cooley, throwing his aim off.

Katelyn grabbed for Ollie, but he took the box and sprinted into the woods.

TWENTY-THREE

Thunder boomed through his chest, followed by a crack as lightning hit a nearby tree and split it open. Half the trunk plunged toward them. Cooley straddled Beck with his fist ready to strike Beck's face, but rolled away as the tree hurtled toward them.

Beck scrambled up and out of harm's way just in time. The trunk thudded against the ground, wood chips splintering and flying as the trunk bounced. Beck gave the tree a wide berth and caught a glimpse of Cooley sprinting into the woods.

"Ollie!" Beck shouted. "Ollie, run. Get far away. You know your way around. You can do this!"

The man was going after Ollie and the Pokémon box. Beck raced after Cooley and entered the woods that grew darker by the minute. The storm winds picked up and the evergreens rustled with the wind, sounding like a thousand whispers.

Lightning flashed again and again, coupled with thunder claps.

Would any of them survive this?

"Ollie!" Beck called out to his son, but if Ollie answered, then Cooley could find him, too.

"Ollie, run. Get away. Cooley's coming."

In reality he'd been running around in the dark for five minutes, but it felt like hours. He paused next to a tree to catch his breath. Where would Ollie go? He was scared but smart. Strong like his dad. He'd done his best to instill confidence in the boy and this was the time he needed to rely on that. Then he thought he knew where Ollie would go.

Lightning flashed and he spotted Cooley's silhouette in the distance. The man had retrieved his gun and held it at the ready.

Good. Cooley was heading in the wrong direction. Beck kept going, jogging as fast as he could, though the underbrush was thick in places. His heart pounded but he kept going and wouldn't stop until he found Ollie. Beck climbed over the boulders at the base of the crags where Ollie could hide and dashed around them, searching for his son.

Beck hoped he was the only one struggling to find a way out of this, and that Ollie was well on his way to safety. At the same time, he wanted to find his son. Needed to know he was safe. He thought he knew where Ollie would go, but so far he hadn't found him. *Where are you, Ollie?*

He was thinking about this all wrong.

Ollie wouldn't simply hide, he would try to climb to escape.

Beck's heart hammered at the thought.

Beck changed course and headed for Vista Point Trail, running through cedars and dogwoods. If he was Ollie, that's what he would have done, and his kid was enough like him to think the same way. But nothing in life had prepared either of them to face off with this sort of evil. Beck ran toward the base of the jagged granite spirals, the place he'd taken Ollie in the past to start their climb. Only they had protective gear and ropes. This—this was dangerous, and part of him hoped that Ollie had gone a different way.

Part of him hoped Ollie wouldn't try to free climb. One mistake could kill.

Finally, he reached the heart of the Crags. He glanced up. Castle Dome stood tall and lofty like a sentinel over the region.

Ollie…

He worried about Katelyn but trusted she was out there searching for Ollie, too. He hoped she'd already found him and secured his safety. That he'd grabbed the box and taken off like that had surprised them all, and served as the distraction that Beck had needed. Up to that point, he had been flailing to find a way to distract Cooley without causing more harm to Ollie.

Ollie had been the one to give them a chance.

Beck was sure God had something to do with it, too. He always did.

Don't worry, Ollie, Katelyn. I'm coming.

Beck weaved up the steep wall of the dome's first section, then paused to look around.

No Ollie.

Bending over his thighs, he caught his breath. "Ollie… Where…are you?"

"Here, Dad. I'm here." The voice was small.

He whirled and spotted his son huddled in a space between two boulders. Shivering, Ollie held out the opened Pokémon box, Pokémon cards spilling out. Tears rushed down his cheeks.

Beck ran forward and drew him into his arms. "Oh, Ollie. I'm so proud of you. You got away. You got to safety."

He released Ollie and crouched at eye level. "Are you okay?"

Ollie's eyes remained huge. "I think so. Mimi and Pops will be worried, though."

Beck tensed. He hadn't wanted to ask about them yet. "You mean Cooley didn't harm them?"

Ollie shook his head. "Pops got sick so we had to go home. Mimi was taking care of him. I went outside— Pikachu was missing." Mimi's cat. "And then, he took me. He let Pikachu get away, but he took me."

Mom and Dad would have tried to call Beck. So what Ollie said didn't make sense. They could be tied up somewhere. He had to focus on getting Ollie to safety, but he could call the police and get someone to his parents' home. He held up his cell. No signal.

"Dad, I thought the box held some of Mom's things."

Beck ruffled Ollie's hair. "I'll explain everything, I promise, but right now Cooley wants to kill us. He wants to kill Katelyn, too. We have to get somewhere safe. You understand, don't you?"

The anger and confusion in Ollie's eyes seemed to clear as he nodded. "Okay. I came here to climb and get away. I thought… I thought I could climb, but I don't have the ropes. I didn't have you. I can't go without you."

"But you did the right thing. I suspected you would come here, and I came to find you. Cooley is out there in those woods with a gun. If we can make it up to our spot we'll be safe from him. We've done this a hundred times, Ollie." And Beck could possibly get that signal.

Ollie nodded. "I'll leave the box here. I don't think Cooley wanted the cards. We'll come back for it, won't we?"

"Yes, we will."

Beck grabbed Ollie's hand and together they headed up the dome—where Beck had trained for free climbing many times. "You got this," he said.

They followed the quartz vein along the granite toward the porch on the dome's east side. There the ground would drop away, down sheer cliffs. After the porch came the gully, and then the final pitch, which was a class four. They'd need rope for that.

"We're stopping here, Ollie."

"I know. We need rope. You haven't taken me yet."

"Maybe one day."

They found a place to rest, where they often would come to look at the view.

Father and son. And talk about the deeper things of life. Here all was quiet and the world was right again. Here Beck could be closer to God, and to his son.

Here Cooley couldn't get to them.

Beck wished Katelyn was with them, and guilt warred inside that he was here with Ollie but had left her to fend for herself. But she'd reminded him a hundred times she was an ex-cop. One had to pick and choose their battles, and right now, Beck wanted to get Ollie away from the madman who had killed Beck's wife, and was gunning to kill them all.

He tugged out his cell phone to call 911 and then Katelyn.

A big drop hit Beck in the face. Then another. Then the storm clouds released a downpour.

"Dad!" Ollie slipped.

Rain hammered the forest. Though the trees shielded her from the brunt of it, Katelyn was hit with a few pine needles, along with water drops, as rivulets washed debris away in places. Splashing through them, she searched for Ollie.

That had been her only job, the most important job she would ever have—to keep that little boy safe.

That a bullet had grazed Katelyn shouldn't have stopped her. That wound bled profusely now because her heart pounded and adrenaline surged. Gasping for breath, she leaned against a tree, ripped the sleeve from her soaked blouse and wrapped her arm. At least the rain had washed the wound a bit. She should have done that to begin with, but she thought she could catch up with the boy. He had somehow disappeared—and not just him.

She'd heard Beck shouting for Ollie, but she hadn't seen him. She'd been beyond relieved to hear his voice because she'd left him fighting with Cooley. She had no doubt that Beck could get the best of Cooley, the coward.

She'd heard Beck shout that Cooley was coming. So he was out here, too.

The cold wind and rain whipped around her. She couldn't remember the last time it had stormed like this.

Ollie had made a run for it more than twenty minutes ago, she guessed. Good for him. Good for him that he got away and gave them a distraction, but now what? She wiped the rain from her eyes and face, then pushed from the tree trunk, ready to search again.

She remained wary of Cooley, who would still be out here searching, too. He wanted that box. And he wanted them dead. They were the only witnesses. She wished he would leave. Clearly he hadn't won this battle, which only meant he would come for them again when they least expected it.

No. That couldn't happen. They had to get him today. Take him down today.

The rain slowed to a steady beat instead of a tumultuous hammering downpour. Katelyn ignored her shivering and tried to hold her weapon steady. The forest was dark in the shadow of the crags. Lightning flashed in the distance as the storm moved on. She strained to see well and needed to pull out her flashlight, but feared that would definitely give her away to Cooley.

A branch caught her foot and she stumbled forward and fell into the wet pine needles face-first. Her gun slid across the needles beneath a fallen, rotting tree trunk

With the rain trickling through the trees and the rumbling thunder in the distance, she struggled to hear any sounds that would warn of approaching danger.

She scrambled to her feet.

Cooley stood near and held a gun. He'd seen her too. She dove behind a tree as gunfire ricocheted through the forest. Katelyn gasped for breath. Her weapon was somewhere beneath that fallen trunk. Somehow she had to make her way around to get the gun.

Forget her burning arm.

She was moments away from certain death.

Remaining frozen in place behind the tree, she calmed her breathing and listened. The forest was eerie with shadows cast when lightning flashed and raindrops pattering through the trees and plopping on the needle-laden ground, muting the sound.

She detected the slightest motion.

And held her breath.

Cooley… He was near. He had to be near.

What am I going to do?

Her only choice was to make a dash for her gun and hope he wasn't quick enough to shoot her in the back.

That didn't seem like much of a choice. She needed another choice.

Holding her breath, Katelyn remained as quiet as possible and hoped he wouldn't find her. Heart pounding, her pulse roared in her ears.

Then Cooley stepped directly in front of her, the muzzle of his gun pointed in her face.

Oh, God, help me...

He lifted the weapon and swung the grip toward her head.

TWENTY-FOUR

"You're doing great, Ollie."

At least up on the crags, darkness hadn't yet descended. They had barely enough light and needed to get down while they still could. As they made their way down the Castle Dome, the rocks were slippery, but Beck and Ollie had trained on this climb before and knew every place to step. He wanted to stay so that Ollie would be safe, but with the wind so harsh, Ollie had slipped. Beck had caught him. But the crags weren't safe, either, after all, so they made their way down. Beck had thought this was the best way to escape Cooley. At the top, Beck had called 911 and explained their emergency as succinctly as he could.

A man with a gun with intent to harm was on the trails.

He didn't go into the fact the man was a CIA operative or supervisor—that would make it sound like a crank call. Katelyn's brothers could hear the news on the police radio and come for them.

Then he'd texted Katelyn. He needed to know if she was okay. He waited for her reply for a few minutes. She could be hiding or in a bad situation. Or she could simply be searching and lost.

He'd heard gunfire and his gut clenched.

He'd left Katelyn to fend for herself. Guilt suffused him. How did he keep Ollie safe and help Katelyn? Sure, she'd been a former cop, but cops depended on backup.

Friends never leave friends...

His only thought for his son, he'd left Katelyn behind, trusting that she would be okay.

Had the gunfire been from her gun? Or Cooley's?

He led the way down, and if Ollie slipped again, he would once again reinforce his moves. Reposition him if necessary. Granite could be climbed wet or dry, so the rain didn't hinder them too much.

"Only a little more, Ollie. You've got this."

Finally Beck hopped down and reached up to grab his boy from the rocks. He held him long and hard. "Ollie, I need to find Katelyn. I'm worried about her. But I don't want to take you into danger."

"You want me to hide, don't you?"

He released Ollie and gripped his arms. "Hide and wait for me."

Tears streamed from Ollie's face. "I can't, Dad. Take me with you. That's the safest place for me."

Beck thought he'd never heard wiser words. "You know something, you're right."

He tugged his son to him, hoping for life to return to normal. He hadn't even told Ollie about the house. Considering how he acted over the box he thought contained his mother's things, news of the house fire would be devastating.

But first things first. They weren't out of this yet.

Beck took a long breath. "We just have to take the trail down now."

They continued along the trail that led out of the area at the base of the crags and drew near the woods.

Beck stopped and eyed the forest.

"What are we doing, Dad?"

Ollie's eyes were big and round and blue, and Beck saw Mia there, in his son. How did he make him understand? How did he keep his boy safe and also save the girl?

Ollie's eyes widened. "Dad!"

Beck whirled around, keeping his body in front of his son. Cooley stood ten yards away, aiming his weapon at them.

"I should kill you now. Blow both your heads off. But I need the box."

"Where's Katelyn?" Beck asked.

"No need to worry about her. I took care of her. You're a failure, Beck. Mia should never have married you. I warned her that she wouldn't be happy settling down, especially with the likes of you. A big dumb athlete."

Beck tried not to let the words cut him, eat away at him. Mia was gone. What did the words matter? But his heart bled, the wound opening back up. And now to hear that he'd let down Katelyn, that she was dead too… Beck's knees almost buckled.

He still had this one last chance. This last chance to save his son. Ollie had to live, no matter the cost.

"What have you done with it, boy?"

"I'll never tell you!" Ollie shouted.

Cooley fired his gun into the ground near Beck's feet. He almost flinched but maintained his composure. "Ollie lost the box. He doesn't know where he left it. You're free to search."

"That's a lie. He wanted his mother's things bad enough to risk everything."

Well, Cooley had been paying attention and that didn't help them right now.

"Boy, the next shot is going into your father's gut. Did you know that's one of the most painful ways to die? You bleed out slowly. It can take—"

"Stop it!" Beck took a step forward.

Cooley lifted his weapon higher, aiming more toward Beck's chest. "You see, if he dies slowly, you'll have time to say goodbye to dear old dad. Otherwise, I could just shoot him in the heart and he dies instantly. Or a bullet to the head."

"Dad." Ollie choked out the word through tears. "I'm scared."

Beck reached over and squeezed Ollie's hand, reassuring him. He had no idea how he was going to get them out of this. If he could draw Cooley in a little closer, then he could ram him and Ollie could once again run. This time he could run to find a ranger station. But he could keep running until he was somewhere safe and never look back.

"I'll give you everything you want. I'll take you to the box right now, only let Ollie go. Let him live his life."

"Deal. You give me everything I asked for, then only one of you has to die *today*."

Beck didn't think he misinterpreted the hidden threat. He would die today, but Ollie didn't have much time to live.

Her vision blurry, she saw two of everything.

Cooley had slammed her with the butt of his gun.

That much she knew because she felt it with every single beat of her heart thundering through her head. All she could think was that he was done wasting bullets trying to kill her. Maybe his last two bullets were meant for Ollie and Beck. Cooley might have finished the job, though, if he'd been able to find *her* gun.

She had to get to Cooley before he used the last of his ammunition to kill two people she cared deeply about.

The voices had sounded through the trees and stirred her. Motivated her to get up and save Beck and Ollie. So she'd scrambled to her feet and found her gun, despite her throbbing head and double vision. Aching back and burning arm. That would all heal. But lives could not be recovered.

She could do this. She had to save them. This was the moment she could make it all right. She'd never wanted this moment or asked for it, but it was here. Katelyn had to help them.

Using the trees for support, she moved from one to the next until she finally got her balance and her double vision eased up.

The voices echoed against the crags leading her to them. Katelyn held her weapon high. She knew exactly what she had to do. But what she didn't know was if this was like the scene from *True Grit*, where the ranger helped save the others but was mortally wounded and died in the effort.

She couldn't think about that.

Beck and Ollie had to live even if she died.

As she crept forward, she finally saw the two men she had to save and blurred images of Cooley's back.

Katelyn crept quietly. Cooley was too busy making threats, and she was about to run out of time.

She wouldn't let them down.

But how did she shoot if her aim was definitely going to be off? She couldn't see straight.

God, help me take the shot. Help me make it right. I have no other choice. When I walk through the water...

"Cooley!" she called. "You should have killed me when you had the chance!"

Cooley whirled around and fired his weapon at the same moment Katelyn fired twice.

The man fell forward. Katelyn dropped to her knees. She could have missed and killed Beck or Ollie.

They ran toward her. Beck dropped next to her, and Ollie, too. The rock-climbing master held them both in his arms.

Beck gripped Katelyn to peer at her. "Are you okay?"

"He hit me in the head. I could have killed you just now. My vision is blurred. I feel sick."

"You've got a concussion. I called the police. Some-one should be here." He glanced around. "But the woods are growing darker. I should get you out of here."

She rose. "Wait. We can't leave Cooley." Katelyn stumbled toward the man. If he wasn't dead, he was dying. "We should try to save him. Keep him alive until help can arrive. Call for an ambulance, too."

Cooley rolled to his side and aimed his gun at Kate-lyn.

"Katelyn!" Beck shouted.

She whirled as Beck rushed forward to block the shot, putting himself in harm's way and kicking the gun from Cooley's hand. Beck pressed his booted foot on the man's wrist. "Good news, Cooley, you're not going to die today. Not if we have anything to do with it."

A couple of rangers rushed forward from the woods. Deputies, too.

"We were responding to your emergency call near the crags," one ranger said, "and heard the gunfire."

Reece, Ben and Ryan emerged from the woods then too. Tori jogged right behind them.

Oh, great. Her whole family had come. Then again, what would she do without them? The rangers gave Cooley medical attention and called for a helicopter to lift him out and fly him to the nearest trauma center. Her family gathered around and hugged her.

"You need to see a doctor and fast. Maybe you should fly in the helicopter with Cooley," Ryan said.

"No. Just no, thank you."

"I'll take her." Beck stepped up, holding tight to Ollie.

"And your parents are okay, Beck. They were tied up and were able to free themselves. We received the emergency call from them moments ago."

Relief whooshed from Beck. "Thank you for letting me know."

Her brothers left her alone with Beck and Ollie while they spoke with the rangers. Detective Manning informed Cooley he was under arrest.

"There's still the matter of handing over this material to the right person," Beck said.

"You're afraid it's not over yet."

He nodded.

Beck's cell rang. An unknown number. Why was he getting a cell signal now, of all times? He held her gaze. "Here we go again."

"You should answer it, Beck. Let's get this over with.

No more hiding now. Everyone is going to know about this soon enough."

He put the phone on Speaker and answered. "Beck Goodwin."

"Mr. Goodwin. This is the Deputy Director of the CIA, Martin Kendall, speaking." Beck gave her an incredulous look.

She understood his shock. How did this guy know to call *him*?

She shrugged. He was the director of the CIA, after all. She was glad that he already knew enough to call Beck.

Katelyn smiled at Beck as they listened—it was over now. Truly over.

For the moment, she ignored the sudden fear that her time with Beck would be coming to an end. They would say their goodbyes and he would probably move away. Who would want to stay here near the Mount Shasta region after everything?

TWENTY-FIVE

Tori and Ryan's ceremony was as beautiful and special as any wedding could be. Katelyn fought the tears as she stood in her place as maid of honor next to the bride and watched her brother exchange vows with Tori. The Goodwin family had joined them today upon her invitation, and she kept wanting to glance out into the gathering at Beck.

Katelyn's mind kept going back to that moment when Beck had stepped in front of her to block Cooley's shot. He'd been ready to give his life for her, and in the end he'd saved her. He'd been ready to give his life for his son. A man like that could be trusted with her heart. She hadn't thought she could trust again, but there was nothing she wanted more than to give Beck her heart. But he'd struggled with trust himself after what he'd been through with his wife. So Katelyn should put aside her hopes. Besides, this wasn't her day. This was Ryan and Tori's day.

Katelyn might not ever get a wedding day—she didn't think she would ever find another man like Beck.

After the pastor pronounced Tori and Ryan as man and wife and introduced Mr. and Mrs. Bradley to the crowd, Katelyn waited for her turn and then followed the wedding couple down the aisle and out into the foyer of the church. A reception was to follow in the fellowship hall.

Joy filled Katelyn's heart. *Thank You, God.* She'd made it through the ordeal of this week and Tori and Ryan had made it to the altar. Katelyn hugged and congratulated family members and swiped at the tears that kept escaping. Weddings always made her cry, and she wasn't sure why.

In her peripheral vision she spotted Beck standing back in the hallway with his family, as if preparing to leave. Katelyn excused herself and rushed to catch up with them. She tugged Beck's jacket and he turned.

Beck's eyes brimmed with admiration and so much more. "Katelyn, you look so beautiful." He leaned in and whispered, "More beautiful than the bride."

Then he stepped back and smiled. Her cheeks warmed. "Thank you. Um… You're not leaving already, are you?"

"Mom and Dad are taking Ollie out. I was deliberating on what to do next. I wanted to at least say hi to you before I left, but…"

Beck had wanted her to believe in him and had often waited for her to say things. Well, this time, she wanted to hear him say it. She could invite him to stay, but she would hear it from him first.

"But?"

He studied her, searching her gaze, looking right through her soul like only he could. Had she truly only gotten to know this man so well in a week? Her throat grew tight and tears welled. The wedding stuff getting to her again.

Stepping closer, Beck pressed his hands against the bare skin of her arms. Fortunately the bullet-grazed part of her arm was partially covered. Considering the current that had always sparked between them, she wasn't sure she wanted him so close, touching her arms. A hum started in her belly.

"I wasn't sure if you wanted me to stay, Katelyn."

"Of course I want you to stay. You're all invited to the reception. But only if you want to be here, Beck. No pressure." Katelyn wanted to tell him more, but she needed to hear this from him.

"You believed me when no one else would," he said. "Not even my parents."

"I believed you."

"When I thought Cooley had taken you out, all I could think about was how I would give anything to have a chance with you. Because…"

He gently lifted her chin and leaned closer. "I'm free to trust now, Katelyn. All because of you. Free to trust, and free to love."

Again he searched her eyes and his gaze dropped to her lips. "What do you think about you and me? Is there a future for us?"

"I'm free to trust, too, Beck. I'm free to love." Exploring the possibility of love and a future with this man was all Katelyn wanted and joy filled her heart.

His lips found hers and slowly he wrapped his arms around her, drawing her closer, and kissed her with the promise of so much more.

When he ended the kiss, Katelyn found family members watching. Tori and Ryan clapped and the others joined in the applause. Katelyn's cheeks grew hot.

Tori tossed Katelyn her flowers, which, according

to tradition, meant she would be the next among the bridesmaids to marry. She hoped Beck wasn't clued in to those traditions and flicked a glance at him.

"No pressure," he said and winked.

* * * * *

Get 4 FREE REWARDS!

We'll send you 2 FREE Books plus 2 FREE Mystery Gifts.

FREE
Value Over
$20

Both the **Love Inspired**® and **Love Inspired**® Suspense series feature compelling novels filled with inspirational romance, faith, forgiveness, and hope.

HARLEQUIN
PLUS

Announcing a **BRAND-NEW**
multimedia subscription service
for romance fans like you!

Read, Watch and Play.

Experience the easiest way to get
the romance content you crave.

Start your **FREE 7 DAY TRIAL** at
<u>www.harlequinplus.com/freetrial</u>.

LOVE INSPIRED

Stories to uplift and inspire

Fall in love with Love Inspired—
inspirational and uplifting stories of faith
and hope. Find strength and comfort in
the bonds of friendship and community.
Revel in the warmth of possibility and the
promise of new beginnings.

Sign up for the Love Inspired newsletter
at **LoveInspired.com** to be the first
to find out about upcoming titles,
special promotions and exclusive content.

CONNECT WITH US AT:

f Facebook.com/LoveInspiredBooks

🐦 Twitter.com/LoveInspiredBks

LISOCIAL2021